The Silent Years

PETER HOLDROYD

Published by NVP Publications
Norwich
www.nvppublications.uk

2nd edition published 2015
Copyright © 2015 Peter Holdroyd
All rights reserved.

ISBN-13: 978-0-9933409-4-9

DEDICATION

To my wonderful and supportive wife, Dee

FOREWORD TO THE 2ND EDITION

'The Silent Years' was my first venture into self-publishing, which followed a long learning-curve. Once the first edition of The Silent Years appeared on the Amazon and CreateSpace.com websites, and I finally got to hold my first printed novel in my hand, I began to wonder if it could be improved.

Consequently, this second edition has a new cover, a new 'Prologue' and a new ending. I hope those who bought the first edition will forgive the rapid publication of the second.

ALSO BY PETER HOLDROYD

In print

BRAIN FEVER

Kindle e-books:

Summer Island
Bio-Morph
Coming to Terms

Don Carter, cover-name Laroux, made his way stealthily towards the landing ground. He'd formed a good relationship with the local group of maquis. It went against the grain to be out tonight, alone, with no one else aware of his task. An 'eyes-only' message from London had chilled his blood – a traitor somewhere in their midst – but at least the people at SOE were taking urgent action.

The sound of a light aircraft came to him from the north. Carter reached the edge of the trees and checked the clearing for signs of the enemy. Beyond the trees, to the west, was an old farmhouse. It had been in darkness as he'd cycled past, so the chances were the old man and his daughter whom he knew lived there were sound asleep.

The plane approached, low. Carter ran forward, pulling the red-filtered torch, intended to mark the drop-zone, from his pack. As he positioned it on the ground, its beam point-ing upwards, a single shot rang out from the encompassing trees and he fell, his kneecap shattered. He reached for the torch, to switch it off, knowing that it would make the pilot suspicious and hopefully cancel the drop, but it was beyond his reach.

He saw two men emerge from cover and run towards him. One was in the uniform of an SS officer, and carried a sniper rifle, while the other wore a long overcoat and a slouch hat. Carter pulled a pistol from the pocket of his old jacket.

It must be true, he realised: there *was* a traitor. How else could these men have found him if they hadn't been told who he was, and followed him to this field? He had only a few seconds before they reached him. He could shoot these two, he knew, but there would be other Germans in the area. With his shattered leg, there was no escape. He took careful aim and squeezed the trigger twice in quick succession. Both targets fell to the ground.

Something made him glance upwards, and he saw a container, the sort which SOE packed with supplies, descend on a parachute and land at the edge of the field. Another parachute, possibly a couple of fields away, was coming down fast

More soldiers burst from the trees, coming towards him. He could not take the risk of capture and torture. Heart aching with the pain of a future he would never see, and thoughts of his wife and children back home, he placed the capsule he carried for just such a situation in his mouth, and crushed it hard between his teeth.

PART ONE

CHAPTER 1 – SPRING, 1943

Ann Greatorix had no idea, when she woke to find the bed beside her cold, that her life, and that of her unborn child would never be the same again.

She stared at the empty space on her husband's pillow and blinked as tears pricked her eyes. She felt the usual morning queasiness begin in her abdomen, and dragged herself out of bed, grabbing one of the Rich Tea biscuits David must have brought upstairs before leaving, and taking large bites of it. It seemed to help her stomach adapt to the changes her body was beginning to face. Sometimes she would avoid being sick by this means.

She felt settled enough in a few moments to go downstairs and make herself some tea.

It was still early, only just past seven by the clock near the kitchen window, but she was due to be at work at eight, so there was no time to lose. She made some toast and more tea and put a cardigan on over her blouse. Her eye caught sight of the fruit dish on the table. Empty more often than not, this morning it contained a large orange, fat with juice, and a note. She stared at the fruit, her mouth watering at the rare sight. Where did he find that, she wondered.

She picked up the note: All my love, ever yours, David.

She felt tears prick her eyes, but the warmth the note generated in her easily overcame the deficiencies of the jacket and skirt she wore for work – 'austerity' garments in light-weight fabric, not really warm enough for early Spring. She was nevertheless shivering by the time she mounted her bicycle and pedalled to work at the top secret decryption unit at Bletchley Park.

She had warmed up again by the time she parked the bike outside the hut in which she worked. Her in-tray was already full of envelopes containing decryptions when she reached her desk, which stood alone in a dark corner of the hut. Even on the brightest days, she had a lamp on her desk to cast light on some of the Code Breakers' scrawls. They were often in pencil, involved crossings-out, and were sometimes difficult to read. It was important that she transcribed them accurately.

She worked for an hour before she was interrupted by anything apart from the arrival of more envelopes in her in-tray.

'How're you feeling today?'

Ann looked up to see one of the other women, Mary Hamilton, beaming at her over spectacles which kept clouding in the steam rising from a cup of tea she was holding to her lips. She was friendly towards the women, like Ann, with husbands and boyfriends in the armed forces.

'Fine. Well, fine once I stop wanting to be sick.'

Mary rolled her eyes. 'Don't remind me. I had terrible morning sickness when I was pregnant. Seemed to go on forever.'

'I hope mine doesn't. It's been four weeks now, and I shan't miss it when it stops.' Ann regarded Mary curiously. 'I didn't know you had a child.'

'Lost it at three months. You want some tea?' She seemed to dismiss her tragedy.

Ann sat back. 'I'm sorry about the child,' she said. 'Tea sounds like a good idea, but you know the effect *that* has – and it seems to be getting worse.'

'No problem. The toilets are handy,' Mary grinned. 'Don't want you dehydrating.' She looked at Ann askance. 'I was young. Natural causes, they said.'

'Still, it must have been terrible.' Ann tried to imagine how she'd feel if she lost her baby, and knew she'd never be as sanguine about it as Mary seemed. She tried to put the matter behind her. 'I'll be bloated if I drink too much.'

'Shouldn't worry about it, I don't,' said Mary breezily. 'You're going to get really fat in the next few months, so a bit of bloating won't make a jot of difference.'

'When the pregnancy starts to show, does it put your husband off?'

Mary sipped her tea. 'It depends on the husband, I'd think. On whether they like you with a bump or prefer you flat-tummied. And it depends on you, too.' She leaned closer. 'Some women seem to enjoy doing it a lot while they're pregnant – I suppose it's the knowledge that they can't get any more pregnant. Others don't.'

'Doesn't it hurt the baby?'

Mary coughed politely into her hand and glanced around to make sure they were not being overheard. 'Not in my experience, dear. Not at all.' She straightened up. 'Now you grab some tea while I take a cup to our leader.'

Lunchtime came and went. Signal traffic was heavy and Ann was kept busy all afternoon. It was evening before Mary appeared beside Ann's desk again.

'I expect you'll be glad to get home to that nice husband of yours.'

Ann grinned wryly. 'I think I've been abandoned. Not sure, but it wasn't personal.'

Mary put a concerned hand, the fingers laden with costume jewellery, on Ann's arm. 'Been called away on a bit of war service?'

'So I believe, but you know how it is: nobody tells you anything.'

'I know,' said Mary, shaking her head. 'I do enjoy a gossip, but I can only do it here, with people I know. Honestly, my friends think I'm in training to be a nun, what with Frank being away and me not daring hardly to speak to them in case my mouth runs away when I'm not thinking.'

'Secrecy can be a bit wearing.'

Mary glanced round the room at the other staff. Their colleagues were tidying their desks and reaching for coats as the night shift began to take over.

'Well, this kind is, I agree,' she said.

'What do you mean?'

Mary chuckled. 'Well, there are some secrets which are no problem to keep.'

'Such as?'

Mary glanced round and lowered her voice. 'Well, while the cat's away, you know. You could be living dangerously, with no fear of pregnancy. At least for a month or two. David might be back by then.'

Ann stared at her. 'Are you – !' she gasped. 'I know what you're suggesting,' she said as she stood up and lifted her coat off the peg near her chair. 'But it's not for me. I'm a one-man kind of woman.'

'Well, and that's fine, love. I do hope you won't think worse of me for it.'

'Is that what you do when Frank's away?'

The twitch of Mary's eyebrows and her wry smile seemed to answer the question.

Ann glanced at the clock. 'Time to go. See you in the morning.'

'Yes. Goodnight, dear.'

Ann was more surprised than shocked at Mary's implication. A few married women, mostly the younger ones, were known to be playing fast and loose with some of the men, while their husbands were away. She was surprised to learn that Mary, at twenty-seven, was apparently one of them.

Ann arrived home to a cold house, and kept her outdoor clothes on until she had a fire burning in the grate. Her dinner was frugal, mindful of the fact that while David was away, her food rations could be cut – not in half, exactly, because of the baby, but close enough.

Later, with the washing-up done and a cup of tea at her elbow, she listened to Harry Lauder on the radio.

She missed the comforting presence of David that night, and when the BBC played the record of Vera Lynn singing *We'll Meet Again,* she almost wept.

* * *

On the second day after David's unannounced disappearance from their home, Ann arrived at work and was met by Callum Macbeth, the man in charge of her section.

'Come into my office, Ann,' he said, waiting until she'd hung up her coat. She followed him, at first simply curious. He poured her some coffee from a jug and waved her to a chair.

'Er, Ann,' he began in his carefully enunciated Scots brogue, as warm as the taste of a lowland malt slipping over the tongue. He settled behind his desk, 'I have some information, or rather none, about your husband.'

Her senses went on the alert. 'What do you mean?'

He interleaved his large, banana-shaped fingers, his eyes lowered. 'It may not be a problem, of course, but I felt you should know: there's no report of his arrival in France.'

So that was where he'd been sent, she thought.

'In fact, there's no word at all from the groups in the area, so we don't know what's happened.'

'Can I ask – what's supposed to have happened?'

Macbeth hesitated as if deciding what he could tell her.

'This is between you and me, and within these four walls. A resistance group has been penetrated by a Gestapo spy. At least, we think so. All – every one! – of its leaders has been arrested. Your husband's job was not to join them, exactly, but to try to winkle out the spy from outside the group.'

'But you've heard nothing?' A pit of terrible darkness was beginning to form inside her.

'No. So we don't know at this moment whether he's made contact. He had his own radio so he wouldn't be reliant on someone else, but it could have been damaged in the drop.'

'So, what happens now?' There was a tremor in her voice which she tried hard to control.

He shrugged. 'It may be a few days before we get any more news. Anyway, I thought you'd want to know.' At last he raised his eyes to meet hers, as if, now the unpleasantness was done, he could bear to meet her troubled gaze.

'Th-thank you, Callum,' she said.

Reason told her that there were many possible explanations for the lack of news, but at the same time, for the powers-that-be to have told her what they had, this soon after David's mission had started, seemed to suggest that they were convinced he had run into trouble.

'Keep it to yourself for now, Ann,' Macbeth told her.

She sensed dismissal and rose from her chair. 'Don't worry about me. I'll stay quiet.'

'Even around here,' he reminded her.

'Even around here,' she agreed.

She returned to her desk, still clutching the coffee that Macbeth had provided – it was a better blend than she could normally afford – and attacked the pile of decryptions in her in-tray.

Mary came over. There were times she was glad to chat with Mary, but this wasn't one of them. Ann braced herself. It was not in her to be unkind to someone just because she wasn't feeling particularly sociable. She managed a smile as she sat back from the typewriter and routinely closed the box file into which she placed the decrypted messages she typed out. Every half-hour, she would take the box file through into Callum's office and empty the papers into his in-tray.

'You're in to see Callum very early, dear. Any problems?' asked Mary.

'No.'

Mary regarded her for a second, perhaps waiting for amplification of her response.

'I think that's a *mind your own business* No,' she said shortly.

'You know what this place is like, Mary, lots of secrets.'

'Even from those of your friends who work here?'

Ann would have categorized Mary as a work colleague, rather than friend. She simply arched an eyebrow in reply.

'Hmm!' Mary turned away, not trying to hide her disgust. Behind her, Ann shrugged. She had more important things to worry about. Despite Callum's seeming assurance and her own rationality, she couldn't shake the growing concern she felt for David as every hour passed without news of him.

* * *

It was three days later that Callum called her into his office again. The look on his face was enough to tip her over the edge, and tears, which she'd denied herself while there might still be hope, spilled down her cheeks.

He came round his desk, stood behind her chair and rested comforting hands on her shoulders.

'I'm sorry, lass, but there's been word from another group. One of our men, who should have met your husband, didn't make it. His body was found the next day. And we don't know where David is. He hasn't contacted any of the safe houses in the area.'

Ann closed her eyes and folded her arms across her belly, rocking gently backwards and forwards as if cradling the child inside her while Callum stood by, helpless in the face of her growing grief.

'It's still early to be sure of anything,' she said, making her words sound like a question, in need of reassurance.

'Yes it is. I just don't want you left any more in the dark than you have to be.'

She nodded her thanks.

'But say nothing to anyone else.'

She agreed.

'If by any chance the Germans caught him – and I'm not saying they have, mind – we'd get word through the Red Cross. Should do, anyway. From that point of view, no news is good news.'

She smiled, dried her tears. 'That's right. If they'd caught him, we'd have heard.'

'Don't give up hope. There's time yet for him to pop up somewhere and wonder what all the fuss was about.'

She gave a watery chuckle. 'That would be just like him.'

Callum returned to his chair.

'That's the spirit. Never say die.'

She bit her lip and rose to her feet, thanking him again for his kindness. She guessed he'd probably gone further than he should in what he'd said, but then she knew he had a soft spot for her.

At the door she turned round. 'We'd also hear from the Red Cross if he'd been killed, wouldn't we?'

He waved his hand dismissively. 'Oh, never say that, my dear. But you're right. More of that "no news is good news" stuff.'

She nodded and managed a smile before returning to her desk. She was aware that Mary, who sat on the other side of the room but facing her, was staring, and schooled her features into a bland expression. She didn't want the older woman prying further into her private life.

Penny Sanderson still wasn't used to not having to go to work.

She opened the wardrobe door and caught sight of herself in the long mirror mounted inside: not much grey among the cornfield blonde, figure still quite trim and – where it counted – firm.

Not that *that* mattered any more: since leukaemia had taken John a year ago, she dressed more for comfort than style these days. Their son was working for an oil company in the Middle East, leaving Penny to rattle around the big old house, on the outskirts of Bletchley, all alone.

After thirty-five years of being at someone else's beck and call, in a job which was undoubtedly stressful from time to time, the sudden end of such obligations following her early retirement was taking a lot of getting used to, as was the idea – even a year on – that every month, her Police pension arrived in her bank account.

She bent to pull a box of shoes out from the bottom of the wardrobe. As she did so, her eye was caught by a small envelope. She recognised it at once as part of her late mother's possessions, which had been turned over to her by the care home after the old lady had died – just weeks before her eighty-first birthday in 1990.

She'd had an awful time of going through her mother's private papers. Stuff that could wait to be looked at, she put on one side. Even now, nine years later, she hesitated. She had nothing else to do, and enough time had passed for her to get over the guilt she'd felt at having decided a care home specialising in the needs of patients with dementia was the best place for her mother to spend her remaining years. There had been no choice, really: it was that or risk her marriage. John had tried hard to handle having a mother-in-law with severe and worsening dementia in the house twenty-four-seven, but the stresses it caused had almost rent them apart.

She picked up the envelope and finished dressing.

Downstairs, over her first coffee of the day, she slit it open with a knife from the breakfast table.

A small dog-eared notebook fell into her hand. She flipped the pages and opened it at the beginning. It was written in her mother's hand – the elegance of her cursive script unmistakable. The first section was dated December, 1943.

Our first Christmas, and no word of David. He is missing all the joy Penny has brought into our lives, but I shall take photographs to show him when he returns.

Penny felt tears prick her eyes. Her father had never returned from France, but here was evidence that nine months after he had disappeared, it was obvious her mother had not given up on seeing him again. She scanned through several pages. The notes had been added at irregular intervals, often months apart.

September 1945, Penny's second birthday. She asks where her daddy is, and I don't know what to say. Callum tells me he has been posted as 'Missing, Presumed Dead', and that if he doesn't come home now that the war is over, it will help if I want to apply to have him declared dead.

The writing became wobbly at this point, and Penny could imagine her mother having great difficulty in setting down on paper the probability of her father's death. She turned to the final entry, dated September, 1950. A black and white wedding photograph was tucked in the page. It showed herself, her mother and new Step-father, all smiling for the camera.

Penny looked so pretty in her bridesmaid's dress. I think it was a good idea to remarry on her birthday. She is looking forward to starting at Junior School next week, one of the National Schools. She can already read very well, and Miss Stewart, her last teacher at Priory Road Infants', said she thought Penny would do very well.

Penny thought about that: reaching the rank of Detective Inspector *had* been 'doing reasonably well'. Maybe she could have gone further, but it had become obvious that men were preferred in the higher ranks. And there was the fact that as she entered her fifties, the idea of retiring and being able to pursue her own interests and agendas instead of someone else's had become more and more attractive.

She looked back at the notebook and saw her mother had penned another line, this time in very shaky writing, suggesting it was written as the Alzheimer's was taking hold.

I want to be buried with both my husbands, and pray that Penny will bring David home from wherever he is.

It was a wish she'd never expressed to Penny. By the time she died, she'd been incapable of communicating, and had clearly left it too late to convey her desire verbally to her daughter.

She made a mental note to take flowers to the cemetery where her mother's and step-father's grave markers lay side by side.

The idea came to her slowly. *"Bring David home."* Her mother's last coherent wish.

She had time on her hands.

Her father would have been in his eighties, had he lived. But undoubtedly, he had died in 1943.

She would find her father's grave.

She replaced the notebook in its envelope, changed into her track suit and trainers and took herself off for a run while she figured out how to go about her task.

* * *

David Greatorix's war record arrived in the post just before lunchtime a week later. Penny had spent two days going through the rest of her mother's papers, to see if there was anything else that might assist her, but found nothing. She'd known from her police days how to obtain old military records, and sent for her father's. She slit open the envelope. It contained two large sheets of paper which she was spreading out on the kitchen table when the telephone rang.

'Mrs Sanderson?' A man's voice, warm and friendly, but not one she recognised.

'Yes?'

'Geoffrey Pearson. You don't know me, but we have something in common and I'd like us to meet and talk about it.'

'Oh?'

'My father knew your father.'

She frowned. 'Yes? So?' She was determined to offer him no encouragement.

'I believe you've applied for a copy of his army record. But you won't find anything useful there.'

She considered that. 'How do you know that?'

'Because I know that service with SOE isn't mentioned.'

'SOE?'

'The Special Operations Executive. The "Baker Street Irregulars". The people who ran Station X.'

'Station X?'

He chuckled. 'All very cloak and dagger isn't it. Could we meet? I'd rather we talked face to face than on an open telephone line.'

'Where are you?'

'In your area,' he said.

She suggested a coffee shop. 'How will I recognise you?'

'*I'll* recognise *you*, Mrs Sanderson. See you around two?'

He asked her to bring her father's war record with her.

She rang off, not liking the idea that he knew what she looked like when the reverse wasn't true. In all her working life, she'd always known the people she was meeting. Suddenly the boot was on the other foot and it was uncomfortable. Still, he'd succeeded in arousing her curiosity, and he had said enough to convince her that she should talk to him.

* * *

'Got any identification?' Penny asked when a tall, straight-backed man with salt 'n' pepper hair came to her table and introduced himself.

'I have a driver's licence. Passport at home.' He showed her his licence, with his name and photograph clear.

'How do you know I applied for my father's service records?'

'My father mentioned it.'

'And how would he know?'

'I think he still has a few drams with his old War Office buddies.'

She studied him calculatingly. 'What's your father's name?'

'Colonel Derek Pearson.'

'There hasn't been a War Office for years, so which bit of its successors are we talking about?'

'You want to know a lot.' He looked amused more than annoyed.

'I know nothing about you – or your father. You know something about me nobody else would, unless they were on the inside, somewhere. So I assume either you or your father have connections within the Ministry of Defence. So, which service is it, in which your father met mine?'

'During the last war it was SOE.'

'And now?'

He smiled. It was a warm smile, the kind which said "trust me". And all the more dangerous, she thought.

'I thought we were only concerned with the last war?' he said. He smiled at a waitress who had appeared beside them. 'Shall we order?'

When the girl had gone to fetch straightforward filter coffees – they'd both rejected suggestions of latte, mocha and cappuccino – he turned back to Penny and spoke quietly.

'Personally, I'm retired, like you, and looking for something to occupy my time. I'm just a bit of an odd-job man.'

Anyone looking less like the mental image she had of an odd-job man would be hard to find. She smiled.

'So why are you here, really?'

'I heard you are looking, and I'd been through all this myself. So I thought you might welcome a bit of help with your research. I find it quite interesting, and we might be able to help each other.'

Penny regarded him askance. 'Oh, come on! You don't expect me to believe that, do you?'

He shrugged. 'I haven't lied to you. I've been tracing my family history, and that includes my father's wartime service in SOE.'

The coffee arrived, and Penny studied him over the rim of her cup. 'How do I know I can trust you?'

He opened his hands, palm-up, a gesture inviting her to have faith in him. 'Perhaps for now you'll just give me the benefit of the doubt.'

'I thought I was doing that already.'

He stirred a sweetener into his coffee, slowly. 'And I'm grateful,' he said. He sipped. 'Let me put it this way: you want to find your father, I want to find out about my father's wartime activities. It makes sense to me, if we work together.'

She thought about his words. They made sense to her, too. But.

'I thought your father was still alive. Can't you just ask him?'

Geoffrey sipped his coffee and looked at her over the rim of his cup. 'He's still a bit secretive. To be honest, I thought it a bit unusual for him to tell me about you.'

'Why do you think he did that?'

Geoffrey shrugged. 'All he said to me was that your father's file is apparently still open.'

'Isn't that unusual after all this time?'

'I think it might be due to pressure from the French Government. They still have a case file themselves that your father was supposed to resolve.'

'About what?' she asked. 'How could my father be involved in solving a *French* case file?

Geoffrey shrugged and wrinkled his brow. 'I think you'd have to be a card-carrying member of the secret services to know that.'

Penny held her cup to her lips and sipped while she studied him. She thought he probably *was* a card-carrying member of the secret services, but he obviously wasn't going to admit it easily. She guessed he was probably about the same age as herself, within a couple of years more or less. Pale blue eyes rested on her, flicked up to meet her gaze. On the whole, she decided, it was an honest face – but how many of the people she'd locked up during her police career had had honest faces? An "honest face" was an asset to certain criminals… and to people who worked in the half-world of espionage.

'Okay,' she said, the tone of her voice and demeanour calculated to make him think she accepted what he'd told her at face value. 'So where do you think we should begin?'

'Did you bring your father's war record with you?'

'Yes.' She unsnapped the fastening on her handbag and reached inside, pulling out the manila envelope and placing it on the table between them.

'Mind if I read it?' he asked while she sipped more coffee.

'Don't you know what it says?'

'Of course not, no. You've not read it yourself yet?'

'It only arrived a few minutes before you rang. I haven't had time.'

He pulled the two sheets out of the envelope and smoothed them on the table top.

'What's so special about my father's SOE service?' she asked. 'What did he do that other spies didn't?'

Geoffrey signalled with his hand to keep her voice down.

'Sorry. Well?'

'I can only assume there was something special about your father's mission, which must have been different in some way from those undertaken by our other agents.'

'Not a whisper of which will appear on his military record, I guess?'

Geoffrey shrugged. 'For obvious reasons, clandestine activities don't appear in official service records. See for yourself.' He turned the army record round so she could read it.

'You see here, David's progress from Second Lieutenant to Major is recorded in fair detail, and the places he was posted.'

She scanned the entries from her father's join-up in 1940 to the Autumn of 1942. The penultimate entry simply said, *Detached Duty, Government Service.* Below it, she read the bald statement, dated September, 1943, *Missing.* Entries in other parts of the form showed that Ann Greatorix, née Hacker, Penny's mother, had applied for and received a formal presumption of her father's death, and authorised payment of a war widow's pension. She swallowed, her mouth suddenly dry, and glanced up to meet Geoffrey's gaze.

'And where does your father fit into this? You said our fathers knew each other.'

He'd been sipping his coffee while she read. Now he put the cup down.

'They met at Sandhurst. After their officer training, they went to different regiments, but met again within a few weeks of being sent on "detached duty" – to SOE. You see, they had this need for men like them. You knew your father was a mathematician and fluent in French, thanks to a French mother who brought him up to speak both languages?'

Penny hadn't seen *that* in the record in front of them.

'They'd got their hands on a new Enigma coding machine. The first one they got, in 1939, was what they called a three-rotor machine. The number of rotors determines the complexity of the code. In 1942, the German navy contrived to add a fourth rotor to their machines, and suddenly the people at Station X – Bletchley Park – couldn't crack the German High Command's instructions to their submarines in the Atlantic.

'They acquired one of the new machines eventually, but in the meantime, they were having to go to great lengths using the brain power of people like your father.'

'So he went to work for SOE. But still he was in Britain. Why would he have gone to France?'

'I can't say. I don't know. It seems odd on the face of it. It was the hell of a risk: if the Germans had got hold of him, he would have been able to tell them exactly how well SOE had been able to decrypt their Enigma cipher.'

Penny understood. 'They could have stopped using it for the proper messages and carried on using it for fake messages, designed to mislead the Allies.'

Pearson smiled and looked at her with respect.

'Quite. Whatever reason they had for sending him has to have been a damn' good one.'

'How could I find out? I'd wondered about approaching the PRO.'

Geoffrey grimaced. 'The Public Record Office won't be any help, I think. If your father's mission file is still open, it won't be available. The PFs – that's Personnel Files – of SOE operatives still living are sealed, and you'd only be able to obtain a copy of a deceased operative's record if you can prove that they're dead and that you're next of kin.' He scratched his head. 'And anyway, there was a big fire at SOE HQ in 1945 which destroyed most of the files.'

He glanced at his watch.

'Can I take you to lunch? I don't have much time today, and we can continue talking.'

Penny thought for a moment then nodded. 'There's a pub at the junction just along the road from here which does good food.'

'Sounds good to me.'

He paid their tab, and they left the coffee bar.

'You must be finding retired life very quiet?' he asked, turning to her.

She glanced up at him. 'My garden's never looked so good,' she replied. 'It's something I never had much time for before.'

'You had a fairly active working life, I believe,' he said as they approached the pub.

'You seem very well informed, not only about my father, but also about me.'

He smiled. It was the first proper smile she'd seen. It dimpled his cheeks and suddenly she realised he was quite good looking. He kept his back straight, and his small, neatly trimmed moustache gave him very much a military bearing.

'You're an interesting lady. I suppose I might have read beyond the strict boundaries of my research and discovered you were a police inspector.'

'Who set the boundaries of your research?' she asked, her mind alert.

'Me, mainly.'

She stole another glance at his profile, the firm jaw giving him a resolute appearance.

'Were you a soldier?'

He glanced sideways at her. 'SAS.'

'It sounds as though special forces runs in your family.'

'Only me and my father.'

They reached the pub, found a table and sat down. Pearson ordered wine for both of them. She almost objected on principle, but decided she would not have chosen differently in this instance, so decided to bide her time before pointing out that she was entitled to be consulted before he made decisions involving her.

'Do you have a family?' she asked.

'A son and daughter. Both married. Two grandchildren and one on the way.'

'A wife?'

'Dead. She died five years ago. Hit and run.'

'I'm sorry. Did they catch whoever did it?'

He shook his head, his focus inward for a moment. Then he looked up at her.

'No. Probably some drunk. I'm over it.' He brandished the menu. 'What're we going to have?'

The way he brushed his widowhood aside suggested to her that he wasn't as "over it" as he claimed. She kept the thought to herself. They ate their main course in companionable silence. Afterwards, he refilled their glasses.

'You asked me about my family: do you have one?' he asked.

She told him about Sandy, helping Kuwait recover from the invasion by Iraq and the destruction of its oilfields.

'And husband?'

'Died of leukaemia last year.'

'Sorry,' he said.

They were silent for a moment.

She wondered briefly what John would have thought of her, lunching with a stranger. Probably he wouldn't have given it a second thought.

'Desserts are on the blackboard over the fireplace,' Pearson said, bringing her mind back to the present.

She shook her head. 'Not for me,' she told him.

'Nor me. Too much sugar.' He sipped his wine and raised his eyes to hers. 'So, if the PRO is not going to be helpful, where do you think we should look first?'

Suddenly, she noted, it was "we". Her brow furrowed as she pondered his question.

'I wonder if there's anyone around still who might have known him.'

His eyebrows arched. 'That's a good idea. Look, I'm not going to foist myself on you if you prefer to go it alone, but I might be able to help you, if you let me.'

She glanced at him, aware of some degree of diffidence she'd not seen in him before.

'What will you get out of this?' she asked.

He raised his eyes, and for once seemed uncertain. 'I'm interested. I'd like to know what your father was supposed to do in France. It's a bit of a puzzle and it'll keep the grey matter in working order.'

She didn't think he really needed any additional stimulus in that area.

'I can manage, thanks.'

She glimpsed a sudden flash of disappointment in his eyes and for no reason she could have identified, reconsidered her answer.

'But, if you want to, I don't mind that, either.'

He smiled. 'Thank you. I will.'

She felt unexpectedly glad that he would be with her.

If only she felt confident his interest was friendly. He didn't seem threatening, she decided, and so would suspend judgement of him until she knew him better.

* * *

'What did David do in the war?'

The speaker was Stephanie Tabor, a detective sergeant who had been on Penny's team. The two women had become friends, despite the twenty year age difference. They sat either side of a shiny-topped circular table outside a pavement café, clutching large earthenware cups of coffee.

Penny shrugged. 'I don't know much about it. I sent for his war record from the army archives – God! they take so long when you make a civilian request,' she added, with obvious frustration which made Steph grin.

'So what have you learned about him?'

'He volunteered in 1940, was sent to Sandhurst, and became an officer.'

Penny sighed.

'So where was he killed?'

'Mother said it was somewhere in France. I know it was 1943, because I was born in the September.'

Steph seemed hesitant.

'What?'

'I was wondering how to ask… but you're definitely David's daughter? I mean, quite a few wives and girlfriends…'

She left the sentence unfinished, but her meaning was clear.

Penny shrugged. 'Who's to say? My mother never hinted at having an affair. As long as I've known her, she's remained true to my father's memory, and he's named on my birth certificate. I don't know how much more sure I could be.'

'Probably not much. It's not worth trying to get a DNA match yet, even assuming you could find something which might bear traces of your father's DNA. It's expensive to get done.'

Penny nodded. 'I was thinking; I'll probably go to France to see his grave, when I know where it is.'

'*If* you find it at all. You think he's dead, then?'

'If he wasn't, he'd be eighty. I know we're all living longer, and sixty is the new forty, and so on, but for a man born in 1919, eighty would be quite a lot beyond what he might have expected to live.'

Steph looked at her. 'You're in your fifties, aren't you?'

'Yes, but I feel as fit as I was at your age,' replied Penny tartly. 'I suppose you'll tell me you actually feel like a twenty-five year-old.'

Steph grinned. 'Darned right!' She rested a hand on Penny's. 'But I want you to know I fully intend growing up disgracefully – like you.'

Penny drew her hand away and attempted a severe look, but it didn't work well and Steph laughed.

'It's like trying to investigate a murder when you have no body and any potential witnesses have gone to ground.'

'That's why we call those, "Missing Persons" cases, not murders,' Steph said.

Penny smiled. 'I know. I'm not in any great hurry so I can take my time.' She drained her cup. 'Even if he survived the war, he could easily be dead by now.'

Steph abandoned the cold dregs of her coffee and stood up. 'If he'd survived the war, I feel sure you'd have heard about it. And now, since *I'm* not a lady of leisure, yet, I'd better get back to work. If there's anything I can do to help, let me know.'

Penny watched her walk away, tall and slender, in the direction of the central police station. There was shopping to do before she returned home and figured out where to begin.

CHAPTER 3 – LATE 1943

'Papa! Il se réveille!'

He became aware of sounds, voices. The crackle of logs on a fire. Footsteps on a wooden floor, a door opening. A man's voice. Comprehension was gradual but eventually he understood.

'C'est merveilleux, Delphine.'

Her voice in his ear, her lips so close he could feel her breath on his cheek.

'Marcel? Marcel, Vous m'entendez?' He knew he should say something. He recognized the language and the words at last and tried to reply. His lips were dry and he tried to move his tongue to wet them.

'Papa, passe-moi de l'eau,' the woman called Delphine said. 'Pass me some water, papa.'

A moment later, he felt her finger, damp, touch his lips, moistening them.

'Give me a spoon, Papa.'

She spilled a little cold water into his mouth. It ran icily into his throat and made him cough. She put an arm under his neck and lifted his head gently. The woman's father came to his other side and between them, they propped him up into something close to a sitting position.

He really must make the effort to open his eyes. He tried, but could see nothing. His breathing became panicky, and he lifted a hand to feel his eyes. She stopped him, her delicate fingers wrapped round his.

'Wait a moment and I will remove the bandage,' she said.

She slipped the spoon between his lips again and more cold water wetted his tongue. This time he swallowed. It was painful, but the water gradually soothed the pain away.

'I must take the feeding tube out of your nose,' she said.

A moment later he felt something being pulled down his nose. He felt the movement in his throat and it seemed to go on a long time. He felt a trickle of warmth on his upper lip which ran down his chin before she mopped it up.

'It is only a little blood,' she said, 'the tube has made your nose bleed.'

If only he could see.

Could he speak?

He tried to form words. The sound was a croak.

She gave him more water, mopped his nose, which seemed to be drying up.

This time when he tried, his voice was there, but rasping.

'Delphine,' he said.

'Yes, Marcel, Delphine.' He could hear happiness in her voice.

Her next question was directed at her father.

'Shall I take off the bandage, Papa?'

'Slowly, my dear. The doctor was clear on that: too quick and he will be blinded by the light.'

Marcel – Marcel was his name? – felt her hands delicately loosening a bandage which circled his head. Perhaps, he thought, he was *not* blind.

Light.

He began to see light.

At first dull and red-tinted, the colour of dried blood. Then, as another layer of the bandage was removed, brighter and the colour shifted to yellow as light from the room proved stronger than the bandage stain. He tried to move his hand, but it was painful.

'Ssh,' she said. 'Be easy. You have to learn to do things again.'

He frowned. At least, he thought he did. Just one layer of the bandage remained. He looked through the gauze and saw her, silhouetted against the flames of the fire. Her hair was neat, and appeared to be tied back. It was the style of a young woman, which concurred with her voice.

She unwound the last of the bandage and let him look at her.

Her hand lay near his, on the bed. He gritted his teeth with effort and managed to move his fingers until they touched hers. She glanced down, and gently enfolded his hand in hers. For the first time, they looked into each other's eyes.

Her hair was dark and her complexion olive, he now saw. Brown eyes studied his, as he now studied her. In her twenties, he guessed. He wondered if he knew her, he couldn't remember. With rising panic, he realised he could remember nothing of his life. He looked at her in fear.

'Who am I?'

She returned his look with a measure of puzzlement. 'Marcel Dubois.' She went to a cupboard beside the fireplace. From below a loose board in the bottom, in a small cavity, she took a small piece of folded card and gave it to him.

It was an identity document, containing his photograph, and printed in both French and German, which named him as Marcel Dubois, with a date of birth in 1919 in Hameau Belchamps and occupation of schoolteacher.

He blew dust from the card. 'How long have I been here?'

'Almost six months.'

He stared at her, incredulous. 'I don't remember... '

'You've been unconscious.' Delphine glanced at her father.

'I'll go and look,' the old man said, leaving the room.

Marcel looked from the door to Delphine. 'At what?'

'There are German patrols out here. We must be careful. They mustn't find you.'

'German...?'

She sighed. 'Do you know we are at war with Germany?'

He stared at her, and shook his head sadly. 'I don't know where I am, or anything about Germany.'

She smiled sadly. 'You're on a farm, not far from Sainte Marguerite-en-Bessin, in Normandy.'

'Normandy?'

'Normandy, France.'

He shook his head again, and covered his face with his hands.

'I know nothing. Oh, what has happened to me?' His voice rose in a wail of despair.

Delphine rested her hands on his shoulders. 'Don't worry. We'll look after you, as we have since I found you.'

'Found me?'

She sat on the bed and touched the card. 'I don't believe this.'

'Why? I don't understand.' His brain was reeling from the information he was gathering.

'Because you dropped from the sky. When I found you, in the Spring, you were unconscious and attached to a parachute. You had a terrible head injury, and we've been looking after you since then.'

He was aware that he was very thin. He examined his body. Every rib, every bone, was visible. He found he was wearing a diaper.

She smiled gently. 'We had to do something. We fed you through a tube.' She nodded at it, now lying on the table beside the bed. 'I'm afraid you'll be very weak. I can't give you much to eat: for one thing, we don't have much. The Germans control the food supplies, but we do have some eggs, which will be good for you. For another, it will not be good for you to eat too much all at once.'

As movement came back to his arms and hands, Marcel explored his body, becoming quickly aware that his skull showed signs of damage. Part of it, near the crown, was concave. There was no pain, his wound having long since healed. The rest of his body, apart from the thinness, displayed no obvious injuries.

Returning to what she'd said earlier, he asked her, 'So why do you think I was parachuted onto your land?'

She leaned close so she could lower her voice. Her breath was sweet and warm, and she smelled of soap. He noted that he had suddenly remembered soap, and that it could be scented, and pigeon-holed the fact.

'I think you are English, though your use of the French language is fluent. But you have a Parisian accent, which is how the English learn our language. According to your papers,' she nodded at the identity card, 'you are from round here, so you should have a local accent. And, of course, your arrival here was not that of a local.' She smiled. 'We tend to use bicycles.'

'Then, I am not Marcel Dubois?'

She shrugged. 'Unless we ever find out otherwise, I'm afraid you are.' Her expression became serious. 'If the Germans come, we shall try to hide you. We have succeeded on earlier occasions, and fortunately, they haven't bothered us much. We do what they ask us to do: grow food as best we can, and take it to town where they pay us very little for it – in Reichmarks, too – and sell it dearly. But people are fed.' She met his gaze levelly. 'We appear to collaborate, but we do not. Do you believe me?'

He shrugged. 'The fact I'm still here suggests you are being truthful.'

'Only me, Papa and Doctor Lafarge know you're here, and neither of them knows about the parachute. I buried it, though it grieved me not to take at least some of the silk.'

He frowned. 'What for?'

She grinned at him, her cheeks pinking. 'Certain types of clothing are in very short supply, due to the war.'

He gazed at her, baffled, but he didn't pursue the matter.

'For how long have – we – been at war with Germany?'

'The British declared war in September 1939. The following year, the Germans overran northern France.'

'And how long ago is that?'

'This is September 1943. Three years we have had to put up with the Boche.'

For the first time, he detected bitterness in her voice.

'And I have been here six months?'

She nodded. 'You should have gone to a hospital, but Papa and I dare not let you. Our doctor is trustworthy, though, and he has been coming to see you. He said you might suffer damage to your brain. I suppose your loss of memory is the sort of thing he meant.'

He was silent for a moment.

'And the war goes on? Are there any signs it will end soon?'

'We – the patriots – hope and pray that the Allies – the British and Americans, and our Free French soldiers – will one day soon return and drive the Germans out of our country. But, naturally, no-one knows when that might happen.'

Suddenly, he yawned. She noticed.

'You should sleep now. I am tiring you.'

'It sounds as though I've been asleep for half a year.'

She smiled and he noticed a pair of dimples appear adjacent to her lips. 'That is true, but I think you need a more natural form of sleep now. Don't worry: we'll soon have you up and about.'

* * *

On Christmas Eve, with snow covering the farmyard in thick drifts, a truck swept in through the gate and ground to a halt outside. Delphine peered through the window.

'It is the Boche!'

She stared in turn at her father and Marcel, who had risen to their feet from their chairs either side of the fireplace. Before anyone could do more, the door burst open and a jack-booted officer in the grey uniform of the Wehrmacht stepped inside. Behind him, two helmeted soldiers entered, their sub machine guns pointed at the room's three occupants.

The officer glanced quickly round the room, his eyes coming to rest on the table, still bearing the remains of dinner.

'I see you are contriving to keep yourself and your family well-fed, Monsieur Delacourt.'

'Yes, Captain.'

'Leutnant.'

'Yes, Leutnant.'

The officer turned towards Delphine and allowed his eyes to travel down her body from head to foot.

His gaze, in Marcel's view, was insolent. He was about to step forward and say something, when Delacourt grabbed him.

'No, Marcel!'

The lieutenant stepped in front of Marcel and drew his Luger pistol.

'No, indeed not!' he growled. His eyes strayed upwards to the indentation on Marcel's skull which remained as a reminder of his injuries.

Delacourt took Marcel's arm. 'Please, Leutnant, you can see he has been badly injured. He is not fully healed ...'

The officer hesitated a moment. 'You know there are people who think it would be kinder to put imbeciles out of their misery.'

'He is not an imbecile, Leutnant, merely recovering from a terrible injury.'

Behind Delphine's father, one of the two armed soldiers had been looking in drawers and ornaments, eventually finding something in the bottom of a ceramic vase. He threw the vase to the floor and picked a shiny gold necklace from the shattered pieces. The lieutenant sheathed his pistol in the holster fixed to his belt and held out his hand for the trinket. The soldier placed the necklace in it.

The lieutenant turned back to Delphine and held it up.

'This is yours?'

She nodded. 'It was my mother's. She left it to me when she died.'

He smiled. 'Then allow me to place it where it no doubt belongs.'

He gestured to her to turn round while he opened the necklace and arranged it round her throat, where a small pulse beat. His fingers lingered on her creamy skin which trembled in response. His grin broadened and he took his time with the clasp, until the jewel was fixed in place.

Delphine had kept her eyes downcast, but now raised them and found Marcel watching her. There was anger in his gaze. She shook her head briefly and the German glanced mockingly at him.

'You would do well to put away your anger. Is she yours?'

'No.'

The lieutenant pushed Delphine aside and moved to confront Marcel.

'So who are you? I had thought you her husband.' He jerked his head towards Delphine before holding out his hand. 'Papers!'

Marcel felt in the pocket of the dungarees he was wearing and produced his ID card. The lieutenant studied it and looked up.

'How long have you been here?'

'Two months, I think.'

'You *think*?'

Delphine stepped forward. 'He had an accident and doesn't remember everything,' she said. 'He has been here longer, but was unconscious.'

'What sort of accident?'

'He fell and hit his head on a rock. You can see,' she told him, pointing at Marcel's indented skull.

The lieutenant looked and appeared satisfied. He glanced once more at the ID card.

'You should register at the *Mairie*,' he said. 'You will get more rations that way.'

Marcel dropped his gaze in a show of humility. 'Thank you, Leutnant.' He took the card and replaced it in his pocket.

The officer turned back to Delacourt. 'I see you have eaten. My men are hungry. Please provide them with some food.'

The farmer's eyebrows arched. He shrugged.

'We have little to eat, Leutnant, but I will get it.'

Delacourt shuffled towards the door, the picture of a subservient peasant. The lieutenant jerked his head at one of the soldiers, who turned and went out with the old man.

The lieutenant strutted round the large kitchen, his eyes falling on the iron oven which drew its heat from the fire. He reached out to the handle.

'Leutnant!' Delphine cried.

He stopped and turned towards her, hand reaching for his pistol again.

She held out a cloth. 'The handle is hot.'

He looked from her to the oven and back. 'Please open it,' he told her.

She nodded and moved past him. She twisted the handle and the door swung back. Inside were three potatoes, which had been baking for some time. The aroma of their crisping skins filled the room.

'Thank you, they will be very welcome,' said the lieutenant. He gestured to the remaining soldier to remove his helmet and use it to hold the hot tubers.

Behind them, the door opened and Delacourt came in holding a dead rabbit, stiff with cold, followed by the soldier.

The lieutenant addressed the soldier. 'That was all they have?'

The soldier's heels snapped together and he stood to attention. 'Ja, Herr Leutnant.'

'Or all he let you see!' The lieutenant shifted his attention to Delphine and Marcel. 'Tell me, do you have any more to eat than this? After all, this is Christmas, the season of giving.'

Near the door, the soldier relaxed his stance, but held Delacourt's thin arm.

Delphine shook her head. 'That was to have been our Christmas meal,' she told him.

The lieutenant took a step towards her and gripped her chin, his eyes boring into hers.

'I'm not sure I believe you. This is your last chance. Tell me where your food supply is or one of you will be punished.'

Delphine tried to shake her head, tears beginning to fill her eyes. 'There is nothing else. We take all our food into Sainte Marguerite as we have to.'

'This is a farm. Of course you keep food back so you have plenty to eat.'

'No, Herr Leutnant. If we had any more we would show it to you.'

The officer shook his head. He maintained his grip while he darted a glance at Marcel before turning to the soldier holding Delacourt's arm and jerking his head towards the door. The soldier yanked the old man outside and the door slammed. Delphine sobbed.

Moments later, a shot rang out. The soldier returned, alone.

The lieutenant turned back to Delphine. 'I warned you what would happen. You still maintain you have no more food?'

"No,' she cried through her spilling tears.

Marcel, who had been perfectly still during this display of barbarity suddenly sprang to life and moved towards the German officer.

'Bastard!' he cried, but before he reached him the lieutenant pulled out his Luger and pressed it against Delphine's temple.

'Be quiet, or she will join her father. You will be next.'

When Marcel backed off, the lieutenant pushed Delphine away from him so that she fell against a small writing table under the window. The three Germans moved backwards to the door.

'Gute nacht.'

The door slammed behind them.

Delphine ran to it, but Marcel grabbed her round the waist. 'Wait until they're gone!'

The engine of the truck burst into life and they waited as it turned in the yard and finally drove away.

Silence fell.

Delphine clung to Marcel, her breasts crushed against him in a way that let him feel every one of her sobs as they wracked her. Her tears soaked the rough fabric of his shirt. He gently lowered her onto a chair.

With a glance to make sure she stayed there, he went to the door and stepped out into the moonlit snow. The body was not many yards away and plainly visible. Marcel availed himself of a big wooden wheelbarrow and loaded the farmer's remains into it before pushing it, its wheel squeaking, into an old byre. With the old man's corpse arranged respectfully on a bed of straw, Marcel returned to the house.

Delphine was where he'd left her. Her face, when he saw it in the firelight, seemed to have lost its colour, and her grief was palpable. Marcel found a clean handkerchief and dried her cheeks. She raised her eyes to look at him.

He clasped her arms lightly and shook his head.

'I'm sorry,' he told her, 'but your father is dead. I have left him comfortable and out of the weather, and tomorrow we will send for the priest.'

That night, for the first time, they lay together, both feeling the need to affirm life in the aftermath of death. When the priest came in the morning, they talked not only about a funeral, but also about arranging their marriage. In another era, such proximity would not be seemly, but in wartime, the normal rules, and often the timescales, sometimes have to be set aside.

CHAPTER 4 – 1999

Colonel Derek Pearson, CMG, MC, was a man of great presence, even at the age of 91. He still lived independently, though he employed a woman to come to his bungalow two mornings a week to help with the ironing and cleaning. He was also a man of great charm, Penny decided, when he bowed low over her hand and allowed his lips to brush her fingers.

'What can I do for you, Ms Sanderson?' he asked, waving her and Geoffrey to chairs facing his in the snug sitting room.

'Geoffrey says you knew my father, which is more than I did,' she began, and explained her desire to discover what became of him.

'David Greatorix was a good man,' he told her. 'He was a good mathematician, and not only that, but he was a gifted linguist too. Fluent in French.' He settled himself more comfortably in the worn leather armchair he occupied. 'Of course, it was the maths that attracted SOE's interest.'

' And is that important?'

' Very much so,' he said. 'Mathematics involves a great deal of logic, and logic is key to unravelling ciphers. Before they found a four rotor Enigma machine, logic was about the only thing we had.'

'What can you tell me about why my father was sent to France?'

'Ah, well, there I can't be too helpful, I'm afraid. I know there was something which was upsetting the powers-that-be, but I'm not quite sure what.'

'Wouldn't it be unusual to send a person like David Greatorix into France?' asked Geoffrey. 'They would be running a terrible risk, if he'd been arrested.'

'Yes that's true. I can only suppose that the need must have been great, and they must have required someone who wasn't known to other agents.'

The Colonel thought for a few moments. 'You see, normally, those agents who were recruited specifically to work in France were trained in groups, so they often knew each other. The fact that they decided to send your father, who hadn't trained in any group – well, not only suggests a bit of a hurry, but also – and I'm only guessing,' he added, 'it makes me think they didn't want anyone to recognise him.'

Geoffrey stood up and went over to the sideboard. 'You have any of that lowland malt here, dad?' he asked.

'Left-hand cupboard.' The Colonel turned to Penny. 'Would you like a drop?'

'Just a small one, please. I thought when they dropped agents into France, that a member of the local resistance group would meet them.'

'That would be the normal practice,' said the Colonel, 'which leaves us with the possibility that either the person who was sent to meet them betrayed your father, or he or she was arrested before your father was met.'

Penny wrinkled her brow. 'But surely my father would have made contact with someone, even if the person he should have met wasn't there when he landed?'

Geoffrey set shot glasses down on the small table between them, keeping one in his hand.

'I think it would be normal practice for there to be a fallback position,' said the Colonel. 'The thing is, so much else in this case didn't fly by the normal rules, we can't be certain they applied them.'

'Even so,' said Penny, 'whatever happened, surely he would have tried to contact SOE?'

The Colonel sipped his malt. 'I agree. And there, as the Bard probably said, is the rub. Surely, he would, *if* he'd been able.'

There was a silence while they considered the obvious conclusion.

'So the chances are, he was killed around the time he landed?' She glanced from one to the other.

'It was, of course, the official view,' said the Colonel.

'So what I need to find out is where he was dropped,' she said. 'I suppose if someone found his body, he would have been buried nearby?'

'That is often what happened at the time,' said the Colonel. 'After the war, the War Graves Commission exhumed the bodies of soldiers, sailors and airmen, and buried them in military cemeteries.' His eyes moistened. 'I saw the graves of a lot of my old comrades when I visited some of the cemeteries in France, after the war.'

Penny took a small sip of her whisky, while father and son both drained their glasses in unison.

'Of course, if David followed normal practice, he went to France under a false identity, and might not have been reburied by the War Graves Commission if they didn't recognise him as a British agent.'

'Which is most likely what happened,' said the Colonel.

He studied Penny for a moment, then seemed to come to a conclusion.

'Leave it with me until tomorrow, and I'll see if I can find anything out from one of my old contacts.'

Penny glanced at Geoff and saw a small, satisfied smile on his face. She guessed this was what he'd expected to happen. Declining the offer of a refill, ten minutes later, she found herself walking along a neat suburban pavement, Geoff positioning himself always between her and the road, as if it was the most natural thing in the world to do.

He looked round at her. 'Fancy some lunch?'

Penny glanced at him and grinned wryly. 'I'm not going to make a habit of dining out,' she told him. 'Since I retired I find I have to work at not putting weight on.'

'If it bothers you, I give you full permission to watch me eat lunch while you chew on a piece of lettuce.'

'I give you full permission to chew on a piece of lettuce with me,' she said.

She was amused by the look of disgust which crossed his face as he took her elbow and guided her over the road towards a pub from which issued an appetising aroma of chips and real ale.

It was when he picked up his beef burger in its bun, using both hands, and took a large bite out of it that she abandoned her intention to saw through her salad-filled baguette with the dull knife she'd been given, and picked it up in like manner. It was, she knew, not the most elegant way to tackle her food, and it was good, she thought, that, whatever reservations she might still harbour about Geoff Pearson, she felt able in his company to behave more naturally, more as she would have in the comfort and safety of her own home.

She watched him apply himself to his food, with single-minded determination. The word which came to her was trencherman. She wondered what sort of father he had been when his children were still at home, what kind of husband. If he'd been working undercover, she knew from her own experience in the police service, there would have been times he'd gone "to work" and his wife wouldn't have seen him for weeks, with no explanation ever given to her. Such behaviour put a great strain on a marriage, and demanded much understanding from one's partner. How had he coped when his wife had been killed? Competently, she guessed. Geoff would be extremely *competent*, she figured, in any situation.

It was something of a surprise to her to realise she had begun to think of him as "Geoff", rather than Geoffrey.

She raised her eyes and found he was gazing at her. For some reason, it made her feel self-conscious, which surprised her even more. Penny was not the kind of woman who routinely worried about what other people were thinking, so something was different, her detective's mind told her, about the present situation. The lines which joined his nose to the corners of his mouth deepened and his lips parted in a smile which revealed even teeth. A jolt of lust rocked her, causing her to suck in her stomach and inhale deeply.

Good God! she told herself, let's not go there!

But the signs were real, and she knew she would have to squash such feelings if she was to make progress with her quest. At the moment, Geoff – Geoffrey! – was a man with contacts, who had conveniently offered to use them on her behalf. She refused to contemplate what *he* might hope to gain from their partnership.

'Penny for them,' he said.

'If I had a penny – make it a pound – for every time I've heard that.'

He grinned. 'Sorry, it was just a figure of speech. Must in future remember to engage brain before opening mouth.'

She smiled.

'You've been very quiet,' he said, 'I just wondered what you were thinking about.'

She shrugged. It gave her time to think what to say. 'I do have other things to consider,' she said. 'But I was remembering this morning and how nice it would have been if I'd been able to visit my father like you can visit yours.'

'Do you have any photographs of him?'

'One. Taken in 1940 in his first uniform. He looked very dashing, but I wonder what he was really like.'

'I'd like to see it sometime.'

'Why?'

He glanced at her. 'Just interested.'

His reply left her wondering again. Was it an innocent request or did he have some other purpose? She mentally shook herself. Such a suspicion, she thought, must be down to her years as a police officer: that made a person suspect just about everybody of almost anything.

She finished her meal and sat back, away from the table.

'If the PRO's no use to us, and while your father is trying to find out where mine was dropped, what other channels of enquiry do we have?' she asked.

He considered the matter for a moment, before looking up at her and grinning. 'I have a couple of tickets to see that new show, *Mamma Mia* tonight, so my next channel of enquiry is, how'd you feel about going to see it?'

The suggestion took her by surprise. It was a show she wanted to see, though the thought of doing so with Geoff beside her gave her pause. But, she told herself, she hadn't been out in male company for a long time. She knew her feelings about him were ambivalent: she sensed he could be dangerous, but at the same time, quite paradoxically, she felt safe with him.

'That will hardly progress the matter.' It was amazing how she could still slip back into "police mode speech" without thinking. She pulled herself up suddenly and opened her mouth to paraphrase the sentence in words less formal, but he nodded and spoke first.

'No, it won't, but I'd like to get to know you better, if you don't mind, and discovering whether you have the same interests as me is quite important. To me, at any rate.'

Penny found herself agreeing, but keeping the knowledge private. However, she'd made a decision.

'Yes, okay. Where shall I meet you?'

Geoff 's smile was as broad as a teenage swain's. She had to fight hard to stop herself laughing out loud, not only at his obvious pleasure but at the feeling she'd almost forgotten, of the power she could wield over a man. She spared a thought for what should happen after the theatre. What *usually* happened after a night out? Would he want to take her somewhere afterwards and have sex? She felt very out of touch with current practices and expectations.

She blew out her cheeks. There was no way *that* would happen, but it would be wonderful if he asked…

In the event, when Penny glanced sideways at Geoff in the half-light of the theatre, she saw with surprise that he was watching her, not the stage, and quietly smiling.

If he'd asked her then to spend the night with him, she knew she'd more likely than not have agreed.

Chapter 5 – Spring, 1944

It was doing things like this that made him feel alive.

Marcel glanced to his left through the foliage to see that Delphine was unhurt. She pulled her beret on even tighter having nearly lost it as they rolled down the bank. Above them, the roar of engines indicated the passing of the German patrol.

He raised his eyebrows in a silent question. She smiled and nodded. She was okay.

When the patrol had passed, they climbed the bank again and looked across the road at the railway track which ran parallel to it. The line ran from the Normandy coast east towards Paris, and was used by the Germans to reinforce and supply the troops in northern France.

Word had been received through coded messages broadcast by the BBC that the longed-for invasion was imminent, though not precisely when. The resistance group of which Delphine and Marcel were now an integral part had the job of destroying this rail link, and keeping it destroyed until the area was liberated by the invasion force. The competence with which the German military could repair damaged track was well-known, but it was hoped that when many different lines were cut at the same time, even the enemy's efficiency would take a hit.

A dozen members of the Sainte Marguerite group were now in position, either side of the line, ready to install explosives to the rails.

The Germans were as aware as anyone of the strategic importance of the rail link, hence the regular patrols on the road which ran beside the track. The group knew from previous observation that they had a window of ten minutes before the patrol came back, and a short whistle from the leader indicated that it was time to move up to the track and begin their dangerous work.

Marcel's backpack was full of explosive. With increasing frequency, British aircraft would fly over and drop "plastique", which the groups could use against tough objectives, like bridges and dams.

Marcel ran across the road, Delphine at his left, until he was beside the railway line. Unfastening his pack, he began to fix the shaped charges against the rails. Into each charge, Delphine pushed a detonator. With all the explosives in place, Marcel connected each of the detonators together, and all of them to the long cable they would use to trigger the explosion.

Paying out the cable, Delphine and Marcel moved back across the road and slithered down the bank. Delphine took the box with the plunger, which would detonate the charges, from her backpack, and Marcel connected the wires from the detonators. The group leader whistled once more. Delphine pulled up the plunger and pressed it hard. The ground shook as above them both rails of the line were torn apart along a one-hundred-metre stretch.

For a while at least, the Germans would be denied the use of the line to reinforce their troops on the coast.

Delphine, Marcel and the rest of the group melted into the darkness.

The next morning, it seemed as if the entire German army had saturated the area. Before dawn, two lorry-loads of infantrymen turned up at the farm and searched every outbuilding, scattering the remains of the harvest, and the few hens they still owned, in all directions. They left empty-handed. Marcel and Delphine watched them go before beginning the process of tidying up and recapturing the hens.

It took them until the middle of the day. The hens were their first priority, and they were rounded up in little more than half an hour. Re-stacking the clamps of vegetables took much longer and involved harder work. When they had finished, he closed the door of the barn and padlocked it while she watched. He stood beside her and put his arm round her shoulders.

'Let's go in.'

He led her to the door of the farmhouse and opened it. Before she entered, she turned round to look at the yard.

'I love this place, Marcel,' she said, 'almost as much as I love you, but there are times I wish we lived somewhere else, somewhere we could bring up our children in peace, where there would be no fear of soldiers turning up at any time of the day and night; where life often seems to hang by a thread.'

He held her close. 'So do I, my love.' As he spoke, the sun emerged from behind a cloud and shone its dappled light, filtered through the leaf-filled branches of a horse chestnut tree, onto the hard earth of the yard. 'The war won't last forever. The liberation will be soon.'

She sighed and laid her head comfortably on his shoulder. 'I know, but when? How soon?'

He shrugged. 'We only know what we hear. Speaking of which...' He cocked his head on one side, listening. 'We have a visitor.'

Delphine straightened up, alert. 'They're coming back?'

'No. I don't think so.'

A lone cyclist rode into the yard. Marcel recognised him as the leader of the Resistance group they'd been out with, Albert Lebrun.

'Good afternoon, M'sieur, Madame,' he said, touching a finger to his beret when he addressed Delphine. He glanced round. 'We're alone?'

Assured on this point, he said, 'It will be the next full moon when they come.'

Marcel lifted a sceptical eyebrow. 'They said that in May.'

Albert looked at him in some exasperation. 'I *know* that! But this seems to be the real thing. It's taken a bit of time to find an SOE radio operator, since the last one was taken.' He pushed his cap up and scratched his head. 'The full moon is the sixth of June. All the resistance groups will be working to destroy bridges, telegraph and telephone lines, the railways and anything else that might otherwise be useful to von Rundstedt.'

His expression softened as he turned to Delphine. 'How are you?'

He lowered his gaze to the swelling of the young woman's belly.

Delphine smiled wryly. 'It would be better for him' – she tapped her stomach – 'if we had a bit more good food, but we seem to be all right.'

Albert was still looking at the visible signs of Marcel and Delphine's heir. 'How far along are you?' he asked.

'Twenty-five weeks, I think.'

'I don't want to worry you, Madame, but have you seen the doctor? You look a little small for someone so far gone. Smaller than my sister did at four months.'

Delphine and Marcel both looked at Albert, worried.

'We've seen no need to fetch the doctor,' said Marcel, but his voice was doubtful.

'He's kicking all right?' asked Albert. 'I think he's all right if you can feel him moving.' He lifted her eyes to meet Delphine's anxious gaze and shrugged apologetically. 'Oh, don't mind me, I'm just a man. What would I know about it? Put it down to the war.'

Marcel spoke. 'Do you want some coffee?'

Albert wrinkled his nose. 'You mean that stuff they make out of acorns?'

Delphine nodded, shrugging. 'Of course.'

'Thank you, but I'll just have some water.'

After he was gone, his bicycle bouncing across the uneven ruts of the farmyard, Delphine turned to Marcel. He saw pain in her eyes.

'What's the matter, my love?'

She chewed her lip for a moment. 'I – I don't feel him move,' she told him, and burst into tears.

He took her in his arms. 'Delphine, my darling, don't blame yourself. If God has seen fit to take our little one so soon, He must have really needed him – or her.' He kissed the top of her head. 'And he may just be having a rest. We'll go and see the doctor.'

But the news, when they went into town the next day, was as bad as it could be. Doctor Lafarge dried his hands and rolled down his sleeves while Delphine dressed behind a screen.

'I'm sorry, Madame Dubois, but I think the child is dead,' he said, when she was once again sitting beside his roll-top desk.

Delphine could not speak. She closed her eyes and tears flowed, hot and wet, down her cheeks, dripping onto her blouse. The doctor leaned forward and tenderly dabbed at them with a clean linen handkerchief which he relinquished into her hands. With her face covered, suddenly a howl rose in her throat, followed by gusty sobs.

The door burst open and Marcel entered, rushing to his wife's side.

'Delphine! Oh, my love!' he cried, holding her tightly.

She tried to control her breathing. 'Our baby! Our baby's dead.'

Marcel glanced at the doctor for confirmation and received a shrug. Tears filled his own eyes. The doctor rose to his feet.

'I will be back shortly, there is something I need to do.'

After the door closed behind him, Marcel and Delphine struggled to control their grief.

He wiped his tears away with a sleeve. 'We can have more children,' he said.

She dabbed at her cheeks again and looked up at him. The pain of loss was clear to see.

'What if we can't? We might not be able to. Maybe any child we make will die before he or she is born?'

'Oh, I know it's possible, but it's far more likely that not having enough to eat, coupled with our way of life' – he glanced round to make sure they weren't being overheard – 'have caused this to happen.'

When the doctor returned, they were ready to leave.

'You have my sympathy – both of you,' he said.

'What happens now?' Delphine asked, looking down at her slightly-rounded belly.

'If indeed the child has died – there isn't much hope it hasn't, if I'm honest about it – then you will abort in the next few days. When you are no longer pregnant, your body will return to its natural rhythms, and expel the lining of the womb as it does each month. This time, it will be quite painful, however. You can go into hospital at Bayeux, if I can find you a place, or you could stay at home. My nurse, Simone, could attend you. I'll let you have some morphine.'

He got up and went to a cupboard, returning with one of the Syrettes he kept on a shelf, which had a long neck containing a needle. He gave it to Marcel.

'When your wife cannot bear the pain any longer, you break the seal and slip the needle in just under the skin, at a very shallow angle.'

Delphine shut her eyes and shed tears again at the thought.

'I'm so sorry,' the doctor added.

'We'll be able to have another child, won't we, Doctor?' asked Marcel.

'More than likely. I can see no reason why not.' He turned to Delphine. 'You should not blame anyone for this, Madame. It is the war. They say it will be over by Christmas.'

He turned to Marcel. 'And you, M'sieur, how are you?' His fingers touched the depression at the rear of Marcel's skull.

'I am well, thank you, but still remember nothing before being at the farm.'

'It's possible your memory will return, but it may be patchy. Something done or said, or a place or thing, might just trigger some recollection. Then again,' he shrugged, 'it might not. It is rather like trying to light a fire with a tinderbox: the flint, the steel and the kindling have to be in just the right place relative to each other when the spark is struck in order for the tinder to catch. One day, something you've said or done, or felt or seen numerous times before may suddenly cause the right kind of spark and you will remember something.'

'I hope I do.'

The doctor had moved away to his desk and sat down. 'Be careful what you wish for, M'sieur.' He looked up. 'But it would be interesting to know how you got your Parisian accent. There are not many of those in Sainte Marguerite-en-Bessin or Hameau Belchamps these days.'

Marcel turned as he ushered his wife out of the room. 'You have a far better memory than I, Doctor, if you can remember where I was born.'

The doctor smiled. 'Ah, but I haven't had a very bad bang on the head.'

* * *

Every day, the pile of paper in Ann Greatorix's in-tray seemed bigger than before. The quantity of Ultra, the name given to Enigma-encoded messages, was growing, and it didn't take much brain to work out that something was exercising the mind of the German High Command.

Fortunately, the code breakers of Station X were by now able to decode the messages very quickly and keep the planners of military strategies au fait with the enemy's intentions.

More than a year had passed since she had last seen her husband and still nothing had been heard from or about him. She had never quite given up hope of seeing him again, but every day that passed, she told herself she must look to the future for both herself and her daughter.

She had named the child Penelope because it was the name, in Greek mythology, of the wife of Odysseus, who waited for him faithfully for twenty years while he fought at Troy and then got lost going home. Ann figured naming her daughter Penelope might somehow bring her husband back to her.

If he was still alive.

She felt certain she would have known if he was dead.

In the meantime, she buried her feelings under a mountain of work. In her dark corner of the hut, she tapped away at her typewriter, barely stopping for sustenance. Mary Hamilton had noticed and kept her supplied with tea.

'Mustn't neglect the inner woman,' she said with a tight little smile as she placed a brimming cup on just about the last clear space on Ann's desk.

She stopped typing and tugged the paper out of the platen with a rasping sound, putting it face-down in her out-tray.

'Thanks, Mary,' she said, pressing her shoulders back and shaking her fingers to relax the muscles.

The older woman was about to move away when she seemed to change her mind.

'Look, it can't be much fun for you, bringing up Penny on your own, and working twelve-hour shifts here, day in, day out. Why don't you come to my house one evening, and let me do dinner.' She sighed. 'It's so long since I had company, and it's so tedious, cooking just for one.'

Ann considered the offer. Having only her small daughter for company at home and work colleagues to talk to during the day was undoubtedly not the recipe for a great life. Adult company would be welcome, she decided.

'Thanks. That's very good of you. I can bring some food round.'

Mary waved away the offer. 'No, that's all right. Keep what you've got. You have a growing girl, who needs all the grub she can get. I've plenty for us, and Penny, too, if you want to bring her.' She smiled. 'Of course, if you can get a babysitter, we can be just the two of us.'

Ann thought about her mother, who looked after Penny while she was at work, and figured she'd probably agree to a few extra hours with her only grandchild.

'Sounds good to me, Mary,' she said. 'A night out would be wonderful. I've forgotten what they're like.'

Her attention switched to the man who had burst into the hut behind Mary and was staring round as if the place was unfamiliar to him. He was not someone Ann recognised.

Mary turned to follow her gaze. 'Can we help you?' she asked.

'Ann Greatorix?' asked the man.

Ann's heart leapt. News of David? 'I'm Ann.'

He pulled a strip of paper from his pocket and held it out. With a sinking feeling, she recognised it as one more Ultra decode.

'Can you type this up at once – sorry about my writing.' He glanced at Mary. 'I get so nervous, sometimes,' he told her with a twitchy little grin.

Mary smiled at him and took the message while Ann fitted a clean sheet of paper into her typewriter.

'It must be very important,' Mary said, her eyes wide in admiration.

The young man blushed. 'Oh, I think so.'

'You must be awfully clever,' she said.

Ann glanced at her and smiled inwardly. Mary was trying very hard to engage the man's interest, but then, it was no surprise: Frank was still a prisoner in Germany, and she'd made no secret of the fact that she enjoyed the company of young men – given what Ann knew about her, that could easily include bed-and-breakfasting them.

Mary hitched her bottom onto the corner of Ann's desk and allowed one foot to swing, until the heel of her shoe slipped off leaving it to hang only by the toe. She also made sure she leaned forward often, allowing the young man to glimpse her breasts when he glanced down at her.

Ann concentrated on the message. She deliberately tried not to remember what was in most of the them, but it was sometimes hard to ignore what some of them said. The one in front of her included a reference to eastern England, and was a directive by the High Command to *counter the build-up of FUSAG by moving all available troops to the Pas de Calais*. She'd never heard of FUSAG, but guessed that it was something to do with the invasion of Europe, which everyone knew would happen soon.

She finished typing and pulled the page from her type-writer. The young man held out his hand for it, but she shook her head.

'Sorry. This has to go to my boss now.'

She felt sorry for him as his face took on a crestfallen look, but orders were orders, and her duty was clear. As she locked away the papers on her desk, she saw Mary stand up, extend an arm and run her fingers lightly down his cheek.

'She's right, you know. There are procedures to follow. Still, if you've decoded something really useful, I'm sure you will be... properly rewarded.'

Ann grinned to herself, and thought she could guess what kind of reward Mary might have in mind. She knocked on Callum's door, opening it in response to his invitation.

'Ah, and what have you brought for me, Ann?' His eyes were fixed on the papers in her hand.

'One of the decoders brought this through in person, so I guess it might be urgent.' She held the message and her tran-scription of it out so he could take them.

He read both pieces of paper and then stood and looked at her, excitedly. He came round the desk.

'It's excellent news, Ann,' he said, and grabbing her round the waist with one hand, the other, containing the messages still, on her shoulder, he whirled her round the room in a frenzied reel. She tripped as he spun her and felt her ankle twist. Fortunately she was near a chair and able to sit down, wincing as pain shot up her leg.

He was all contrition. Dropping the papers on his desk, he fell to his knees and took her foot in his warm hands.

The action caused her to suck in her breath sharply, and he looked up into her face, alarm and concern all over his.

'Och! I'm sorry, Ann. I didna mean to hurt you, girl.'

Now he'd stopped actually trying to move her ankle, she discovered there was some pleasure in having his hand simp-ly support her foot.

'I think I've twisted it,' she said, feeling foolish.

He bowed his head. 'Och! Ann, I'm so clumsy.' He looked up at her, devastated. 'And I should have realised, you didna know the steps.'

The statement struck her as very funny, and she felt a bubble of laughter grow in her chest until she had to let it out.

'Oh, Callum!' she said, wiping her eyes, 'if you could see your face!'

He seemed puzzled by her response at first, but gradually her laughter infected him and he grinned.

'Okay, so now we both know I'm an idiot. Can you walk?'

He supported her arm as she stood up, but when she tried to put some weight on the injured ankle, pain struck again, and she would have fallen had he not held her.

His sudden proximity, the pressure of his body against hers, caused her to feel something she'd not experienced since she and David had spent their last night together. A rush of heat balled in her stomach and spread upwards, causing her breasts to tingle and a rush of blood to darken the flesh of her chest, slowly extending to her neck. Her breathing became ragged and she looked at him to see if he'd noticed.

She realised from a growing pressure on her hip that whether he had or hadn't, their closeness was affecting him in a similar way. She forced herself to swallow and slip out of his arms so she could sit down.

She looked up at him. 'No,' she said.

He looked puzzled.

'No, it appears I can't walk,' she said in amplification.

'Oh! Oh, well, you'd better let me take you home.'

'I have my bike.'

'I'll stick it in the boot.'

'What about my work?'

'I'll get Mary to take over.'

She felt surprised at his choice of deputy, as Mary had not done the work before, but acquiesced, waiting for him to collect her coat and handbag and make the arrangements to cover both their absences, and then, still feeling a mixture of foolishness and arousal, which refused to go away, she slipped one arm round his broad shoulders and leaned on him all the way to his car.

CHAPTER 6 – 1999

In the event, Geoff had taken Penny home after the show and only kissed her chastely on the cheek. He hadn't touched her in the three days since, and she found herself wondering if she'd misunderstood, and he didn't like her as much as she'd thought he did. But apart from that, he continued to behave just as he had before, with courtesy and the occasional flash of humour.

Then yesterday, he'd gone into London without her, and without much in the way of explanation. And when he'd called for her today, to take her to see his father, he hadn't referred to the trip at all.

What, she wondered, was going on?

But then, no doubt Geoff had a private life, his own business. Maybe he had a girlfriend somewhere. She'd not detected any evidence of one, which meant either he was very good at removing all trace – not something men were, in her opinion – or he didn't have one. It was teasingly frustrating not to know. Of greater concern to her was the feeling of listlessness that had not left her all the day. Surely, she told herself, she didn't miss him?

Anyway, she thought, what business is it of mine what he does in London?

Even so, she knew she wanted it to be.

They were seated in the Colonel's lounge, each with a glass of his Glenkinchie. It was obviously something of a regular ritual when Geoff visited.

'Have you been able to find anything out, Dad?'

The old man turned to look at Penny, tilting his head slightly, which gave him a quizzical air.

'It wasn't easy,' he began, 'but I did get to talk to someone. Your father was deployed on rather an unusual mission,' he continued.

Penny waited. 'Oh yes?'

'Yes, someone had been betraying the leaders of the resistance group, based at Sainte Marguerite-en-Bessin, in *Normandie-basse* – Lower Normandy – and your father's job was to try to find out who the traitor was.'

'I thought my father was involved in code breaking, not employed as a field agent?'

'That is so,' replied the Colonel, 'but I believe it was his fluent French is the reason he was considered suitable. And because he was not known to other agents.' He paused and studied her expression. 'He volunteered, you know.'

'I didn't know, no,' Penny said. 'I suppose a lot of people volunteered to do things they didn't have to do, during the war.'

'That's true,' said the Colonel, 'but what your father did was particularly brave. He knew he would be very much on his own, though another SOE agent should have met him when he landed. We know that didn't happen, because that agent was shot by the Gestapo.'

Penny sipped her drink. 'Do you know where he landed?'

The Colonel took a draught of his whisky and smiled. 'I know where he was supposed to be dropped,' he said. 'The only person who knows for a fact where he was really dropped is the pilot of the aircraft, but he is no longer with us.' He turned to his son. 'Pass me the Michelin Atlas, will you, Geoff.'

A moment later, with the atlas open at the appropriate page, the Colonel indicated an area between Sainte Marguerite-en-Bessin and Bayeux.

'As far as my old friend in the SOE is concerned,' he said, 'that's where your father should have been dropped.' He took another sip of his whisky. 'But you have to be aware that in those days, navigation was far from being an accurate science. Weather conditions and the exigencies of war could have conspired to put the aircraft off course.'

'But it would be the place to start,' said Geoff.

* * *

It took them a week to organise their journey. With no hotels in Sainte Marguerite-en-Bessin itself, they booked rooms at the DeVries Hotel in Bayeux, which they reached in the evening after spending most of the day at sea. Next morning, they drove the short distance to the hamlet. It was built around the junction of two roads, and had been by-passed in recent years by the main road between Bayeux and Carentan. It was little more than a few farmsteads, and homes for people who worked in the nearby town. There was, however, a bar near the junction. Penny and Geoffrey parked and went in.

On their immediate right, a polished wood bar counter curved round to the wall. *Le Patron,* a stout man wearing a clean white apron stood by the open access flap in the counter at the far end, nursing a glass of wine. On the left, a long bench seat ran, in front of which were three substantial rectangular wooden tables. More tables and chairs filled the far end of the room. Being so small, the place seemed crowded and yet there weren't that many customers. Two elderly men sat at the middle of the left-hand tables, whilst a group of younger people sat at the far end. Penny thought they would be unlikely to have the kind of information she wanted, whereas the older men might.

'How good's your French?' she asked Geoff in a low voice.

He sucked his cheeks in for a moment, a glint of amusement in his eyes.

'If we're talking about the language, not particularly. Schoolroom stuff, and I haven't been near a schoolroom for thirty-odd years.'

'What else would I be talking about?' she demanded with mock severity. 'No! Don't answer that.'

She got up and crossed the room towards the two elderly men, smiling as they looked up. The one on the left was clean-shaven, prosperous-looking, with round, wire-rimmed glasses and brushed-back, thinning grey hair, while the one to her right was more wizened in appearance, with a trimmed half-inch of beard and deep laughter-lines around his eyes, which twinkled with azure lucidity. Penny thought they were beautiful.

'*Pardon, Messieurs,*' she began, '*mais est-ce que vous connaissez ceux qui étaient dans la résistance en dix-neuf cent quarante-quatre?*'

The one on the left replied. 'You are English?'

'Yes,' Penny replied, relieved that she would not have the burden of all the language work.

'What do you want to know?'

She explained about her father.

'What was his name?'

'David. David Greatorix.'

She noticed peripherally the bearded man was looking at her, but when she turned to face him fully, she realised his eyes were focussed slightly to one side. She had a sudden intuition that he was blind.

'Do you know of him?'

The one on the left translated the question for the benefit of the other. Both men shook their heads.

'You are Miss Greatorix? I am Doctor Lafarge and this is my friend Albert Lebrun. We both lived here in 1944, and Albert led the local resistance group.'

'Penny Sanderson, these days, Doctor, though I'm a widow.'

The doctor glanced across the room at Geoff. 'And he is your paramour?'

That's a better question than you know, she thought. 'We're just friends with a similar interest.'

'Well, Madame Sanderson,' he said, 'there were several agents of your SOE parachuted into this area in the months before *Jour-J*, or D-Day, and one thing about all of them: they had French names and identity papers. There is no possibility that when Monsieur Greatorix landed, he was not similarly equipped.'

Penny felt deflated. It must have shown in her expression because the doctor spoke again, kindly.

'You did not know? But it is obvious now, *n'est-ce pas?'*

Geoff brought her drink across and introduced himself.

The doctor invited them to bring a couple of chairs over and sit down.

Penny related the doctor's comment to Geoff.

'I'll ask my father if he can discover David's cover name.'

'Your father?' The doctor tilted his head slightly in query.

'He worked for SOE as well during the war. There are still some others alive.'

'Oh,' replied the doctor.

It seemed to Penny that he had thought better of making some comment or other.

'Do you know when your father was sent here?'

'March, 1943,' she told him.

'Albert,' said the doctor, turning to the other, *'Est-ce que tu connais-tu un agent anglais qui est arrivé en mars, dix-neuf cents quarante-trois?'*

The bearded man shrugged and drained his glass.

'Est-ce que vous voudriez encore quelque chose à boire, Albert?' Penny asked. Would you like another drink?

He smiled and asked her in careful French for a glass of Pastis.

Geoff got to his feet. 'I'll get it. And for you, sir?' he added, looking at the doctor.

'A glass of Merlot, if you please.'

Penny declined another drink. When Geoff had gone to the bar, she turned back to Albert.

The wrinkles covering his forehead deepened. After a moment's thought, he spoke rapidly in French to the doctor. *"Il n'y avait aucun agent britannique qui est venu s'engager avec nous à ce moment-là'*

'Albert does not remember any British agent joining the local group at that time,' he translated.

Penny felt disappointed that her enquiry seemed to have fallen at the first fence. 'Oh,' she sighed. 'That seems to be that... unless there was another group round here?' She glanced back at Albert, whose clear but sightless eyes appeared to be fixed on hers. 'A group which had lost most of its leaders?'

The doctor put the question for her.

Albert's brow wrinkled again.

But after a moment, he nodded.

Penny felt her heart leap. Albert spoke.

Again, the doctor translated. 'He says there was a group of *maquis* like that. In fact, several.'

'Is there anyone we could talk to who would have been connected with them? Someone who was in one of them?'

There was a long conversation in the local patois Penny found so difficult to understand before the doctor turned to her and shook his head.

'Not as far as we know,' he told her. 'All the ones Albert knew were killed by a German patrol trying to escape from the Falaise Pocket some time after D-Day.'

'*Beaucoup de chefs de groupes de résistance ont été pris et tués a ce temps-là*' added Albert, speaking directly to Penny. The doctor didn't translate. Geoff, who had returned bearing drinks, looked an enquiry at her.

'I think he said that many resistance group leaders were caught and killed around that time.'

Albert nodded imperceptibly.

'Thank you,' Geoff said politely.

Penny turned back to the doctor. 'What is the Falaise Pocket?'

Geoff explained that in the August following D-Day, Allied troops, including some airborne brigades who had been dropped inland from the coast, had been able to sweep round to the south of the town of Falaise and encircle German army units. The British, who had been held up by strong resistance from the occupying army at Caen, finally managed to push through, and between them, the Allies closed the last remaining gap on the Paris side of Falaise, capturing huge numbers of enemy personnel and their equipment in the process.

The doctor smiled. 'It was one of the first strategies in which Free French soldiers, the Second Armoured Division under the command of General Leclerc, played a full and vital role.'

Geoff nodded politely. 'And let's not forget the Canadians and Poles.'

The smile disappeared from the doctor's face. 'No, indeed. Let us not forget them, nor the fact that for most of the war, we French were an occupied nation, deprived of our freedoms, and unable to join our allies in the struggle to overthrow Hitler.'

Penny glanced from him to Geoff and sensed that a conflict of national pride was about to arise.

'I'm sure it was a matter of great rejoicing to all the allied forces that the French army was able to take its place alongside them in the battle to liberate their own country.'

The doctor smiled again, and the level of tension fell. 'Indeed, it was a proud moment for the French.'

'But somewhere, in the process of "closing the Falaise Pocket", many resistance fighters were wiped out?'

'So Albert says.'

Penny thought for a moment. 'Does he know where?'

She was, by now, used to Albert's sightless eyes tracking her voice.

The doctor frowned. 'Why would you want to know that?'

'In case my father was among them. I could look in the local graveyard.' She grimaced. 'I want to have a look at the ones round here. It's why I'm here, to find my father's grave.'

'Oh, yes, yes, of course,' said the doctor.

Another series of questions and answers passed between the two old men.

'Albert thinks it was near the crossing of the N13 and the railway line.'

'We could travel over there and see if we can find out anything from the locals,' suggested Geoff.

The doctor lifted his glass. 'You could try.'

CHAPTER 7 – JUNE, 1944

Marcel grieved: not only for his unborn, dead child, but also for the effect it was having on his wife, as each day, she waited for her body to expel the foetus.

There was a knock at the door, startling him. He left his wife's side and crossed the room.

'Who's there?' he said through the door.

'Pineapple,' came the reply.

'Orange,' said Marcel, pulling the bolts, satisfied the code word was correct.

Albert was standing on the threshold.

'Come in,' said Marcel, glancing round the yard to see if they were being watched by anyone.

Albert crossed the floor to the fireside where he could warm his hands, dry out clothes which, Marcel could now see, were quite wet, and look at Delphine.

'You seem sad, Madame. Is there a problem with the pregnancy?'

'After you mentioned that the child seemed small, Delphine and I decided to let Doctor Lafarge examine her,' said Marcel. Delphine looked up at them, her eyes dull.

'And?'

'The baby was dead. He said the foetus would be expelled naturally in a few days. We hope that will be soon.'

Albert reached out to touch Delphine's shoulder comfortingly.

'I am sorry, to hear of your troubles, Madame,' he said. 'I had better go, I need to find another woman.'

Delphine raised her arm to stop him. 'Why do you need a woman?'

'It is the full moon tonight. You know what that means. I shall need all the men, and a woman to tend to our wounded.'

Delphine stood up. 'I will do it.'

Marcel stepped forward and placed a hand on her arm. 'But my darling, are you sure you are up to it? Surely you should rest?'

She covered his hand with hers. 'I have been sitting around, resting, for days now. I want to do something useful.'

'With any luck, there won't *be* many wounded,' said Albert.

On the verge of protesting more, Marcel looked into his wife's face and saw animation he had not seen in a while. She smiled at him, reassuringly.

'Well, I suppose you had better,' he said. He turned to Albert. 'What's the plan?'

'Tonight, we must destroy as many as possible of the Germans' lines of communication. Bridges must be blown, telegraph lines destroyed, roads mined and blocked by trees. In fact, we must do anything and everything we can to stop the Germans reinforcing the coast.'

'What you want me to do?' asked Marcel.

Albert glanced from him to Delphine and scratched his head.

'I think in view of the situation here we three will travel to the nearest section of the railway line, and the rest of my group can go to Ranchy, to sabotage the Bridge where the N13 crosses the line. They can travel by bicycle, I think it's best if we walk. We can take enough explosive to take out some telegraph poles as well.'

Marcel looked at him thoughtfully. 'You know, most military telephone cables are laid underground. Telegraph poles wouldn't necessarily stop military traffic.'

Albert nodded. 'I don't think it's practical to try and do anything about buried cables,' he said. 'Hopefully, the bombardment will take care of it, but I'm sure that every little helps.' He looked from one to the other of them. 'Shall we get ready?'

* * *

They had been travelling south for an hour, their way lit only intermittently by the occasional flash of lightning, and each of them, including Delphine, was burdened with a back-pack full of explosives. It was raining and heavily overcast. Somewhere behind the clouds, the moon was full, but down on the ground, they could barely see their hands in front of their faces.

She had complained at first, pointing out that if she was supposed to be tending any wounded, they were more likely to be with the bigger group heading for Ranchy than with just the three of them.

Albert shrugged. 'Your husband would not let you go without him, Madame, and we have a perfectly good objective just a few kilometres away, which we can reach on foot.'

Delphine knew he spoke out of consideration for her, but sometimes, she thought a bumpy bike ride might be just what she needed. She was beginning to accept what had happened, and thought less about how their dead child might have been, had he – or she – survived. Such morbid thoughts were being slowly replaced by more forward looking ones. The doctor had said she should be able to conceive and bear a child again, and probably, if she waited until the peace, which now seemed not so far distant, that's what would happen. Better anyway, she told herself, to have a child born to peace than war.

The sound of heavy engines suddenly grew coming along the road behind them. Albert ushered them swiftly into the trees where they waited, weapons cocked and ready.

The vehicle turned out to be a small armoured personnel carrier, with rubber-tyred front wheels and two wheels behind connected by light tracks. Delphine expected it to pass them, but it slowed and stopped about forty metres away. The soldiers in the back looked like Wehrmacht regulars. They climbed down, their rifles and machine guns held loosely by the barrels. Some lit cigarettes, others moved into the trees. Two came and stood by trees close to her, and a moment later, in the darkness, she heard the sound of them pissing. The smell of their urine drifted past her nostrils and when the smoke from a cigarette added its acrid scent to the other, she had to fight to keep her stomach contents in place, and not make a noise.

She never heard him arrive, but was suddenly aware that Albert was at her side. He put a warning finger to his lips. In time, the men buttoned up and returned to the road. The engine started up and they boarded the vehicle again before it trundled off into the night, in the same direction the saboteurs were themselves headed.

Delphine felt she could breathe again. The three of them returned to the road and set off in the direction taken by the truck. As they neared the railway line, they heard the sound of men talking. They edged forward until they could see small encampment at the bottom of the raised ground on which lay the railway line. Albert turned round and led them away from the Germans. Unable to use torches, each step they took was fraught with danger. Some hundred metres from the camp, Marcel stepped on a twig, which cracked underfoot.

Albert held up his hand, and they froze, listening for any sign of pursuit. They heard nothing and Albert gave the signal to move off. Delphine suddenly experienced a sharp cramp in her stomach. The pain was almost enough to cause her to moan. She bit her lip and sucked in air, willing the pain to go away. Marcel moved to her side, and whispered.

'What's the matter?'

'Just cramp,' she said, 'it was nothing.'

'It's not the…?' His hand rested briefly on her swollen belly.

Another wave of pain hit her. She pushed a knuckle against her lips.

'It could be,' she whispered.

He muttered something she didn't quite hear and tugged on her arm. A few metres further on, Albert stopped them.

'This is a good spot,' he said, 'see, the land falls away here, down to the stream, and there is a culvert, where the stream runs below the railway line.'

Delphine knelt down, her arms crossed over her stomach.

'Are you all right?' he asked.

Marcel knelt beside his wife. He glanced up. 'I think it is the matter we talked about.'

Albert nodded. 'Give me your backpacks,' he said, 'you stay and look after your wife, I will deal with the bridge.'

As Albert disappeared into the darkness, Delphine curled up again as another wave the pain hit her. They were becoming more frequent.

'Shall I get the morphine?' asked Marcel.

Delphine shook her head but he saw that her teeth were gritted. He laid his coat on the ground, behind her, and helped her lay down. He realised he had left the morphine ampoules in his backpack.

He brushed her forehead with his hand. 'I'll be back in a minute.'

He went quickly after Albert, hoping to catch him up.

Delphine experienced another excruciating cramp, which caused her to lift her knees towards her chest. She could not stop a brief cry of pain emerging from her lips. She realised she was experiencing kind of contractions normally felt when delivering a baby, and wondered how long they would last in her case.

It seemed like hours before she heard a footstep just behind her. She twisted her head and strained to see through the darkness. Suddenly, a figure loomed close to her and she recognized the shape of the distinctive helmet worn by German soldiers. During a short break in the clouds, he was silhouetted against the moon, and she was sure he was looking at her.

There was a burst of gunfire from the direction Marcel and Albert had taken and the soldier fell, his machine weapon firing in reply as he did so. At almost the same moment, Delphine found herself pushing hard. Even as she screamed again, she felt the foetus leave her. Marcel burst through the trees and knelt at her side, pulling a Syrette of morphine from his kit and squeezing the drug into her thigh. Behind him, Albert appeared, and in the faint moonlight. She could see blood streaming from a wound on his temple.

In the meantime, Marcel had confirmed that she had delivered the foetus.

'We have to go,' he told her urgently, 'we can't stay here.'

He slipped one arm under her shoulders, the other under her knees and picked her up. 'Can you manage, Albert?' he asked.

'Yes. You look after Delphine, don't worry about me.'

They made haste to leave the spot before more Germans came to discover what had become of their lookout. Marcel carried Delphine for about 15 minutes before she reached up and kissed him.

'You can put me down now, Marcel, thank you,' she said.

He was not reluctant to obey. There was no sign of Albert, but after resting a few moments, they decided to press on. Albert, he thought, was capable of looking after himself.

Dawn was breaking by the time they arrived back at the farm. In the early light filtering through the kitchen curtains, Marcel saw that Delphine's face was stained with tears. He held her close to him.

'I was stupid to go out with you when I knew I could have the baby any time,' she said.

'You weren't to know that would happen,' he soothed her. 'Albert needed both of us, and if you'd stayed here, I would not have gone with him and left you. You've known for weeks that the foetus was dead and would be delivered eventually, but when Albert called on us, you gave no more thought to the possibility of delivery tonight than you did twenty-four hours ago. And it isn't as if you looked pregnant: unless someone knew you well, like I do, your bump could easily have been due to other causes.'

She grinned sadly. 'Are you trying to tell me I'm fat?'

He shook his head, smiling. 'I'm trying to tell you that it's bad enough we lost a child, but you mustn't blame yourself for what happened out there.'

She chewed her cheek. 'You killed a German.'

He nodded. 'Yes, I did, didn't I. Somewhere in Germany, parents will grieve for a son, a sister for a brother; possibly a wife for a husband and children for a father. But I couldn't let him shoot you.'

He told her to go to bed and rest. In the kitchen, he put another log on the fire's embers and waited for water to boil. In a chair, waiting, he suddenly realised that tears were coursing down his cheeks.

In part it was relief from the tensions of the night, but mainly, it was his dim recollection in the pale moonlight of the tiny, yet perfectly formed, foetus, lying between his wife's legs. He told himself he should have brought the body with them, but a more detached part of his mind assured him that it had been more important to get Delphine away to safety.

The kettle was boiling. He made mugs of tea, put the rest of the water into a bowl, and managed to carry everything into the bedroom. He set them down beside the bed and soaked a cloth in the warm water. Delphine was still fully clothed, and he gently unbuttoned her dress. She lay still, watching him. He glanced at her face and saw that like his, her cheeks glistened with shed tears.

Setting the cloth aside, he leaned down, took her face between his hands, and kissed her gently on the lips.

* * *

Callum turned out to have a deft technique with children. Penny was still a babe-in-arms, not yet a year old, and a seemingly contented baby. She was looked after by her grandmother during the time Ann was at work, but Ann had had her at home while she'd been waiting for her ankle to heal.

It had taken all Callum's persuasion to convince her that the war would not suddenly be lost if she took a few days off work.

'You can get to know your daughter better, and besides,' he added, 'Mary needs a little more time learning what to do so she can deputize for you.'

Ann had frowned at this, worried that he might be going to replace her.

'I like my job, Callum,' she told him. 'And I think I'm good at it. Very few errors in the transcriptions that I've been made aware of.'

He took one of her hands in his and smiled gently. 'You *are* very good at it, and your job is quite safe while I have any say in the matter. Now look here: Penny is blowing bubbles at you. I think that means she likes having you around.'

He picked the child out of her cradle and held her safely in his arms, rocking her gently and talking to her in those soft, cooing tones adults use when talking to babies.

Ann watched him. 'Have you any children of your own, Callum?' She realised she knew nothing about him. All their talk was about work.

He spared her a glance. 'Och, no. I'd have to find the right woman to marry first.'

'I don't think that would be difficult,' she said, smiling.

'And, of course, there's one major drawback to having one's own children.'

'What's that?'

'You can't hand them back to their mother when their nappy needs changing,' he replied, holding Penny out to her.

She took the child and the hint, and laid Penny on a towel on the floor. 'Have you ever changed a nappy, Callum?'

He actually took a step back and held up his hands as if to ward off the suggestion. 'No, no. Nappy-changing is women's work, just in case you thought it was time I had a lesson in the subject.'

She laughed. 'Please yourself. I think changing a baby's nappy is a great privilege, even when it's all stinky – like this one!' She pulled the messy terry-towelling out from under the girl and asked Callum to wet the flannel she kept to clean the baby. He disappeared into the kitchen and returned with the cloth dampened.

'You're sure you don't want to do this?' Ann asked him.

He laughed. 'I'll tell you what I'll do: I'll take us out for a meal.'

'I can't. I can't get a sitter for Penny at such short notice.'

'She could come with us?'

'Not if you expect to eat civilised. She throws stuff all over. I'm sure other diners wouldn't appreciate it.

'So, we're back to eating here.'

Ann shook her head. 'I don't think there's enough in the larder. I only eat small meals myself.'

He silenced her with a gesture. 'Leave it to me. I'll just go down to the shops.'

'My ration card is on the sideboard. But really, Callum, I don't know what I can get before Saturday.'

'Leave it to me,' he repeated enigmatically. He picked up Ann's Ration Card, slipped it in his pocket, and went out.

Ann looked at her baby, who appeared to be deciding whether or not to cry.

'Did you think I was neglecting you, darling Penelope?' She kissed the child's forehead but her reward was the sight of the baby's face crinkling up and a loud wail being emitted. Penny's colour had suddenly deepened, her face red and blotchy.

Ann was alarmed. 'What is it, my love? Oh, let me wipe your nose!' She dabbed with her handkerchief, tucked it away up her sleeve and finished wrapping the child in a clean nappy, completing her daughter's toilette by pulling on the little set of pyjamas her mother had made.

'Is that another tooth putting in an appearance?'

Penny remained fractious for nearly half an hour, and was still grizzling when Callum returned with a brown paper wrapper under his arm. He raised his eyebrows when he heard the little girl cry and looked questioningly at Ann.

'She's teething again,' she said.

'Och! the poor wee bairn,' he replied, shaking his head sadly.

'She'll get over it,' said Ann, laying Penny down. 'What's in the parcel?'

Callum rubbed his ear. 'I managed to get a piece of meat. Beef. Think you could do something with it?'

He passed her the package. It felt heavy. She opened it carefully and her eyes widened.

'Callum! Is this... beef fillet?' She could scarcely believe her eyes. She hadn't seen such a wonderful, lean piece of beef in four years.

'Aye. I believe that's what the man in the funny apron said.'

She gazed at him, stunned. 'It must have cost an absolute fortune!'

Callum's brow furrowed and he shrugged as if to say it was all a mystery to him.

'I was thinking, if you had the makings of a shortcrust pastry, we could have a Beef Wellington.' He hesitated. 'But only if you feel like making one, of course.'

Still almost speechless with shock, Ann got to her feet and walked shakily towards the kitchen. 'I'll see what I can do,' she said faintly.

It took an hour. While Ann worked in the kitchen, Callum played with Penny. She laid the table, getting out a clean cloth and even unwrapping a pair of silver-plated candlesticks a friend of David's had given them as a wedding present.

The reminder that she had a husband – possibly – somewhere in France gave her pause, but she told herself firmly that she and Callum had done nothing wrong, she had not betrayed David. But the line between betrayal in the flesh and betrayal in mind was becoming very tightly stretched, and she foresaw that one day, she might cross it.

When the meal was ready, she brought it to the table and sat in her place, staring, feeling her mouth water at the plateful of vegetables, and especially the small, pastry-covered lump in the middle of the plate. Callum sat opposite her and she looked up at him.

'Callum! I still don't know how you managed to find fillet steak. For God's sake, how?'

He smiled at her. 'I have my sources,' he said, tapping the side of his nose. He replaced her ration card on the sideboard.

'I'd better find some decent wine, hadn't I?' Ann said.

She went into the hallway, opened the cupboard below the stairs and returned carrying a dusty bottle of claret.

As they sat down to eat, Penny began to grizzle again. Ann had propped her against some cushions on the settee. She picked her up. Penny was blotchy and hot again. She walked her up and down for a while but the baby would not be quieted. Callum was smiling at her.

'I know what will help, if she's teething,' he said. He pulled a hip flask from his pocket, unscrewed the cap, whetted the tip of his finger, and let the baby suck on it. The whetted his finger again, and this time ran the tip along the budding lines of Penny's gums. Penny screwed up her face at the taste, grizzled some more, but suddenly stopped and smiled at him. He tickled her cheek briefly and turned back to his food.

'Well, it's not what I would have recommended, but it seems to work,' said Ann, sitting opposite him again.

'We'd better eat while she's in a good mood,' he said.

The room fell silent while they concentrated on their meal. At the end, Ann apologised for not having any dessert. She made them coffee using some of her precious, hoarded supply, and whilst it was brewing, took Penny upstairs to her cot. By the time she returned, Callum had poured out a cup for each of them.

Ann leaned back in her armchair and looked up at him.

'Callum, what are you up to? Do you want us to be… a couple?'

He blushed. 'Ah, no. You know me, confirmed bachelor.'

'No, I *don't* know you. But every day since I turned my ankle, you've dropped in. That's nice, that's caring. Then you manage to find a delicious piece of fillet steak, like I haven't seen for years. And no, I'm not going to ask where it came from. And finally, you stop Penny's discomfort from her teething. More points. I'm not green enough to believe you could keep that sort of thoughtfulness up forever, but I have to admit, you put the case to be my... consort... very well. Is that what you want?'

He stared at the ground, like a naughty schoolboy, she thought.

'Aye, well. Aye.'

'You're a man of few words, Callum, when a few words might get you a long way. Come here.'

She reached up as he bent towards her and pulled him down so that his moustache tickled her nose. Then she kissed him on the lips. For a moment, he pulled away, then holding the back of her head in one large hand, he returned the kiss firmly. She felt the same heat balling inside her she'd felt before, the day she'd had her accident in his office.

'There, Callum,' she said when she came up for air, 'it's official. We are together. Friends.'

'But I do not want to marry ye.'

' David is only "presumed dead". I'm not looking for another marriage yet – I don't think I've totally given up hoping that David will come back – but I do miss the company of a man, sometimes.'

'Aye,' he said again. 'Ye'll no mind being discreet round the office?'

'I think that would be for the best,' she agreed.

'There's another reason I want you to be discreet,' he said, shuffling uncomfortably on his feet.

'What's that?' She frowned.

'I want you to do something, and it might be difficult for you.'

'I take it you mean at work?'

'Aye.' He sat down near her but did not attempt to take her hand. 'I'm going to tell ye something which is top, top secret. Never mention it outside this room. Official Secrets Act and everything.'

She raised her eyebrows in surprise. 'Are you sure you're talking to the right person? I mean, my security clearance ⟩ '

'Has been raised. At any other time, you'd be promoted, but just now, it's important you stay in your present job.'

'This is getting more and more mysterious, Callum. What's it all about?'

'Mary Hamilton.'

She stared at him. 'What about her?'

'We think she's spying for the Germans.'

For a long time, she said nothing, as the idea sank in. 'Why?' she demanded, 'whatever makes you think that? I presume it isn't just you who thinks it?'

'No,' he said, shaking his head. 'But we've discovered something. Or one of our agents in the field has. What do you know about her husband?'

'I thought he was a POW. She gets a letter from him every week. I've seen them.'

'He is a prisoner, that much is true, but he's not in a POW camp. According to our agent, he's being held by the Gestapo, in what they call *Schutzhaft*, and we call detention without charge. They get the prisoners to sign their own detention warrants, in which they "request" to be held in protective custody.'

'And Mary's husband?'

'To the best of our knowledge, he is being held in Paris, in the Fresnes prison at Val-de-Marne.'

'But why does that make Mary a spy?'

'Because while she provides them with information gleaned from Bletchley, they let her husband live. If you can call the sort of conditions the prisoners are kept in at Fresnes, living.'

Ann was silent.

'Does this explain why she often takes a lot of interest in the messages which came across my desk?'

'Almost certainly,' he replied. 'Her interest in the message ordering German troops to move to the Pas de Calais to counter the build-up of FUSAG in the south-east of England made me very suspicious when I heard about it. I arranged to have her checked out, and her husband. And then, when you stayed home with a sprained ankle, I gave her your job.'

'Yes. Was that wise?'

He grinned at her. 'Well, I didn't give her *all* your job. What she saw were a few inconsequential messages, and then one which seemed to suggest that the Germans would invade Britain, giving orders to land on the Suffolk coast, in Sole Bay.'

'And the point of that was...?'

'More Ultra, displaying confusion about the date and location for this German invasion.'

'Meaning,' Ann said thoughtfully, 'that the original message, which I presume was false, had been relayed back to the Gestapo as if true, in the form of a warning that the Allies knew about the German intention?'

'Precisely!' He grinned at her again. 'You can see why I want you to work with me. Never miss a trick.'

'And Mary?'

'I've had her watched and her communications monitored. When she wrote to her husband, supposedly, her letter was carefully checked by our counter-espionage experts and it contained a simple little code and a microdot. Of course, we let it go. Didn't want the Jerries to suspect she'd been rumbled. But after that, you'll recall, she was moved out of the section and for a while put where she could do no harm.'

'Wouldn't that have affected her husband's safety, if she couldn't provide them with any more useful data?'

'Poor Mary. She was frantic when she was cut off from her usual sources. I'm afraid she began sleeping around more, trying to glean information from pillow talk. I – we – provided young men with information for her to target and told them to make it very difficult for her to extract it. She would be more convinced of its importance if she had to work hard to get it, and would make a better job of convincing her masters. I've never known a team of young men exhibit a more personal interest in their work.'

Ann frowned at him. 'It doesn't sound very ethical,' she said.

'Neither was what the Gestapo were doing. You know what they say about love and war.'

She thought for a moment before looking up. 'Callum, did you… ?'

'No! Far too old for that sort of thing. Besides, I was her boss. *That* wouldn't have been ethical.'

'So her husband survived?'

'Although his letters purported to come from a POW camp in Germany, our agent, as I say, was able to discover he is in France.'

'How did he do that?'

'*She* made a friend of a senior Gestapo officer who worked at the prison.'

'A friend?' She raised her eyebrow wonderingly.

'War finds us strange bedfellows. Literally, in her case, I understand. Still, it was not for long.'

'She left him?'

'Permanently. Fortunately, she managed to get her information back to us before he found her and shot her.'

Ann muffled an impromptu cry with a hand. When she could speak again, she asked, 'Why was the message about FUSAG so important?'

'Because it doesn't exist. The acronym stands for "First US Army Group", and it was created as part of a scheme to persuade the Germans that we meant the invasion to be at the narrowest part of the Channel, at the Pas de Calais. So when they ordered their troops to that area – taking them away from Normandy – we were delighted. The ruse had succeeded.'

'Do you know what happened to Mary's husband?'

He bowed his head. 'Like just about everyone else in the Fresnes, as soon as the Allies broke out of Normandy, the Gestapo went about killing everyone in there. Covering up their crimes.'

'Poor Mary,' Ann said.

'At least she hasn't been shot. She'll get a few years in Holloway.'

'And then what'll become of her?'

'How should I know?' he asked with a touch of asperity. 'If she'd managed to tell the Germans that we could decode their messages, Ultra would have been ruined.'

'Maybe it's to her credit that she didn't,' said Ann. 'I can't believe she was truly a traitor, she was such a nice person.'

'Maybe you're right. Anyway, I'd better be going.'

He didn't move. Ann glanced at the clock on the sideboard. 'Callum, it's late. There's a bed in the spare room. You're welcome to use it.'

'Are you sure you won't mind? I'll leave early so the neighbours don't see.'

'Bugger the neighbours,' she said.

CHAPTER 8 - 1999

Geoffrey followed Penny into her room at the hotel in Bayeux. They were hot, exhausted and disappointed after spending most of a day visiting Ranchy and searching graveyards and war cemeteries within several miles' radius where they found no sign of any gravestone belonging to any person they recognized.

She sat on the bed, kicked off her shoes and swung her legs up, wriggling her toes.

'I could use a drink,' said Geoff.

'Me too,' Penny said, 'is there anything in the minibar?'

Geoff opened it. 'There's gin and tonic,' he said, moving bottles so he could see labels. 'And a couple of miniatures of blended whisky.'

'I'll have G&T, please, but go easy on the gin,' she said.

'I'll have the whisky.'

He found some ice, poured the drinks and sat on the other side the bed. 'Well what are we going to do now?'

Penny sipped her gin and tonic thoughtfully. 'What do you think of the idea of visiting farms southeast of Sainte Marguerite-en-Bessin, where dad should have landed?'

He shrugged. 'Not a bad one. Tomorrow?'

'Yes. Now, do you think we have time to be tourists before then, and go see the Tapestry. Can't visit Bayeux and not do.'

Geoff straightened a leg and studied his foot inside the brown Oxford brogues he habitually wore. 'Is it far? I mean, do we have to do more walking, or could I be delivered in a sedan chair, right to the door?'

'That's a point,' Penny said. On the other side of the bed, she straightened both her legs and looked at her hot feet. She'd slipped off her shoes whilst Geoff had been getting the drinks. 'I'd forgotten how far we walked today. Anyway, what I want more than anything is a bath before dinner, so when you've finished your drink...' She inclined her head towards the door.

He drank the rest of his whisky in one swallow and got to his feet. 'A bath sounds like a good idea. See you later at dinner.'

The next morning a visit to see the Bayeux tapestry was postponed when they decided not to waste any more time but to seek out farmhouses near the intended landing-site. The first two farms they visited yielded no helpful information. The third, at first glance, seemed unoccupied.

Penny drove past a large duck-pond into the yard and parked outside a cow byre on the left. Without much hope she knocked on the door. The sound echoed between the enclosing buildings. She noticed there was no sound of animals and, indeed, the atmosphere was thick with abandonment. She was on the verge of leaving when she realised there were fresh footprints beside an overnight puddle, between the house and the barn. Someone was there, or had been there recently, since the rain.

She used a fist to bang on the door loudly.

'Anyone here?' she called, *"Il y a quelqu'un ?'*

The barn door creaked open and a woman wearing dungarees and rubber boots stepped out and looked at them with suspicion. Penny crossed the yard towards her, smiling, and introduced herself.

'Oui? Qu'est-ce que vous voulez?' Penny gritted her teeth and attempted in her less-than-adequate French to explain what they were looking for.

The woman, who she'd originally guessed was in her late thirties or early forties, was, she saw as she got closer, ten years younger than that.

'Venez chez moi,' the woman said. 'I do not live here. Come to my house.'

'Merci, Madame,' Penny replied.

She and Geoff returned to their car while the woman walked out of the gate of the farmyard and round the corner to the left. Penny followed her slowly. The woman's 2CV was parked against the wall. She led the way down a rutted cart track to the next-door farm, a kilometre away.

There, she led them into the kitchen, sat them at the table and poured each of them a glass of wine.

'I will fetch my 'usband.' She smiled at them before disappearing outside.

Penny took a sip of her wine and glanced round the room. The walls for the most part were plain brick, with the occasional vein of timber running through them. The kitchen range was placed at the far end and down the sides were more modern appliances. The large, white, scrubbed table at which they sat dominated the centre of the room and was surrounded by eight plain and sturdy wooden dining chairs. Cut flowers wilted gently on the windowsill.

Geoff tapped his foot impatiently on one of the large flagstones that formed the floor.

The door suddenly opened and the woman returned followed by a man. He was dressed in an old tweed jacket and corduroy trousers tucked into rubber boots which he pulled off just inside the door. He held a cap his left hand and Penny noted his swift scrutiny of the visitors.

'You are English?'

'Yes,' said Penny, ' I'm trying to find out what happened to my father after he was parachuted into this area in 1943.'

'What was his name?' asked the man, sitting opposite them.

'David Greatorix,' replied Penny, 'but I understand that when he arrived here, he would have been supplied with false French identity papers. I do not know what name these were in.'

He shrugged. 'Without a name, what can I tell you?'

She smiled at him understandingly. 'I'm sorry. I knew it would be unlikely. I suppose I really need to speak to someone who was here at the time – and that clearly wasn't you,' she added with a smile intended to placate him.

'It was twenty years before my time,' he said, breaking into an answering grin. He frowned. 'Was there a particular reason for going to the Delacourt farm?'

'No, it was just one of a number we planned on. We were going to visit them all,' she added, glancing at Geoff.

He nodded.

'The man who owns the other farm is Oliver Delacourt,' said the farmer, 'it's been in his family forever.'

Penny touched her fingertips together. 'The farm looked unoccupied. Doesn't M'sieur Delacourt live there?'

The farmer grinned. 'No, no. He lives in Paris and Caen. He is a businessman.'

'What does he do?' asked Geoff. '*Que fait-il?*'

The farmer waved his hands helplessly and shook his head. 'He owns a chain of car dealerships. Luxury cars. Mercedes, Ferrari, even your Rolls-Royce and Bentleys.'

Penny looked at Geoff. 'He probably won't be difficult to find, in that case,' she said.

'No. Thank you very much, M'sieur.'

'There's just one last thing,' Penny asked, 'do you know anyone in the area who would have been around possibly in the Resistance, in 1943?'

The farmer shook his head. 'No, I'm very sorry, I don't.'

The afternoon was getting late when Penny and Geoff returned to Bayeux, passing the Delacourt place on their way.

* * *

Oliver Delacourt put down the phone, his face impassive.

'What is the matter, *ma chère*?' asked the woman who had draped herself seductively on his bed. She spoke French with a German accent.

He turned to look at her, considering whether the news he had received from Le Greq, the farmer who rented his fields in Normandy, was more or less important than the opportunity of sexual gratification she presented. She wore a short black leather skirt and a matching bustier, through small holes in which her rosy nipples protruded. Her black, shiny hair was cut severely, curls clinging to her scalp and revealing the shape of her head. One hand had drifted up the nylon covering her legs, and was busy beneath the skirt. She sighed softly, a hint of her arousal.

He felt his own, and decided that tomorrow would be soon enough to consider a return to the farm near Sainte Marguerite-en-Bessin.

'Nothing that need bother you,' he replied, crossing the room until he stood beside her. He felt in his pocket and produced a small plastic bag containing a white crystalline powder. 'If you're good, this is for you,' he told her.

Her eyes focussed on the bag as he returned it to his pocket and began removing his clothes.

Six hours later, he woke in the dishevelled bed. He twisted his head and saw that the woman, now naked from the waist up, was lying beside him, mostly on top of the duvet. His nostrils caught the scent of cold sex and he screwed up his face in disgust. He showered and noted the time while he dressed. It was still early, not quite seven o'clock, but there was no part of his business which couldn't manage without his presence. The woman stirred and opened her eyes slowly. The kohl which coated her lashes had smudged, giving her eyes deep shadows which extended down her cheeks, and left black marks on the pillow.

'Good morning, darling,' she said as she stretched her body sensually.

'Good morning, Eloise, I shall be going away for a few days. Can you survive without me for perhaps a week?' he asked with a touch of cynicism.

'Of course, darling.'

He drew another small bag of cocaine from his pocket. 'Can you survive without *this* for a week?'

'You could leave me a little,' she said. 'I'll make it up to you when you get back.'

He tossed the bag on the pillow beside her. 'Make this last.' He wrinkled his nose. 'I suggest you have a shower before you leave,' he added.

An hour later, after croissants, *pain-au-chocolat* and coffee in the restaurant of the hotel, he was in his car, heading south-west, having paid a short visit to his local car dealership. He stopped at a hypermarket for food, and arrived at the farm in time for a late lunch. While in Paris, he lived a life of sophistication and modernity, but at the farm, he preferred the simpler lifestyle of his youth.

He dumped his shopping bag on the kitchen table and went upstairs to the master bedroom, which he'd taken over when his father had moved out in 1974 to go live in Vire with his new wife. He sometimes wondered what had become of him: if he was still alive, he would be eighty. The chances were, Oliver thought, that he was dead. As long as he stayed away, Oliver did not have to confront the black demon which had occupied his soul ever since discovering he was half English.

After changing out of his suit into denim jeans and a short-sleeved checked shirt, he made himself a simple lunch, thick slices of Brie on halves of baguette, and ate it at the kitchen table. Over coffee, he telephoned the nearby farm and spoke to Madame Le Greq.

'I was collecting the eggs,' she told him. 'This woman and a man arrived. They were English, and they were looking for anyone who could give them information about a man she said was her father, who was parachuted into this area in 1943.'

'What did you tell them?'

'What could I tell them? I know nothing, Jean knows nothing. I didn't think he should have bothered you last night,' she added.

Oliver waved a hand dismissively. 'That's quite all right,' he said. 'Did they say where they were staying?'

'The DeVries Hotel in Bayeux.'

He thanked her and hung up thoughtfully. He rubbed his chin, feeling the stubble regrowing already after shaving only a few hours earlier.

Anything involving English people suggested some connection with his father. He felt bile rise in his throat. He stood and crossed to the old stone sink, believing for a moment that he was going to be physically sick.

Later, he drove into Bayeux as the time approached when people would be beginning to think about where to eat, and parked outside the hotel, hoping to see the visitors, wondering whether, while they were out, he could find out which room they were in and gain access to it. He went to a nearby ATM and withdrew what he thought would be sufficient cash to persuade a member of staff to part with information and a key.

* * *

Penny met Geoff in the vestibule of the hotel. She'd spent more time than usual in choosing what to wear from the limited selection of garments she'd brought with her. Eventually, having regard for the warmth of the evening, she settled for a figure-hugging, long-sleeved black dress, with a grey top in a glittery fabric and low-heeled black shoes. She realised, somewhat wryly, that she was putting more effort into her appearance than she normally did, especially when she applied some shadow to her eyes and colour to her cheeks and lips. She regarded her standard of dress quite adequate most of the time, but this evening, for no reason she wanted to examine too closely, she felt like dressing up.

She emerged from the elevator and saw Geoff waiting for her near the door. He was wearing a charcoal grey lounge suit and white shirt with a dark red tie. His black shoes gleamed and he had an altogether scrubbed look. Penny was pleased she was not the only one of them to have made an effort with their appearance.

'Shall we walk or ride?' he asked.

'It's a lovely evening. Let's walk,' she replied.

He held out his arm and she took it, and they went out into the evening

There were quite a few people walking in the town. Penny and Geoff strolled along the street to a corner, where they turned left, arriving at the brasserie where they'd decided earlier they would have their meal. As they paused outside the door to study the menu, Penny suddenly felt the hairs on her neck rise. She looked back towards the corner and received the fleeting impression of a figure darting back out of sight.

Geoff caught her frown reflected in the window. He turned. 'What's up?'

'The strangest thing,' she said. 'It was as if we were being followed. If I was still working, I'd be sure of it.' She told him what she had seen.

'I'll go and look,' he said. 'Wait here.'

Before she could remonstrate over his peremptory manner, he had gone swiftly to the corner and peered round it. A moment later, he returned, holding out his hands in a gesture of emptiness.

'Nobody I could see,' he reported. 'No-one running or even walking away quickly. There're a number of shop doorways where someone could have hidden, but I'm not dressed for chasing people around on spec. It's something akin to having a bird in the hand,' he added, looking pointedly at her but with his tongue jammed firmly in his cheek, 'being decidedly more desirable than any number of shadows on the street.'

'Are you casting me in the role of bird?' Penny asked.

'Almost without hesitation. A few years ago, there'd have been none at all.'

She smiled, not angry. In fact, she was wondering whether he meant *she* was "desirable", or the fact that she was *with* him.

Their meal began well enough. Savoury *galettes* to begin, then marinated roast pork with apples, followed by a dessert of profiteroles smothered in a dark chocolate sauce and bursting with Normandy cream. A bottle of sauvignon took the richness out of the sauce served with the meat, and both were experiencing a warm glow by the time they had finished and were walking back to the hotel.

The happy mood lasted until they reached Penny's room. She slipped her key card into the slot and opened the door. For a moment, Geoff hesitated in the corridor. She smiled.

'You can come in, if you like. There'll be a nightcap in the minibar.'

He smiled, and she noticed the diffidence was back. 'If you're sure,' he said. 'But I'm not sure I like the idea of you in a nightcap?'

'Not that sort of nightcap,' she said as he followed her into the room and closed the door.

It was then she took her first good look round the room and felt the hairs on her neck stand up again. She turned to him. 'The maids don't come into the rooms in the evening, do they?' she asked.

'Don't they turn the beds down?'

'You're confusing this place with somewhere posher. Besides, no-one's turned down *my* bed.'

'What's the matter?'

'I just have the feeling someone's been in here. Stuff's been moved and not put back where I left it.'

CHAPTER 9 – 1946

Normandy was recovering from the ravages resulting from the allied invasion of its northern shore. Roads and railways had been repaired, the shells of buildings damaged by fire and bombing had been pulled down and new ones built in their place.

It was the end of term, Marcel walked out of the school where he'd finished his last day before the summer break. He drove home through the countryside, enjoying the beauty of the sunlight on its fields and orchards, and noting how nature was gradually reclaiming the land from the damage inflicted by the fighting. Where once there had been dilapidated dwellings, fresh coats of paint and neat flowerbeds had appeared. An old wooden wheelbarrow stood by the door of one, brimming with scarlet geraniums which trailed over rickety back legs.

In the fields around the Delacourt farm, sheep grazed and crops ripened. Marcel parked outside the cow byre, and noticed a bicycle had been abandoned on the ground in apparent haste, near the back door. He entered quickly and heard voices upstairs. As he headed for his bedroom, the wail of a new-born child filled the air. He took the last steps two at time, at the last moment hesitating at the door, and knocking before entering.

His gaze went immediately to the bed where Delphine sat against pillows, smiling, but obviously tired, and gazing with such tender love at the child in her arms. Beside the bed, Madame Le Greq, their neighbour's mother, sat watching. Both women turned to look at him as he came to a halt at the foot of the bed.

'It's a boy, M'sieur,' said Madame, with quiet satisfaction.

'Meet your new son, Marcel,' said Delphine, holding out a small bundle towards him.

Marcel took his son in his arms as if he was the most precious and delicate object in the universe. The child was barely bigger than one of his hands, and nestled comfortably in the crook of his elbow. His eyes were closed but he lay there and whimpered. Marcel instinctively rocked him and the child quietened almost at once.

Delphine grinned. 'It is his papa's magic touch, I think,' she said to the woman beside her.

The old woman looked at Marcel sceptically. 'And how long do you think that will last?'

'Oh, for years yet,' replied Delphine, with a weary laugh.

'How are you, my dear?' asked Marcel, perching on the edge of the bed beside her, so they could both gaze upon the miracle they had wrought.

'Very well, and very happy,' she replied.

'We should take the child away for a while,' said Madame Le Greq. 'Whatever she says, your wife needs a little sleep.' She stood up and ushered Marcel towards the door. 'The Lord knows, you will both need your sleep in the next few months,' she added. As she preceded Marcel down the stairs, she continued, 'Have you decided what you will call him?'

The truth was Marcel and Delphine were undecided on the matter. In the large farmhouse kitchen, their neighbour asked him if he could cook dinner and change a nappy.

'I can certainly cook dinner,' he replied, grinning.

'And no doubt your wife will let you,' replied the woman. 'I must be going,' she said, opening the door, 'will Delphine's grandparents be coming to help?'

Marcel frowned. Delphine had never mentioned grandparents. 'I don't know. I'll ask her.'

Their neighbour collected her bicycle. Marcel watched her from the door and closed it as she cycled away.

'Well I think I can guess what you're having for dinner, son,' he said softly to the child, 'but what are your mother and I going to eat?'

Later that evening, in the light of a single candle placed near the crib, he lay beside Delphine and talked with her. They decided to call the boy Oliver.

For a month, the little family stayed mostly around the farm. Eventually, Marcel suggested they should take him on his first visit to the town of Bayeux. He loaded their perambulator on the roof of the car, and soon they were pushing it and its valuable burden around the parts of the town which were once again beginning to experience visitors. Tourists were once again eager to see the 11th century tapestry recently returned to the citizens of Bayeux from the depths of the Louvre in Paris where it had spent the war. Not far from the Hotel de Doyen, the museum where it was displayed, they found a cafe where they could have lunch outdoors.

Oliver, who had been asleep whilst he was wheeled past many of Bayeux's attractions, awoke on cue and demanded to be fed. Delphine wrapped her coat round the child and held him close while she pushed her jumper out of the way so he could get to her breast. Marcel became aware that a party of English tourists at another table were glancing at his wife disapprovingly. One of the men scowled at him.

'Typical French behaviour,' he said to the woman beside him, but loudly enough for Marcel to hear him.

Marcel looked at his wife, whose modesty was preserved by the coat, and could see no reason for the remark.

'But this is quite a rural part of France,' said the woman who looked as if she could have been the man's wife, 'I expect this is how the peasants behave.'

Marcel turned and stared at her through narrowed eyes.

The man turned round and spoke to him. 'I say,' he said, speaking loudly and slowly, 'do you understand English?'

Marcel stared at him as he realised, for the first time, he did. It was the first time he'd heard it. He licked his lips. 'Every word you've said.'

The man seemed taken aback. He looked apologetic. 'Sorry, old man, didn't realise you *were* English. Been here long?'

'I live here,' Marcel replied, 'and neither my wife nor myself, nor our son, are peasants. Do your women not feed their babies?'

The man glanced at his wife, whose expression was one of mild interest in his answer.

'Er, yes of course. They just use bottles.'

'Not all of us, dear,' said his wife in a manner which Marcel thought was calculated to make up for her earlier solecism. He saw a blush spread across her face as she added, 'I suppose that makes some of us peasants as well.'

Marcel stared at the two of them.

The tourist got to his feet and grasped his wife's arm. 'Come along dear, I think we have more sightseeing to do.' He nodded at Marcel and led her hastily away.

Marcel finished his drink and lifted his eyes to his wife's. Delphine was watching him expressionlessly.

'You told me once,' he said, 'that you found me in a field, attached to a parachute.'

She nodded. 'That's right. I thought you were English, and the tourist has confirmed that.'

He stared at her. 'But I only know I am Marcel Dubois from Hameau Belchamps. I must be someone else, too – an Englishman, with perhaps a family – parents at least – in England.'

Delphine did not answer him while she switched Oliver to her other breast. When she did, she spoke softly. 'You are Marcel Dubois. You are my husband.'

'I have no recollection of ever being English.'

She gazed down at their son, sucking lustily at her breast. 'Maybe it's something you will remember one day,' she said dully.

He had a flash of perception and knelt beside her. 'Delphine, you are my wife and I love only you – well, and Oliver, of course. But you must know that whatever I might one day find out about my earlier life in England, you are still the woman I love, the mother of my son, and my wife forever. You mustn't fear that I would ever leave you.'

She looked at him with moist eyes and reddened cheeks.

'I love you, Marcel. You are my husband, father of my son, and the man I will love forever. And now you should get up, people are staring.'

He glanced round and saw that, indeed, they were being observed. He stood.

'As soon as you finish feeding Oliver, perhaps we should go and look at the Tapestry.'

Three quarters of an hour later they were part of a line of people, shuffling admiringly past the enormous work of embroidery which pictured the conquest of England by Duke William of Normandy in 1066. Oliver, Marcel noticed, was not paying attention, having fallen asleep almost as soon as he had finished his feed.

Life was good, he thought. After five years of war and the oppression of the Occupation, the freedoms of peacetime, to travel, to speak one's mind, and to see again such artefacts as the Tapestry, were still taking some time to get used to.

Before they reached the last panel of the great work, Delphine was showing signs of tiredness. Marcel noticed at once, and led his family outside to where he had parked their small Citroen.

'Come on, let's go home,' he said. 'We can always come back another day.'

* * *

That evening, Delphine sat beside the fire in the farmhouse, cradling Oliver in her arms. She stared at the flames as the logs in the grate crackled and spat the occasional puff of smoke into the room. Marcel finished dealing with some end-of-term papers and moved to the chair opposite her.

Delphine broke the silence.

'It had been a quiet night, up to the point when I heard the aircraft,' she began, still watching the flames. 'Then there were several shots. I got out of bed and looked across the fields. I couldn't see anything, so I got dressed and went out.'

'That was dangerous,' Marcel said. 'You could have been killed.'

'There were a dozen German soldiers in the biggest east field. We had planted oats there that year, and the shoots were coming through nicely. Anyway, I stayed out of sight and watched to see what happened. There were three bodies on the ground, one in uniform – SS I think. The soldiers picked them up and carried them into the back of their truck, which arrived while they were there.' She looked up at him. 'I think they had been expecting the plane, and someone to meet it. After a bit, they threw one of the bodies out of the truck. Then two of the them went to the side of the field and picked up one of the metal cylinders – the kind of thing SOE would drop weapons and equipment in. They put that in the truck and drove away.

'I went to look at the body they'd left. It was Laroux. He'd been in Sainte Marguerite a couple of weeks. I didn't know where he came from, or anything about him. I left him' – she broke off and looked away – 'I know I probably should have done something about him, but it was dangerous, and I don't know that I could. Anyway, I came away, meaning to come back here, but I saw a flash of moonlight on something in the north field. I went, and it was you, bleeding from a head wound, and as I told you, you were still attached to your parachute. How the Germans didn't see it, I have no idea.

'But you were still breathing. I managed to get the parachute off you, and buried that in the copse behind the duck pond.' She smiled softly. 'It's probably still there. Then I went to get papa to help me bring you back to the houses. We used the wheelbarrow.' She stopped and looked at him. 'The same one you carried poor papa's body in that Christmas.'

She turned back to the fire, where the flames were beginning to die away while the logs glowed redly.

'We managed to stop the bleeding and in the morning, we fetched Doctor Lafarge and told him you'd been found in the field and appeared to have fallen and hit your head on a rock. It was most likely the truth. The doctor didn't question it, anyway. When it was clear you weren't going to come round, he showed us how to put a tube in your stomach and feed you through it.

'The only identification papers you had on you are the ones you know about: they said you were Marcel Dubois, born in Hameau Belchamps in 1919. And that is who you have been to me, ever since.'

She studied his face for a moment in silence. Muscles twitched in his cheeks as if he was clenching his teeth.

'I never told anyone about the parachute. Not even Papa knew about it.'

She dropped her gaze and looked at her sleeping son. 'I think it's while you were still unconscious with that I began to fall in love with you,' she said.

She looked up and found his gaze on her, and felt a blush rise up her throat into her cheeks. Suddenly, he smiled. Relief swept through her, making her feel giddy.

'I was already totally indebted to you for nursing me back to health,' he said, 'but I see I owe you a good deal more than that.' He got up from his chair and knelt beside her, resting one hand on the back of her neck and the other on the child. He kissed Oliver gently on the cheek, then Delphine on the lips. 'And how could I fail to fall in love with you, my beloved sweetheart.'

She pressed her lips against his again, passionately this time. 'Do you know, that despite everything you've done for me there's one thing you've never done?'

He tilted his head on one side. 'What's that?'

She prodded him in the chest with her forefinger. 'You have never bought me flowers.'

'I shall fetch some at once,' he replied, contritely.

She laughed. 'Perhaps next time you go into Bayeux,' she said.

'But that may not be until school begins again,' he said.

'I'm not going anywhere.'

* * *

Ann looked round the hut for the last time before leaving. It had acquired a forlorn air since all the staff, not just in her hut, but throughout the site, had begun to leave. SOE had passed on Churchill's orders, to destroy all evidence of their secret work, and it had broken her heart to see the huge Colossus computer, first of its kind in the world, in pieces. She turned round to find Callum by her side.

'What will you do now?' he asked.

She shrugged. She had no vision of the future. David had been officially declared dead, leaving her free to remarry, if she wished, though she felt no desire to do so. She had to find work, to keep herself and Penny, and supposed there might be secretarial vacancies. She told Callum.

He shuffled his feet. She recognised it as the prelude to his saying something he felt diffident about, and waited.

'I, uh, might be able to take you on as my secretary.'

'I'm not some pretty young thing you can bounce on your knee when no-one's looking,' she said.

He shook his head vigorously. 'No, no! I mean a real secretary. Typing, shorthand, telephone. More of a Personal Assistant, really.'

She felt her curiosity rise. 'Personal Assistant doesn't sound bad, as long as you weren't planning on getting too personal.'

He blushed and his moustache quivered. 'Er, no. It'd be rather like here, only with more responsibility.'

'What sort of business is it?'

He glanced round to make sure no-one was listening. 'Er, well: more of the same, I suppose.'

She cocked her head and looked at him sharply. 'You mean MI – '

' – Six. Yes.' He sucked in his cheeks. 'Of course, it will mean working in London.'

Ann sat down. Her head was in a whirl. 'I suppose there are buses and trains, so I wouldn't have to move house.'

'No. That'll be good for Penny, too.'

She rested a hand on her hip. 'There you go again. You could have made some woman a really good husband and father to her children. Why do you waste your time on me?'

'Haven't you guessed yet?'

'No?'

'I'm enjoying being a father-surrogate to Penny. Of course, that means I have to keep you sweet so you won't chase me away, but – och! – that's a small price to pay.'

She found herself bereft of a suitable response except for a tendency to chuckle, which she tried to bottle up. He was, she thought, a lovely and charming man. She liked him, enjoyed working with him, but as for anything else... Besides, he'd had plenty of opportunities to make any ambitions in that direction plain, and she could only assume that he really didn't want to form any closer a relationship than the one they currently enjoyed.

As the months and years slipped by, she was finding it easier to accept that David was not coming home, and that she might one day feel ready for a new permanent partnership. When that day came, if it did, she had no idea whether Callum would want to be the man in her life or not. The signs were not hopeful, but for now, she was happy with the arrangement they had, as long as he wanted it to continue.

* * *

In September, 1948, Penny Greatorix started school. Callum and Ann took her to the school gate and saw her safely taken in charge by a teacher. On the third day, the little girl insisted she didn't need them to take her to school. It was, she declared, in the serious way of the very young, quite sissy to be seen in the company of one's parents. She knew Callum was not her father, but he was the nearest thing to one, and she treated him as if he were.

Callum was secretly tickled, pleased she accepted him. He thought it the ideal kind of parenthood, the kind he could walk away from whenever he wanted, knowing that there was a real parent for the child. He had not, so far, found a need to do so, and in fact enjoyed his position *in loco parentis.*

Besides, it was clear that Ann enjoyed his company and the benefit of his advice, and it didn't seem fair simply to leave her to sort out problems when he could help.

Occasionally, he considered whether he should ask her to marry him, but each time he shied away from the idea because he thought she would think him very stupid. He had a good thing going, so why rock the boat? She was still in love with David Greatorix, and if she needed reminding of him, there was little Penelope, his child.

More frequently than he considered proposing to Ann, Callum considered trying to seduce her. But again, there was the fear that if he tried and she turned him down, it would be enough not only to rock the boat of their friendship but to swamp it altogether. If the price of being allowed to visit her on an almost daily basis, to act as a male parent to Penelope, was celibacy, then he was prepared to be celibate. He directed most of his energy, when he wasn't with Ann and the child, into his work, which with the start of the Cold War and the realignment of nations into east and west alliances, began to take on a new kind of importance.

CHAPTER 10 – 1999

Penny checked her suitcase and the clothing she had unpacked into the wardrobe. Geoff watched her, concerned.

'Is anything missing?' he asked.

'Not that I can see,' she replied. 'It is still not a nice feeling.'

Geoff went to the minibar and found a miniature bottle of brandy. He shared it between two glasses and passed one to her.

'I'd better go and see if my room has been touched. Would you be okay by yourself a few minutes?'

'I'll come with you,' she said.

Five minutes later, they were back. Geoff 's room was as he'd left it, with no signs of disturbance.

'Shall we tell the hotel management?' he asked.

'I'll phone them. There might have been other instances of pilfering.'

She called the reception desk and told them what had happened. When they offered to send for the police, she declined on the basis that nothing had been taken and she did not want to become embroiled in French police procedures. The management assured her that it was their policy that if any member of staff was caught misusing their access to guests' rooms, they would instantly be dismissed. They added that in this case, notwithstanding the police were not to be informed, enquiries would be made among the staff.

Penny hung up and turned to Geoff. 'Let's go and ask if we can see their CCTV.'

They let themselves out of her room and went down to the foyer, where they asked to see the manager.

CCTV coverage of the hotel was not comprehensive, but one camera gave a wide view of the foyer, and a few minutes after Penny and Geoff saw themselves leave the hotel, among the many other movements in the area, she noted a moustachioed, dark haired man in a suit entering the building. He chose a path through the foyer at the furthest edges of the camera's view and made no attempt to approach the reception desk.

'Is that man one of your guests?' Penny asked the manager.

The manager studied the indistinct images before shaking his head slowly. 'I do not think so, Madame,' he told her.

'Do you recognize him?'

He shook his head again. 'No, I am sorry, Madame.'

In response to her request, he manoeuvred the tape to get the best view of the man's face, and captured the image. The definition was too poor to allow for much enlargement, but he did what he could. The end result was a blurred picture of a man with dark hair, dark eyebrows, and clean-shaven except for a thin moustache.

Penny accepted a print of the photograph and thanked him. She and Geoff returned thoughtfully to her room.

Once inside, Geoff asked her, 'Why'd you pick him? There were other people in the foyer who didn't approach the reception desk.'

She smiled. 'He just seemed a bit more suspicious than the others,' she said. 'Must be my years in the police service.'

Geoff seemed hesitant about something.

'What's bothering you?' she asked.

'Do you think he might come back?'

'No. Why? Do you?'

He shrugged. 'I suppose you can take care of yourself.'

She glanced at his expression before sitting on the bed and pulling off her shoes. 'Were you meaning, might he come back while I'm in here?'

'Uh-huh.'

'What would you do about it?'

'Er, well, I was going to suggest that I sleep in the chair.'

'Ready to spring to my defence?'

He shrugged. 'Something like that.'

She chuckled. 'If you think you should, I don't mind. Do you want to go and get your toothbrush, and maybe a change of clothing for the morning? And bandages, sticking plasters… '

He blushed and laughed ruefully. 'Okay, okay. So not very likely. No worries. I'll be off.' He headed for the door.

Penny touched his arm. 'Just bring the toothbrush.'

He gazed into her eyes for a moment, trying to read their depths. 'You're sure?'

'If you are. I'm certain that chair will be very uncomfortable, but if you think you should… well… '

She opened the door for him and watched for a moment as he trod quietly along the corridor carpet. Then she closed the door, wondering at her decision, whether it was wise to allow him the intimacy of sleeping in the same room. She had little doubt that she could defend herself from an unwelcome intruder, but if Geoff became amorous, could she defend herself against him? She grabbed her nightdress from under the bedclothes and quickly changed into it. Her clothes had been folded and put aside by the time she heard Geoff tap on the door. She checked through the spyhole before letting him in.

'There's some spare bedding in the wardrobe,' she told him. 'Help yourself. I won't be a minute.'

She closed the bathroom door behind her, leaving him to find a blanket and pillow. He placed them neatly on the chair, and took off his jacket, laying it neatly on top of her folded clothes, removed his tie and unfastened a few shirt buttons.

Penny came out of the bathroom, suddenly conscious of his eyes on her. The full-length nightdress she wore was layered cool blue-green gauzes, with oriental birds embroidered on it in warm reddish colours. It was the most expensive nightdress she'd bought in a long time, and she knew it was a very feminine garment, swirling as she moved.

Geoff went to clean his teeth, and by the time he came out of the bathroom, Penny was demurely covered up in the big king-size bed, with a copy of *Cosmopolitan* open in her hand.

As Geoff took his place in the chair and wrapped the blanket around him, she glanced up at him and put the magazine aside. 'Do you mind if I turn the light off now?' she asked.

'It's a long time since I was frightened of the dark,' Geoff said.

She grinned and reached across to the switches on the headboard, plunging the room into darkness except for the thin line of light at the bottom of the corridor door. She wriggled down, under the duvet, and listened to Geoff trying to make himself comfortable across the room.

She lay there, trying to ignore an idea in her mind which refused to go away. She heard Geoff try turning onto his other side.

The silence which ensued was nerve-wracking, as she strained to hear him breathe, but he was quite still. She waited a few minutes more before she could stand the silence no longer.

'Are you awake, Geoff?' she whispered.

'Yes,' he replied softly.

'Oh. Okay,' she said.

Silence filled the room until she heard him move again. She waited a few minutes longer. The time dragged. She licked her lips.

'Are you still awake?' she whispered.

'Yes, of course.'

'Is the chair really uncomfortable? It looked uncomfortable to sleep in.'

'I'll be fine. Go to sleep.'

She heard him move in the chair once more.

It was maybe ten minutes later when she spoke again. 'Geoff?'

'Yes?'

'For God's sake, come over here and get into bed.'

'Are you sure?' He sounded pleased, she noted.

'Yes. Which side do you prefer?'

'I have no idea. I used to sleep on the right before my wife died. These days, I sleep down the middle.'

'Well, get in on the right side. I don't mind the left. John always slept on the right, so I'm used to it. I hope you don't snore.'

'And they say romance is dead!'

She giggled. 'I just don't want my generous gesture repaid with a night spent listening to you snoring.'

'If I snore, you have my permission to wake me up,' he said, as she felt him touching the bed to find his way round it in the dark. 'Provided, of course, that I have yours to do likewise.'

'*I* don't snore,' she told him primly.

'Then it won't hurt to give me that permission,' he said. She felt him slip under the duvet and for a moment, his leg brushed her foot. She moved away, into the chilly, unoccupied left side of the bed.

'Very well, if I must.'

He laughed softly. 'Don't be such a grouch,' he said.

'What more do you want?' she asked, turning towards him.

He rolled over until she could smell the toothpaste on his breath. 'Maybe that's for another time,' he said.

She made no response. His meaning was plain, but did she want their relationship to become a personal one? At least, not at this moment. The thought in her mind was still lurking in the shadows. A few minutes later, she heard Geoff's breathing become even and shallow.

'Geoff?' she asked quietly.

No answer.

'Geoff?' She prodded his shoulder lightly. He woke up with a snort.

'Geoff?'

'Wha – yes?'

'Don't you think you should take your trousers off in bed?' she asked.

* * *

Once she had fallen asleep, she didn't wake until half-past eight the following morning. When she did open her eyes, she lay in a drowsy state, comfortable and relaxed.

Then she woke up properly and rolled over to find Geoff was laying quietly beside her, watching her.

'Good morning,' he said.

She stared at him. Such formality was unexpected.

'Do you need the bathroom first, or shall I... ?'

'Uh-huh,' she said, still trying to clear her mind. In the cold light of day, she had to wonder what had prompted her to accept his offer to stay the night, and secondly, to let him share her bed?

Probably, she decided ruefully, too much wine with dinner. She'd only had one glass, but plainly, she'd better stick to water in future. As Geoff swung his legs out from under the duvet and stood up to pull his trousers on, Penny allowed herself the briefest of glances and concluded that he was in good physical condition. There was a firmness that she approved of. Thereafter, she paid little attention while he dressed, slipped on his shoes, and grabbed his jacket and tie.

'I'll see you downstairs for breakfast in about half an hour?' he said.

She smiled at him. 'Okay.'

She waited until the door closed behind him before sitting up and pulling the duvet up to her neck. But the only thing she had to hide from now was her own recollection of the night. It really would not do! she told herself. Geoff must be discouraged from any idea that sleeping together should mark the beginning of a more intimate relationship. They were colleagues, not friends, she argued, and they'd slept in the same bed for entirely professional reasons.

It didn't sound professional, when she thought about it, but it would have to do. Nothing had happened, and she'd had the best night's sleep she'd had for a year or more. Surely, she thought, that alone suggested that their sleeping arrangement had been business, not pleasure?

She failed to convince herself entirely. It didn't help either that when she went into the bathroom for a quick shower, the first thing she saw was Geoff's toothbrush and paste. That was a bad sign, wasn't it? Did he think he'd sort-of moved in, or was it just that he'd forgotten to take them with him.

Her thoughts were still spiralling in the same sort of pattern when she met Geoff again in the dining room. It was only slightly gratifying that he seemed as embarrassed as she felt, and several times appeared to be on the verge of saying something but drew back. As she ate the last piece of toast, softened by melted butter, she took pity on him.

'It's all right, you know, Geoff. About last night.'

'It is? Oh, good,' he replied. 'Can I have my toothbrush back?'

She gazed at him in wonder. Even after more than fifty years, the fact that a man's thoughts were not on the same track as her own could sometimes still surprise her.

* * *

Oliver had spent a restless night. His search of Penny's room having revealed nothing of interest, he had returned to the farm. In the morning, he went to the hamlet of Sainte Marguerite-en-Bessin. Doctor Henri Lafarge lived in a modest house in the middle of the row of buildings on the main street. Oliver parked outside and knocked on the door, letting himself in.

'Henri?'

The doctor emerged from the kitchen. 'Oliver!' He went up to the younger man and embraced him in the continental fashion. Oliver suffered this invasion of his personal space in silence. It was happening less often in Paris, being replaced by the simple handshake.

'What brings you here?' asked Lafarge.

'May we sit down?' Oliver followed the Doctor into the living room.

'Glass of wine to set you up for the day?' asked Lafarge.

'Too early for me,' said Oliver settling back in a chair.

The doctor sat opposite him and waited patiently.

'There's a couple of English people asking questions about the war,' Oliver said.

Lafarge placed his fingertips together. 'Ah, yes, it's possible that I've met them. They came into the bar at the end of the street a couple of days ago. I was there with Albert.'

'What did they want to know?'

'The woman is looking for her father. It appears he was parachuted into this area in the spring of 1943, as far as I could gather.'

Oliver considered this. 'You were around at the time, weren't you?'

'Indeed, I was.' He scratched his head. 'To the best of my recollection, the only stranger who appeared here at that time was, in fact, your father, and he was from Hameau Belchamps.'

'You're sure of that?'

The doctor shrugged and held both hands palm upwards, in a helpless gesture. 'But of course,' he said. 'I saw no reason to question his identity.'

Oliver leaned forward, resting his elbows on his knees and staring at the worn carpet. 'You never enquired?'

'No. Your mother and grandfather accepted him. I think she was most concerned about a terrible head injury he had received.'

'How'd he come by that?'

'I think he was crossing one of their fields in the dark, fell and hit his head on a large stone. He should have gone to hospital, really, but, you know, the country was in a terrible state by then. Hospitals full of injured Germans as well as local people, insufficient medicines and equipment due to the war… Your mother wanted to look after him, and I managed to get some of the necessary equipment from the hospital at Bayeux so she could feed your father through a tube, and so on. He was in a coma for nearly six months.'

Oliver looked up. 'So I heard. And then, in January, they married.'

Lafarge shrugged. 'It was the war. The Germans shot your grandfather on Christmas Eve. Delphine – your mother – inherited the farm, and, when she and Marcel fell in love, it worked in just right. Two years later, you came along.'

'At least it wasn't a shotgun wedding.'

The doctor raised an eyebrow. 'I didn't say that.'

'What do you mean?' Oliver sat up and frowned. 'I wasn't born until 1946.'

'No. But your mother miscarried on the 5th June, 1944, as near as I recall.'

Something in his tone made Oliver pause. 'Weren't you there when it happened?'

'No. I suppose I can say this, now she's dead, God rest her soul, but I think she was out and about with the rest of the Resistance, that night, preparing the way for the invasion the next day.'

'If she was pregnant – stupid woman!'

The doctor shook his head in disagreement. 'I think I will have that wine. Sure you won't join me?'

'No.' Oliver waited until the old man sat down again, clutching a small goblet of his favourite Merlot. 'Well?'

'The baby was already dead. We were simply waiting for the foetus to be expelled. It happened that particular night. I shouldn't be surprised if she didn't go out with the thought in her mind that all the rough and tumble of blowing up railway lines might encourage the delivery. It must have been frightening, and fairly horrible, when it did happen,' he added, ruminatively. 'Women go through so much as they fulfil their destinies as the bearers of children. Most men don't notice, but I, as their doctor, saw much of it. Delphine spared me her pain: I didn't have to watch. In time, of course, you came along.' He smiled at Oliver, who sensed the revelations were at an end. He got up.

'Thank you. You think there is nothing to fear from the two curious English?'

'Nothing at all. If they see you they will only ask if you know anything about a stranger who appeared in the Spring of 1943. You will tell them only what you think you should, which might amount to nothing.'

CHAPTER 11 – 1951

Even in the small towns of northern France, they'd heard about the Festival of Britain. The King declared it open on the third of May and the local papers around Bayeux included a few photographs. Marcel bought a newspaper on his way home from school and sat in the front seat of his car looking at them.

The festival was set to last until the autumn. With the long vacation looming, Marcel saw it as an excuse for the family to visit England.

'But, why?' asked Delphine, when he got home to the farm and told her his idea.

'The Festival of Britain should be interesting anyway,' he said, 'and besides…'

'Besides, what?'

He sat by the fire and stared into the embers. 'I remember… I remember a life in England.'

Delphine came to his side. She was biting her lip, and he thought she was about to cry. He took her hand, kissed it briefly and pressed it to his cheek.

'I used to wonder if you would ever remember your early life,' she said quietly. 'What do you remember about it?'

He gripped her hand. 'Just bits and pieces,' he said. 'A place name, Bletchley; a woman's name, Ann.' He looked up at her, frowning. 'I am Marcel Dubois, I was born in Hameau Belchamps in 1919…' He shook his head. 'My name is David. I can't remember the rest of it. Everything's a jumble.' He released her hand and stared into the fire again before standing up and turning towards her. 'I must go to England, to try and find out who I am. I thought we might all enjoy visiting this festival.'

Delphine put a hand on his shoulders comfortingly. 'This woman, Ann, sounds as if she is special. What will you do if you discover she is your wife?'

Marcel turned to her and rested his hand on hers. 'You are my wife, Delphine. If I ever had another, I do not have her now. It is you I love, you and Oliver.'

'What if you left a child behind in England?'

He shrugged. 'Then, I left it. I have no idea if I have a child in England.'

'But what if you have one?'

'He or she would have to be older than Oliver, and do you think he or she would thank me if I suddenly turned up out of the past? Both the child and its mother will have made their lives without me.'

'But if you discovered you had a wife and possibly a child, could you really leave them alone?' Delphine walked towards the other chair and turned to face him.

'I have only one wife, and only one child,' he told her. 'You and Oliver are my life, and France is my country.'

Delphine sat. 'But in the meantime, you want to go to England to find out what you can.'

He looked up at her and nodded. 'Yes,' he said, simply.

* * *

'Why is my name different from yours, daddy?'

Callum sat down and lifted Penny onto his knee. He and Ann had accepted that, eventually, Penny would start asking questions about her unconventional family, and agreed that honesty would be best, even if the truth had to be explained by instalments, suitable for the child's level of understanding.

'That's because your real daddy was called David Greatorix, so you are Penny Greatorix. Because girls and boys have their daddy's last name, usually.'

'Why is David Greatorix my real daddy? Aren't you my real daddy?'

'Because your real daddy was killed in the war, sweetheart,' said Ann, who had appeared in the kitchen doorway with a mug of coffee for Callum. 'Callum is your real daddy now, but you're still Penny Greatorix, because we don't want to forget you once had another daddy.'

Penny pouted. 'Why did my other daddy get killed? I don't remember him.'

Ann put the mug down on a coffee table near Callum's elbow and sat on the floor beside her daughter. 'Your other daddy died before you were born, sweetheart, so that's why you don't remember him. He never saw you, so he never knew what a pretty little girl we had.'

'Why did he get killed?'

Ann's eyes had filled with tears. Even after eight years, she still occasionally grieved for David. With no body to bury, and only a stark presumption that he was dead, she had found it difficult to move on. Only with Callum's constant and reassuring companionship had she managed to make something approaching a normal home life for her daughter.

'We don't know,' he said. 'He went to France, and never came home.'

'So how d'you know he's dead?'

Callum glanced at Ann before continuing. 'In war, love, lots of people go away and never come home, just like your real daddy. After a while, the government decides they must be dead.'

'Oh. Poor daddy.' The pout returned.

'Yes, indeed. Poor daddy,' echoed Callum.

Ann patted her daughter's knee. 'But Callum is your daddy now.' She looked at him. 'And a better daddy no little girl could wish for.'

Penny looked at Ann. 'Do you kiss Callum?'

Ann smiled uncertainly. She did, but only ever on the cheek or forehead, brief friendly greetings or expressions of gratitude for something he'd done. In her mind it raised the question of just what Callum's status was in her life.

Constant, that's what. She realised suddenly, he'd been her companion far longer than David, and it really was time to recognise that he was a more important part of hers and Penny's life than David had ever been. Suddenly, she felt a lump in her throat as her conscience pointed out ruthlessly that she had accepted his companionship and support, and allowed him almost total parental rights over Penny, and he had never over-stepped the mark.

He'd never tried to seduce her either. Maybe, she thought, he doesn't find me attractive enough.

'Very occasionally, I kiss him,' she told Penny with a smile. 'When he's been particularly good. Like I kiss you when you're particularly good.'

'Sylvia Armstrong's mummy kisses her daddy a lot, she says. They're always doing it, then they rush upstairs to bed for half an hour.'

Penny had to restrain a laugh. Sylvia was Penny's current best friend at school. 'Do you think that's what mummies and daddies should do, Penny?'

The child nodded solemnly.

Ann glanced at Callum. 'We'll have to brush up our act, won't we, Callum.'

She saw him blush, and thought maybe there was life in the old dog. He was only a year older than her own thirty-two years, though his demeanour was that of a much older man.

'Aye,' he said. 'Why don't you go out and play, sweetheart. I'll come out in half an hour and we'll see if you can ride that bike of yours without stabilisers.'

Penny slipped off his knee. 'Ooh, yes!' A moment later, they heard the crash as she grabbed her bike from the pile of toys they kept in the outhouse, and took it outside.

Ann watched Callum's face as his eyes followed the little girl until she was out of sight. 'It's a pity you aren't her real father,' she said.

'Aye. Well, I do what I can so she doesn't feel the loss.'

Ann got up off the floor and sat on his lap, grinning. 'I think you just like having little girls sitting on your knee.'

He blushed again. 'I think, given a choice, I'd prefer bigger girls,' he replied, slipping his arm round her waist.

She leaned into him, so that her breasts were under his nose. 'There's more to get hold of, I suppose.'

His gaze disappeared down her neckline. She waited a moment before coughing gently to draw his attention back to her face.

'Callum,' she said contritely, 'I've taken you so much for granted, and you've been such a perfect companion to me and daddy for Penny. Don't you think it's time you made an honest woman of me?'

For a moment, he stared into her eyes before a grin broke out and spread across his face.

'Does this mean that, if I was to press my suit, you might be minded to accept me?' His Scottish burr was very pronounced, which she put down to a pleasing degree of nervousness.

'I might be minded to accept you even in your wrinkled suit,' she told him with mock gravitas.

'This is a serious matter,' he said sternly. 'Now, will you marry me, Ann my love?'

She put both arms round his shoulders and studied his face. She was surprised how easily she had prompted a proposal from him. Surprised and gratified.

'That will depend on whether we are completely compatible,' she told him.

He looked uncertain. 'I – I'd have thought we were after all these years. What can I do to convince you?'

'Would you invest in a new car without taking it for a test drive?'

'What?' He looked baffled.

She smiled again. 'Kiss me, Callum.'

'Och, aye!' He leaned forward and gave her the usual sort of peck on the cheek.

She shook her head. 'That's not quite what I had in mind. How do you think Sylvia Armstrong's dad kisses her mum before they disappear upstairs for half an hour?'

While he was still pondering that, she took his face in her hands and pressed her lips against his. Tongues met and explored. In a much shorter time than she had expected, she felt him stiffen. She wriggled to make herself more comfortable, but only succeeded in waking her long-forgotten desire.

Breaking the kiss, she said, 'Time for the next step in Sylvia's dad and mum's menu, I think.' She stood up and took his arm, leading him towards the door to the hallway.

'Penny's expecting me to teach her how to ride her bike,' he protested feebly.

'After you've taught me a thing or two,' Ann said, amazed at her own boldness. She was glad nobody else could hear her. She took his hand and led him up to her bedroom.

* * *

'Do you remember Mary Hamilton?'

'Of course,' Ann replied. 'What about her?'

She was perched on the corner of Callum's desk in the anonymous building where they both worked for the Secret Intelligence Service, or SIS. There had been pressure from 'above' when they had married – a quiet little ceremony at the Register Office – aimed at transferring Ann somewhere else, away from her husband, as couples working together were thought to be less efficient – spending time discussing domestic matters instead of work – than if they worked separately. They had stood firm, and continued to work together as a team, albeit with Ann being technically Callum's Personal Assistant.

He held up a typed memo. 'She's due to be released from Holloway. Time off for good behaviour.'

'Oh,' said Ann. 'Poor Mary. I wonder what she'll do now.'

Callum rested his elbows on the desk and touched his fingertips together. 'I was thinking we should offer her a job.'

Ann stood up and faced him, surprised. 'After what she did…?'

'Uh-huh. Think about it – she's trained. She always was willing to put herself out for the cause. I think we could make use of her.'

'But she was a spy for the Germans!'

'I know, but we're not at war with the Germans now. The Soviet Union – you know, the ones we fought with and for during World War Two – is being very bolshie, which I suppose is appropriate. Churchill's Iron Curtain grows more substantial every day.'

'So? Where does Mary come into this?'

'She can spy for us. Wonder if she speaks Russian?'

'Are you thinking of sending her to Russia?'

He sat back in his chair, shaking his head. 'Oh, no. There are plenty of Russians here in London.'

'But don't they all speak English?'

He touched his fingertips together again and smiled lop-sidedly. 'Not necessarily in their sleep.'

Ann stared at him. 'Callum!' she exclaimed, 'That's a shocking thing to say.'

He grinned. 'Really? I thought it was providing her with an opportunity to shine – and do something for *this* country's benefit, for a change.'

Ann shook her head. 'I suppose she did have lots of boy-friends when her husband was a prisoner and she was alone.'

'Quite. Are you with me on this?'

'I suppose so.'

'Good. We'll go over to Holloway first thing tomorrow and pick her up when she comes out.'

In the event, Ann and Callum had to wait for over ninety minutes outside the prison. It was a little after ten when the huge doors opened just wide enough for a person and Mary Hamilton stepped outside. Her skin was grey. Her face was more lined than when they had last seen each other, in fact she looked years older.

Ann got out of the car and walked slowly towards the prison. Mary looked round and recognised her.

'What are you doing here?' She bent down to look inside the car. 'And Callum, too?'

'Yes. We came to meet you.'

Mary looked down at her plain grey skirt and jacket. 'I'm not really dressed for entertaining.'

'It's just as well, then, that we're not really your guests. Would you like to get in.'

Ann picked up Mary's bag and dropped it on the back seat of the car. Mary was puzzled, but followed it in. Ann shut the door and got in beside Callum.

Mary looked from one to the other of them. 'Well? Why are you here? It's not as if you bothered to visit me while I was inside, so I detect a bit of self-interest, but I'm blowed if I can figure out what it is.'

'We figured you'd need a job,' said Callum.

'Oh?'

'Yes. So first-off, I need to know, would you like to take it, in which case I'll take you to the house that goes with it, or if you don't want it, just tell me where you'd like to go and I'll take you there.'

Ann turned round and watched Mary's face reflect astonishment. 'Wait a minute! You're offering me a job that goes with a house?'

'The pay's not good, but there are one or two perks,' he said.

'What's the job?'

'Can't tell you until you've signed the Official Secrets Act, which would be after you've decided to accept the offer, of course.'

'Official Sec— ? Wait a minute! Are you two still working for SOE?'

'SOE no longer exists,' Callum told her. 'Closed in 1946. Don't they tell you anything in there?' He nodded towards the looming walls of the prison.

'They didn't tell me that,' replied Mary. She looked from one to the other of them. 'And you're both doing… whatever it is you do?'

'We are a team,' said Callum, resting his left hand on Ann's shoulder.

Mary caught the glint of gold on his finger. 'Callum! You're married?'

'You sound surprised,' he said, smiling. 'May I introduce my wife.'

Mary transferred her astonished gaze to Ann. 'Ann? But what about David?'

'He never came back from France. We, uh, we've only been married a week.'

'Did you save me any wedding cake?'

'We – well, I – wasn't expecting to see you. This is Callum's idea, and I'm not sure you'll like it.'

'When do I get to find out?'

'Are you going to sign up?' asked Callum.

Mary looked from one to the other. 'Either of you got a cigarette?'

When both of them shook their heads, she shrugged. 'Oh, what the hell! Give me the bloody paper.'

Callum reached into his inside pocket and pulled out a folded piece of paper on which the words of section 1 of the 1911 Act were printed, along with an acknowledgement that the undersigned understood the section applied to them.

'Sign at the bottom,' he told her.

'Got a pen?'

Ann opened her handbag and searched inside. 'Did they take everything off you?'

Mary opened her own handbag and took out a packet of cigarettes, tapped one out and lit it. 'No, I just got into the habit of scrounging things off other people.' She put the cigarette packet away and produced a cheap fountain pen. 'Bloody difficult getting ink for this,' she said. 'They only allow you a pencil in there. Do you know, the Governor's the only one with ink in his bottle.'

She pursed her lips as she spoke, and grinned saucily, leaving Ann wondering exactly what she meant. It was a sudden glimpse of the Mary of old. She signed the paper and handed it back to Callum.

'Well, what have I let myself in for?'

Callum started the engine and the car moved off. 'First things first, eh, Mary. Let me take you to your new home. It's right in the middle of the Diplomatic quarter. I'm sure you'll like it.'

'And what do you expect me to do?'

'Do you like diplomats?'

'I don't know, I've never tried one.'

Callum smiled, but Ann noticed it didn't reach his eyes. 'I'll have to see if I can introduce you to some. One at a time, of course.' He met Mary's eyes in the mirror. 'Or maybe two, if you're feeling up to it.' He drive along Regent Street. 'And I would like you to learn Russian.'

Mary stared hard at the back of his head. 'You'd better tell me the other side of this – this *deal!* What if it turns out I don't like diplomats?'

'I could see my way to changing your address again – back to where you've just come from. Remission can be cancelled, you know.'

Ann had turned round in her seat and saw the sudden flicker of vulnerability in Mary's eyes, something she'd never expected to see.

'So, in plain terms, Callum,' said Mary, 'you want me to sleep with Russian diplomats and extract their secrets?'

Callum entered a fine old Georgian square and pulled up outside a terrace of four-storey town houses. 'That's it, more or less is exactly,' he said. 'Tell me, do you like your new home?'

They got out of the car. He led the way up a short flight of steps to an anonymous front door, and rang the bell. A woman opened it.

'Ah, Freda,' said Callum, 'this is Mary. Mary, Freda is your housekeeper. She'll ensure your life runs smoothly and you don't have to worry about things like cooking, cleaning or shopping. You can concentrate on your, um, work. Freda will take you shopping this afternoon for some new clothes. Prison issue is so very drab, don't you think, and tomorrow night there's a cocktail party at the American Embassy.'

'American?'

'Don't worry, dear, it'll be teeming with Russians, all trying to plant bugs or search the place. I'll see you there.'

A few minutes later, he and Ann left the house.

'Had you forgotten it's Penny's school play tomorrow?'

'Er, I had, but it'll be over before the cocktails start flowing at the Embassy.'

'Is this new project with Mary going to affect our private lives much?'

'No. Once Mary has actually got something useful out of a Russian, I think we'll be able to ensure that she'll continue. Then I can hand her over to one of the regular Field Officers, and I'll be back to nine-to-five all over again.'

'I hope so,' said Ann.

CHAPTER 12 – 1999

It was an odd feeling when Penny found herself face to face with the man in the CCTV. She was sure it was him, and Geoff thought so too, but the fact that the man had been in the hotel was not proof that he had been the one to search her room.

'Oliver Delacourt,' he said, holding out his hand. His English was only slightly accented. 'I've ordered us some coffee. Hope you don't mind?'

'Penny,' she said, deliberately omitting her surname. 'No, of course not. Thank you.' They shook hands briefly.

'I believe you were looking for me at my parents' farm?'

'Not specifically,' she replied. 'I was trying to find someone who might have known something about my father, who came hereabouts in 1943.'

Oliver smiled and shrugged. 'Three years before I was born.'

They were in the foyer of the hotel. A waiter brought coffee to the low table between them.

'Your neighbour told us that,' said Penny, 'but thought you might have information anyway, perhaps from your parents.'

'My mother's dead,' he said.

'I'm sorry to hear that. And your father?'

Penny caught the movement of his eyes as he looked away.

'He's gone away.'

'Do you know where?'

'No.'

She glanced at Geoff, who was sipping coffee. His slightly lifted eyebrow told her he'd noticed the lie as well.

'He was the farmer, was he?' she asked.

Oliver seemed surprised by her question. He responded quickly. 'Not really. He helped out, I think, in the early days, just after the war, but he and my mother let the fields out to the next-door farm.'

'What did your father do, then, if he didn't work the fields?'

'He was a teacher.'

Penny looked suitably impressed. 'Quite a change for someone whose family had been farmers for generations.'

'It was my mother's family that had been farmers. My father's ... weren't.'

'But the farm... it's the Delacourt Farm. Monsieur Le Greq said that Delacourts had farmed it, but that would mean your father was a Delacourt, if you are?'

Oliver stared at her, seeming to be angry. 'I use my mother's name.'

She drew back from him. 'Oh. Why? What was your father's name?'

'That,' said Oliver, 'is none of your business.'

Penny backed off further. 'Sorry, M'sieur. I'm just naturally nosey. Inquisitive,' she amplified, seeing his puzzlement at the idiom.

He spread his hands in apology. 'I am sorry, Madame. I was rude. Please forgive me.' He stood up. 'Let me get some more coffee, or perhaps you would like something else?' He snapped his fingers at a waiter as he spoke, and refused to listen when Penny politely declined.

'More coffee!' he demanded, sitting again.

'M'sieur.'

He threw his credit card on the waiter's tray as the man picked up the used cups and coffee pot and took them away.

'That's very kind of you,' said Geoff.

'Not at all, you are guests of my country.'

Penny smiled, feeling somewhat embarrassed by his sudden effusiveness.

'May I ask, what do you do? M'sieur Le Greq said you spend much of your time in Paris and Caen.'

'Yes. I run a chain of motor dealerships. We sell luxury cars and have bases in most of the big towns and cities.' He grinned. 'Actually, they more or less run themselves these days. I get all the free time I want.'

'Do you manage to fill it?'

'One likes to keep busy,' he replied, 'but also one likes to… chill out, I think is the phrase.'

She chuckled. 'Yes, I think it is.'

Oliver looked from one to the other of them. 'And you two, you are an item, yes?'

Geoff's smile in response was muted. 'We're colleagues, simply looking into Penny's family background. After all, everyone likes to know where they're from, don't they?' he added as the waiter arrived with a fresh supply of coffee, handing the credit card slip to Oliver for signature and returning the card.

'You said your father was a teacher: what did he teach?' asked Penny.

'Mathematics. He got a job here in Bayeux after the war.'

She watched his face while he spoke and got the feeling that Oliver neither wanted nor enjoyed speaking about his father. She wondered why.

'Were you proud to have a father who was clever enough to be a teacher. Was he the first in your family to be university educated?'

'No, no. That was me. My parents sent me to *Science Po*.'

'What is that?' asked Penny encouragingly.

'It is a university specialising in social sciences, politics. I wanted to become a politician, once.'

'Oh? What happened?'

He glanced at her and compressed his lips. 'It didn't work out. I decided to go into commerce instead.'

'Obviously a good decision,' she said.

'Why? Do you think I would have been a bad politician?' He frowned at her.

'I have no idea whether you would make a good politician or not,' she said, 'I was merely thinking, in the light of what you said, that you can't have done badly – sorry, that's English for "you have succeeded", only we tend not to think that way – at it.'

He forced a smile. 'Ah, yes, I see.'

Geoff leaned forward. 'I was thinking, you'd probably have been at university during the Paris riots of 1968?'

'I had just left.'

'You weren't minded to join in the protests?'

'No. Pardon, M'sieur, but I fail to see…?'

Geoff backed off. 'Sorry, M'sieur, I guess I'm nearly as nosey as Penny. But if we don't talk and ask each other questions, how do we communicate, and about what?'

'Well, and that is so. But we are here only so I can tell you I know nothing about Penny's father.'

Penny stood up. 'It has been interesting talking with you, M'sieur Delacourt. We may see you in the hotel or the town again before we leave.'

Oliver and Geoff both stood. Oliver inclined his head graciously. 'I, too, have found our meeting interesting. You are not likely to find me in the hotel, but perhaps we will see each other around town.'

'I must apologise again. One of the waiters said he thought you'd been in here a couple of nights ago.'

Oliver stared at her coldly. 'He was clearly mistaken, Madame.'

Penny and Geoff watched him leave.

'There's a drop of coffee left,' said Geoff. He sat again and refilled their cups. Penny sat down slowly, frowning.

'He's strange,' she remarked. 'A man of many secrets.'

'Doesn't want to think about his father,' said Geoff, 'and refuses to use his name; doesn't like to talk about his student politics – seems odd for a would-be politician.'

'Didn't really like to talk about himself at all, except when it came to boasting that he was the first person in his family to go to university.'

'Wonder where his father taught? I'll bet there's a record of school-teachers in Bayeux somewhere.'

'I'd think the *mairie,* the town hall, would be a good place to start,' said Penny.

Geoff drank the cooling coffee in one swallow. 'I'm sure he's the man in the CCTV pictures. In which case, why would he lie about being in the hotel?'

'Yes, I wondered about that.'

'And another thing, Pen, I'll bet his father's name was Dubois. If we're going looking for schoolteachers, we might need to know.'

'How did you find out?'

'Credit cards generally show your legal name.'

'Hmm. I couldn't read it from where I was sitting,' she grinned.

'Let's go find the town hall.'

As they stepped out into the street, she turned to him. 'You know, Geoff, I quite like the fact that we often think about the same things.'

He glanced down at her at his shoulder. 'I might put that idea to the test a bit later.'

She looked up at him, saw the little gleam of mischief in his eye, and smiled.

'Nothing to say?' he asked.

'Surely, you weren't expecting anything?'

They were directed to the custodian of the town's records. It took half an hour to find the record of employment of one Marcel Dubois, of Delacourt Farm, Sainte Margue-rite-en-Bessin, from shortly after the liberation until 1969. Next of kin was shown as *Delphine Dubois, wife*, but this had been crossed through and the name *Oliver Dubois* substituted.

'When was this alteration made?' Penny asked the archivist.

He peered at the yellowing page through thick-lensed glasses and produced a magnifier. With his face scarce inches from the page, he screwed up his eyes to read.

'April 1969, Madame.'

Penny thanked him and looked up at Geoff. 'For Oliver to become next of kin, must mean that Delphine, his mother, I suppose, was dead.'

'Perhaps that is why he took his mother's name?'

'Perhaps.' She turned back to the archivist. 'What else can your records tell you about this family?'

'What would you like to know?'

'Births, deaths and marriage? Do you have that sort of information?'

The little archivist drew himself up to his full height, level with Penny's shoulders. 'But of course, Madame. France is not in the dark ages.'

Penny looked as contrite as she could. 'I'm sorry M'sieur, if that is what I seemed to imply. I meant no disrespect.'

He nodded graciously. 'Madame. Come with me, please.' He led the way into another room, full of shelves lined with books of indices to the area's births, marriages and deaths.

'These date from the war. Earlier ones were... incomplete.'

Penny and Geoff glanced at each other over the use of what she certainly thought of as a euphemism for 'war damaged'.

The record of Oliver's birth was found, and his father identified as *Marcel Dubois, farm worker, born in Hameau Belchamps, Calvados.*

'Hameau Belchamps?' Penny asked the archivist.

'A small place, Madame,' he said. He led them to a modern map of the area and tapped with his finger. 'Just there. Not far to visit.'

'Nothing about his parents or when he was born?'

'Not that I can see,' he said. 'But if you go there, you could ask around. It's a small place, there might be someone who knows, or knew, the family Dubois.'

'Can you find a record of his mother's death?' asked Geoff.

'But of course.'

The archivist pulled four volumes off a shelf and placed them on a large table. 'We look for entries for Dubois. You said the mother was Delphine, née Delacourt?'

'Yes.'

They took a volume each and scoured them for the entry. They found it in the first quarter.

'March the twenty-fifth,' said the archivist. 'It appears she died from an accidental drowning on the farm.'

Penny looked sad. 'The poor woman,' she said, angling the page towards her. 'Only forty-six or -seven. It doesn't say how it happened?'

'No, Madame. There may be something in the newspaper archives, though.'

Penny thanked him for his help, and she and Geoff left the building, in search of the newspaper office.

'I suppose it's a bit like old times for you,' Geoff said, 'tracking down clues, following a trail?'

She smiled. 'A bit. But it's not as if we're hunting a murderer.'

They passed a side street where a café had cordoned off part of the pavement for tables under sunshades. Penny glanced at her watch.

'Fancy some lunch before we look at the newspaper clippings?'

* * *

The woman in charge of the newspaper library was dressed in a green tweed suit. She was broad across the shoulders and hips, and her large feet were encased in sensible brown brogues. Heavy, dark horn-rimmed glasses dominated her face. Hair, a mixture of brown and orange, was swept into a pleat and pinned rigidly in place. Her square chin served to set off a wide, thin-lipped mouth.

'*Oui?*' she asked as Penny and Geoff were admitted to her sanctum by one of the younger members of staff.

It was, thought Penny, not a promising start. She answered the woman's frown with a smile. She tried to explain in her inadequate French what they sought. Six words into it, the woman smiled.

'Ah, you are English,' she said, nodding as if that ex- plained as if that explained why Penny was having such difficulty with the world's most elegant language.

Penny admitted it.

'Per'aps we could speak English. I don't get much oppor- tunity to practise it in here.'

Penny smiled and explained they were looking for any re- port of the death on 25th March 1969, of Delphine Dubois.

'Let me see,' said the librarian, tapping her lips with a fin- ger. 'That should not be 'ard to find. It would probably be the day after, or sometime in the week following... Wait here.' She indicated a row of three wooden chairs and faded into the gloom among the poorly-lit shelving units which held filing boxes.

Penny and Geoff sat down to wait, absorbing the atmos- phere of the place, the slight mustiness, the hint of dust in the air, and the acoustic deadness, all sounds being instantly swallowed almost before being created, by the yards of shelves filled with piles of stacked paper. The windows were covered by blinds, probably, thought Penny, to stop sunlight fading the nearer archives, but the effect of that, coupled with the high shelving which filled the room, conspired to make the place feel small and airless.

The woman returned with a box file and put it on the counter which separated her from her visitors. Penny and Geoff went to look at the contents with her.

'The twenty-sixth of March, 1969, was a Wednesday,' said the woman. She riffled through the file and pulled out a dried-up copy of the local newspaper of the day. She scanned it quickly: Penny thought, not only would she know where to look, she would be able to spot anything relevant quicker than herself or Geoff.

There was no mention of the death in that day's edition, and they moved on to the next. On page four of the paper

was a news item. The woman stabbed one entry with her
finger.

'Là! Madame!' she said triumphantly, turning the page so
they could see the entry.

Penny could read French better than she could understand the spoken word.

'You'd better translate for me,' said Geoff. 'I obviously
should have paid more attention in class.'

Penny peered at the words. 'Here goes. Oh, my God! It
says Delphine's body was discovered face-down in the duck
pond at the farm. She had drowned. On the same day, her
husband, Marcel Dubois, disappeared. The police are searching for him. Their son, Oliver, arrived home from Caen, and
was interviewed by police.'

She looked up. 'Is there any more in the next edition?' she
asked the librarian.

The woman handed her a copy of the next day's paper.
The story had been relegated to a side-bar, and reported that
Delphine's death had been determined to be accidental. Marcel had been discovered in hospital in Vire with a fractured
skull. He had been unable to describe his attacker when he
recovered consciousness, and the investigation had fizzled
out.

'Wonder if the police report is still on file?'

It wasn't.

'We would not keep a record of a death which turned out
to be nothing more than an accident and an assault that had
been unsolved through lack of evidence for this length of
time, Madame,' said a tired-looking gendarme at the police
station.

Penny and Geoff made their way back to the hotel at a
leisurely pace. Neither saw a figure who seemed to be paying
them attention on the other side of the street, his face lost in
shadow. He waited a few moments after they entered the
hotel before turning and walking slowly away, his head
bowed.

CHAPTER 13 – 1953

Marcel stood on one of the bridges spanning the River Thames and looked upstream. He and his family, hadn't, in the end, visited the Festival of Britain, but here, two years later, the British were celebrating the enthronement of a new Monarch. The streets of London along the route the fairy-tale Gold State Coach would follow to Westminster Abbey were thronged with people from all over the country, all over the world. Delphine had more or less insisted he go, since in all that time, his recollections had been growing stronger.

He now knew who Ann was.

That had been a terrible moment. The revelation had come to him while he slept. He woke up, Delphine's beloved face inches away from his own on the pillow, her eyes still closed in repose. And he realised his first problem was whether or not to tell her. They shared most things, and it was his natural inclination to do so, but this – *this* – might be a share too far.

It wasn't, he realised, as if he was still in love with Ann. They hadn't been married long when he'd left her. He had a vague recollection of boarding a small aeroplane, burdened down with stuff which hung from his belt, while strapped to his back had been a bulky pack containing a parachute. He remembered nothing after that until he woke up six months later in Delacourt Farm.

Ann was just a distant memory, there was nothing he'd shared with her that he hadn't experienced with Delphine, and Ann certainly hadn't looked after him whilst he lay help-less and comatose as Delphine had.

No, he knew with confidence, his loyalty was to Del-phine, and undivided. She was, as he'd reassured her many times since his memory of Ann had returned, his one and true wife. But there was the question in his mind, what had happened to Ann. One recollection he had not shared with Delphine was that he was almost certain Ann had been pregnant when he left. He wanted to know if he had another child in England.

Earlier in the day, he had found himself in London's Baker Street. He'd read some of the Sherlock Holmes stories, ever since he'd discovered he was comfortable reading and speaking English, and half expected to find a brass plate on the door of 221B. There was a plaque outside where the address would have been, which mentioned Holmes, but the wall to which it was attached belonged to a bank. He found himself wandering aimlessly along the street. At one point he'd stepped out into the road, believing it to be clear, so he could look up towards the high rooflines. A policeman had grabbed him and hauled him back onto the pavement. He'd forgotten the traffic flowed on the left in Britain.

'You all right, guv?' asked the constable, releasing him.

Marcel brushed himself down. 'Yes. Thank you.'

'Need to be a bit more careful, sir.'

'Yes, officer. Thank you.'

The policeman touched his helmet respectfully with a finger. Marcel smiled, and moved away towards number sixty-four. He'd remembered the number while they'd been talking.

Number sixty-four was a nondescript office block, unidentified by any sign.

He contemplated entering and speaking to someone, but figured he'd be told the place had nothing to do with a defunct wartime department, which might or might not be the truth. He certainly wouldn't get further than the front desk, and what did he expect to find anyway.

What he needed to do was to meet someone who'd been far enough up the organisational pyramid, who might be able to tell him how he, Marcel, had become involved in the organisation in the first place. It seemed he was a mathematician and a linguist, and he couldn't see any reason why a person with such qualifications should have been sent into France as a secret agent.

He strolled southwards, along Park Lane, through Green Park and St James's, until he reached Westminster Bridge, from which he had stared westwards along the river.

He decided to visit Bletchley, in the hope that it would stimulate his memory more.

The train took longer than scheduled to reach the town, due to maintenance work just before the station. Marcel took the opportunity to scan the landscape to see if it reminded him of anything. At one point, he thought he recognised a row of houses, but decided it was a phantom memory, his mind playing tricks, trying to put something where something ought to be.

The train approached Bletchley and stopped. He made his way out of the station. The breeze had stiffened and he pulled his trilby down over his eyes more firmly. This time, when he thought he recognised a road, he was suspicious of it. However, lacking anything else to go on, he began to walk roughly north-westwards from the station. Without thinking too much about where he was going, he kept moving. Other views – the way a wall ended, the shape of a roof gable, the configuration of a junction, all suddenly seemed to make sense. He *knew* that, if he went *this* way, he would find houses, if he went *that* way, he would find… a large mansion, with turrets and fanciful architectural features. Bletchley Park.

Suddenly a whole chunk of recollections about the geography of the place came to him. As he approached the old wartime code-breaking centre, more memories came, this time of Ann, whom he remembered now *had* been pregnant last time he'd seen her. He knew where they'd lived.

He reached the mansion. It seemed unoccupied. He stared at it from the road and realised that there was nothing there for him. He turned back, the question in his mind being, should he try to find his old home? There would be a strange sort of nostalgia, seeing a house of which he had few real memories, and knowing he lived there once. Nevertheless, he decided to go. He felt drawn to the place.

The streets were essentially familiar, but here and there, new buildings had appeared and ones that he remembered being there had gone. It was not difficult finding his way, and inside half an hour he had the house in his sights.

Even as he watched, a young girl of about the age his child would be walked round the far corner of the street, entered through the garden gate, and let herself in at the front door. He stopped suddenly and leaned on a convenient lamp post. A moment later, the front door opened again and a woman, obviously the child's mother, came out and closed the gate which the girl had left open. She went back inside.

It took him a moment to recognise Ann. His throat tightened, and his breathing became difficult. His intention, to talk to her, vanished. Ten years had elapsed since he'd left her, and those events were still hazy in his mind. He needed time to consider his next move. He had a new and different life, and didn't doubt that Ann would have, too. She looked up but he turned quickly and walked away. He made his way back to the railway station, wondering what he should do now he knew where Ann lived, and the almost total certainty that the girl was his child.

Should he write to them? Should he go back and knock on the door?

Or should he go home to Delphine, and try his best to forget what he had seen?

By the time the London train arrived, he had decided he would go back to France and seek his wife's opinion.

* * *

'There was a man hanging around outside earlier,' Ann told Callum that evening, after Penny had gone up to her room to read a new adventure of *The Famous Five*. 'Anything to do with work?'

Callum pondered for a moment, then shook his head. 'Not that I know anything about. What was he doing?'

'I saw him from the bedroom window. I was looking out for Penny, coming home from school, and he came round the corner at the end of the road.' She wrinkled her brow with the effort of recollection. 'At first, I thought nothing of it – you know, just another pedestrian. But then he stopped, over by the lamp post, and leaned against it. He was watching the house, I'm certain. Then Penny came home, and… it was the way he looked at her: he seemed to be staring.'

'You didn't recognise him?'

'No. The street lamp hadn't come on, and my eyesight isn't what it was – I really must get my eyes tested. And he had his hat pulled down.'

'A hat?'

'A trilby. Dark brown.'

Callum nodded. 'Like every other man in the street.' He indicated she should continue.

'After Penny came indoors, I went out to have another look. She'd left the gate open – again – so it didn't look too obvious, but when I tried to look more closely at him, he turned and walked back the way he'd come.'

Callum's eyebrows arched but he said nothing.

'That was what seemed really strange,' Ann continued. 'If he'd just been an ordinary passer-by, he would surely have carried on walking past the house, in the same direction he'd been going when he entered the road; but he turned round and walked away. That's why I wondered if the house was under surveillance.'

Callum shook his head. 'Not that I'm aware. Anyway, anyone professionally trained in surveillance wouldn't make such an elementary mistake. As you say, it causes them to stand out a mile. If he'd been Special Branch, or MI5 or 6, he'd not have behaved so suspiciously. Might not have let you see him at all.'

'Which begs the question, then: who was he? And why was he watching us?'

'You're certain he was watching us, not next door?'

She nodded. 'Yes.' She frowned. 'There was something familiar about him, and yet, not. I don't know how to describe the feeling. I suppose it's like that time, shortly after David disappeared, when I kept thinking I saw him in town, but of course, it was just my imagination.'

Callum nodded sympathetically. 'Aye. That often seems to happen to people who've been suddenly bereaved.' He pulled a notebook out of his jacket pocket. 'How was he dressed?' He wrote down the description Ann gave him. 'I'll ask around, but I'm pretty sure he's not one of ours.' He smiled at her. 'He might simply have got lost, and turned back.'

She smiled faintly. 'If you believe in coincidence. I'm quite sure he was looking at this house.'

He patted her hand in a way that was supposed to reassure her. 'Well, I'll see if I can dig anything up.'

* * *

By the time Marcel arrived back in London, it was too late to contemplate returning to France that evening, so it was after lunch the following day when he got back to the farm and Delphine.

On the long journey home, he had come to a decision.

'Until the moment I saw… Ann…' he told his wife, 'I had no clear idea of what I was going to do. I was, I admit, tempted to talk to her, but then…'

His voice tailed off, and he chewed his lips.

'What *did* you do?' Delphine asked. She fetched him a glass of local *cidre bouché*, the sparkling cider made from Normandy apples, and put it on the kitchen table.

'While I was making up my mind, I was watching the house from a distance. A young girl came, probably from school.' His eyes misted and he looked at Delphine sadly. 'I think she might have been my daughter.' He swallowed, picked up the glass, sipped, and swallowed again. 'Then Ann came out and shut the gate. She seemed to look at me, and at that moment… I turned and left.' He drained the glass. 'Thinking about it, on the way home, I realised I cannot recover what is lost. Ann and my daughter are lost to me, and I to them.' He stood up and took Delphine in his arms. 'You must know: you are my one and true wife. I love you, and you only.'

She reached up and pulled his lips down to hers. Tears, which had been building in her eyes, overflowed, and she swallowed. He kissed them away.

'I love you, Marcel,' she told him, 'I always have from the moment you woke up – and a little while before that, if I'm honest.'

He sat down, and pulled her down onto his lap, still keeping her close, leaning his head against her breasts. For a long while they held each other without speaking.

The peace was shattered when the door burst open and seven-year-old Oliver came in carrying a hen by its neck. The bird's feet were scrabbling at his clothes and it was squawking loudly in panic.

'Mama! I can't get it to die,' Oliver complained.

Delphine got up quickly and went to him, taking the hen from his grasp. She made a rapid visual inspection of it and concluded that it was more shocked than injured. She tossed it gently out into the yard.

'Oliver, you mustn't try to kill the hens.'

'Why not? You do.'

'Yes, but you have to do it humanely.'

'What's that mean?' he asked, his bottom lip beginning to protrude.

'Kindly. You kill hens in a way that causes them least distress.'

'Why?'

'Because you don't want to be cruel or unkind to animals. It's not nice.'

Oliver curled his lip. 'Why should I be nice to *hens?*' he demanded.

She squatted down beside him. 'Because people need the animals for food and other things, and to provide us with most of them, we have to kill the animals first. It's a fact of human existence going back thousands of years, but there is nothing to be gained from the manner of killing, so as we now know better than our ancestors did, we kill them as painlessly as possible.'

He looked unconvinced. The bottom lip still stuck out. He shrugged and went back outside. Delphine stood up and went to the door.

'Don't go far away, Oliver, it's nearly your bedtime.'

She watched as he slouched across the yard and entered the old cow-byre, which had gradually become his den and private place. She really must go in there and tidy up, and make sure it wasn't too dirty to let him play in.

She closed the door and turned back towards Marcel, who was watching her.

'Would you like more cider?' she asked.

She held the bottle over his glass. He nodded.

'Perhaps he needs to be taught how hens should be killed?' Marcel said.

'Maybe. I'd be worried, if we did, that we'd come home one day and find the entire flock laid out on the table with their necks stretched.'

Marcel grinned. 'You don't think he'd know when to stop?'

Delphine sat near him at the table. 'Quite honestly, no. Haven't you noticed how he seems quite unfeeling about things?'

'No. But isn't it usual for all small children to be a bit that way?'

'I don't think so. Mostly they seem to enjoy watching animals, having pets, learning about other forms of life on the planet. I'm not convinced most children have the urge to kill.'

'Maybe, in Oliver's case, it's just the result of being brought up on a farm?'

'Perhaps.'

'What are you afraid of, Delphine?' Marcel peered at her over the rim of his glass.

She turned and walked round the table to the opposite side. 'Oh, I don't know. I just don't want Oliver growing up to be... uncivilised.'

Marcel put the empty glass down. 'Perhaps we should take him out more, go to a zoo. Get him a pet.'

Delphine nodded. 'A couple of cats could be useful round here,' she said, thinking they'd keep the rat population of the barn down.

'I'm surprised we didn't get some earlier.'

'With not farming the land, I suppose I feel less connected to it than I did,' she mused.

'Oh? Anyway, next time we go into town, we'll get a couple of cats. See how Oliver takes to them.' He stood up. 'Delphine? I was thinking: perhaps it isn't a good time to tell Oliver about... ' he jerked his head northwards 'England, and whatever might have been my former life there.'

'It's still all very speculative,' she replied. 'No. We'll keep it to ourselves. Perhaps one day...'

'When he's older.'

She nodded. He crossed the room, hesitating when he reached the stairs

'What's the matter?' asked Delphine, noticing.

He glanced at her guiltily. 'I was just wondering if my other child has any pets.'

Delphine turned her head away so he wouldn't see her eyes. She had discovered in herself a fear of losing Marcel, now he had remembered most of his past, and the idea that he was thinking about his other family when he should have been thinking about Oliver caused a pang of jealousy.

Behind her, she heard him go slowly upstairs.

Chapter 14 – 1999

Hameau Belchamps was a small hamlet, even smaller than Sainte Marguerite, though a little further away from Bayeux than the latter. Penny and Geoff arrived there late in the morning.

The place had little going for it. A *boulangerie* was situated near the central crossroad. They parked the car at the side of the road near it and got out. Penny was stiff after the journey, and surreptitiously stretched her back.

There were no people to be seen. The *boulangerie* was closed, all the bread apparently sold.

'Surely *every* French village has a bar or a bistro?' Geoff muttered.

He began strolling along the street, looking left and right down the side-alleys, in the hope of seeing a few tables and chairs set out in the sunshine. A few curtains twitched, and further along the street, a woman stepped outside her cottage with a watering-can and aimed it at some rioting geraniums in tubs beneath her window.

Penny approached her.

'Pardon, Madame,' she asked in her inadequate French, 'but I am trying to find someone who remembers the war years in Hameau Belchamps.'

The woman stopped watering her plants. Penny assessed her as being probably in her forties. No wedding ring on her finger. Dressed dowdily.

'*Moment,*' she said, and went to the door. '*Papa!*' she called.

A man, much older, with thin, grey hair and a few days' growth of stubble, appeared at the door. He regarded Penny and Geoff for a moment, tossed the remains of a Gauloise down and ground it out under the toe of his work boot. The woman explained what Penny wanted.

'What do you want to know about the war years?' he asked.

Penny explained, haltingly, about Marcel Dubois, born in the hamlet in 1919, but turning up at a farm near Sainte Marguerite-en-Bessin in 1943.

'Is there a family Dubois here?' she concluded.

He frowned in concentration, and nodded. 'There was.' He glanced behind the visitors. People had begun to appear in the street while Penny and Geoff hadn't been looking. The man beckoned one of them over. This one appeared to be even older than the first, but he walked easily with some evidence still of a spring in his step. He bowed briefly and politely to Penny and Geoff and touched his beret with a finger.

'M'sieur, 'dame,' he said.

The elderly man spoke to him, too rapidly for Penny to keep up, but she understood enough to know he was simply passing on her request.

The elderly man removed his beret to scratch his shiny pate.

'Yes, there was a family Dubois,' he said, in heavily accented English. 'But *Marcel* Dubois?'

Penny nodded.

The man shook his head. 'I taught the local children before the war, and I would have known a Marcel Dubois. He was not here then.' He looked at them wryly. 'The last Marcel Dubois from this place died in Spain in 1814, fighting for *l'Empereur* against your Lord Wellington.'

'That's very interesting,' said Geoff. 'Thank you very much.'

He took Penny's arm and, after thanking the people for helping them, led her back to the car.

She shook his hand off. 'I can walk all by myself, Geoff,' she told him. She settled behind the wheel. 'Now, what's in your mind?'

He climbed in beside her. 'I think the man we know as Marcel Dubois might well have been your father.'

'What makes you think so?'

'The French didn't make mistakes with ID cards – not of that nature. If there was no real Marcel Dubois, then the one we know of is a false one. And who was provided with false identities during the war? Agents of SOE, that's who.'

'You're saying that Oliver's father is… ' Her voice tailed off and she turned to look at him, her eyes wide. 'That would make Oliver my half-brother.'

Geoff looked at her askance. 'I wouldn't set much store by it. From his behaviour in the hotel, I'd say there's little chance of being remembered in his will.'

She chuckled. 'I wonder if he knows he has a half-sister? Assuming it's true.'

'My guess, from his demeanour, is that he doesn't.'

Geoff fell silent for a moment. Then, 'I wonder what his politics *are*?'

'Why?'

'Just curious,' replied Geoff, sounding ingenuous. 'I mean, he didn't look like your peasant or your communist to me.'

'You're thinking he was – is – right-wing?'

'Wouldn't surprise me.'

'Maybe we'll find out one day,' Penny said.

They drove the rest of the way, almost into town, in companionable silence.

'I've been wondering what became of Marcel Dubois,' she said.

'Oliver said he had gone away, and he didn't know where.'

'Yes, and we know it must have been after he retired as a schoolteacher in 1979.'

'It gives us a span of twenty years. We can't hope to discover anything about him over such a period.'

'The newspaper office?' suggested Penny, parking outside the hotel.

'It's still too much,' said Geoff. 'Even one issue a week over twenty years amounts to more than a thousand newspapers to search through. It'd take us weeks.'

'Don't suppose we could ask Oliver?' asked Penny, more to herself than anything, as they entered the foyer and collected their room keys.

'I didn't get the impression he ever wants to talk to us again,' said Geoff.

Penny hit the button which called the lift. The doors opened and they stepped inside.

'How about that doctor? The one in the bar in Sainte Marguerite. Lafarge, wasn't it?' she suggested.

'I thought he didn't know...'

'He didn't know of a British agent turning up in 1943, but he might well have known Marcel Dubois.'

Geoff nodded. They were in the corridor outside their bedrooms. 'He just didn't think of him as an agent.' He opened his door. 'Coming in?'

'Just for a minute,' replied Penny. 'Weren't you going to ask your father if he knew David's cover name?'

Geoff was opening the minibar. 'Want one?' He held out a miniature of gin and small tin of tonic water. 'I'll give him a ring. I have a few calls to make, anyway.'

Penny poured herself a drink in a tooth glass on the table next to the television. Geoff helped himself to a miniature of Bell's.

'We could go and see Lafarge again tomorrow,' he said.

'We can't be sure of finding him.'

'Somebody in the bar'll know. I think it's that sort of place.'

'Okay,' Penny agreed. 'I don't know where else to look anyway.'

'There's another thought,' Geoff said, 'he might know a bit more about how Delphine died.'

* * *

'Have you spoken to Oliver?'

They had found Lafarge in the bar in Sainte Marguerite-en-Bessin with his friend, Albert. He hadn't looked surprised to see them again.

'We did,' said Geoff, who reckoned the two men met there regularly. 'He said his father had gone away and he didn't know where.'

Lafarge pursed his lips. 'Oh.'

'Is that true?'

'He hasn't been seen round here recently,' said the doctor.

'When did you last see him?'

Lafarge dropped his gaze briefly. 'I can't remember. Maybe it was some time ago.'

Or, thought Penny, reading his body language, maybe you don't want to contradict anything your friend had said.

'Did you know Delphine Dubois?' she asked.

'Ah, the poor woman!' sighed Lafarge, shaking his head.

'Could you tell us what happened to her?'

He shrugged. 'Nobody knows for certain. Oliver came home from Caen one day – it must be, let me see, thirty years ago – and found her dead, face down in the duck pond at the farm. A terrible, tragic accident.'

'It was definitely an accident?' Penny asked.

He looked shocked. 'Are you suggesting it wasn't?'

'No. I just wondered. Did the police ever discover how it happened? Who certified her death?'

Lafarge looked uncomfortable. 'This is the, uh, *third degree*, as the Americans call it?'

'Sorry, I didn't mean to seem to be interrogating you.'

He looked somewhat mollified. 'As a matter of fact, *I* certified her death. The police do not investigate accidental deaths.'

'You're certain it was an accident?'

He gazed at her levelly for a moment. 'Actually, no, I'm not, but there are reasons why I certified it as such.'

'And what are they?'

He shrugged. 'The church frowns on suicides. Had she died a few years earlier, she would have been refused burial in the Catholic cemetery, as until the early 1960s, suicide was regarded as a mortal sin from which she could not have been absolved.'

'You're saying she committed suicide?' asked Geoff.

Lafarge shrugged. 'It's not for me to say. There was no physical evidence, but I believe she had become very depressed.'

'Enough to make suicide a reasonable possibility?'

'In my view, probably.'

'But in 1969, when Delphine died, the Roman Catholic church had changed its view on suicide, and there would have been no problem interring her in a Catholic cemetery, if that's what the family wanted,' said Penny.

'Old traditions die much harder in the countryside than in the towns, Madame.'

Penny gazed at him speculatively, trying to decide whether there might be another reason for the doctor's decision to treat Delphine's death as accidental. Or was it the simple truth? Because of his certification, there had been no substantial police investigation. Her police-trained brain retained its suspicions.

Geoff glanced at Penny before asking the next question. 'Do you know why she was depressed?'

'It was not something she spoke to me about,' replied Lafarge, 'so I am unable to comment.'

'Yet in your view, she was depressed enough to have considered killing herself?'

Lafarge shrugged. 'It is my opinion, M'sieur, based on my observation of her.'

'You saw her about other matters, as her physician?'

'From time to time, M'sieur, but you would not expect me to divulge them to you, surely?'

'As she's dead, you're no longer bound to keep medical confidences, Doctor,' Penny pointed out.

Lafarge smiled with a hint of regret and shrugged again. 'I am a doctor of the very old school, Madame, and choose to keep the business of my patients, past and present, confidential, whatever the law may say.'

'How did Marcel and Delphine meet?' asked Geoff.

Penny appreciated his opening up another subject, far removed from what they'd just been discussing. It was an interviewing technique practised in order to make the interviewee struggle for anything but the truth, since he or she had virtually no time to make up a lie, and especially a detailed one.

'Really, M'sieur! I don't know. When I first saw Marcel, he was in a coma at the farmhouse, and Delphine and her father were taking care of him. I helped them out by supplying the equipment and medicines for feeding him through a tube, when it became obvious he wasn't going to wake up within days. And I also dressed the appalling injury to his head which he'd suffered.'

'Do you know how the injury was caused?'

Lafarge shrugged again. 'Delphine said he had been crossing their fields, lost, and in the darkness, tripped, hitting his head on a stone.'

'And the injury was consistent with that?'

'It had been a mighty blow, but yes, M'sieur. If he fell hard and landed on a large stone in the dark, the sort of injury he had would have been caused.'

'How long was he comatose?'

'It is a long time ago, M'sieur. I believe around six months.'

'Why didn't he go to hospital?'

'Delphine was adamant about looking after him at home. The Germans had equipped the hospital fairly well, but that was mostly for treating their own troops. Still, they gave me the equipment and medicines. They weren't all bad, you know.'

Geoff sat back. 'There were some people in Britain who thought that, too, at the time.'

'Your King Edward, I believe, was among them. The one who married the American divorcée.'

'True enough, but of course, that was before the Holocaust and the discovery of the death camps the Nazis set up.'

Lafarge shrugged. 'Like many régimes, the Nazi one wasn't without its faults, but you can't argue it wasn't efficient.'

'Efficient? Is that– ?'

'Can we move on, gentlemen?' interrupted Penny, foreseeing a quarrel developing. Both Geoff and the doctor, bristling, bit their lips and fell silent. She turned to the doctor.

'What do you know of Marcel's history, before you met him?'

Lafarge frowned with the effort of recollection. 'I suppose, nothing. When he was found, he had on him his identification papers – quite properly. When he woke up, so many months later, I had no cause to enquire.'

'You did not see him in later times about the usual sort of things people see a doctor for?' she asked. 'Would you not then have taken his history.'

'Only his medical history, Madame.'

'Would you not have talked about the past? His life before the war? Yours?'

Lafarge waved his arms helplessly. 'He had no recollection of an earlier life, Madame. His brain had obviously been damaged in the fall. It was not surprising.'

'When did you first see Marcel, after he was found in their field?'

'That was the Spring of 1943,' he replied after a moment's pause.

'But he could have been there earlier than then?'

'Of course it is possible, Madame. People only call for the doctor when there is a medical matter to deal with. Exactly when Marcel appeared at the Delacourt farm is not something known to me, as I told you.'

'Evidemment, je n'avais pas fait sa connaissance avant le mariage' Lafarge, Penny and Geoff all turned to the fourth person present, who had remained silent until that moment.

'Vous avez connu Marcel, Albert?' asked Penny. She caught sight of Geoff's silent request for translation.

'Albert said he didn't meet Marcel until he and Delphine married.' The old man with the bright blue eyes nodded. Penny wondered if that meant he understood more English than he spoke.'

'So Albert knew him? Albert led a resistance group, so I wonder if Marcel was a part of it.'

Albert was nodding. '*Oui.*'

That seemed to confirm it. He understood English. Penny glanced at Lafarge. He appeared to have drawn the same inference and was staring at Albert with astonishment.

'I never knew that!' said the doctor.

Albert simply shrugged and returned to his customary silence.

Penny studied him shrewdly under her lashes, and wondered if it might be profitable to try having conversation with the old man without the doctor present. Clearly, Albert had kept one secret from his friend; perhaps there were more.

Oliver had acquired a Peugeot 504 saloon, nearly new, and on his release from court, after paying his fine, he went to fetch it from the garage he rented, well away from the districts which had seen the riots. He still had a few bruises, some of them from gendarmes trying to prevent the clash of Left- and Right-wing students. He hoped that, by the time he went home to the farm, they would have faded, so no questions would be asked that might oblige him to answer... creatively. In the meantime, there was a private 'graduation party' at the home of one of his friends, a local organiser of the FAF, *Fédération des Amoureux de France*, with which he had become involved during the last two years at university.

It was the first group to which Oliver had ever really felt he belonged. He had contributed to the group's newsletter advocating racial purity, as the nearest thing to his own ideals.

Michel, who was his mentor in the group, welcomed him with open arms at the party. 'Come in, come in. We thought the *flics* were going to do something dreadful to you.'

Oliver explained about the fine as they made their way past several other young men and women into one of the downstairs rooms.

'This is Odile,' Michel said, picking up a girl who was sprawled on the floor, her miniskirt rucked up, and her vacuous expression showing signs of being spaced out on dope. She smiled vaguely at Michel and Oliver.

'Odile, now you be nice to Oliver. He's been through a lot and needs a great deal of care and consideration.'

She tilted her head enquiringly. 'How much "care and consideration"?'

'Just take Oliver up to one of the bedrooms and fuck him, take his mind off his recent woes.'

Odile turned her head with difficulty and focussed on Oliver. She smiled, took him by the hand and led him towards the staircase.

'And Oliver,' Michel called after him, 'don't be all night, there's a good fellow. We have plans to make, with Pompidou about to take possession of the Elysée Palace.'

'I thought he'd be on our side? He's a Gaullist…'

'He's a traitor! Not one of us at all, Oliver. Wants to let the British into the Common Market.' Michel waved him away. 'Still, my friend, we can talk about this later. First things first, eh, Odile?'

She smiled, but to Oliver's gaze, it was still a vacant one. However, she would be compliant. Michel knew how Oliver liked to exert mastery over women, and he was sure to have chosen one who would expect such treatment. He loosened the belt on his trousers and pulled it through the loops as he followed her into the bedroom. He didn't want a girl who was *too* compliant: there was no pleasure if they didn't make an effort to fight back. Resistance piqued him.

* * *

Delphine looked up from the worktop where she was preparing vegetables for the evening meal as Oliver's Peugeot rattled along the stony track into the farm yard. She hoped he'd notice how the farm had been tidied up during the years he'd been away. Once the le Greqs at the adjacent holding had taken over the business of farming, and the rental payments had started coming in, she and Marcel had begun a programme of maintenance and improvement. With tourism becoming more attractive, they had turned his old den, the cow byre, into a *gite* and were trying hard to attract bookings.

'Oliver! How nice that you're home again.'

She crossed the room and wrapped her arms round him in a warm, welcoming hug. He returned the embrace – somewhat half-heartedly, she thought, but that was a man for you.

'How are you, mother?'

He sounded quite formal. Was that an outcome of university education, she wondered.

'I'm fine,' she said.

He looked around the kitchen. 'Where's father?'

'He's on a field trip,' she replied, turning back to the vegetables and picking up a potato to peel.

'Where is he this time?'

'England,' she replied, without looking up. She became aware of him standing by her shoulder, his lips close to her ear.

'Can you tell me how it is that a teacher of mathematics has to visit England… so often? Are French mathematics so bad we have to learn from the English?'

'Of course not, dear. I don't know what the connection is, but I know your father has to go. It's only once a year, after all.' She noticed his frown. 'Why? Is anything intrinsically bothering about your father's trips to England?'

He turned away, muttered something under his breath as he walked over to the fireplace.

'Pardon? Oliver, I didn't hear you.'

He turned back to her. 'I said, it's full of Jews. They went there before the war, and they're *still* there.'

Delphine arched her eyebrows. It wasn't a sentiment she'd heard uttered within the four walls of her home before, though she knew there were people about with strong anti-Semitic views. She was shocked that Oliver seemed to hold them, too.

'It's not too surprising, is it, Oliver?' she said. 'Considering what happened to those left in Germany and the occupied countries during the war, I imagine it will take a long time before they trust the Germans enough to move back there, no matter what the attraction.'

'The British should have forced them out.'

'Thank God the British didn't! Oliver, we know the Nazis murdered six million people, most of them Jews, in death camps like Birkenau-Belsen and Auschwitz. If the Jews who

146

emigrated to Britain and America hadn't been able to do so, we might be looking at millions more.'

Oliver shrugged, uncaringly.

Delphine frowned at him, angry now. 'I didn't realise we'd raised you to hate people just because of their race and religion.'

'Oh, no!' he snapped at her, his lips thin and pressed together whitely. 'You didn't – you and father are very left wing and liberal. It wasn't till I got to university that I realised how weak you both are.'

He hesitated, undecided whether to go on, but it seemed his demons were in control. He drew himself upright. 'France would be a mighty country again, were it not for people like you and father, mother. We could be a major force in the world instead of an amiable puppy at the feet of the Great British Bulldog.'

'France is not like that, Oliver. We're a sovereign nation, and nobody's lapdog. As for the British, well now, *they* want to join *us* in the Common Market. Hardly how a master-race behaves.'

'You forget mother: the other major player in the Common Market is Germany. If the British are allowed in, it will double the number of Anglo-Saxons, meaning the French will be marginalised once again. They will always be able to outvote us in Strasbourg.'

'That isn't how the British are, most of them. They'll judge issues on their merits – of course with an eye to their own interests, same as the rest of us do. What they won't do is vote on racial lines.'

'What makes you so sure? The British are descended from Germans. It's not as if you know anything about the British, except what you read in the papers. You've never been there.'

'The British are also descended from the French – people from round here, in Normandy – and from the Celts, the same people who still live in Brittany, Lesser Britain.'

'*Lesser* Britain! Why is it "Lesser Britain"?'

'Your father says the only real justification for having a *Great* Britain is if there's a lesser one. Centuries ago, people moved freely between the Greater and the Lesser. It was the only way of telling the two areas apart.'

'*He* said that, did he?'

'Yes.'

'And what would he know about it?'

Delphine realised that he had no idea his father was British, and was careful to guard that information. It might be twenty-three years since the war, but that didn't mean there weren't people about who might take serious exception to a British spy who had passed himself off as a Frenchman during all that time.

'It's something he learned on a field trip,' she mumbled.

Oliver sat beside the fire, his fingers together, touching his chin. 'You don't suppose dad has a mistress, do you? All this stuff about "field trips" being just a cover? I mean, why does a mathematics teacher need to go to Britain?'

'I don't know, son. I am sure he does not have a mistress.' She grinned. 'What mistress would be content to see her lover only once a year?'

Oliver lifted his eyes. 'The kind that fills in the other 51 weeks with other lovers.'

Delphine smiled at him. 'Smart answer, but I'm still quite sure your father does not have a mistress.' She stood up. 'And now I must get on with dinner.'

She returned to the worktop under the window and resumed peeling the potato. She would have known, she told herself, if Marcel had a mistress in England – or anywhere else for that matter. No, he was faithful to her, and she loved him for it. But she needed to discuss with him whether it was time that Oliver should be told Marcel's history, learning in the process that he was himself half English.

* * *

Marcel was parked in his hired car, just along the street from the police station in Bletchley. A young woman emerged in the uniform of a police constable. She was accompanied by a male officer, and they began walking towards where Marcel was parked. He considered driving away, but decided that would look even more suspicious than remaining where he was. He took a road map out of the glove compartment and flicked it open to the local page.

There was a tap on the window. He leaned across and wound it down. The woman bent down to look into the car and he found himself staring into bright azure eyes.

'Everything all right, sir?' she asked.

'I'm fine thank you, Officer. Just getting my bearings. Never been here before.'

He kept his French accent in place.

'Where are you looking for?'

He looked down at the map. Everywhere he wanted to go he could find. He pointed at a street at random, on the other side of town. The constable sucked air through her teeth. She reached in and tapped the map.

'You're here at the minute, sir.' She looked at him. 'You need to turn round and go down the street to the second junction.'

She tapped the map again, and proceeded to give him clear directions to a place he had no wish to visit.

'Might I ask, sir, what your business is in Caley Street? It's an area which gives us a lot of trouble, and I'm curious why a French tourist – you are that, aren't you, sir? – should want to visit it?'

'What sort of trouble, *mademoiselle?*'

'It's the Red Light district.'

Marcel felt himself reddening. 'Then perhaps I have made a mistake. I will study the map, Officer.'

'Where else might you go, sir?' she asked.

Marcel admired persistence, but hers was making him very uncomfortable. 'Maybe I shall return home to France.'

She rested her elbows on the car window sill. 'Perhaps someone at the Town Hall could help you? Seems a long way to come and then turn back because Caley Street is in the Red Light area.'

149

'Thank you. Very well, I will go to the Town Hall. Thank you, Officer.'

'It's over there, sir,' she said, pointing.

He thanked her again and started the engine. As he drove away, he was aware that both police officers were watching him.

He parked the car and got out. He hadn't come far, and it was perfectly possible, if they'd found his behaviour at all suspicious, that they could walk in this direction to make sure he really was what he appeared. He headed into the Town Hall and found a tourist office signposted from just inside the entrance. He had an idea, and went to it. When he got there he asked if anyone could tell him what had become of Bletchley Park. He used his English accent.

The person whom he addressed was a man of similar age to himself, with thinning hair not at all disguised by a comb-over, and horn-rimmed glasses, over which he now looked at Marcel.

'Not sure what it's doing these days, sir,' he said. 'Don't know what it ever did, even during the war, if you understand me.'

Marcel understood. 'Oh, the Official Secrets Act still applies, does it?'

'Wouldn't know, sir.'

Clearly, he wasn't going to learn anything from this conscientious citizen. Marcel thanked him and left. He returned to his car. Fortunately, neither of the police officers was anywhere to be seen.

The female would be about the same age as his daughter, he supposed.

For six years, he had not seen her during his annual fleeting drive-bys of the house he'd once shared with Ann and had found no way of discovering where his daughter was, but reason suggested she had probably been away at university. His observation of the house had taught him that Ann had remarried, or at least was living with a man, but he had no idea who. Marcel supposed he should feel grateful to him for taking on his child.

* * *

'John phoned today,' said Penny as she took her place at the dining table.

'Oh, yes? What about?' asked Ann.

'He's found a house. We're going to see it together at the weekend.'

'What sort of house?' asked Callum, looking up from his plate.

'Nothing too fancy for a first home. A three-bedroomed semi.'

'How much are they wanting for it?'

Penny dropped her gaze. It was more expensive than they'd intended, but John's description had made it sound very tempting. 'Four and a half. All-but.'

Callum pursed his lips. 'Four thousand five hundred pounds, all-but. Then you have to furnish it.'

'I know.'

'Where is it?' asked Ann.

'Somewhere off Whaddon Way.'

'That sounds a nice area, dear.'

'We think so.'

'Will it be ready in time for your wedding?'

'It should be. A month before. Give us time to sort out some furniture.'

'You'd better decide what Callum and I can get you as a wedding present.'

Penny grinned sheepishly. 'Well, there's this bed, in Connor's... '

Ann gave an answering smile. 'Most important, I'm sure. Before things like a washing machine?'

'John's mother has promised to get us a Hotpoint Twin-Tub.'

'At least Mrs Sanderson has an eye on something beyond the immediate joys of marriage.'

Penny didn't immediately respond. When she did, it was to change the subject.

'Saw a strange foreign tourist in town today.'

Ann parked her knife and fork. 'What was strange about him?'

'He was French – no, that's not what was strange. He was looking for Caley Road.'

Ann's eyebrows rose with surprise. 'Wouldn't he do better in somewhere like Hamburg or Amsterdam if he wants a Red Light area?'

Penny made a little moue. 'Almost certainly. It's just that when I told him what it was, he seemed to lose interest and said he might return to France.'

Ann frowned. Callum looked up as he finished his dinner and began paying attention.

'Is that what he did?' Ann asked.

'I don't know. Last thing I saw of him he was headed for the Town Hall.'

'Did you find out what he did there?' asked Callum, so casually that Penny knew he was taking a professional interest.

'No. I was out with Ronnie Higgins. We were supposed to be looking for – well, someone – so we really didn't have time to go chasing after shadows.' She looked at Callum. 'Or should that be spooks, dad?'

Callum's eyebrows arched in an expression of innocence. 'That would be ghosts, would it, Pen?'

'That would be spies, dad.'

Callum shook his head with exaggerated distress. 'I don't know what ideas you youngsters have in your heads these days! When I was your age, a spook was definitely a ghost.'

Penny smiled with equally exaggerated sweetness. 'And when you were my age, men with red flags still walked in front of motor cars.'

Callum narrowed his eyes. 'Only when I was very, very young.' He shook his head sorrowfully. 'The Americans have a lot to answer for.'

'The Americans, dear?' asked Ann.

'Spooks. It's another Americanism infecting the English language.'

'Spies, mother,' said Penny, dramatically.

'You think this Frenchman was a spy?' Ann asked Callum.

He rolled his eyes. 'No, dear one. I am – I think the technical term is – pulling Penny's leg.'

Ann pursed her lips. 'I think you should leave that sort of thing for John to do – after they're married!'

Callum and Penny caught each other's glances and each stifled a laugh. Ann chuckled.

'Don't think I don't know you two are ganging up on me!'

'Mother! Don't come the Old Soldier with me! I know perfectly well you and dad work among an entire nest of spies. I'm surprised they haven't trained you up as a modern-day Mata Hari.'

Ann echoed Callum's earlier expression of innocence while she stood up and collected the plates. 'And how do you know they didn't?'

Callum nodded at Penny. 'Quite. I probably wouldn't be here today if your mother hadn't successfully charmed me into it.' He shot a quick glance at Ann then turned back to Penny. 'Of course, her pretty little blue-eyed daughter might have had something to do with it as well.'

'Much more than me,' said Ann, taking things through into the kitchen. 'I think it was you your dad fancied first. I just came along as part of the package.'

Penny glanced at them both and sat back. 'You're both talking a lot of baloney. Dad was always besotted with you, mum. I was lucky if I got five minutes of his attention at any one time. Now you mention it, the Frenchman had blue eyes the same shade as mine. Even bluer than mum's.'

'Really?' said Callum. 'And I suppose blue-eyed people aren't common?'

'Nothing common about us, is there, mum? But we have particularly light-blue eyes.' She peered into Callum's tawny ones. 'Hadn't you noticed?'

'I should have. You batted your lashes at me enough times when you wanted something. And the Frenchman's were the same?'

Penny nodded.

'The only person I ever knew... ' Ann began, then stopped and went back into the kitchen.

Callum watched her go then turned to Penny and finished his wife's sentence. 'The only person we ever knew with eyes the same shade as yours was your father. So maybe you're right, and the Frenchman was more than a little strange.'

Ann came back into the dining room. 'Saturday, we'll go shopping for your trousseau,' she said, changing the subject firmly.

CHAPTER 16 – 1999

Dr Henri Lafarge had suffered several sleepless nights. For a moment, he'd considered it might be something to do with a stirring of his conscience occasioned by his recent meetings with Penny, Geoff and Oliver, but that seemed unlikely. There was, he concluded, nothing which might have given rise to such a cause.

Perhaps it was the discovery that his friend, Albert Lebrun, could actually understand English which had shaken him, somewhat. There was always the possibility that he'd said something disparaging in English about Albert, which he now couldn't remember, in the belief that the old man couldn't understand him. It was not as if Albert was a good friend: Lafarge tolerated him out of a sense of much shared history – they were members of a declining number of people who had lived through the Second World War.

During the war, they had held radically different philosophies. Albert had been out-and-out opposed to the occupation of France by Hitler, and thrown all his effort into confounding the occupying forces. Lafarge, on the other hand, had taken a different view. As long as he was prepared to put his medical skills to use in the local hospital, patching up injured German soldiers along with French civilians, and occasionally carry out a few medical repair jobs for the Political Police, the Gestapo, when their interrogation methods had been too hard on a suspect, he found he had a fairly easy war. Indeed, his contacts had been useful when he needed to obtain a stomach feeding tube, all those months Marcel Dubois had been unable to feed himself.

It was time to go down the street to the bar on the junction. He picked up his hat, black and wide-brimmed, and set it on his head at a rakish angle. He used a finger to smooth his moustache, picked up his walking cane, straightened his shoulders, and left the house. The bar was opposite a marble representation of the Crucifixion. Unusually, he made the Sign of the Cross as he passed it.

For once, Albert was late. The doctor sat in his usual place and *Le Patron* brought him his usual glass of Merlot.

'No Albert today?' asked *Le Patron*.

Lafarge smiled at him briefly. 'Not that I can see, Serge.' He made a point of looking around the bar, and shook his head. 'No! Can't see him anywhere, so I suppose you're right.' His smile became mirthless. 'I am not Albert's keeper.'

'Of course not, Doctor. I merely note that normally, you both arrive at the same time. It is like clockwork, *n'est-ce pas?*'

'If you say so, Serge.'

Serge glanced around, saw no-one waiting to be served, and sat in Albert's usual place, beside the other of his two oldest customers. 'You think those English tourists might come back? The ones who buy you wine and Albert Pastis?'

Lafarge looked at him tiredly. 'Need the boost to your takings, do you?'

Serge rubbed his hands. 'Never turn business away, I say.'

'The pursuit of money, eh, Serge. Could get you into all sorts of trouble.' His own sleepless nights came to mind for some reason.

'Do you mind telling me why you look after poor Albert, Doctor? On the surface, you wouldn't seem to have much in common – you an educated man, and him a farm worker.'

'Retirement is a great leveller, Serge. Our experiences during the war are what mainly bind us.'

Serge looked past him and stood up as Albert entered and came towards them, his white stick feeling his way past the chairs to his regular spot at the table he shared with Lafarge.

'Good morning, Albert,' said Serge, guiding him gently to his seat.

'Good morning, Serge.' He reached to his right and patted Lafarge's knee. 'Good morning, Doctor. I wondered if you'd still be here as I'm a bit late.'

'I'm still here all right, Albert,' replied Lafarge.

Serge had gone over to the bar and returned with a glass containing Albert's favourite aniseed liqueur. He put it in the old man's hand.

'Thank you, Serge,' said Albert. '*Santé!*'

Lafarge raised his glass and echoed Albert's toast.

Serge waited until he had swallowed before speaking again. 'You didn't say, Doctor. Are those tourists likely to be back?'

'I have no idea, Serge. Why – apart from the boost to your takings – are you so interested?'

'Well, as you know, my grandfather was in the Resistance. My mother told me stuff about him I thought they might be interested in.'

'I doubt they would, thank you Serge,' said Lafarge. 'And as it happens, I *didn't* know your grandfather was in the Resistance.'

Serge shrugged, and seemed disappointed.

'I did,' said Albert. 'I knew him.'

Serge and Lafarge both stared at him.

'You knew my grandfather?' Serge said.

Albert nodded.

'What can you tell me about him?'

'What has your mother told you?' asked Albert.

'Only that he was in the Resistance, and she's said about some of the raids he went on with his group.'

'He ran the group in the next district to me,' Albert told him. 'He was a good and brave patriot, a son of the soil, and it was terrible, what happened to him.'

Serge dragged up a chair. 'What did happen to him? My mother has never spoken about it.'

Albert shuffled in his seat and sipped another mouthful. 'Can you put some water in this, please?'

Serge stood up. 'Of course. I'll freshen it up, too – on the house.'

'Thank you.'

Lafarge turned to Albert while Serge was tending to a few other bar-keeping duties as well as getting the old man's drink. 'Who was his grandfather?'

'Bertrand.'

'He was Serge's grandfather? I never knew that. He wasn't the same family.'

'Serge's mother's father,' said Albert, as Serge took his seat back at the table.

At the mention of the man's name, Lafarge had experienced a stab of uneasiness.

'It was in November of forty-two,' Albert began. 'There was a new German radar installation on the coast and several local groups had been organised to work together, to make a co-ordinated raid on it. The British flew in supplies of guns, ammunition and explosives, a female radio operator and a man who did the planning.' Albert paused and looked towards Lafarge, his line-of-sight missing by a few centimetres. Lafarge always found that disconcerting.

'You'll know him, Henri. Well, maybe. Remember him. Maury, we knew him as. She was Yvonne de Tourney. Cover names, of course, but both quickly assimilated into our lives and landscape. Maury damaged a foot chopping firewood two days before the raid, and I brought him to you, because we all knew you were sympathetic and would help a fellow freedom-fighter.'

Lafarge looked as if he was eating a lemon. 'Yes... Yes, of course I remember him. More or less.'

'Then you must remember Bertrand, as he was the one who brought Maury to you. You had lots of questions about how the injury had occurred. I know Bertrand had to give you a hint that Maury had to be fit for the following night.'

'Yes, yes. Then I do remember Bertrand.'

'What was he like?' asked Serge.

Lafarge shrugged. 'He was a big-boned man, very strong, light on his feet though.'

'But a patriot?'

Lafarge smiled briefly. 'A patriot, of course.' He was horrified to see Serge's eyes fill with tears. 'For God's sake, he was only a grandfather you never knew.'

Serge mopped his eyes with the hem of his apron. 'But he defended France against the Boche. He was a hero.'

'He was a good-hearted farm worker,' said Lafarge, feeling exasperated at Serge's emotional response, 'but he was engaged in actions which resulted in the Germans leaning more heavily on the communities round here.'

'I didn't think that was how you saw the Resistance at the time, Henri?' Albert queried.

Lafarge turned to him, surprised to find that, in responding to Serge's upset, he had overlooked the fact that another man of almost identical description was sitting next to him.

'Of course, I mean, the Resistance did good things, but you have to admit that their activities used to upset the Gestapo, and the SS occasionally rounded up scores of French men and women – aye, and children – and shot them in reprisal.'

Albert bowed his head. 'I know. It grieves me still. They made the ultimate sacrifice for their country.' He lifted his empty gaze and turned towards Lafarge again, this time, appearing to stare directly into the doctor's eyes. 'Did you know, someone was suspected of betraying the Resistance members, especially their leaders, to the Gestapo?'

Lafarge stared back. 'I – No. No, I didn't. Who suspected that?'

'London.'

Lafarge ran his fingers round his collar. 'And what did they do about it?'

Albert looked away, down at his hands. 'Alas, nothing. They were supposed to send another agent out, whom none of us knew, whose sole job would be to discover the traitor in our midst.'

'But he, or she, never came?'

'No.'

'So the traitor, whoever it was, was never identified?'

'No.'

Lafarge drank the rest of his wine. 'Pity,' he said. Perhaps it was the wine, but he felt better. 'I'll have to be going. Things to do.' He got to his feet.

'Good day to you, Doctor Lafarge,' said Albert, unusually formal.

'Hope to see you again tomorrow, Doctor,' said Serge, standing also.

Lafarge felt eyes on him all the way to the door. Including Albert's.

* * *

The telephone rang. Penny reached across the pillow beside her to answer it. It was Geoff, in his room, a couple of doors along the corridor.

'Are you decent?' he asked.

'Usually,' she replied. 'Just now, I'm not dressed.'

The telephone went silent for a moment. She figured what he was thinking.

'I mean, I'm still in bed, in my nightdress.'

'Well, get dressed. I'm coming round in five minutes. I've got some information.'

He rang off before she could protest that five minutes was not long enough. She glanced at the clock. It was eight in the morning, late for her to be getting up, but then, she reminded herself, it was only seven o'clock in England. She was still pulling a comb through her hair when he knocked.

'Come in,' she said, pointing him at the chair while she finished making herself presentable.

'Thanks. I think I rather like the tousled look,' he said as he sat.

'I don't,' she said, as much to deter further flirting as because she meant it. 'What's happened?'

'My father has been on the phone. He found out your father's cover name.'

Penny put down the comb and came towards him. 'Well? Do I have to drag it out of you?'

'There are pleasanter ways for a woman to extract information...' he said.

She smiled briefly. 'Geoff: I am not a morning person. One day you might discover how much I'm not, so I am not in Mata Hari mode, nor anywhere near it. Just tell me or I'll punch you.'

'Ah, the direct approach, eh? Well, okay. In my fear of permanent injury, I will tell you what you want to know. Are you ready for this?'

She knew perfectly well he was teasing her. A part of her was pleased, because she'd decided she wanted Geoff to like her, and it showed he did, but the other part was annoyed.

He held up his hands in surrender. 'Okay. Your father was dropped into France with French ID papers identifying him as – Marcel Dubois.'

Penny's gaze drifted past him as, suddenly thoughtful, she sat on the bed. 'So Oliver *is* my half-brother,' she said quietly. She looked at Geoff. 'This makes it a whole lot more personal.'

'I wonder if he knows?'

'It makes finding out what happened to him after 1969 more important.'

She got up and went back to the dressing table where she checked her appearance in the mirror.

* * *

Oliver gazed through the half-frosted glass partition dividing the manager's office from the car showroom, which contained three gleaming high-performance sports cars. He turned to the man behind the desk.

'Sales were down last month.'

The man shrugged. 'It's the credit squeeze. People cut down on luxuries like these' – he indicated the cars – 'as soon as the cash shortage begins to bite. It's a pity the manufacturers can't come up with some incentives.'

Oliver leaned on the desk. 'People who are affected by credit squeezes aren't the kind who buy these cars anyway, Ramon. You should know that. Try a mail shot to our usual customers and anyone like them – any celebrities, or people who like to think they are, living in the area. Throw a party, hold a competition, the winner gets to test drive the car of their choice for a week, say. Runners-up get one for a day. The price of raffle tickets had better cover our costs. Work it out. If someone's driven one of them for a day or a week, shown all their friends, don't you think they'll feel almost obliged to buy when they come to hand it back?'

'Yes, boss.'

'And if one buys, see if you can't persuade the others that to be as good as him – or her – they need to buy one, too.'

'Yes, boss.'

'You need to try more initiatives, Ramon, increase the sales figures, or you'll be selling Citroens. Don't leave it to me all the time.'

'I understand, Oliver. Do you want coffee?' He opened the connecting door to the office, where a couple of young women were handling the paperwork generated by any successful motor dealership, on top of dealing with telephone enquiries. 'Anne-Marie,' he said to the one sitting nearest, 'can you rustle up two coffees, please.'

She turned and Oliver saw her face. It was strikingly white, made even more so by the jet black bob of her hair, dark-lined eyes and crimson lips, which in colour matched her tailored suit. There was something oriental about her appearance which engaged his interest at once.

'I'm rather busy with work stuff, Ramon,' she said to him. 'Perhaps Lisette could help. Or you could do it yourself – the machine's in the corner.' She indicated the filter-coffee maker.

Oliver stepped past Ramon who was trying to decide what to do about the embarrassment he was feeling.

'I will make coffee, Ramon.' He smiled at the woman as he went past the Manager and poured coffee from the jug into two cups. 'Perhaps you and Lisette would like some, too?' he asked her.

She smiled. It seemed genuine. Lisette turned, also smiling, and said she would love a cup.

Oliver filled two more cups, emptying the jug. He glanced at Ramon. 'It's a useful skill, being able to make your own coffee,' he said. 'Glad it's one of mine.'

Ramon dipped his head. Oliver could feel the fury inside him and smiled even more broadly. He turned to the women.

'What time do you finish, ladies?'

'Six,' replied Anne-Marie.

'I'm sure Ramon can spare you a little before then, eh, Ramon? Say half-past five in the Bar at the DeVries Hotel. I shall be expecting both of you.'

The two women exchanged glances. Anne-Marie spoke for them both when she accepted his invitation. Oliver and Ramon returned through the connecting door and closed it behind them.

* * *

The bar at the DeVries was nearly empty when Anne-Marie and Lisette entered it. Lisette ordered fresh orange juice and Anne-Marie a cognac. They had not been waiting very long when Oliver appeared, smiling.

'Can I get you another drink?' he asked. 'Same again?'

The women nodded, curious. He returned from the bar with a tray bearing three glasses, a tonic water to go with his gin, and a part-bottle of orange juice for Lisette.

'I hope neither of you is expected anywhere tonight, or at least nowhere you can't beg off?' he asked them.

'You want us to cancel our dates?' asked Anne-Marie.

Oliver had a strong suspicion that neither had what could be termed a 'date', but he went along with the idea. 'It would please me if you could phone your boyfriends or whatever and agree to spend a few hours here.'

'Why?' asked Lisette.

She, of the two of them, was going to be the one who would make life difficult,.

'I don't usually stay in Bayeux at night and I would like to see its principle delights,' he said, allowing his gaze to travel up from Anne-Marie's pointed patent leather court shoes, along her black-stockinged legs, black skirt and jacket to her smoky black-rimmed eyes.

She drank half of her cognac and lifted an eyebrow. 'Do I take it you include us in that description?' she asked.

His eyes had fixed themselves on Lisette's breasts. They thrust against the confines of her blouse and pushed against the lapels of her unbuttoned jacket so from his angle of view, their ample roundedness was clearly visible. He looked back at Anne-Marie.

'I do,' he said. He drank half of his gin and tonic. 'Hurry up, girls, keep up!' He looked over at the bar and indicated another round to the barman. 'These are on me, because I'm feeling very good,' he told them.

Lisette emptied her glass and moved on to the one Oliver had bought her. Anne-Marie drained her cognac and leaned towards him as she put the empty glass down.

'Tell me,' she said, 'does sir have in mind a *ménage a trois?*'

He touched her white cheeks with his fingertips. 'It would certainly make my trip here worthwhile.'

Anne-Marie glanced at Lisette, who was sipping the drink Oliver had brought her and screwing up her face.

He noticed. 'Anything wrong?'

'Have you put something in this?' she asked.

'It's only a vodka and orange. Isn't that what you had?'

'Oh!' she said. 'It must be the vodka.'

The barman put three more glasses, two more bottles, on the table.

'Sorry,' said Oliver, 'that'll be the same.'

Lisette shrugged. 'I have to drive, so I must be careful what I drink, but two vodkas are not the end of the world.'

'I'm glad you see it that way,' Oliver said, raising his glass again. The three clinked glasses.

Penny and Geoff passed the entrance to the bar on their way up to their rooms. She nudged him.

'There's Oliver,' she said. 'And it looks as if he's picked up a couple of girls.'

Anne-Marie had swallowed half her second glass of cognac. Both women were beginning to get giggly.

'Might not be the moment to go and talk to him,' said Geoff.

Penny glanced at him, unimpressed by his apparent lack of valour, and entered the bar. Oliver saw her and the smile disappeared from his lips.

'Mrs Sanderson,' he said in English. 'Is there something I can help you with? It will have to be quick as I am keeping these young ladies waiting.'

'We'd like to talk to you about some new information,' Penny said. Preferably,' she added, glancing at the two women who were showing signs of becoming increasingly intoxicated, 'tomorrow.'

Oliver nodded. 'Tomorrow. I will meet you here at ten? Okay?'

'That will be fine,' she said, and with a last glance at the two women, returned to the corridor and Geoff.

They got out of the lift and headed for their rooms. 'See you later for dinner,' she said.

Neither Oliver nor the women used the hotel's dining room and the evening passed quietly.

In the early hours, the night receptionist was roused from his contemplation of a taped movie playing on his television in the office behind the desk. Lisette staggered out of the lift and stumbled, sometimes to her knees, towards him. He stood behind the counter and stared as she held on to it and tried to stand upright.

'G-get the p-police!' she demanded. 'I think I've been raped and my friend is d-dead.'

Delphine had been waiting with a growing sense of foreboding for Oliver to come home from university. He had obtained good degrees in politics and business administration from one of the best universities in France, and she was proud of him for doing so. But she was also worried. He had been involved in the Paris riots of the year before, and whilst he hadn't said anything so directly, she had a feeling he had continued to have connections with a neo-fascist group, the FAF. He'd only mentioned the group once, on an early trip home, but there had been the light of enthusiasm in his eyes when he'd spoken of it. He might, of course, have grown out of it, she thought, but then again, he might not. His not mentioning it again might be because he was still a part of it.

She and Marcel had agreed that, as someone born after the war, Oliver needed to be shown that France's wartime experience was not to be judged solely on its capitulation in 1940 and the policies of the puppet regime in the south afterwards.

There was justifiable pride in the resilience shown by individual French men and women, many of whom had laid down their lives for their fellow-citizens. Indeed, thousands had stoically accepted, and even encouraged, allied bombing raids because they believed every one shortened the war, despite the mounting civilian casualties. And pride also, for those who would not accept the Third Reich's mastery over France, who fought against it with every means at their disposal, albeit with the increasing help of agents and *matériel* flown in from England.

By and large, Delphine and Marcel agreed, with a few exceptions, the French population had acquitted itself better than its political masters, with the exception of Charles de

Gaulle, who would always be a hero to those he left behind to deal with the occupation face-to-face.

Oliver had been brought up to recognise that while his country might have been defeated by the Nazis in 1940, the heart of its people had beaten true, and there was no reason at all to feel ashamed of the situation the French had found themselves in during the war.

Delphine suspected that Oliver, in fact, stood at the other extreme, and was worried because she knew what it meant to live under a fascist regime which used the freedoms democracy provided to replace it with totalitarianism.

She heard the crunch of gravel outside and glanced through the window to see his car come to a stop. He climbed out and she saw him fasten the jacket of a new suit while he surveyed the yard, probably looking for any changes. He saw her at the kitchen window and stared.

She opened the door, and he came to her, embracing her perfunctorily.

'How are you, mother?'

It was over their evening meal that he gave her and Marcel the news.

'I am standing in the elections for the National Assembly.'

Both parents sat back and stared at him.

'Really?' asked Marcel, as if finding credibility strained.

Oliver looked from one to the other. 'I thought you'd be pleased.'

'We are,' said Delphine. 'It's just not something we expected. You certainly know how to drop a bombshell.' She smiled to remove any hint of criticism from her words.

'For which party?' asked Marcel.

Oliver stared at him. 'The FAF,' he said, keeping his eyes on his father's face, watching for any hint of disapproval.

'And what is that?' Marcel returned his son's look, levelly.

'The Fédération des Amoureux de France.'

Marcel picked up his knife and fork. 'That's the group that is rather strong in Caen at the moment, isn't it?'

'It's the Caen constituency I'm standing in.'

'Then I suppose you have a good chance.'

'It will be quite something to have an Assembly member in the family,' said Delphine. She was trying to show support, but she knew what the FAF stood for and she hated the thought that her son wanted to represent the party in the French National Assembly. She schooled her expression into one of smiling affection. 'We should go out and celebrate.'

Oliver smiled at her briefly. 'That will be nice, mother. Perhaps at the weekend? I have a meeting to attend tomorrow.'

'A meeting?'

'Of the party.'

'Oh. Right.' She nodded, kept smiling.

Oliver turned to Marcel. 'There's one thing I keep having to try explaining to the others, and that is, why you keep going back to England every year? We can none of us work it out.'

Marcel glanced at Delphine. They had not told Oliver about Marcel's gradual recovery of his memory, maintaining the fiction that the trips were 'field trips' about his work as a teacher. Delphine was as sure as ever that the real reason was a private matter for Marcel only, and it should stay that way.

'It helps your father,' she explained. 'Besides, he likes England – better than I do, in fact.' It wasn't quite true, but she wanted to keep Oliver on side, and thought it a good idea to have him believe she did not find his 'Lovers of France' ideals totally rejected by both parents.

'Well,' said Oliver, staring at Marcel, 'I wish you'd stop going there. Especially after the campaigning starts. You know how the Press tend to look for cracks in the integrity of candidates. To discover that a close member of the family of any candidate was involved in activities which might be seen as undermining his ideals would be seized upon and could cost me the election.'

'How can occasional trips to England be considered undermining your ideals?' asked Marcel.

'We believe in France, father: first and foremost. We believe in the strength and integrity of its people.' He included Delphine in his sweeping glance. 'You've told me often enough about the bravery of the people during the war. We all know how De Gaulle stood against the ideas of foreigners – '

'Although he was glad of their help after he escaped from France?' put in Marcel.

'That was simple expediency. And they offered. He could have turned them down, but didn't choose to.'

'No,' muttered Marcel, arching his eyebrows.

'De Gaulle dreamt of a great France, standing foursquare in the world, afraid of no-one. The FAF has that same dream.'

Oliver's voice had risen as his polemic got the better of him. Delphine's stare must have registered because he suddenly stopped.

'Anyway, it's important for me as the campaign approaches for you to stop having anything to do with England, father,' he added more quietly, looking down at his untouched plate.

Marcel was regarding the top of Oliver's head through tired eyes. 'Very well, Oliver, if that's what you want. After my next trip, I won't go again until you are safely elected.'

'You mustn't go again while I remain a member of the Assembly,' Oliver said, looking into Marcel's eyes. 'In fact, it would be helpful if you were overheard dropping a few anti-British and anti-German remarks.'

'Would anti-Jewish or anti-Gypsy ones help, too?'

'Yes – !' Oliver stopped, seeing the look on his father's face. 'Ah, you're joking!'

'It isn't much of a joke, Oliver,' Marcel said, and this time, Delphine could hear the sadness in his voice.

'Why would anti-British remarks help, Oliver?' asked Delphine, 'They helped us a lot during the war.'

Oliver turned to her, his lips twisting. 'Because of that,' he snarled, 'they seem to think they should be running Europe

169

now. And they are in bed with the Americans. We should have nothing to do with them.'

Delphine nodded slowly. She felt shocked that her son could hold such radical views when he'd been brought up in a household of more liberal ones. It must be, she concluded, the effect of university. Perhaps, she hoped, he would grow out of it.

'What's wrong with the Americans now?' asked Marcel. 'You know France and America have so much in common.'

'Such as?' Oliver started to eat his meal.

'Both countries in their modern form have risen up from Revolution. And do you know that in both cases, an Englishman was in the forefront of ideas, which eventually helped in drafting our Constitutions.'

'We had our own philosophers.'

'Yes, but Thomas Paine played a big part in both the French and, later, the American Revolutions.'

'And the Americans have been sorry ever since.'

'I don't get that impression,' said Marcel. 'In fact, while the Americans seem to prefer being on friendly terms with Britain, they are careful to maintain their independence.'

'Well, then: even Thomas Paine decided that England was a place best shunned.'

'He was just one man, and his life in Britain was not a happy one, so maybe he was prejudiced.'

'He was – and you are not?' demanded Oliver. 'You two are so pro-British, maybe you should go and live there.'

Delphine dropped her gaze and heard Marcel speak.

'It really would be better for you to moderate your stance on the English,' he said quietly.

'Why? I can't see how.'

Delphine heard Marcel suck in a breath.

'Because you are half English yourself.'

There was silence, which dragged on. Delphine looked up. Father's and son's gazes were interlocked, Oliver staring, incredulous, Marcel simply watching, waiting for the reaction.

At last Oliver tore his gaze from his father and stared back and forth between him and Delphine.

'One of you is English?'

'Me,' said Marcel.

Oliver stood up, sending his chair skidding across the flagged floor. 'How the fu— '

'Oliver!' interrupted Marcel loudly. 'Mind your language in front of your mother!'

Oliver leaned across the table towards his father. 'Why did you never tell me?' he hissed.

'Because we decided not to,' said Delphine calmly. 'And I suppose we forgot about it, not seeing it as anything particularly important – especially to you. Anyway, your father didn't know himself until I told him.'

Oliver turned his venom on her. *'You* knew?'

She nodded.

'You knew when you married him?'

'Yes.'

'And *he* didn't?'

'Well, he did by then.' She took Marcel's hand in hers.

'How was that? Tell me!'

She glanced at Marcel who was watching her and his son through narrowed eyes while she told Oliver about finding his father.

'Didn't the Germans come looking?'

'Yes, but we – your grandfather and I – would hide your father, and they never found him. Later, it didn't seem to matter. You came along after the war, and we were just an ordinary French family. Your father had woken up hearing French, and since he was fluent in the language, he simply used it, not realising he was English at first.' She smiled at the recollection. 'It was years before he knew he could speak English. Do you remember,' she asked her husband, 'at the cafe in Bayeux? The day we took Oliver to see the Tapestry at the Hotel du Doyen.'

'I remember,' said Marcel fondly.

'I don't,' said Oliver.

'You were only a few weeks old at the time,' explained Delphine. 'We've always meant to take you back when you grew up, but never seemed to get round to it.'

'And something happened at this cafe to make father think he was English?'

'Not quite,' said Marcel. 'Some English tourists were impolite about your mother feeding you at one of the tables and I heard them. I simply put them straight in English. It was the first time I'd spoken it, and according to one of the tourists, I spoke it like a native. It was the start of my memory returning.'

'So when you go to England each summer, it's to discover your past?'

'That's right.'

'But in the meantime,' Oliver continued, his tone hardening, 'you didn't tell me what was going on?' He turned to direct the question also at his mother.

'We decided not to at the time,' she said. 'We always meant to tell you later.'

'But you wouldn't have told me today if I had not said what I did.'

She looked down at her unfinished meal. 'I suppose that's true.'

Oliver stood and pushed his chair back in place under the table. 'You realise what this means for me?' The colour had gone from his face.

'What?'

'I cannot stand as a candidate for the FAF.'

Delphine felt initial relief. She glanced at Marcel, whose expression was impassive.

'Do you understand?' Oliver demanded, loudly.

'It's a matter for you, son,' said Marcel.

Oliver glared at him. 'Somehow, it may not surprise you to know, I do not any longer feel like a son of yours.'

He turned abruptly and went up to his room.

Delphine heard the bumps and other noises which accompanied his packing. She went after him, knocking on his door.

'Oliver, may I come in?'

The noises stopped. 'It's your house,' he said grudgingly through the door.

She entered and went to him. 'You're not leaving again, are you, Oliver?'

'I can't stay here, under the same roof with *him*!'

'You shouldn't speak of your father that way. He loves you – I love you. We wouldn't do anything deliberately to hurt you.'

'But you've both lied to me, for over twenty years.'

'Not with any intention of hurting you – and not because we were ashamed of the fact, in any way.'

'You did it, though. And now my political career is screwed. I can't even remain a member of the FAF with that sort of blot on my ancestry.'

Delphine almost smiled, and fought the urge hard. 'I'd hardly call being half-English a blot on your ancestry.'

He stopped packing and stared at her. 'Well, that's the difference between us, you see: I would.'

She rested a hand on his. 'I don't want you to go. Your father is booked on the ferry to England on Monday' – she raised her hand to forestall his comment – 'and we can talk about it after he's gone. At the moment, it will only hurt him to hear you say more of the cruel things you've said already.'

'How do you know I don't think the cruellest things about you? After all, you're the French woman who decided to marry a foreigner. For God's sake, mother, why didn't you marry a Frenchman.'

She smiled at him faintly. 'Because it happens that your father is the man who needed me most.' She sat on the bed next to his open suitcase. 'You can't imagine what it was like: I nursed him for six months while he was unconscious.' She met his gaze. 'In a coma, Oliver. We had to feed him through a tube, and we had to do it all in secrecy.'

'Why?'

'The Gestapo. The Germans. If they'd seen him, they might have taken him away. I daren't let that happen.'

'Why?'

'Because I knew he was an English agent.'

'Spy.'

'He came here to help.'

Oliver sat down. 'So what happened next?'

'We set up a bed and sent for the doctor.'

'Lafarge?'

Oliver seemed to relax at the mention of the name.

Delphine continued, 'Yes. We thought he would help. He'd helped members of the Resistance. He supplied the tube and told me what I could pour down it to feed your father.'

'All without the Germans suspecting?'

'That's right. Doctor Lafarge worked at the hospital in Bayeux. He was well-respected there, looking after injured German soldiers as well as local people. I think they tended to look the other way if he needed some equipment.' Her eyes were bright with tears. 'I – we – didn't expect your father to live, but he did. In September, he woke up, able to speak and understand French, but with no memory of anything before that moment.'

Oliver stared at her, but less aggressively. 'And when did you decide to marry him?'

'After the Germans shot my father on Christmas Eve.' This time, tears rolled down her cheeks and she mopped them with the back of her hand. 'Your father and I were married six weeks later. We needed each other by then.'

'And I arrived nine months later? No, wait, I wasn't born for, let's see, 1946 – another two and a half years. Did you spend eighteen months with your legs crossed, mother?'

The tears rolled again. Delphine hung her head. 'No. I – I had a miscarriage in 1944. We decided to wait a while after that – until after the war was over. I became pregnant with you in the autumn of 1945.'

'A miscarriage in 1944?' Oliver leaned towards her. 'You anticipated your marriage, perhaps?'

'It's before your time, Oliver, and none of your business.'

The look he gave her chilled her. It conveyed disgust. She dried her tears and stood up.

'Please don't leave us.'

He studied her for a moment. 'Very well, mother. But I shall be spending the next few days travelling to Caen to sort out my affairs with the Party. God knows what they'll think when they discover what you've finally seen fit to tell me.'

She swallowed, opening the door. 'Actually, Oliver,' she said, 'I only care what you think, not your friends in the FAF.'

'Hope you don't find out, mother.'

* * *

Oliver drove back to the farm on Monday morning, still feeling shame at having to withdraw his candidacy from the elections. Most of his anger was directed at his mother.

The FAF group leader had not uttered a word of condemnation, but his expression said it all. Oliver would have to make a gesture of monumental significance if he was to reinstate himself in the group's good books. The other members, at least those who were privy to his confession of racial impurity, had voiced their disgust and refused to speak to him. Two had muttered darkly, within earshot, that in their opinion, Oliver should be taken outside and shot.

He hadn't believed they were serious, until one pulled a 9mm Luger pistol from his pocket and showed it to the other. He'd torn his gaze away from it at last to find both men were regarding him. There was little doubt in his mind that they meant, at the very least, to frighten him, and possibly to warn him to expect such retribution. It was not in Oliver's nature to feel fear, but the sudden coldness of the group liquefied the contents of his bowels, and sent him rushing for a toilet. For the first time ever in his life, he had found himself in a situation he could not control, and he disliked the feeling intensely.

Cleaning himself on the bidet, he contemplated demonstrating his contempt of those group members who criticised him most severely for his ancestry, despite the fact it was hardly something he could do anything about. Could they not see, he was as truly French as any of them? Born, raised and educated in the motherland; scarcely been out of it. He hadn't known his father was English, for God's sake. Why should that fact, having now come to light, change who he was in any way?

It wasn't as if he had suddenly found out he was Jewish. In fact, he'd not expected the FAF to react to his situation as negatively as they had.

By the time he reached the farm, he knew the blame lay really on his parents. Fury simmered in him, whilst he determinedly appeared calm. His mother came out of the house with a bucket of feed for the hens. She smiled at him and went into the barn. A few moments later, he heard the chickens and hens squawking as they fought over the grain, and his mother came back into the yard, and walked to meet him, her arms outstretched in welcome.

Oliver deliberately avoided being hugged.

'Hello, mother,' he said, his voice distinctly cool.

She stopped, surprised. 'Oliver.'

'I'm back,' he said. 'I have withdrawn my candidacy.'

She took a step towards him, her smile broadening. 'I'm so glad, Oliver. I would have hated—'

'But not my support for the organisation!'

That wiped the stupid, insipid smile from her face.

Delphine stopped, silent. She turned, and went indoors.

Oliver followed her, finding her watering some of the potted plants she had dotted about the place.

'Aren't you at least sorry?' he demanded.

She put down the small watering can and looked at him. 'What should I be sorry about, Oliver? Marrying your father? Having his child? Bringing you up the way you are?' She came towards him. 'Maybe I should regret that: I thought – we thought – we had raised a boy with a decent set of values;

while we expected the usual behaviour of teenagers coping with puberty, we expected that in your twenties, with the self-confidence which comes from living away from home at university, you would mature into the kind of person your father and I could admire. We've always been on your side, Oliver – until we discovered last week that you've apparently become a racist. It seems possible that you are also a fascist, a Neo-Nazi. Please tell me if I'm wrong, but that's how it seems.'

Oliver heard sounds of movement upstairs.

'I thought he would have left by now,' he said, indicating the presumed location of his father.

'He's on a later ferry,' replied Delphine. 'And let me say, I think he is as appalled as I am about your politics, Oliver.'

He took a step until he was almost touching her. 'I don't give a damn, mother, what you or father think. When I leave here, it will be for the last time. I want nothing more to do with either of you. He' – he glanced upwards again – 'might as well be dead as far as I'm concerned; and you…'

'What about me?' Delphine asked, her voice colder than his now.

'You are a traitor to France. I don't want to see you again, either.'

She folded her arms, forcing him to take a step backwards. 'Very well, Oliver. You can get out now.'

'That's it, then, is it?' he demanded. 'Thus proving you don't love me really, or you'd be begging me to stay.'

'If you loved your father and me, you would never have said what you have, so let's not get into an argument about who loves whom. Go away. And when – if – you ever discover what a hateful person you have become, I will be here, waiting for your apology.'

'Don't hold your breath, mother. I'll never change.'

She smiled coldly. 'People do change, whatever you think now. When you're a few years older, you'll be surprised how differently you see the world. I'll wait until your mental maturity catches up with your body.'

Her words had an odd effect on him. Instead of the sharp riposte he could have made, her reference to his body made him look at hers; not as his mother but as a woman. At forty-seven, she was still slender and held herself proudly. He felt a sexual response in himself which he didn't expect. Before he could react, he heard footsteps on the stairs and Marcel came into the kitchen carrying his suitcase.

He held out his arms to Oliver and walked towards him, smiling.

'Oliver, my son. It's good to have you home again so soon.'

Oliver avoided Marcel's touch. 'It was only last week I was here, father.'

Marcel dropped his arms. 'It is always good to see you. You've so rarely come home since you went to university.'

Oliver stared at him. Delphine took a step to her husband's side.

'Oliver is leaving home, dear.'

Marcel raised his eyebrows. 'Oh? For how long this time?'

Oliver backed towards the door. 'Forever,' he said.

Delphine turned to look only at Marcel. 'Apparently, our existence offends his politics. We remind him that he is only half French, and therefore not racially pure.'

Marcel could not conceal his surprise. He turned to Oliver.

'Don't go!' he cried. 'We can—'

'Oh, let him!' said Delphine. 'He wants to feel martyred for the sake of his horrible FAF. Do you realise what they are?'

Marcel stared at her. 'I thought they were one of those political societies that spring up at universities – especially ones specialising in political science like the one Oliver went to. And then were forgotten about?'

'Not this one, apparently,' said Delphine. 'At least, not yet.' She turned fully to face her son. 'Tell me, Oliver, how many candidates were the FAF expecting to field in June?'

Oliver licked his lips. He had not been listening, instead envisaging having his mother bent over the table, pulling her dress up and forcing himself between her thighs.

'Er, three, I think. But the movement will grow.' He lifted his gaze to rest on hers. 'You see why my withdrawal is so important.'

He saw his mother's focus shift to his trousers and real-ised he had sprouted an erection. He turned away abruptly and went outside.

A few moments later, Marcel came out with his suitcase.

'Your mother has explained that you are still shocked at finding you are half English.'

'You could put it that mildly,' said Oliver.

'I am sorry, son. I never imagined it would worry you. I can't apologise for being who and what I am, nor for falling in love with your mother, nor for begetting you. You were conceived in love, because we both wanted a child…'

'Shut up, father!' cried Oliver, his eyes moistening and his face red. 'I don't want to know. Mother is no better than those women you told me about who collaborated with the Germans – *horizontal collaboration,* I think you called it.'

'They did it because they saw it as the best way of surviv-ing a horrible situation.'

'Is that what mother did? Did she see fucking you as the best way of surviving a horrible situation?'

Marcel frowned threateningly. 'Don't you ever speak to me about your mother in those words again.'

'From a purely French point of view, father, she was a slut.'

Marcel drew back his fist and let fly at Oliver's chin. He followed up with another punch to his body. Oliver went down as Delphine appeared in the doorway behind them.

'What are you doing!' she cried, coming forward and reaching down to drag her husband off her son, who climbed groggily to his feet.

For a moment, he stared at his father, shocked, then turned on his heel and went to his car. Delphine and Marcel watched as he drove out of the yard, scattering gravel.

Oliver's blood was up. Just before the track joined the road, out of sight of the farm house, he stopped. For a few moments, he considered how to get his own back. Clearly, he thought, there was no returning to the situation of before he'd known about his origins: he'd just come off worst at the hands of an Englishman, and that was not something he could leave unpunished. He got out of the car, opened the boot and found the wheel brace. Clutching it, he waited for his father's Citroen to come down the track on the way to the ferry port.

* * *

Delphine had seen off Marcel dry-eyed, assuring him he did not have to cancel his trip. She thought it best, in fact, for him to be out of the way for a while, until the incident in the yard was less fresh in everyone's mind. She felt that, whatever Oliver had said about leaving for good, she wanted to see him and talk to him about the situation without Marcel being around, as she felt she might be able to make him see reason.

She picked up the stale bread from yesterday and took it across the yard, out of the gate, to the pond where a pair of Rouen Foncé ducks had made their home. Wherever the mother swam, she was followed by a group of four ducklings, tiny legs and feet working at high speed, to keep up with their mother.

Delphine began breaking the bread up into small pieces and throwing it towards the ducks. Mother and offspring swam towards them, quacking noisily. She heard a sound behind her and turned to find Oliver approaching.

'Oliver…'

He did not reply. His face was still mottled with anger. She'd heard what he thought of her, when Marcel had knocked him down. While she didn't approve of violence in general, she was pleased that he had defended her so succinctly.

'Are you here to apologise, Oliver?'

'No,' he replied, through his teeth.

She barely had time to identify the fact that he was splashed with blood. Without warning, he turned her round facing the water. She felt him press against her, and was horrified to find once again that he had an erection. She was about to protest when he pushed her hard between the shoulder-blades. She lost her footing and slipped face-down into the water. She raised herself on her arms so her head was clear, but even as she did so, she felt him enter the water behind her and prise her legs apart. He grabbed each of them, above the knee, and began to push her, wheelbarrow-style, towards the middle of the pond.

'Oliver! What are you doing? Get me out of here!'

'I was beginning to wonder what father saw in you, mother,' Oliver rasped. 'Is this the sort of thing you did for him – lay with your legs open, encouraging him to fuck you? Is that what you did? And with a foreigner, too.' The thought triggered the red mist in his mind, filling it with hate.

As she was about to reply, she felt him push her forward again. She tried to wriggle out of her son's grasp, but he was too strong. Her arms were tiring and at full stretch. Her neck was strained, holding her mouth and nose out of the water, but still he pushed.

'Oliver!' she screamed.

With one more push, her face disappeared under the surface.

He held her there, his eyes fixed on her, until the bubbles stopped and her struggles ceased.

After a while, he shook his head as if clearing it and dropped his mother's legs into the water. Then he turned and walked back to his car.

PART TWO

CHAPTER *18 – 1999*

Penny and Geoff's rooms, by chance, were on the same floor of the hotel as Oliver's. Penny was wakened around three o'clock by a firm knock on her door. She pulled a robe over her nightdress and peered through the spyhole before unlocking the door.

A gendarme?

'Can I help you?' she asked in English, before groping through her sleepy brain for the French. *'Est-ce que je peux vous aider?'*

'There has been an incident, Madame,' the policeman replied, 'just along the corridor. I am to ask you if you heard or saw anything suspicious.'

Penny shook her head. 'No. I have been asleep. *Je dormais.* What happened? *Qu' est-ce qui s'est pasée?'*

'There 'as been a murder, Madame. A young woman.' He looked at her enquiringly. Penny felt shock, the kind she'd felt throughout her career whenever she'd been told of a killing. 'Did you per'aps see any young women in the hotel last night? Any in this corridor?'

Penny sighed, trying hard to remember. 'The only young women I saw were with one of the other guests.'

'Do you know who?'

'I don't know the women, but the man they were with was M'sieur Oliver Delacourt. Or Oliver Dubois, I think his name really is.'

This time, the gendarme frowned. 'A man with two names?' He produced a pocket notebook and began to write.'

'I think his legal name is Oliver Dubois, but he uses Delacourt.'

' 'Ow do you know this, Madame?'

'My friend and I saw his credit card, which was in the name of Dubois, but he'd introduced himself to us as Delacourt.'

At the mention of a friend, the gendarme moved to peer past her into the bedroom. Why, wondered Penny, did everyone seem to think she'd be sharing a room with the friend in question?

'He's staying two doors along.' She pointed at Geoff's door. 'Mr Pearson,' she added helpfully, as the gendarme's pen flashed over the page. She had to spell the name, and her own, too.

'Would you please come and talk to my superior officer.'

Penny nodded, straightening her hair. She picked up her door key, and followed the gendarme down to the seating area in the foyer. Geoff was already down there, seated in the same place where they'd been earlier. She sat beside him and waited while the gendarme spoke to a man in a brown suit. It was, she noted, not a new one, and showed signs of much wear. The only time she'd seen suits as rumpled as this among her own team had been when they'd worked nights and found time only for cat-naps. Maybe the detective had been called out from his sleep.

He came across the foyer, accompanied by the gendarme.

'Inspecteur Dumonde, Madame,' he said.

The Inspector regarded her without expression as he sat beside her. The gendarme took a seat on the opposite side of the coffee table.

'Mrs… ?'

'Sanderson,' Penny supplied.

The Inspector inclined his head briefly. 'I understand you saw M'sieur Oliver Delacourt, or *Dubois*, as you now say he is called, in the hotel with two young women last night.'

Penny nodded.

'Can you describe the women?' he asked.

She did so.

The Inspector remarked, 'Your description sounds highly accurate.'

She smiled. 'I was trained to be observant. Until I retired last year, I was a Detective Inspector in the British police.'

The policeman arched his eyebrows, then returned her smile. '*Alors! je comprends.* I understand.' His face resumed its business-like expression. 'Did you know either of the women?'

'No, Inspector. I think M'sieur Delacourt intended spending some time in their company. When I saw them last night, the women seemed to be slightly drunk, and it was still quite early.' She shrugged. 'We didn't see any of them after that.'

The Inspector nodded. 'They made a couple of calls on Room Service, and that seems to be that, until one of the girls came down to Reception and said she and the other girl had been raped and the other girl killed.' He leaned forward. 'I hope you will not be broadcasting that information, Madame, which I give you as a courtesy to a former colleague.'

'Thank you. I'll be discreet,' Penny told him. 'Do you know anything about the girls?'

Dumonde shook his head. 'Not yet, Mrs Sanderson.' He tapped his notebook. 'Could you tell me please why you seem to know Oliver Delacourt so well?'

She told him of her self-imposed mission. 'So far, we've learned that there might be a – a connection with Oliver's father.'

'What sort of connection, Madame?'

'It's possible Oliver is my half-brother.'

'*Vraiment!*' Dumonde exclaimed. He tapped the table-top with a neatly manicured finger, then looked up at her. 'So, you have reason to believe that your father is also that of Oliver?'

Penny nodded. 'Seems very likely.' She told the policeman what she and Geoff had learned since they'd been in France.

'Perhaps the most surprising information is that M'sieur Dubois' mother, Delphine, was killed in an accidental drowning in 1969, and at the same time, his father was attacked and spent time in hospital.'

'But his father – per'aps *your* father – was he not considered a suspect? '

Penny glanced at Geoff. 'We understand from the doctor who examined her body that it was his view her death was due to an accident.'

'Ah!' replied the Inspector, 'then that is undoubtedly so.'

Penny studied his face for a moment. 'The doctor had considered suicide a possibility,' she said.

'But decided it was unlikely?'

'Yes.'

Geoff leaned forward. 'What would it take to have her body exhumed?'

The Inspector turned to regard him thoughtfully. 'Why would you like Madame Dubois' body exhumed after thirty years?'

'It could be that the doctor missed something that modern forensic methods might turn up.'

'What do you think that might be?'

'I suppose,' Penny interrupted, 'I feel some doubt about the doctor's diagnosis, and I'd like to be more certain that Delphine died accidentally, and wasn't murdered. A new post mortem might be able to establish what one thirty years ago couldn't.'

'Why do you think she might have been murdered, Madame?'

'Because we're talking about the same Oliver Dubois, or Delacourt, who spent the night in this hotel, apparently with those two young women.' She glanced at him tight-lipped. 'I suppose if it were me, I'd just want to be sure about the findings of the post mortem on his mother.' She shrugged. 'But it's your investigation, not mine.'

The Inspector nodded, rose to his feet. 'I will consider the points you make, Madame. I personally believe it unlikely a fresh post mortem would yield any more information than the original, after all this time, but thank you for your help.'

Penny and Geoff watched him re-join his colleagues.

'It all seems a bit relaxed,' she observed. 'The only person showing signs of emotion is the surviving girl, and she is still here. I'd have thought they'd have taken her somewhere for a thorough examination by now.'

Geoff shrugged. 'Diff'rent courses, diff'rent horses.'

A waiter offered the girl something hot to drink. She took it, her shaking hands causing the cup and saucer to clatter together, the waiter moved away and she was left alone. Penny glanced at Geoff, got up and went over to her.

'Hello,' she said. '*Salut!*'

The girl looked up. Mascara had smudged into dark shadows round her eyes, with streaks down her cheeks where tears had run. Penny pulled up a chair and sat beside her, and told the girl who she was. Between them, they had enough grasp of each other's languages to communicate. The girl told Penny her name, Lisette.

'The Inspector told me what happened – in confidence, of course. Is there anyone I could call for you? Mother, perhaps? Father?'

Lisette shook her head. 'They must not know,' she said.

'But, Lisette, you've suffered a most serious assault. If you were my daughter, no matter what our history, I would want to know, and be with you.'

Tears squeezed down Lisette's cheeks. 'But I am not your daughter, and my mother is not you. She is a dancer, and just now she and her troupe are in Dubai, so, you see, she is not coming to see me any time soon.' Her father, she added, was with his new wife and child, down south in Provence.

Penny wanted to get the girl to talk to her, but shied away from the direct approach.

'Has a doctor seen you?'

'Not yet. I have been told not to wash until one has.' She looked into Penny's eyes, her expression one of great sadness, almost of desperation.

'I'm sure it won't be long,' said Penny, sounding more confident than she felt, having observed the apparent lack of urgency being exhibited by the police. The Inspector glanced their way and frowned. Penny reckoned her chat was about to be cut short. She ventured a direct question.

'Have you known Oliver long?'

'You know him?' asked Lisette, and Penny could sense her drawing back.

'Only a little. We met just this week.'

Lisette pursed her lips, scowling. 'He owns the company Anne-Marie and I work for. Worked for. Oh! Poor Anne-Marie!'

She bowed her head, covering her face with her hands, and sobbed noisily. Penny instinctively moved over and put her arm round the girl comfortingly. When she glanced up, the Inspector was at her side.

'Pardon, Mrs Sanderson, but this lady has been through a great distress. I'd be obliged if you would return to your place.' He jerked his head in Geoff's direction.

Penny didn't relinquish her gentle hold of Lisette at once.

'I was comforting her. I understand she has been through a terrible trauma, and yet, she is still waiting to be seen by your police surgeon. Doctor; medical examiner,' she added in case her meaning wasn't clear.

'That will be soon, Madame. In the meantime…'

She nodded. 'I'll be here if you want to talk, Lisette,' she said softly, getting to her feet.

She smiled at the Inspector to show she harboured no hard feelings, and returned to her seat beside Geoff.

'Wonder what's happened to Oliver,' he said quietly.

'I haven't seen him about,' replied Penny, glancing round what she could see of the large foyer lounge.

Inspector Dumonde was talking on his mobile phone in the corner near the door. He closed the lid and came towards them.

'M'sieur Pearson, Madame Sanderson, may I join you a moment?'

He took a chair opposite them and laid his notebook and a pen on the table.

'M'sieur Delacourt, or Dubois, seems to have interesting friends,' he began.

Penny arched her eyebrows. 'Oh? Who?'

'You do not know, Madame?'

'As I told you, we only met this week, and we haven't spoken much in that time.' She noticed Geoff's eyes were on his coffee cup, whilst he sipped.

Dumonde glanced from one to the other before continuing.

'He was a member of a neo-Nazi group, thirty years ago.'

Penny wondered why she didn't feel more surprised. 'Really?'

'A friend of mine in the DST – *Direction de la surveillance du territoire*, one of our security services – has been taking an interest, and discovered this fact.'

Geoff gave Dumonde an old-fashioned look. 'Taking an interest, eh? Why, after thirty years?'

The Inspector regarded him askance. 'I have no idea.' He looked at Penny again. 'And you didn't know that Oliver had such connections?'

'I did not, Inspector.'

He appeared to be satisfied and rose to his feet. Penny stopped him.

'Do you think there's some connection with your current case?'

He hesitated before answering. She was beginning to notice that he rarely spoke without thinking about the possible ramifications of doing so.

'No, Madame. Whatever he did in the past seems in no way connected with the present.'

'Thank you, Inspector,' she smiled. She watched him cross the room to join some of his colleagues, then turned to find Geoff watching her.

'Well?' she said.

'Seems odd to me that that another event involving Oliver in 1969 should suddenly surface,' he said.

* * *

Oliver had fled to the farm.

The little cow had deserved it. He could tell her kind the moment he met her, when Ramon had asked her to make coffee for them and she'd refused. But he'd seen the glint in her eye, and known she liked pitting herself against men. Well, he, Oliver Delacourt, successful businessman and patriot, was up to teaching her who was master and who was servant.

The GHB in her drink had softened her up – softened both of them up. By the time they'd made it to his bedroom in the hotel, they'd both been largely out of it. He couldn't remember who originally said it, but the phrase "get your reprisals in first" kept flitting through his mind. Of course, it had been an easy matter then to let her fall back on the bed, her feet still on the floor and her knees already apart. If the other hadn't tried to interfere, he'd have been able to move in on the dark-haired one straight away, a simple matter of pulling open her blouse, pushing her skirt out of the way and tearing off her underwear.

He felt himself getting hard again at the recollection.

But then the other one had more or less jumped on him, pushing him forward until his shins struck the bed and he overbalanced onto it beside dark-hair.

What the hell were their names? Ah! He remembered.

He'd had to punish Lisette. He'd swung at her. His knuckles were still bruised, but she'd gone down, and simply laid on the carpet whimpering while he'd turned his attention to the one beside him, Anne-Marie.

He realised that while he'd been dealing with the blonde, he'd lost his erection. Removing his jacket and trousers, he reached out for Anne-Marie's breasts to provide him with the kind of stimulation he needed. She was staring at him, with that vacant look they got from the Roofie, as he ravished her, pinching the nipples, bruising the firm flesh of her tits. With his penis in one hand, he'd used the other to pull her panties out of the way then thrust himself into her.

She'd moaned then, he recalled with satisfaction. He'd forced himself into her repeatedly until he felt his crisis approach. Vaguely, he wondered whether he might be impregnating her. The thought quickened his motions.

Lisette was picking herself up slowly as he shuddered and jerked above Anne-Marie. He pulled himself free of her and turned to the other girl. She was trying to focus on him, but the drug was obviously too powerful to resist. He pushed her down easily, to lay on the bed beside her friend. He left them for a moment while he went into the bathroom, where he cleaned himself up before opening his toilet bag and finding a pack of small blue tablets. He swallowed one and took a drink of water before returning to the bedroom.

Lisette had pulled Anne-Marie's clothes back into some sort of order. He hadn't minded, because he was done with Anne-Marie. The blonde turned her head as he approached her. She was, he saw, shedding tears. There was a bruise blooming on her cheek, a patch of red where he'd hit her. Despite her obvious grogginess, he saw her actions as in some way defying him.

It seemed she needed a lesson as well. He felt his arousal.

'No!' she'd screamed.

It was the first time any of them had spoken since reaching the bedroom. He'd had to slap her again to shut her up. He didn't want interruptions from curious guests or hotel staff. Her lip began to bleed. The sight of her blood inspired him to tear the buttons on her blouse, and when he'd opened it, he pushed her bra roughly up, above her breasts, knocking aside the crucifix she wore round her neck. He admitted to a fascination with women's breasts, knew they were very sensitive, and easy targets if he felt the need to inflict a little pain or punishment. He pushed her skirt up, enjoying the sight of her stockinged legs, then yanked her lacy thong down, not caring that it ripped.

She'd shaken her head as if trying to clear it, drawn her legs together and began to struggle upright.

'Fuck you!' he'd spat at her, drawn back his right arm and delivered a punch which seriously hurt his knuckles. She fell back on the bed, apparently unconscious, while he used the pain in his hand to bolster his aggression. He recalled enjoying the moment he'd driven himself into her, thrusting hard to bring on his crisis, watching her face all the time for signs of a return to consciousness. And when he'd finally emptied himself into her, he'd felt victorious. He felt excitement at the possibility he might have impregnated Lisette, too, if she was the kind of good Catholic girl the crucifix suggested.

Well, he could always offer to take care of such an eventuality. Lafarge could be relied upon to get rid of a foetus. Oliver smiled. Lafarge could be relied upon to do anything Oliver wanted.

And then it had all gone wrong.

Anne-Marie seemed to be coming round. He'd intended slipping her a reasonable payment for her discomfort – big enough perhaps to tempt her to a repeat event another time – but she was staring between him and Lisette, seeing the blood on the other girl's lips, the bruise; and then she'd started to scream at him. He'd had no choice but to shut her up.

He'd hit her quite deliberately on the breasts. She'd screamed again, and he'd had to clamp his hand over her mouth. He'd held her firmly against her struggles, even when her heels had repeatedly kicked at the floor and the toes of her shoes had bruised his legs. He held on, and suddenly the movements stopped. He glanced down at her and saw the blankness of her gaze, which suggested that the influence of the drug was still strong.

It was when he'd gradually removed his hand from the lower half of her face and allowed her head to slip back onto the bed and her eyes never moved, never blinked, that he realised there was something wrong. He slapped her cheeks lightly. Her head rolled with the blows, but still she did not react, did not blink.

Lisette was showing signs of a return to consciousness.

'Oh, fuck!' he muttered, as the gravity of the situation began to hit him.

He grabbed his clothes and dressed hurriedly, packed his bag and prepared to leave. Something close to panic was tunnelling his thoughts. He couldn't think what needed to be done to get rid of any traces of him. But then, it was *his* room. He couldn't cover that up. He suddenly needed time to think, somewhere he could be safe. Lisette was leaning over Anne-Marie's body, trying to wake her. He'd taken the two strides towards her and punched her again.

Without waiting to find out what effect his blow had had, he grabbed his suitcase and let himself out of the room, leaving the hotel surreptitiously by the fire stairs.

* * *

He realised he was sweating, in need of a shower, and went up to the bathroom.

Standing under the powerful jets of hot water, he knew he needed to take some urgent decisions. Should he leave the area? Was there any point, since the hotel room had been in his name? So, no. He would have to face the inevitable enquiries.

He didn't fear them too much: he was, after all, a highly successful local businessman, owner of a nationwide chain of car dealerships, and a man who still had friends in politics. He felt sure the police could be persuaded the death had simply been an accident.

He decided he should return to Bayeux and turn himself in.

CHAPTER 19 – 1969

The pain was excruciating. David opened his eyes and found himself face down in the grass and weeds below a hedge. He felt stickiness on his face and touched it. His hand came away scarlet with blood. He knuckled more blood out of his eyes then gingerly rolled over so he could sit up. At the same time, he felt the top of his head, where the pain was seated. He could feel the jagged edges of a gash, but much more frightening, he could feel the sharp edges of cracked cranium below the surface.

God! The pain!

It speared into him. He wondered if moving might do more damage. He needed a hospital. He kept seeing double, and something was making a noise in his head that matched the waves of pain. He realised it was his heart, racing.

Where the hell was he? Through eyes which kept blurring with blood he thought he saw a car. A moment later, he saw two. The double vision kept shifting: sometimes there was one, and a moment later he'd be looking at two. Moving very slowly and cautiously, he looked around him. He had no idea where he was. There were no signs of the war, no guns or heavy aircraft engines, just birdsong and the sound of motor vehicles passing, somewhere nearby. The hedge came to an end a few yards away. Any movement was threatening to make him vomit, and he didn't think that would do a head injury like his any good at all. But could he get at least as far as the gap in the hedge?

He needed a place to hide from German patrols. Where the hell was his parachute? It slowly dawned on him that he was wearing civilian clothes unlike those he remembered putting on before leaving North Weald. His vision slowly sorted itself out. Okay: only one car, for definite. But unlike any he'd seen before. It looked like a small Citroen, with its trademark chevrons, but smoother, more streamlined than those he'd seen pictures of. Compared with his Austin Seven at home, this was a very stylish motor.

He realised there must be a road, presumably the other side of the hedge, and he determined to get himself as far as the gap. The headache was settling into a constant throb that made his breath catch in his throat, and kept the taste of bile in his mouth. He couldn't see anybody in the field, and set out on his hands and knees towards the gap. Would his contact find him? Was he off course? A couple of fields could make a lot of difference. And time. He should have arrived in the middle of the night, but, judging from the sun, it was nearer to the middle of the day. He glanced at his watch.

It wasn't his. It wasn't even one they'd given him at SOE when he'd been kitted out with his French identity. But then, he realised, the wrist and arm the watch was strapped to didn't look like his either. He pinched himself. He was real enough, he concluded. But his arm looked like an older man's, the skin's elasticity beginning to break down and a few permanent wrinkles appear. The hairs on it included some grey ones.

He changed direction and headed for the car. It had wing mirrors, but mounted on the doors. In fact, it didn't have what he'd call wings, nor a running board. The wheels being all inside an aerodynamic body shell. And the headlights weren't masked to minimise their light.

He rose on his knees beside the right-hand door until he could see himself in the mirror. The image was distorted by its convex surface, but the face which looked back at him was of a middle-aged man. There was blood staining the whole of his scalp, still running under his chin and staining his shirt.

He felt as though he was staring at an apparition. He searched his pockets and found a wallet. It was full of currency notes – New Francs, issued by the *République Français* – and a chequebook in the name of *Marcel Dubois*. His cover name. There was a French passport in another pocket, and tickets which appeared to be for a ferry to England.

That was when he saw the date of the crossing, and realised he had no idea, no memory at all, of the last twenty-six years. If the Gestapo were still about, they might want to know about the ferry trip to England.

He managed to stand up, his mind spinning and walked unsteadily as far as the gap in the hedge, where he tore the tickets up and buried them before stepping unsteadily onto the roadside verge beyond. Traffic, such as he had never seen, roared past. His heart went into overdrive, pumping the depleted volume of blood around his body, but it wasn't enough to stop him fainting at the edge of the road.

* * *

Lafarge looked up as the surgery door opened. He was surprised because he'd checked not many minutes before that the last patient had left. Oliver Dubois stood in front of him, obviously disturbed.

Lafarge rose to his feet. 'Oliver, what's happened?'

'There's been an accident,' he said. 'My mother's dead – and my father is missing.'

Lafarge gaped. 'Delphine is dead?'

'It was an accident. I'm sure it was,' Oliver replied, nodding. 'My father was around but he's not now, so I can't ask him what happened.'

Lafarge looked at him through narrowed eyes. 'Did you see her die, Oliver?'

Dubois looked at him. 'No, of course not. I could have saved her if I'd been there.'

'How do you know it was an accident if you weren't there?'

Oliver sat in the chair reserved for patients and held out both palms over the table. 'Because the alternative is too terrible to think about. I mean, work it out for yourself: my father was there earlier in the day, and now he's missing and mother's dead. What alternative is there to an accident? It's unthinkable that father would have done anything like kill her, even if they were going through a bit of a bad patch. No, it *must* have been an accident.'

Lafarge felt shocked. He could see exactly what Oliver meant: Marcel was a good man, and he loved his wife, regardless of whether they were not seeing eye to eye on everything just at the moment…

'What sort of "bad patch" were your parents going through?' he asked as the thought occurred to him.

Oliver looked down at his hands, sadly. 'To be frank, I think it might be me – my fault. I've been around more since coming down from university. I think mother has been happy to see more of me but dad had become used to seeing me only six times a year and was finding it difficult to adjust.'

'That's hardly what I'd call a "bad patch".'

Oliver frowned. 'Well, maybe there were other things as well. You know how niggles – hardly anything to worry about individually – can pile up into one big heap of dissatisfaction? Maybe there were other things driving them apart.'

'Such as?'

'Well, think about father's Parisian accent.'

'What about it? He's always had it.' From the day he woke up in 1943, thought Lafarge.

'Well, it must be an affectation he's kept all these years,' said Oliver. 'I mean, the man's a local, from Hameau Belchamps, for God's sake. They don't speak with a Parisian accent in Hameau Belchamps.'

'I'll give you that,' said Lafarge, nodding. He recalled it had been a slight puzzle when he'd first met Marcel, after he'd woken from his coma, but he'd scarcely thought about it since. Marcel's accent was just… Marcel's accent.

He had a sudden thought which caused the hairs on the back of his neck to stand up. He was amazed he hadn't thought of it before: he'd never looked into Marcel's background. During those awful months before the liberation, his caring vocation had been to the fore, and matters which seemed unimportant had been pushed to the back of his mind. Marcel spoke with a Parisian accent: in the early days, after he woke up, he'd occasionally – apparently – forgotten the meaning of words. On the other hand, he had never given anyone cause to question his nationality.

Suppose, thought Lafarge, the cold shiver still running up and down his spine, suppose Marcel had not been from Hameau Belchamps. Suppose he had not been French at all, but only someone who spoke the language well.

Suppose also, he thought, his hands unconsciously trembling, Marcel had been another British agent.

Surely Delphine would have known, if she'd found him. She never voiced any such suspicion, but Marcel's head-wound could be explained by a bad landing by parachute.

Oliver was looking at him strangely. The stress caused by his thoughts had cut out the sound of the young man's voice. He dragged his mind back to the present.

'I'm sorry. What were you saying?'

'Only that I'm sure my mother had an accident, and I'd be glad if you would do the necessary certification.'

Lafarge eyed him beadily. 'You want me to certify her death was an accident, so the police don't look for a killer?'

Oliver nodded. 'Anything else would be unthinkable.'

'I should do a post mortem.'

'I'm sure it will only confirm that she drowned.'

'How did she do that?'

Oliver looked down at his hands again. 'I told you, I wasn't there. Her body was found in the duck pond outside the yard.'

Lafarge stared. 'She drowned, by accident, in the duck pond?' he repeated, almost as if learning a part.

'That's right, doctor. I'm pretty sure a post mortem won't reveal anything else.'

Just before leaving the surgery, Oliver had turned to Lafarge, his eyes moist. 'I'm going to use my mother's name in future, doctor. Please amend your records.'

For two days, Lafarge debated with himself over whether to comply with Oliver's request. Delphine's body was brought in to the mortuary in Bayeux, and he carried out a post mortem because that was the law.

Her body was that of a normal, healthy woman of her age. As Oliver had said, there was water in her lungs which confirmed death by drowning, and no other marks that caused him to wonder about how she'd died. There was slight bruising on her thighs, near her knees, but her flesh was mottled with the bruise-like patches, the marks just more signs of hypostasis, or blood-settling.

In the end, he signed the certificate to the effect that there were no signs of foul play and that in his opinion, Delphine's death had been an accident.

The local police closed their file before it was scarcely open.

Marcel did not show up in the month following his wife's death, and Lafarge began to wonder if in fact he might have had something to do with Delphine's drowning. But then, there was no evidence on her body that she'd done anything but fall, somehow, into the water and been unable to get out. Perhaps, he thought, she'd suffered a bout of cramp. It sometimes happened. Perhaps Marcel had simply gone to England on one of his regular trips, and hadn't yet heard the news.

That thought brought back Lafarge's initial worry, that Marcel was in fact a British agent. But why had he been sent to France? The man's loss of memory had been both a curse and a blessing – a curse because whatever his purpose, it had not been carried out, and a blessing because... well the same thing really. Lafarge had helped his fellow-countrymen out – of course he had – but he had firmly believed that the activities of the Resistance groups had resulted in the civilian population being treated more harshly than they otherwise would. Marcel had begun to help out the local Resistance, but only as the lowly, unskilled peasant, they thought him to be. Lafarge knew enough about that to know that Marcel was certainly not guiding the group in any way like he'd expect a SOE agent to do.

A scenario occurred to him then. Perhaps Marcel *had* been an agent, who had lost his memory – Lafarge had tested him, and was satisfied it was genuine. Since the war, much had been learned of a condition called Post Traumatic Stress Disorder, and how this could involve memory loss, even without a skull injury. And Lafarge had read that such lost memories might, in time, given the right stimuli, be recovered to a greater or lesser extent.

It fitted the facts as he knew them, and possibly accounted for the increasing number of trips to England Marcel had made over the last dozen or more years. He'd nearly always travelled alone, and it was possible to see this as supporting Oliver's assertion that his parents had been drifting apart over a period of time.

Six days after Oliver had come to see him at his surgery, and two days after signing off Delphine's death as an accident, Lafarge was in his local bar with Albert Lebrun, and picked up the weekly newspaper. A small item on page five contained Oliver's name and caught his eye.

He wondered if Oliver's membership of a neo-Nazi political party, and the withdrawal of his candidacy from the forthcoming election, might have had any bearing on events of the last week.

Whilst he'd once thought Hitler's Third Reich might not be such a bad thing for France, that was long ago. Since the war, France had made peace with Germany, and prospered under the European agreements on atomic energy, coal and steel, leading twelve years past to the formation of the European Economic Community. On the whole, he didn't want a return to the bad old days and the jackboots. He wanted nothing to do with anyone who did.

'What's that you're reading?' asked Albert.

Lafarge took a good sip of his Merlot and read the paragraph aloud.

* * *

He woke up in a hospital. At least it looked like a hospital. Moments after he opened his eyes, a nurse came into his field of view.

'M'sieur Dubois! Comment ça va?'

So he was definitely in France. Yes, the cars had been driving on the right. He remembered that.

'Where am I?' he asked her in French.

'The hospital at Vire.'

His head, he realised, was bandaged and his clothes had been removed. He was wearing only a thin hospital gown.

He wracked his brains, trying to remember the geography of the area he was supposed to be dropped into. He couldn't remember a place called Vire. The nurse must have seen his puzzlement.

'In Lower Normandy,' she added. 'About a hundred kilometres from the beaches.'

He deduced from the way she spoke that "the beaches" should have meant something.

His blank expression must have persuaded her that more help was needed.

'Don't try to move. You have a bad injury to your head. I am going to find the doctor.'

After she'd moved out of his field of view, he carefully looked around the room, moving his head as little as possible. He saw equipment he'd never seen before. Things that looked like radar screens, but thin, and filled with coloured lines which seemed to flow and pulse from one side to the other. A regular and quiet beep was emitted by one of the machines.

A few minutes later, a tall, slim woman in a smart suit came into view and sat beside him where he could see her easily.

'M'sieur Dubois, I am Édith Solon. I am a doctor, a neurosurgeon. Do you know what that is?'

David resisted the urge to shake his head: it felt too tender for that. 'No.'

'I'm concerned with trying to repair damaged brains. You were unconscious when you were brought in and I operated to realign your skull fracture. My purpose now is to find out, if I can, whether the injury has affected your brain.

'My brain seems to be working just fine—'

'Good. But it might seem fine to you even if it was damaged, in certain ways, anyway.'

'I was going to say, it seems to be working fine except that I have no memory of the last twenty-six years.' He'd been about to tell her the last thing he remembered was being brought to France in a small aircraft, to be dropped by parachute into a field near Sainte Marguerite-en-Bessin. It occurred to him, that he should keep such information to himself until he discovered the outcome of the war, and what had happened in the years since.

Édith Solon chewed her lip for a moment.

David smiled. 'My wife does that when she is undecided about something,' he said.

She lifted an eyebrow interrogatively. 'What?'

'Chew her lip near the corner, like you were.'

She was a very handsome woman. He guessed she was in her early forties, with soft brown eyes and sleekly coiffed brown hair, pinned back in a pleat. The suit hugged her figure pleasingly.

'Do you remember being attacked?'

'No. What happened?'

'Nobody is quite sure, but it looked, from the shape of the injury, as if you had been struck with a wheel brace.'

David stared at her. 'Are you sure?'

'The marks on your skull were consistent with the size and shape of the cup-shaped spanner on the end of a wheel brace.'

David blew out his cheeks. 'I don't remember any of that.'

She tried another tack. 'You remember your wife's name?'

'Of course,' he replied unhesitatingly. The thought suddenly hit him that he'd already said too much. Was the woman Gestapo? He felt sweat begin to bead his forehead and armpits.

'What is it?' Solon asked.

He swallowed. 'Did Hitler win?'

She gazed at him thoughtfully. 'Don't you know?'

'I told you: yesterday, I was in 1943.'

She didn't reply, but stood up and went over to the document box on the wall near the door and took out his medical file. From it she pulled an X-ray of a skull – *his* skull, he supposed – and pushed it into the clips of a light box. The light came on and for a few moments, she studied the image.

She returned to his side but remained standing. 'All right. Tell me what you think your wife's name was.'

He looked away, wondering if he'd already said too much. 'I made a mistake. I don't have a wife. I am Marcel Dubois from Hameau Belchamps. Born in 1919.'

'Do you know who hit you?'

'No. No!'

Dr Solon sat again. 'From the position of your injury, a problem with your memory is perfectly feasible. The human brain is an amazing thing, M'sieur Dubois. But this is not the first time you've been struck on that spot and suffered a cranial fracture. I found evidence of an old fracture which had not been reset properly.

'I have pulled all the pieces of your cranium into place and they have been set. Over the next few weeks, I expect the bones to knit together until you are as good as new.'

'And my memory?' he asked.

'There's every chance that it will return, but we don't know how quickly.' She glanced up as a movement outside the half-glazed door caught her eye. 'I must go. In a few minutes a policeman is going to want to talk to you. I shall warn him not to take long, because you're not up to a stressful interview yet. May I tell him about your condition?'

The thought of a police interrogation had sent a surge of adrenaline through David's body. This was it, then? They'd warned him, in training, about thumbscrews, nails being pulled, electrical wires being attached… He swallowed hard.

Dr Solon smiled. It seemed friendly, but professional. Almost, it was reassuring. But that was all part of the plan, he guessed. She left him and shortly, he heard voices outside the door. A moment later, a man in a leather jacket, blue jeans and black ankle boots occupied the chair she'd been sitting in, and lifted one leg over the other. He produced an ID card, but removed it before David could focus on the details.

It was very different from the ID card SOE had provided him with before his journey to France.

'M'sieur Dubois, I am Sergeant Christophe André. Doctor Solon tells me you cannot remember your wife's name, nor anything which has happened since 1943. The year I was born,' he added with a small grin.

David stared at him. Of course! Ann had been pregnant when he left. Somewhere, he had a son or daughter the same age as the policeman in front of him. He dragged his mind back to the present.

'That is correct,' he said.

'Do you remember who you are?'

'I am Marcel Dubois from Hameau Belchamps. Born in 1919.'

André nodded. 'You're sure about that, M'sieur?'

David stared at him, thinking it was an easy question at the start of his interrogation. 'Yes,' he said.

'Very well. It is a start.'

'What do you mean, "a start"?'

'We know almost nothing about you, M'sieur. Where is your home? Where is your family – do you *have* a family, in fact?'

'I – I don't know, David gasped.

'I gather Doctor Solon has told you what you were hit with.'

'A wheel brace, she said.'

'Well, I want you to keep that bit of information to yourself. It will not be made public, so only you, me and the doctor will know. Oh, and the person who did it, of course.'

David could see the logic of that. 'Very well.'

André stared at him without speaking for a few moments, then picking up his brief case, he got to his feet.

'I shall be back shortly.'

David watched him leave the room, closing the door behind him. A few minutes later, the nurse returned and brought him a cup of tea and a croissant, which she fed to him slowly. By the time she'd finished, the policeman was back from his errand.

'Let me show you something, M'sieur,' said André, coming towards the bed and sitting on the chair vacated by the nurse. He reached into his brief case and produced some sheets of paper which he held so David could read them.

'I've just had the official record of the births in 1919 in Hameau Belchamps faxed through to me,' said André. 'Can you see your name on the list?'

David, wondering what 'faxed' meant, ran his eye down the page. It had a certain photographic quality, and plainly wasn't an original document. The word 'facsimile' came to mind: maybe that was what the detective meant? Nevertheless, the document looked official.

His name was not on it, of course. 'No.'

The policeman sat back. 'Do you want to see the births in 1918, or 1920? Very short lists, like the 1919 one. In three years, only twenty-seven babies were born. None of them called Marcel Dubois. You can look, or take my word for it.'

David tried to shrug. 'Somehow, it has been missed off the list. But you've seen my identity card, my passport?'

'I have indeed.'

David didn't reply. He wondered how long he would be held prisoner.

Sergeant André gazed at him as if he were trying to decide something.

'My colleagues in Bayeux seem to know who you are. Indeed, they're anxious to speak to you. Do you recognise the name Delphine?'

'No. I told you, I don't remember anything since 1943.'

'How about Oliver?'

'No.'

'Why do you think I am asking about these names?'

'I don't know. I don't know these people.'

André watched him carefully. 'Do you speak English, M'sieur Dubois?' asked the officer, switching to that language.

'Non.'

'Enough to understand the question though?'

David swore under his breath. It was carelessness like that which got agents killed.

'Un petit peu.'

'Delphine and Oliver may be your wife and son.'

David stared at him. 'No! My wife is… not Delphine.' He spoke in English, having decided there was little point in pretending he didn't understand the language.

André smiled approval of the admission. 'Really? We'll soon find out. We're checking your fingerprints against those found at a farm belonging to Marcel and Delphine Dubois. We think you and Delphine Delacourt were married in January 1944. Oliver was born two years later.'

David stared at him.

'What do you think your wife is called?'

David clamped his lips together and shook his head slightly. André reached into his brief case again and pulled out a bulky object. It looked like a camera, but not like any he'd seen before. He pointed it at David who blinked as the integral flashgun fired, followed a moment later by the whine of a motor and the ejection of a small square of thick paper from a slot under the lens.

'I'll see if the British police can put a name to your face,' André said. 'You speak English very well, enough to make me wonder about you.'

205

A chemical smell filled the room as he peeled the print apart a couple of minutes later. David could not keep the surprised look off his face at seeing the resultant coloured picture.

André leaned towards David. 'You know, in the absence of any information from you, I am trying to work out how you come to be here.' He tapped the sheaf of papers. 'You've seen that there's no record of your birth where and when you say it took place, and the last thing you remember was 1943. Tell me, M'sieur Dubois, what do you remember of 1943?'

David began to doubt his resolution at that point. There had been no thumbscrews, no electrical wires, just a series of polite questions. And undoubtedly, he'd lost his recollections of all the years between then and 1969. Nevertheless, until he found out if he was among friends and allies, or enemies, he had to be circumspect.

'Germany was at war with Britain, America and Russia and had occupied France.'

André nodded. 'Do you know who won?'

'No.'

André grinned. 'We did. That's to say, the allies. The British, Americans, Canadians, the Free French, the Russians. Hitler shot himself in May 1945.'

'And the Third Reich?'

'Died with him.'

David knew the Americans and Canadians had been gathering in Britain before he left, and there were plenty of Free French around, especially in London, where de Gaulle had been attempting to rally the French civilian population – and, of course, the Resistance – by broadcasts on the BBC. His sigh of relief had been heard by André.

'You know what I think, M'sieur?'

'No.'

'I think you were a British agent in 1943, and parachuted into France with false papers, which were so good, everyone accepted them as genuine.'

David sucked in a breath. 'I don't remember,' he said, and it was, for the moment, the truth.

'You will have to hire replacements,' said Oliver.

'Neither of them – well, Lisette – will be coming back?' asked Ramon, twisting his fingers together.

'I'm not having her back,' growled Oliver, 'she's a liar and a slut.'

'Slut…?' Ramon was openly sceptical.

Oliver glared at him. 'She was happy enough to go with me to my room – both of them were. And you don't think we simply read magazines and tourist information while we were there, do you?'

'Well, no. You said she's accused you of rape… rape and murder.' He couldn't look Oliver in the eye.

'Exactly. They went with me, voluntarily. When things went a bit wrong, and Anne-Marie had her accident, Lisette panicked and started rushing around the hotel blaming me and making a lot of serious but unfounded accusations.'

'Of course, of course,' Ramon nodded. 'I will place an advertisement in the newspaper today.' He glanced up shiftily and met Oliver's gaze. 'And what are the police doing about it?'

'It would seem, not much.'

Oliver had called in at the gendarmerie earlier that morning, after spending much of the night awake, while his mind considered his decision to take the attack to the enemy. Better to go to them, he decided, and, his mind made up, he'd slept for a couple of hours until the early morning sunlight lancing in at the window woke him.

'Inspector Dumonde please,' he'd said to the officer on the front desk.

He'd been obliged to wait for almost ten minutes, while other people came and went, but at last Dumonde appeared and took him into an interview room.

It was a bleak place, containing a table and four chairs. A uniformed police officer joined them, sitting next to the Inspector.

'I rather thought we might speak confidentially, in your office,' Oliver complained.

Dumonde glanced at the gendarme. 'We can speak freely in front of Jérôme, M'sieur Delacourt. Or M'sieur Dubois. Which is it to be?'

'I use my mother's maiden name,' Oliver told him. 'I... do not like Dubois.'

'But that is your legal name, is it not?'

'Yes.'

'And it is a perfectly common surname, is it not? No connotations...? Not *Jewish* for instance?'

Oliver half rose out of his chair, livid. 'How dare you say that? No! No! I am not Jewish, my name is not Jewish, I do not attend synagogue!'

Dumonde sat back and waited, gazing mildly, until Oliver's tirade had burnt itself out and he resumed his seat. Dumonde picked up a manila file which had been laying on the table and opened it, holding it up so Oliver could not see the contents, though *Oliver Dubois* was written in black permanent marker on the cover. Dumonde peered over it at Oliver.

'I believe you wished to tell me about events in the Hotel DeVries the night before last, M'sieur.'

Oliver frowned at him. 'What are you doing with that file? Why does it have my name on it?'

Dumonde arched his eyebrows and stared at the file as if seeing it for the first time.

'This file, M'sieur?' He waved one hand in the air, while continuing to hold the file with the other. 'This isn't a police file. It's not even current. I mean, there's nothing about you in here since 1969.'

Oliver's frown deepened. 'What does it say about me in 1969?'

Dumonde closed the file and laid it flat on the table, the long fingers of his hands interlaced on it. He shook his head. 'I can't go into that, M'sieur. Not without the permission of the DST.' He tapped the logo of France's internal security service on the cover.

Oliver stared at him. 'What have I ever done to interest the DST?' he demanded.

'I can't tell you that, either, M'sieur,' replied the policeman. 'What do *you* think might have brought you to the attention of the DST' – he peered at the front of the file – 'in 1968?'

Oliver's jaw muscles tightened. 'I thought you said 1969.'

'The file was opened in 1968.'

'Either way, I don't know.'

Dumonde smiled at him. It was bereft of warmth. 'Let us move on to the night before last. Tell me your version of what happened.'

'My version?'

Dumonde ignored Oliver's annoyance. 'Just tell me what happened.'

Oliver placed his hands on the table, fingers interlaced. 'The two women went with me to my room, where we engaged in some… some sexual behaviour. There was an accident. One of them died.'

'As simple and straightforward as that?' asked Dumonde. His expression said he didn't believe it. 'Most people engage in *sexual behaviour*, as you put it, but rarely does it kill anyone. Perhaps you would describe this apparently lethal form of it to me.'

Oliver's lower lip protruded for a moment. 'This is embarrassing, Inspector,' he said.

Dumonde shrugged. 'I understand how this might be, M'sieur, but we are both men of France. Men of the world, even. Nothing will go beyond these four walls if it has no bearing on the manner of the lady's death.'

'Well… but it does.'

Dumonde angled his head attentively. 'How, M'sieur?'

'We were engaging in a well-known, if little practised, form of increasing the intensity of sexual pleasure.'

'Go on,' urged Dumonde, resting his elbows on the table and his chin on his hands.

'You must understand, Anne-Marie consented to this.'

'To what, M'sieur? You still haven't told me.'

'Asphyxiophilia.'

Dumonde sat back briefly while he absorbed this, before resuming his position at the table. 'Perhaps you could just run through what that involves – just so I can check that it is what I think it is.'

'Cutting off the oxygen supply to the brain – briefly. It, uh, enhances… sexual pleasure.'

'How was this achieved with Anne-Marie?'

Oliver looked down at his hands. 'I covered her nose and mouth.'

'How were you positioned in relation to her at the time?'

Oliver raised one eyebrow as if he didn't quite believe the naïveté of the question. 'I was on top of her, giving her a fucking. What did you think?'

Dumonde held up his hands defensively. 'I have no pre-conceptions of the process, M'sieur.'

'The point of it is to enhance the pleasure of the orgasm. So, obviously, I was bringing her to orgasm at the same time.'

Dumonde nodded. 'As, indeed, you would.'

Oliver regarded him silently for a moment. 'As a matter of honour.'

Dumonde flipped open the file and glanced down. 'Of course, M'sieur.' He looked up, closing the file. 'How did Mademoiselle Anne-Marie feel about being suffocated?'

'She didn't mind. Didn't object.'

'Did she know what you intended before you began to suffocate her?'

Oliver shrugged. 'I suppose so. There was no secret about it.'

Dumonde leaned closer. 'Would she have been able to object *after* you started to suffocate her?'

'Of course.'

'How?'

'She would simply have to remove my hand from her face.'

'And she did not?'

'No.'

'Where were her hands while you were depriving her of oxygen?'

Oliver scowled. 'Around my waist. Encouraging me.'

'How do you account for the bruising around Anne-Marie's wrists?'

Oliver's scowl deepened. 'I have no idea how she got them. Look, Inspector, I am not a criminal. I grant that how I enjoy myself with young women isn't to everyone's liking, but the risks are understood, and she consented. Hell, they *both* consented to sex. Anne-Marie was happy about the asphyxia.'

'So you tell me.'

'She was! Do you realize that less than one per cent of accidental deaths arising from it occur to women?'

'Er, no. It's not the sort of information I would have at my fingertips,' replied Dumonde blandly. 'Perhaps you could tell me what percentage of all those on the receiving end of asphyxiophilia are women?'

Oliver stared at him. 'No, Inspector. I don't have such information at *my* fingertips.'

Dumonde sat back and touched the surface of the file as if seeking a new path of interrogation.

'Turning to the woman who survived, Lisette. She alleges that you raped her and Anne-Marie: you had sex with them without their consent. She is mistaken, then?'

'The girls met me in the hotel foyer. We had a couple of drinks then went up to my room. We had room service bring food. Afterwards, we had a few more drinks, and undressed. I suppose I was not at my best when I had sex with Lisette: I think I had overdone the alcohol, but in any case, she was first – and, I don't know if you find this, Inspector, but a first fuck is always a quick one with me. So, less satisfying for the girl. If she'd stayed a little longer, I would have taken more time with her after Anne-Marie.'

'Are you suggesting that Lisette's accusation arises from a feeling of dissatisfaction with your performance?'

Oliver shrugged. 'Perhaps. Who knows what is in the mind of a woman when she says such things.'

'She might be telling the truth.'

'Ah, but could you prove it, Inspector?'

'I haven't finished investigating the case yet, M'sieur Dubois – '

'Delacourt, if you please.'

'M'sieur Delacourt.' Dumonde frowned. 'That is still a matter of interest to me, you know. Why did you change your name?'

'It is a matter of personal choice, and none of your business, Inspector.'

Dumonde sat back and considered Oliver silently before telling him he could go, but not to leave the area without informing the police of his whereabouts.

A smile played around Oliver's lips as, a short time later, he stepped out into the street.

* * *

Two days after the events in the Hotel DeVries, Penny called Inspector Dumonde.

'I'm not trying to interfere, Inspector,' she told him, 'but I am worried about Lisette. She told me she has no family close enough to be with her, and I wondered if you could let me know where I might find her. I think she might appreciate a bit of company. She's been through a terrible ordeal.'

Dumonde was silent for a moment. 'I will contact her and see if she is prepared to talk to you. And, Madame Sanderson, do not think you can, uh, pull the wool over my eyes.

213

Please let me know if you discover anything that relates to the case.'

Half an hour later, Penny and Geoff met Lisette by the bronze statue of Catherine de Saint Augustin outside the Palais de Justice in Bayeux. Lisette wore large sunglasses, which did not completely obscure the bruises around her eyes. Her left cheekbone was swollen.

'Let's walk along the river,' suggested Penny. She glanced at Geoff. 'If you wanted to sit this out, you could park yourself over there on that bench.'

'I can take a hint,' said Geoff, leaving them.

They crossed the square to the wall which guarded the drop to the shallow river which flowed through the town, past what appeared to be an old *lavoir*.

'He seems a nice man,' Lisette observed when they were out of earshot.

Penny chewed her cheek. 'He *is,* but I don't know if I know him as well as I'd like.'

Lisette was silent for a moment. 'Like Oliver Delacourt,' she said. She glanced at Penny. 'Why did you want to see me?'

'Because you told me your parents were not around, and you have been through a dreadful experience, and I thought you might like to have someone to talk to who understands something of what it was like.'

Lisette stared at the ground as they strolled slowly along the riverside wall, avoiding occasional low-hanging tree branches. A hundred yards away, beyond the buildings which separated the square from the town, traffic and pedestrians made their way along a narrow, medieval street where small shops and cafés jostled for space.

'How is it that you can understand? Have you ever… ?'

Penny shook her head. 'Not personally, but until last year, when I retired, I had spent thirty years in the police service in Britain. I've spoken to a lot of rape victims and listened to their stories. I think I know how you must feel.'

'What do you expect me to tell you?'

Penny stopped and turned to her. 'Anything. Nothing? If you don't want to talk, that's fine, I understand. I thought, being a disinterested party in this, you might simply want to talk about it.'

There was a moment while Penny hitched herself onto the wall. Lisette sat beside her and clasped her hands.

'Anne-Marie and I worked for Oliver's company – you know he's a main distributor for luxury cars? There are showrooms all over France.' She waited for Penny's nod before continuing. 'He came into the office and seemed to be having a bit of a moan at our manager, Ramon, for not selling more cars. Ramon is a bit idle and a bit unimaginative when it comes to encouraging customers to sign on the dotted line, and Oliver more or less told him to buck his ideas up.'

'Bit of an "alpha male", was he?' Penny suggested.

Lisette blushed. 'Oh, yes! I have to admit, Anne-Marie and I were both fascinated by him.'

'He was a challenge to your femininity?'

The younger woman blushed, grinning. 'I think so. Oh, I admit it. We were both keen.'

'So – did he ask you both out?'

Lisette nodded. 'We both knew there was a strong likelihood of finishing up in bed with him, but… but, well, we've done it before. It's not illegal or anything.'

'I'm sure it isn't,' said Penny. 'So you all met up at the Hotel DeVries, and then? When did it begin to go wrong?'

'I don't drink alcohol that much, and I was drinking a straight fruit juice. Oliver ordered a couple of rounds of drinks, and he put vodka in mine. I noticed, of course, but I didn't want to upset the evening, so I drank it. After the second, both Anne-Marie and I were feeling very woozy, and by the time Oliver got us up to his room, we were both almost in a state of collapse.'

She licked her lips. 'I don't remember much after that, until early the next morning. By then, the police were all over the place. Apparently I'd raised the alarm with the Reception desk, but I don't remember any of it.'

'But you knew you'd been raped?'

'I'm sure. There were… signs.'

Penny nodded. 'Enough for a prosecution?'

'The police said not. The doctor who examined me couldn't rule out… you know… '

'Rough sex?'

Lisette pressed her lips together. 'Yes.' Without warning, her face crumpled, she covered her eyes with her hands and sobbed. 'Poor Anne-Marie. She was my friend.'

Penny put a comforting arm round the younger woman's shoulders and held her until she regained control.

'Was this the only time you'd been with Oliver?' she asked.

'Oh, yes. Other times he's visited the showroom, he would chat with Ramon for a while and then leave. It was just that, well, I think on this occasion, he was angry because of a fall-off in sales and he wanted to annoy Ramon enough to encourage him to do something about it. He used us – forced Ramon to agree to let us off work early to be with him – to make a point about who was really the boss.' She clasped her fingers in her lap again. 'We were stupid, I suppose, but he was powerful, attractive, and charming.'

'Altogether, irresistible to women,' said Penny.

Lisette rolled her eyes. 'We were fools – and now, Anne-Marie's dead.' She began to sob again, pulling a small handkerchief from the pocket of her coat.

Penny waited for the storm to abate before putting a final question.

'Do you remember seeing Oliver kill her?'

Lisette gulped air and swallowed, shaking her head. 'No. As I said, I don't remember anything between going upstairs with Oliver and Anne-Marie and sometime next morning, when the police were there and… and… '

'Okay,' said Penny, gently.

She'd heard enough to be fairly certain no prosecution for rape would be forthcoming. She didn't know how Oliver would fare in the matter of Anne-Marie's death. There were no reliable witnesses, and she'd been involved in enough cases of apparent murder to know that there was often a fine line between murder and manslaughter – and manslaughter and accidental homicide. She wondered what the police would be able to prove. She told Lisette none of these thoughts.

A nearby restaurant whose name celebrated the eleventh century Duke of Normandy and his wife, Mathilde, provided the three of them with coffee and *pains au chocolat,* after which, Lisette left Penny and Geoff.

'Well? What did you find out?' he asked.

She told him, concluding with her pessimistic view of any effective prosecution.

'I wish I knew how Dumonde's interview with Oliver went,' she continued.

Geoff nodded. His mobile phone rang. He glanced at the caller's name on its screen and excused himself, going to stand outside. Penny watched through plate glass windows decorated with small figures of Norman soldiers in the style of the Bayeux Tapestry. He seemed to be listening, and didn't appear to say much.

She decided it was time she tried to find out a bit more about her companion.

Christophe André had gone out of his way to take David home. The London Metropolitan Police had not been able to identify him from the Polaroid photograph he'd sent them. The hospital had pronounced him fit enough to leave their care, and André had taken him back to the farm.

They'd turned in at the gate through the hedge, where David had lain until picked up and taken into Vire. His car was still parked at the side of the track. André pulled up next to it.

'Recognise it?' he asked.

David, his head still swathed in bandage, looked at the vehicle blankly. 'No. Should I?'

'It's your car.'

David gave no sign of recognition, and André moved off, slowing as they approached the duck pond outside the walled yard of the farm.

'They found your wife's body in the water, M'sieur. Apparently accidental.'

David was sure he should be feeling very upset about the death of a wife, but he didn't, and it seemed shameful, almost inhuman, that he didn't even know how she looked. And somewhere, he had a twenty-three-year-old son, and couldn't remember anything about him, either.

André parked outside the house and rattled the door. It was locked. He turned an expectant look on David, who felt in the pockets of his jacket and found keys. He tried the likely ones until he found the one which worked. The door opened.

Both men stepped inside and André closed the door, switching on the light.

The room was cool though there were signs of recent occupation, and in a corner of the kitchen a large refrigerator hummed. David had to ask André what all the new appliances – fridge, microwave oven, television and even the modern cooker – were. André took the opportunity afforded by an ostensible search for instruction manuals to see if there were any more clues to David's life since 1943.

He checked inside the fridge to see that there was a stock of food, some obviously bought fairly recently. He supposed Delphine might have been shopping in the days just before her death.

'You will be all right here, alone, M'sieur?' he asked David.

'I'm sure I shall sort this lot out.' David suddenly frowned. 'This is definitely my place?'

'Quite definitely,' replied André, grinning. He moved towards the door and turned back. 'There is just one thing, M'sieur.'

David faced him. 'Yes?'

'When I asked your name, you told me it was Marcel Dubois. Indeed, this property is owned by Marcel and Delphine Dubois – well, only Marcel, I suppose, now.'

'Yes?'

'Do you remember your real name? Your English name?'

It would, thought David, have been so simple to answer him. He was no longer concerned about whether the Gestapo were still at large in western Europe – there was no denying the passage of time and the friendliness of the European nations towards each other... But if he gave André his real name, checks would be made in Britain, and that might result in further complications, and not only for himself. There was the certainty that he had married Ann Hacker in 1942, and that when he had left for France, she had been three months pregnant with a child due in the Autumn of '43. There was every chance they were still alive, every chance that, like himself, they had made fresh lives for themselves.

It would not be right, he reasoned, for them to be shaken out of the accepted certainties of their pasts and faced with the prospect of taking back into their family the man who had gone out of their lives twenty-five years before.

He gazed levelly at André. 'No,' he said.

The policeman held his gaze for a moment, then nodded, turned and left.

David decided that he must go to Britain, back to Bletchley and the house he'd shared with Ann, and see what he could learn about his English wife and their child. Always assuming they hadn't moved away.

But his first job would be to figure out how to work the cooker so he could make himself a meal.

* * *

A week passed. David had mastered the equipment found in a modern kitchen and discovered documents and other things in the house which indicated that he had been a schoolteacher in the years since the war. He marvelled at the fact that so much had happened to him in that period ... and then felt depressed because he could not remember them.

He had recovered his car. Even that had been something of a learning experience because the controls had changed. He used the ignition key to start the engine, instead of a button. He did not have to double-declutch as he changed down a gear. Acceleration and braking were both much more positive than his old pre-war Austin Seven. He'd driven into Vire, remembering to drive on the right, for food, and discovered that not only was there a good deal more motor traffic than he'd ever seen before, but food shopping was a different experience altogether, everything these days under the one roof.

As the shock of being attacked, and the injuries he had sustained, began to wear off, he had become increasingly concerned about his new present and the future. Two days earlier, some of his worries were answered.

A large black saloon pulled into the yard and parked next to his Citroen. The squarish radiator grill was distinctive, and the car mascot, a small silver circle containing a three-pointed star, confirmed the car as being a Mercedes Benz. David watched from the kitchen window as the dark-haired man with a small moustache climbed out from behind the wheel and, with a glance at the Citroen, strode into the farm-house.

David had expected him to knock and was surprised when he walked straight in.

The man saw David and stopped. 'What are you doing here, father?'

David, struggling with his own shock at meeting his son, registered a flicker of fear crossing the young man's face. Sergeant André had told him Oliver had been questioned in connection with the death of Delphine Dubois.

'I believe I live here.'

'I thought you'd gone – ' Oliver began, but stopped himself abruptly. 'Where've you been?'

'In hospital in Vire. Seems someone attacked me.'

'Do you know who?'

David shook his head. 'No.' He filled the kettle and set it to boil. 'Do you want some tea? For the record, I can't re-member anything between 1943 and coming round four or five days ago – I'm a bit muzzy about the time still.'

It didn't escape his notice that Oliver looked brighter.

'You can't remember *anything*?'

'No. If I think back a week, I remember a day in 1943.'

Oliver's eyebrows arched. 'Really? You don't know who attacked you? But you remember 1943 clearly?'

'Much of it. Till I was sent here.'

'Sent? Who sent you?'

'The British Government.'

Oliver sat at the table and waited while his father brewed the tea and put milk in two mugs. 'Oh, yes! Of course, you're British.' There was a sneer in his voice which was not lost on David.

'Does that bother you?' he asked.

'Not so much now,' Oliver replied.

'Did it once?'

Oliver dropped his gaze briefly. 'It was a surprise when I found out.'

David sipped. He was very curious to learn something of the last twenty-six years, but for a reason he couldn't quite fathom, was unwilling to ask outright. There was something odd about Oliver's behaviour: it might simply be that, in his mid-twenties, he was well past the age at which he could be thought to have become his own man, and would have formed his own patterns of behaviour and personality. Yet, David felt sure there should be something of himself in his son, and he couldn't see it. Maybe, he thought, it was simply because Oliver had no context in his mind, appearing, as it were, fully-formed, with all his youth and upbringing, and the experiences of childhood, completely hidden.

'When was that?' he asked.

Oliver stared at him, his colour deepening. 'A couple of weeks ago.'

David was amused at what seemed to be a growing embarrassment on the part of his son. 'Really? You had no idea until then?'

'None.'

Perhaps not so much embarrassment as anger.

'So your mother kept my secret.' He felt touched that the woman whom he could not remember must have loved him greatly to keep a secret, which could have seen her shot by the Gestapo, for all these years.

'Yes, she did,' Oliver suddenly spat, banging his mug so hard down onto the table that tea spilled in a large puddle. 'And ruined my political ambitions. You and she together!'

'What on earth – ? How could that have "ruined your political ambitions", son? What "political ambitions" are these?'

Oliver scowled and sipped his tea, not bothering to mop up the spillage. He screwed up his face.

'Ugh! I hate tea. It's so *English!*'

'Actually, it's Indian or Chinese in the main.'

Oliver set his mug down and pointed a finger at him. 'You see! That's just what I mean. You British seem to think you can tell the rest of the world what to think!'

David sat back in his chair, slightly amused. 'I was only pointing out that tea itself isn't English. And plenty of French people enjoy drinking it, too – or did, last I remember.'

He waited a moment, but his son showed no signs of answering his question.

'Tell me honestly, Oliver: did we not get on well?'

Oliver looked down at his empty mug. 'Not that well. No.'

'That's a pity,' said David.

'Why?'

'Fathers and sons should get on reasonably well. So should sons and mothers.' It was David's turn to stare into his mug of tea. 'Tell me about your mother.'

The ensuing silence was so long he looked up to see if Oliver was all right. It occurred to him that his son might be missing her enormously, just as he felt sure he would be missing her himself, if he could remember her. But Oliver was looking angry again, and his colour was deepening. Not the reactions David would have expected. Suddenly his son pushed his chair back, away from the table, and strode out of the door. By the time David reached the kitchen window, Oliver was gunning the Mercedes into life and turning it round in a flurry of yard dirt. A moment later, the car shot through the gate and turned towards the highway.

Damn! thought David. He'd wanted to find out about his past life, and now this chance had gone. He expected there'd be others. In the meantime, Oliver's aberrant behaviour raised a few questions of its own.

He washed up and went upstairs to his bedroom, the one he must have shared with Delphine for so long.

He sat on the bed. He'd slept there since his release from hospital. This time, he simply sat there and slowly turned his head, looking at every square inch of the walls, the floor, the ceiling, the furniture. He had looked before, but now there was an added intensity in his scrutiny. So far, he'd accepted his loss of memory as a fact of life, a side-effect of the injury to his head. Now, he began desperately to wish he could remember the missing years.

There had to be answers to questions like: who attacked him? What caused Oliver's strange behaviour? What had happened to Delphine? He'd spent twenty-six years with her, and had absolutely no recollection of them. For them to have been together so long, he reasoned, they must have been happy years. He wanted to know what she was like, how much they loved each other; about his son's childhood… All the answers, he felt sure, were locked inside his mind, if only he could find the key. The most pressing question, the one he'd meant to ask Oliver, was when and where was Delphine's funeral? Was somebody – Oliver? – arranging it?

He found himself staring at a chest of drawers full of Delphine's things. He had not felt like touching them since he'd come home, but now he realised he needed the stimulus to his memory touching, feeling, smelling her things might provide. He crossed the room, slowly, and pulled open the top drawer.

He found himself looking at two trays, one containing little pots of perfume and cosmetics, the other pieces of jewellery – earrings, some set with pearls, one pair sparkling with what looked like genuine diamond, though David wasn't expert enough to be sure. A pair of gold chains, one with a gold crucifix, the other with a locket. He flicked it open with a thumbnail and saw pictures of himself and a boy who was probably Oliver in the two halves.

He found a lump had grown in his throat, and he had to swallow hard. He put the chain back and closed the drawer.

The second and third drawers contained clothing – lingerie, blouses and jumpers, and some T-shirts, all neatly ironed and folded. He let his fingers rub gently on the fabrics, feeling the different textures, and inhaled the scent of washing powder. Then he opened the bottom drawer.

Two large photograph albums filled half of it, and the other half contained five five-year diaries. He lifted them all out, and took them over to the bed.

The oldest photographs dated from the beginning of 1944. They were pictures of his and Delphine's wedding. Black and white, and still fresh – David guessed they'd been kept in the darkness of the drawer for most of the time, which had protected them from the bleaching effect of sunlight – they had been taken by someone who clearly had skills in wedding portraiture. *Genet fils* was printed on the reverse of one picture which had fallen out of its mounts, with an address in Sainte Marguerite-en-Bessin. He wondered if Monsieur Genet or his sons were still around.

Somebody, probably Delphine, he guessed, had captioned the photographs, writing in a neat hand, in ink.

Here, at least, was some kind of past. If he couldn't remember himself, there were the photographs. By reference to them, he could begin to piece together bits of his life since the war.

He set the albums aside, meaning to go through them systematically, later, and turned to the diaries. They were completed in the same neat handwriting as the captions, and began with two notes written out of order, the year after the war ended. In the first, Delphine had described finding him in a field on the farm in early 1943, unconscious, bleeding from a bad injury to his head, and a parachute flapping in the breeze. She'd released the parachute and hastily buried it, then gone back to the farm to fetch her father, to help carry their unconscious visitor indoors. This note also mentioned how she'd nursed David, and then, at Christmas, a small group of German soldiers had arrived at the farm and shot her father.

In the second, he read of Delphine's miscarriage, when they'd been out with the local Resistance on the eve of D-Day, and that the leader, a young Communist called Albert

Lebrun, had suffered a glancing blow to the temple from a German soldier. They had still managed to lay explosives and blow up the railway line, though had had to leave the area rapidly, without seeing the extent of the damage they'd caused.

David flicked through later entries, and decided that his next few days would be spent trying to catch up on his past. Before putting the diaries away, he found the last one, and read Delphine's final entry.

I cannot understand what has become of my dear son. Marcel and I tried hard to raise him as a good and respectful child, considerate of others – and especially of his family. But he has come home in a strange mood. We have not seen him for many months, and all he wants to talk about is a political party he belongs to, the FAF. From what he's said, they sound thoroughly unpleasant, neo-Nazis. Oliver intends to stand as their candidate in the July elections.

Marcel finally got round to telling Oliver he was English, and that Oliver therefore is half English. You would have thought the sky was falling in! Oliver was furious, and began spouting some terrible Nazi-type things about racial purity, finally concluding that he would have to withdraw his candidacy in the election.

He went back to Caen, I suppose, to tell the party members, but before he left, I suggested to Oliver that he might like to come back and let us talk, just the two of us, after Marcel has gone on his annual trip to England on Monday..

Only blank pages followed. So, thought David, he had been going to England… Of course! The ferry tickets! And Oliver had been due to return home. André had said that Delphine's body was discovered by a neighbour called Le Greq, as near as anyone could figure, on the same day David had been attacked. It seemed an odd coincidence, he thought, but one he would sleep on. His head was beginning to ache and the scars beneath the bandages itched. He put the diaries and albums back in the drawer and got ready for bed.

* * *

There were moments in the past twenty-five years when Albert Lebrun had been tempted to reveal his slight deception. If it had not been for the better treatment given the totally blind over the partially sighted in 1944, he might never have lied about his vision. As often happened when he dozed in a chair, listening to music on his old radio, he recalled the night before D-Day, when he'd taken Marcel and Delphine Dubois with him on a mission to destroy a small railway bridge.

There had been no real problem until Delphine went into labour. The child, he recalled, was already dead. They'd been expecting her to deliver the remains and placenta sometime soon, and he'd been dubious about having her along for exactly the reason that she might drop while they were out.

Still, they'd been friends and patriots, and he'd allowed Delphine to go, mainly because he needed Marcel as back-up and he wouldn't leave her. But at the critical moment, with German patrols about, she started with the stomach cramps. He told Marcel to stay with her, in the event, but he had to come after him because he had the back-packs containing not only the explosives, but also the morphine Delphine now needed.

As Marcel felt for the morphine in the darkness, they heard a twig crack away to their right. Albert put a finger to his lips and used signals to direct Marcel back along the track and into the cover offered by the leafy branches. He pressed himself close to the bole of a tree, merging into its shadow. A moment later, a German soldier, clutching a machine pistol emerged from the undergrowth between them. He moved a couple of yards towards Albert, who had slipped a fisherman's knife from his belt and was clutching it in his right hand, ready to strike.

Suddenly, there was a muffled sneeze which Albert guessed was Marcel. The soldier turned and began to move

227

towards the sound. Albert sprang out of hiding, ran up behind the soldier and grabbed his face with his left hand, covering the man's mouth and nose, while simultaneously driving the sharp point of his blade into the soldier's back. He followed the first stab with a second to the man's neck, feeling blood spurt over his hand. The man fell, still clutching his gun. As the butt hit the ground, a single shot burst from its muzzle, striking Albert on the temple and making him see stars for a moment. He shook his head as Marcel rejoined him.

'Go! Go!' Albert commanded in a loud whisper, pointing Marcel back up the track towards where they'd left Delphine. Marcel grabbed the dead soldier's machine pistol as he went past him, while Albert turned and headed for the railway track. He did his best to plant his charges where experience had taught him they would do most damage, set the timers and ran quickly to his friends.

At the edge of the trees, where Delphine crouched, he caught up with Marcel in time to see a tableau in which another German was pointing his gun at her. Marcel aimed the captured machine pistol from his hip and fired.

Albert barely had time to notice Delphine's *déshabillée*, while he stared hard into the darkness to see if any more soldiers were coming their way. The shots would have alerted them and they would be there soon. He glanced down. Marcel had injected morphine into Delphine's leg and a moment later, the foetus appeared. Albert had never seen anything like the emergence of that proto-child and the sight threatened to hold his attention. He dragged his eyes back and scanned the surrounding darkness. Eventually, Marcel tapped his elbow.

'We're done. Let's go.' He threw the machine pistol down beside the dead soldier, picked up his wife and began carrying her back to the farm.

They had not gone far along the road when a massive growl and crack behind them, which caused the ground to shake, indicated that the explosives had blown. Albert only hoped they'd done their job and destroyed the railway bridge.

An hour before dawn, Albert, having barely paused to strip off his clothes before climbing between the cold sheets, had been in his bed barely thirty minutes. Downstairs, the door was smashed in and boots trampled up the bare wooden stairs to his room. Four German soldiers dragged him from his bed and threw him on the floor. He looked up to see a man in a civilian overcoat and black fedora staring down at him.

'You are under arrest, M'sieur Lebrun, charged with conspiring to carry out acts of terrorism against the lawful authority. Treason against the German Reich, in other words, M'sieur Lebrun.' He glanced at the soldiers. 'Bring him!' he said, turned, and led the way outside to the waiting van.

Albert was dragged downstairs and thrown in the back.

After an uncomfortable journey, the van stopped and backed up before the doors were opened and Albert dragged out. His knees and feet were bleeding, but he had a good idea this was only the first blood of much.

They were in a building in Bayeux, one of the ancient ones. He guessed as they dragged him down a flight of worn stone steps they were probably in the basement as there was no natural light. The place smelt damp, and the odour of excrement and urine drifted in the fetid air.

He was taken into a room containing two chairs. One, on which he was made to sit, was bolted to the floor. It was of tubular steel construction, and the bare metal was cold against his naked body. The man in the fedora sat opposite him while one of the soldiers finished tying his ankles and wrists to the chair.

The soldiers finished and at a sign from the man whom Albert guessed was Gestapo, they left the room. The sound of their footsteps faded away down the long corridor outside.

For a few moments, Fedora, as Albert thought of him, kept very still and simply gazed at his prisoner. Albert gazed back. The gunshot wound at his temple had begun to bleed again. His head ached, the grazes on his knees and feet were bleeding and painful.

Suddenly, the ground shook repeatedly with a series of detonations Albert guessed were not too far away. Fedora did not react to them at first, but the silence was broken and he began to speak, in fluent French.

'I don't want to make this any more painful that it has to be, M'sieur Lebrun, but I need some information from you.'

Albert simply gazed at him.

'You will be aware, perhaps, that you are the last of several leaders of the local Maquis.'

Albert stared, silent.

'We have been meaning to pick you up for some time, but to be frank, more important things have kept us busy. You were never dangerous enough to warrant much effort. We knew who you were, where you were and what you were doing. Several times, we nearly caught you red-handed.

'So, you see, we know all the important stuff.'

'Then why are you talking to me? Why not simply take me outside and shoot me, so you can get on with anything you think is more important?'

'Albert, Albert! Do you mind if I call you Albert? No? Good.' He stood up and looked down on his prisoner. 'You think the British are your friends, don't you?'

Albert said nothing, kept his face expressionless.

'You think that when the war is over, they'll be the winners, and thank you for everything you've done?' He got up and went to a corner of the room, returning with a switch of the type used by horse riders, and, resuming his seat, he lightly whipped the palm of one hand with the loop of leather at the end.

'I think you will be disappointed. Indeed, our meeting was inevitable, whether today, tomorrow or in a few days' time.'

Albert squinted through the blood which had run into his eye, shaking his head to try to clear it, but making it spin and throb as the price. Everything, he realised, would now have a price. For anything useful he gave Fedora, there would be some kind of small reward – a drink of water, some food, a cloth with which to wipe himself. Every refusal to help would be met by punishments, and the rumours were that on that front, at least, the Gestapo did not stint.

'So, you must want something,' he said, 'or I'd be dead already.'

There were more detonations and this time running footsteps along the corridor outside the room. Fedora glanced at the door. Suddenly, he moved past Albert, who heard the door open. The running footsteps were louder. Fedora spoke to someone in German, then the door closed and he came back into the room.

'It seems your British and American friends have launched a raid on our coastline. Unfortunately, their plan, to draw our troops away from the Pas de Calais, westwards into Normandy, will fail, as *Generalfeldmarschall* von Rundstedt knows that the invasion will land in the east, where it will be met by his massed battalions. Would you agree with his assessment?'

He bent until his face was close to Albert's.

'Of course,' said Albert, realising that perhaps what Fedora needed was some confirmation of where the invasion forces would make landfall. The tip of the switch lashed against his cheek.

'I really do not have time for gentle persuasion, Albert. Now tell me: is the raid on the Normandy beaches the invasion, or just a diversion? I have to tell you that *Feldmarschall* Rommel thinks – or at least thought, before he went off on leave – that the invasion is coming here. Who is right, Albert? Von Rundstedt or Rommel?'

Albert suddenly realised that he might hold the key to the deployment of a lot of German troops, or he might not. But it seemed, without a doubt, the longer he could hold out without telling Fedora what he wanted to know, the better chance the Allies would have of confirming their bridgehead.

Inside, he exulted in the knowledge that the bombing marked the beginning of the liberation of France. He had only to hang on, teasing Fedora as much as possible, for as long as he could. It was going to be even more painful and unpleasant, he knew, but France's freedom could not be bought cheaply.

He smiled at Fedora. The German stared as if surprised. An alarm bell was ringing somewhere in the building, and more explosions could be heard, creeping nearer. Fedora whipped the switch across Albert's face. He did it again, and a third time. Blood was dripping into both eyes now, with the bullet wound fully opened-up again, and a deep gash over his other eye.

Someone banged at the door and shouted. Albert shook his head to clear his vision. Fedora was finally showing emotion, his face reddened and his lips open in a snarl.

'This is your last chance, Lebrun,' he screamed, all pretence of civility gone. 'Tell me, are we being invaded here?'

Albert couldn't shrug because of his bonds, so he just smiled mutely at his interrogator.

'Would you believe me if I said von Runstedt is right? Or would it be more credible if I supported Rommel's view?' he asked. 'One thing I think is true.'

'What?'

Albert summoned up a smile from somewhere. 'We are definitely being invaded.'

'I know that!' snapped Fedora.

Albert was pleased to hear it. 'Your commanders will have to decide where – whatever I say – assuming I know the answer to your question, which of course I don't, being only a poor French farm worker – you will not believe. But one thing I know.'

Fedora glowered at him. The noise in the corridor had resolved itself into a series of isolated shouts, perhaps orders, and instances of running feet. Suddenly the building shook with a loud detonation.

Fedora grabbed Albert's balls. 'What? What do you know?' he screamed.

'That if the British or Americans catch you here with me, you'll die.'

Fedora, to Albert's relief, released his grip. Spittle was running from his lips down his chin and his eyes were reddened and staring. He brushed his face with the back of his hand. Footsteps stopped in the doorway and an order was barked. Albert understood only the word, *schnell!* – quickly! Fedora responded by putting down the switch. For a moment, Albert felt relief wash through him.

The last thing he saw was the Gestapo man's pulling two long hatpins from the top of his lapel. He jammed them into Albert's eyes.

He could see nothing. The din filling the building was growing to deafening intensity. Footsteps ran along the corridor and Albert, wracked with pain, more than he'd ever thought possible, nevertheless registered that the door was still open. He felt alone, as if Fedora had gone. He could not blink properly or shut his eyes because of the pins skewering his eyeballs, and at some point he lost control of his bladder.

Gradually, the footsteps faded and the noises died away. From time to time, another stick of bombs would land somewhere nearby and make the floor shudder. Albert, unable to move from his chair, sat and waited for the end he was sure would come.

It had been hours, he remembered, before English voices filled the corridor. Moments later, he felt someone near him, and the man yelled for a medic. He remembered his bonds being released, but they wouldn't let him touch his eyes or remove the hatpins. He was put on a stretcher and taken outside, gratified that at least he could tell it was daylight.

He found out later that his rescuers had been British soldiers who had entered Bayeux early in the morning of the 7th June, making it the first town in France to be liberated. His eyes gradually recovered to an extent, but his vision was restricted to very close range. It had been shortly after that he'd heard somebody saying the totally blind were being given better benefits than the partially sighted. It was hardly difficult to persuade the authorities to certify him as totally blind thereafter.

He felt that, apart from the tangible benefits, keeping his true condition a secret might one day help him find the person who had obviously betrayed him, and caused the arrest and murder of many others in the resistance movement.

He glanced at the clock. Time to join Lafarge in the bar for their regular lunchtime tryst. He was a good raconteur, and when he talked about the war, it helped Albert remember what the world looked like before his time in the Gestapo cell. And while Lafarge hadn't been a formal member of any resistance group, he knew most of them because he would patch them up when they were injured during their subversive activities. One day, thought Albert, he might have a story to tell which might point the finger at one or other of the Maquis, probably someone not a Leader themselves.

He put on his jacket and beret, picked up his white stick from the place it occupied beside the door, and let himself out into the street.

The English Channel was having one of its better days, the water only slightly choppy, due to a light westerly breeze, and the *Pride of The Manche*, a diplomatic choice of name if ever Penny'd heard one, was as steady as a rock. She had ventured on part of the deck almost unoccupied except for an elderly man some distance away who seemed to be travelling alone, apparently lost in thought. She leant against the rail and peered down into the white foam caused by the ship's forward motion. Behind her, Geoff emerged from the bar clutching a pint of beer in one hand and a brandy and soda in the other. He held out the small balloon glass.

'Here – good for settling the stomach,' he said, shaking his head in what looked like amazement that she thought it still possible she might suffer from motion sickness, even in a flat calm.

'Thanks,' she said, standing up to face him. 'I daresay you find it amusing, but I was built for dry land. Preferably, *hot* and dry land. Here, it's neither.'

'We could have stayed on,' he said.

'No I couldn't. I didn't think we'd be away as long as we have,' Penny replied. 'I have things to do at home.'

'Shame,' he muttered laconically. 'I was enjoying our little holiday. Will we ever know what becomes of your half-brother?'

She turned to look down at the passing sea. 'I doubt he'll be prosecuted for either matter. From what I gather, there's just not going to be sufficient evidence.'

Geoff sipped more beer. 'I wonder what became of your father.'

'I was wondering that. After all, I set myself the task of finding his grave, or at least what happened to him, and it seems he went missing the same day Delphine's body was found.' She drained her glass. 'If it was anyone else, I'd certainly suspect him of killing her and running away to hide.'

'But you don't think that?'

'No. It doesn't fit in – he was a hero, the sort of bloke his country turned to when it needed him. From what my mother told me, he was a loving and gentle man. He wouldn't have killed his wife.'

'Something must have happened when he parachuted into France, so that he didn't make contact to say he'd arrived, either then or any time later. And if he was married, and such a good bloke, why did he marry again?'

Penny was silent for a moment, considering. 'Here's a thought: in 1943, parachute design was still new technology. There'd been very little use of them, except among daredevils doing circus stunts from balloons. I know the first use by British soldiers was a commando-style raid on a German radar post near the Normandy coast, not very distant in time from when my father was sent there.

'Anyway, I was wondering if he had an accident, a bad landing. There were many instances of that happening, especially during the massive air drops on D-Day. Did he lose his memory? That would account for failing to make contact, and probably marrying again, if he couldn't remember his past life.'

'The only ID he'd be carrying was the forged one he'd be supplied with by SOE.'

'Yes. Of course, I'm guessing that he retained his knowledge of the language, and was simply accepted as a native.'

'But what happened to his parachute? If he landed badly and lost his memory, he'd wonder what he was doing attached to that.'

'Or he landed badly and was knocked out, and found by someone...' Penny looked at him. 'Someone like Delphine, who realised what and who he was, and got rid of the evidence, then somehow managed to look after him until he came round.'

Geoff turned back and looked westwards, his grey eyes catching the sunlight reflected off the water in silvery flashes.

'Chances are, we'll never find out exactly.'

'I'd be happy enough to find out what became of him.'

They watched a cargo ship trundle through their wake. The old man appeared to be snoozing in the dappled sunlight, his hat pulled down over his face.

Penny looked sideways at Geoff, leaning on the rail, and felt a moment's envy that he should look so comfortable, as if he belonged.

'Tell me about your time in the SAS,' she asked him, turning to stare at the same horizon.

He glanced at her briefly. 'Oh, you know. Just the odd foray into hot places. Joined the army in 1968 after a few years bumming around in civvies. Got accepted into The Regiment in 1973. Nearly killed me, getting in,' he added, punctuating the remark with a long swig of his beer.

Penny had locked on to his use of the word "civvies". He hadn't said, "civvy street", which would be service slang for a civilian occupation. The word he'd used simply meant, in jargon, that he was not wearing uniform. She was not going to pursue the matter at this stage, she decided. Better just to let him talk.

'Hot places? How hot?'

'Tropical.' He turned to face her. 'I spent a lot of my time in Belize.'

'Why was the SAS in Belize?'

'There was trouble with Guatemala, next door. They'd been squabbling over the border and Guatemala's claim to most of the country for over a century. The army was there to try and prevent their fight upsetting trade, especially with the mother country.'

'That would be Britain?'

'Belize used be British Honduras and part of the empire right up to 1981. Even then, British troops were stationed there for some time afterwards.'

'All of which sounds like work for the regular army. What was the SAS doing?'

Geoff sipped his beer again and turned to stare westwards, towards the Atlantic Ocean. 'Just keeping an eye on things.'

Penny sensed he would say no more about his own involvement, either its nature or extent.

'Did you operate in any other theatres?' she asked. Apparently, "theatre" was the appropriate word to use for places of combat. She thought it sounded like yet another military and political euphemism, like referring to soldiers who were killed as "the fallen", making war sound less grim than it was. She used the word because she didn't want to make her revulsion at the thought of warfare obvious, at least not while she was trying to get Geoff to tell her about his past.

'Zimbabwe – Southern Rhodesia. You'll remember Ian Smith declaring UDI, and the country deciding to be a Republic in 1970.'

'Vaguely,' she smiled.

'Well, the British Government was torn. Some were sympathetic to the white minority, led by Smith, and others saw black majority rule in a new democracy as the way ahead. These feelings were echoed in the country itself, and on top of that, there were the tribal differences dating back to before the whites arrived, with half the country being Shona and the other half being predominantly Matabele. For some years after UDI, we were there trying to keep the peace, to some extent, but mainly to do what we could to protect the white farmers, who drove the country's economy, from predations by the black activists.'

'And then? What did you do after Zimbabwean independence?'

'Oh, I was back to London for a desk job.'

She looked at him, studying his expression, its blandness not convincing her that he had told her everything of interest.

'Will you ever tell me what you did?' she asked him, a hint of the frustration she felt in her voice.

He grinned at her. 'Would you ever tell me all that you've done?'

'Most of it,' she told him. Of course, she couldn't talk about her spell in Special Branch, when for a time she'd been part of the Royal Protection Team. 'All right!' she added, 'I suppose I have to accept that some of what you did was confidential. But surely not as much as all that?'

He smiled enigmatically and finished his beer.

Penny turned to look out to sea as well. She'd see if her former colleague, Stephanie Tabor, could find out anything about him. They'd done a spell in SB together, so she might still have some influence there, and surely Special Branch should have some way of finding out stuff about former SAS officers?

It was always entirely possible that Geoff Pearson was simply teasing her. But why would he do that? she wondered.

* * *

'The real question is, why you're so interested.' Stephanie Tabor studied Penny over the rim of her coffee cup at their favourite pavement café.

'Because he's not telling me everything, and I want to know. Is he hiding something I wouldn't approve of, or is he just… well, teasing me?'

Stephanie arched her eyebrows. 'Oh! You've reached the teasing-each-other stage? Must be getting serious.' She looked down into the depths of her coffee. 'Have you been practising signing your cheques *Penny Pearson?*'

Penny pursed her lips. 'Don't be ridiculous. I don't think of Geoff that way.'

Stephanie smiled. 'How *do* you think of him?' She poked the fleshy part of Penny's arm. 'Hey, have you two done the deed? You know, slept with him?'

Penny frowned. 'No we have not.' A twinge of conscience got to her and honesty made her admit, 'Well, we haven't actually done the deed, as you put it. But we did actually spend a night in the same bed.' She saw the smirk spread across Steph's face. 'And before you say a word, it wasn't True Romance or anything, Geoff was simply staying over because somebody had been through my stuff while we were out. Sort of on guard dog detail.'

'Oh, I love it. Was he all masterful and protective?'

'No, he just lay there beside me. He was still wearing his trousers when he got under the covers, and I had to tell him to take them off.'

Stephanie couldn't hold back a snort into her coffee, which splashed onto her blouse and trousers.

'Serves you right!' said Penny. 'You're reading far too much into a minor incident.'

Steph dabbed herself dry with a paper tissue from her jacket pocket. She appeared to be struggling to maintain her composure. 'So after you got him out of his pants, did you – you know! – well, accidents can happen under the bedclothes when you can't quite see where everything is. Was he, like, hard?' She leaned close to Penny's ear. 'Big?'

'Stephanie Tabor! I have no idea. We just turned over and went to sleep. I told you, we haven't done anything yet.'

'Yet? Not even kissed?'

Penny rested her hands on her hips. 'No! Well, once. He kissed me goodnight after we'd been to the theatre, but I reckon he was all stirred up by the leading actress.'

'If he was stirred up outside your house, it was because of you, nobody else. I'm sorry, Penny – perhaps you've forgotten – but they don't stay stirred up for that long without continual encouragement.'

'Well, it was only a kiss on the cheek, nothing passionate.'

Steph put her empty cup down in its saucer. 'Okay: I can see you're very resistant to this line of questioning – which is, of course, very suspicious in itself – so let's change the subject and get to business. I'll see what I can find out, if anything, but you know what SB are like – not very forthcoming. Why do you want to know, really?'

'I want to feel able to trust him, and I don't know whether I can. Also, he gets phone calls he won't take in front of me, and I wonder what's going on. With his background in the SAS, my guess is he has been involved in covert work for years. He says he's retired now, but from what? And is he really retired or is he still working for somebody.'

'Somebody?'

'MI5 or 6.'

Stephanie arched her fine eyebrows. 'You don't want much, do you! Okay, I'll see what I can find out.'

Penny put a hand on Steph's arm. 'You know it's only information I want, I'm not trying to interfere in anything?'

'I understand. Give me a few days. I'll call you.'

Penny nodded and smiled. 'Shame about the coffee stains on your blouse.'

'I should really send you the laundry bill,' replied Steph as she rose to her feet. 'See you later.'

Penny took a while longer to finish her coffee. As she drained the cup, she barely registered a man who seemed to be window shopping a hundred yards away, where the paved pedestrian area met the traffic. It seemed as though he looked at her, but a moment later he had disappeared round the corner.

David closed the last of Delphine's diaries and placed it carefully back in the box which now contained all the others. Tears ran down his face, and not for the first time. He looked around the warm kitchen, where the log fire crackled cosily, belching occasional puffs of smoke into the room. He felt the need to get away. The logical place, it seemed to him, was to pay another visit to England, as two years had elapsed since the last time he'd been.

But first, he needed to get the all-clear to travel from Doctor Solon, who had continued to see him at monthly clinics, following his discharge from the hospital. This time, she'd phoned to say she would drop in at the farm, since she was in the area. David's existence was a fairly lonely one, and he had begun to enjoy his meetings with the doctor.

He heard the sound of tyres on the gravel in the farm yard and went over to the window. Édith Solon drove a black Mercedes, similar to Oliver's. He hadn't been near the place for five months, David reflected, opening the door as the doctor approached it. For once, she was not carrying her customary slim briefcase, and had dispensed with her usual business suit. Today she was wearing a dress in a plain deep yellow colour, with a brown jacket he thought seemed much more fashionable than anything he'd seen her wear before. It suited her very well, he decided appreciatively.

'Welcome, Doctor,' he said in French, as he allowed her past him into the room. He shut the door and picked up a newspaper.

'I'm sorry about the smoke,' he said, waving the paper around to dispel the cloud.

Édith sat in one of the dining chairs, smiling. 'As your doctor, I feel sure I should advise you to stop smoking,' she said.

He sat opposite her with an answering smile. 'You need to direct your advice to the fire: I already gave up.' He put the paper down. 'Can I get you a drink?'

She seemed somewhat diffident, he thought, unlike her normal, professional manner.

'Is something the matter?' he asked.

'No – no! I am fine.' She looked up, into his eyes. Her hands clasped and unclasped each other nervously. He placed a hand over one of hers to still it, but withdrew it at once, as inappropriate behaviour.

'David,' she began, and seemed to hesitate.

'Yes?'

'I have some good news for you.'

He smiled. 'Oh, yes? What?'

'You are well again.'

'I knew that,' he said.

'This means, I will not be seeing you again, professionally. You are no longer my patient.'

His mile broadened. 'Thank you. That *is* good news,' he said. 'I am deeply appreciative of the care you've given me – I've felt quite well for a couple of months, once my skull was reset, and the memories began to return. I wouldn't have been surprised if you'd signed me off weeks ago.'

Her gaze fell. 'I know. I should have, perhaps, but I confess I have enjoyed our meetings and knew they would have to stop when – when you were no longer my patient.'

David realised how much he looked forward to her visits to the farm, and how he would miss them in the future. The smile left his face.

'Maybe I'll see you in town, if you ever come up to Bayeux, or I visit Vire.'

She glanced up briefly before rising to her feet. She was no longer smiling, either, as she held out her hand. 'I hope so.'

He took her hand in his, appreciating her slender surgeon's fingers as he'd often done before, his grip firm but gentle.

A moment later she left, and he watched her drive out of the yard. It occurred to him that she had come a long distance simply in order to tell him he was no longer her patient. Damn! If he'd been quicker, he could have persuaded her to stay a little longer for the drink he'd offered.

He returned to the chair he'd been sitting in, on the way tucking the one she'd used back under the table. He could smell her perfume, which was strange, because he'd never noticed it before. Perhaps, he thought, recalling how much more feminine and attractive she'd looked than was usually the case when she was seeing patients, she was on her way to an appointment – maybe with a lover: he'd noticed the absence of a wedding ring. Or maybe with a colleague, a fellow-professional, he added, rebuking himself for excluding such a meeting from his suppositions.

He got up and made coffee.

If he was no longer Édith's patient – and he realised he always thought of her as Édith, not Doctor Solon – then presumably it was in order for him to take the ferry over to England. He drove into Bayeux later in the day and visited a travel agent.

* * *

Years before, when Ann had told him she thought the house was being watched, Callum had set a few metaphorical tripwires. He'd known for some time that every summer, someone called Marcel Dubois, David Greatorix's wartime cover name, had been visiting England on a French passport. There was more than one Frenchman of that name, and he'd had to ask the immigration people to let him have copies of the passport photographs and details until he found one that could have been David Greatorix.

This visitor had been covertly watched, and his interest in Callum and Ann's home noted. Never in all the years had Dubois attempted to make contact. Callum had made sure that Dubois saw him at the house, or going about with Penny or Ann, or both of them, in order to get the message across that Ann and Penny were *his* family now. It must have worked, thought Callum, because Dubois had always kept a distance, and usually returned to France within a day or two.

In 1969, a different trip-wire had been tugged. An enquiry had been received from the French police at Vire concerning David Greatorix. Callum had fortunately seen the fax, and accompanying photograph, very soon after it arrived, and made sure it was not seen by anyone else. Now he picked up the enquiry again and dialled a long, international number.

' Direction de la surveillance du territoire,' said a voice.

'Can I speak to Philippe, please,' he asked in English.

'A moment, M'sieur.'

He heard the sounds of the call being transferred.

'Is that you, Callum?' asked a voice with scarcely a hint of French accent.

After the pleasantries, Callum said, 'I'm looking for a small favour, Philippe.'

'Oh, yes?'

'There's a police officer – *Police Judiciaire*, I think – at Vire in Normandy. He made an enquiry about one of our, uh, soldiers who went missing and was presumed dead in the 1940s.'

'Oh?'

'I was just wondering whether this gendarme could be trusted. His name's Christophe André, a Sergeant.'

'Do I take it you don't want him to know you've been asking?'

'There's no need,' replied Callum.

There was a short silence on the line before the Frenchman continued. 'Any particular reason why you seem interested in someone who died a long time ago?'

'I'm married to his wife and have adopted his daughter. I need to protect them from sudden shocks – such as, for instance, my wife's first husband whom she believes to be dead, turning up at the house wanting to carry on from where he left off.'

Philippe chuckled. 'And the English think the French invented complex love-lives!'

Callum grinned. 'Of course you did, but like good wine, it's a bit of French culture we've imported. I can do without that, thank-you-very-much, and I'm proposing to turn away this enquiry.'

'Just so I know,' said Philippe slowly, 'what is the name of this, uh, soldier, who went missing in nineteen forty…?'

'Three. David Greatorix.'

'Is he likely to be a problem for us?'

'Shouldn't think so. If you like, as a *quid pro quo*, I'll send you over an abstract of his file. One sheet of paper. It'll have to be delivered by Queen's Messenger, by hand, and I trust you will keep it to yourself.'

'But, you're telling me, I have nothing about which to worry?'

'I'd have said you have nothing to worry *about*, but then people who learn English as a second language tend to pay more attention to the placing of their prepositions.'

'Isn't English *your* second language? And Gaelic your first?'

Callum chuckled. 'No. Despite the accent, English is my first language.'

'My mistake. Very well, I'll look forward to your file abstract arriving, and in the meantime, I'll make one or two discreet enquires about Sergeant André.'

'Many thanks.'

Callum hung up and pulled a sheet of paper towards him.

* * *

Callum was torn between confronting David Greatorix, telling his wife that her former husband was in fact still alive, or doing nothing.

A slim file had arrived by Diplomatic Messenger from Philippe, a few days after Callum's request. It contained a brief biography of Sergeant André and a copy of his photograph on file. There was nothing to suggest the man might prove an irritant. He had a good clear-up rate and seemed diligent, but not to the point of obsession. Callum wondered about whether to visit the man and enlist his help in trying to piece together David Greatorix's history since he'd gone to France.

But first, Greatorix was back, after a two year gap. It might it be a good time to get him to talk. Callum realised he might be recognised, but there was someone who had proved adept at getting men to talk, over the years.

He picked up the phone and called Mary Hamilton.

She did not sound happy to hear him. 'I thought I'd paid my debt to society, Callum.'

'Well, and so you have – mostly,' he said. 'I was wondering if you'd do me a little personal favour—'

'You've never been my type, Callum,' she said.

'Mary, you've never let your personal tastes get in the way of your objectives, so listen to me.' He transferred the phone to his left hand and ear so he could doodle with his right hand, as he spoke. 'Do you remember David Greatorix?'

'Ann's husband? First husband, that is?'

'Yes. What if I told you there's a man who uses his cover name, Marcel Dubois, and he's in the UK for a few days from his home in France?'

'You're telling me, David wasn't killed?'

'Possibly not. But something obviously happened, as he never made contact after he went to France.'

'What do you want me to do?'

'I want you to find out if he *is* "our" David, and if so what he's been doing for the last twenty-seven years. Why he never made contact.'

'And just how are you proposing to do this? It's a while since you relied on my bedroom skills, I don't know if they'd still work.'

'This man is your age, so you're not dealing with the young and keen ones you used to. I'd suggest just talk and companionship, but it's a matter for you. I don't think you ever met back at Bletchley, did you?'

'I only ever saw him from a distance,' Mary said with a hint of regret. 'I don't think Ann liked to think of him and me achieving close quarters…'

'Good. I don't want him to recognise you.'

They arranged to meet.

* * *

Mary Hamilton, in what was for her a fairly dowdy floral print dress, flat shoes and no makeup, stood on Blackfriars Bridge, staring over the parapet into the calm waters of the Thames, which, being at the turn of the tide, reflected her own image and that of Callum Macbeth beside her. River traffic passed beneath their feet.

Callum turned to her. 'You seem concerned about something?'

She was very worried, enough for her to ask to see Callum urgently. 'You remember Oleg? Secretary to the umpteenth Trade Attaché at the Russian Embassy?'

'He's the one who never stops eating during the day, smokes Cuban cigars in bed and emits quantities of methane all through the night?'

Mary allowed herself a small smile. 'You make it sound amusing: it wasn't.'

Callum apologised. 'What about him?'

'I think he's spotted me.'

Callum turned and focussed his full attention on her. 'Why do you think that?'

'He stays sober when he's with me, and doesn't seem as keen to stay around as he used to. It's as though he's been told to carry on seeing me, but not to say anything.'

'Think we should cut the contact? Do you feel in danger?'

'I don't know about danger, but I am definitely feeling less comfortable with him; less in control.'

Callum drew in a breath while he studied her. He came to a decision. 'Stop seeing him. Forthwith.'

'He'll think it odd. It might confirm his suspicions – if he's got any – or make him suspicious if he wasn't already.'

'You can move out of town for a bit. I'll get you a place up in Suffolk or Norfolk or somewhere till the heat dies down, or we find an excuse to put Oleg on the next plane home.'

'If you send me into the back of beyond, I won't be able to keep in touch with David Greatorix.'

'He's still here?'

'As if you wouldn't know.'

Callum chewed the inside of his cheek.

'How important is it that you find out what he's thinking?' she asked.

'He obviously knows where Ann and I live, but so far he's kept his distance. I can guess why. He'll know that he'll have been presumed dead, and that, as a widow, Ann has remarried. There's our daughter – his daughter, really – who's never known her father, and he probably thinks that to reappear in their lives after all this time would be too disruptive, too much of a shock. And maybe he's got a life in France.'

'If he's merely interested in keeping a watching brief, maybe I could help. Perhaps he only wants to know what happened here when he failed to make contact. I could help there, too. But I don't want him disrupting Ann and Penny's lives.'

'You think it's all right for you to know that David's still alive – if it *is* him – but that it isn't for his wife and daughter?'

Callum stared unseeingly down the river. 'Ann grieved for him for a long time. It took her more than six years to accept that he was gone. For nearly twenty years, she's been married to me. I think it's right to let the past stay in the past. There's nothing to be gained by reintroducing David into her life.'

Mary studied his profile while he spoke. When he finished speaking, she sighed.

'I'll see what I can find out, but not if you send me off into the sticks.'

Callum looked round at her, thoughtfully. 'There's one thing I'd be very interested to find out, and that's whether he ever succeeded in his mission.'

'What was it?'

'It's still a live file, Mary, so I won't go into it just yet. If he did succeed, then I might want to arrange a meeting with him, a debriefing.'

'Better late than never,' she quipped.

'I'll find you a place near Bletchley. Better use another name.'

'I'll use Kate Newsome.'

Detective Sergeant Stephanie Tabor faced a dilemma. She was in the office of Detective Superintendent Furness, a fifty-year-old man with further promotion in mind. By the window, two storeys above the busy street, stood another man, dividing his attention between events outside and inside the room. He was well-groomed, clean-shaven, mid-thirties, wearing an open-necked white shirt and faded blue jeans, and, though she couldn't see them clearly, he appeared to be wearing cowboy boots. He seemed relaxed, which was more than she felt.

The DS offered her another cream cake from a plate on the edge of his desk, next to her cardboard beaker of coffee. She shook her head and declined politely, but took another sip of the coffee.

'So, if I've understood you correctly, DI Tanner,' Stephanie began, 'you're inviting me to transfer to Special Branch?'

Mark Tanner turned away from the window and looked at her. 'Not exactly Special Branch, but close.'

She turned towards Furness. 'And you'd rather I stayed where I am?'

'I think I can safely say that if you do, you'll make DI within a year.'

Tanner shrugged. 'We don't actually *do* ranks, but you'd be on rank-equivalent pay.'

'I'd continue to be paid what I am at the moment.'

He smiled briefly. 'If DS Furness considers you to be DI material, then we'd put you on DI pay from day one.'

'Your friends – and I – would be sorry to see you go,' Furness told her.

There was a flattering hint of desperation in his voice. In fact, the idea that the two men, on behalf their respective

251

departments, were vying to have her on their teams was immensely gratifying.

'How long have I got to decide?'

Furness glanced at his watch. 'I have another meeting in twenty minutes, so you have around a quarter of an hour.'

She stared at him with alarm. 'You want me to decide *now?*

' 'Fraid so.'

She looked at Tanner. He had very long legs, she noticed, and his shoulders seemed broad and strong – all of which was irrelevant. She wriggled slightly to make herself more comfortable on the thinly-padded chair.

All this because she'd asked an old colleague in SB about Geoff Pearson. There had been no hint that she was opening a can of worms, or any other kind of invertebrate, yet two days later, here she was, effectively being invited to join the mysterious world of covert operations: MI6, in other words. She had few illusions about where Tanner worked. SB wouldn't have been so coy, and besides, they still had ranks. Her enquiry had obviously got as far as the Secret Services and rung some kind of bell on Mark Tanner's desk.

She couldn't resist another glance at him, under her lashes. She was worried about the boots. The only men she'd met who favoured cowboy boots with two-inch heels were either short or gay. She figured Tanner was not short, as, in his boots, he towered some six inches over her, which meant that even out of them, he would top her five feet ten. Which left the other possibility, or simple prejudice. She would have liked some time alone with him to find out. Maybe ten minutes would be long enough.

She realised her study of him had been noticed. He was leaning against the frame of the floor-to-ceiling window with his ankles crossed, his left thumb wedged in the pocket of his jeans, long fingers loosely curled. He turned back to the view of the street, which he seemed to find fascinating.

Her ambition urged her to accept Tanner's offer. Not only was he offering her a good pay rise from day one, she suspected the nature of the work would be more interesting and challenging even than that of a police officer – and that was interesting and challenging enough.

She was aware that Furness had been resting his chin on his hands, his elbows on the desk, gazing at her. He looked unhappy, and he'd been right to remind her of the friends and colleagues she'd be putting behind her if she left the Bletchley station. She turned to Tanner.

'The thing I most enjoy about my work here is being among a team of good officers, and working in and for the community. I find the work challenging, and I enjoy taking part in operations that net some of society's parasites, and seeing the dangerous ones put away. I'm not very good behind a desk.'

Furness was smiling, relief showing on his face. He thinks I'm arguing in favour of staying, whereas I'm trying to get some assurance from Tanner that I won't be bored if I join his lot, she thought.

Tanner stood up straight and took a couple of steps towards the desk.

'You'd still be involved in operations that take down the parasites and others who threaten the rule of law or the security of the state. You'd still be working to an extent with the police. But we deal almost exclusively with serious threats, and not everyone we target is a law-breaker, so we have to find other ways of defusing them. Would that be challenging enough for you?'

'I wouldn't be stuck behind a desk?'

He smiled at her again, making her feel suddenly warm. 'Not a lot.'

Why did Six have to send a hottie like Tanner to recruit her, she wondered. She was well aware of the dangers of lusting after colleagues, or of giving any of them an inch in terms of forming personal attachments. But obviously, her body had seen something it liked, and she would have to draw on her reserves of professionalism and detachment if she was going to be working anywhere near this man.

And she knew she would be – because if she turned down the opportunity, she'd regret it forever, and spend her days wondering what she'd passed up. After all, she could always transfer back into the police, if she didn't like it. She turned to Furness.

'Then, sir, I'll take up Mr Tanner's offer.'

He rested his clasped hands on the desk and shrugged. 'I thought you might,' he said ruefully. He pulled a file – her personal file, she saw – from a tray on top of a filing cabinet beside him, flipped it open and scribbled something on the last page before signing it and handing the file to Tanner.

He stood up and held out his hand. 'That's it, then, Stephanie. You're off our books and onto' – he glanced at Tanner – 'his. You've been a great member of the team here, and I wish you all the best for your future.'

She shook his hand, feeling stunned at the speed at which the transfer had apparently been effected.

'I'll need your Warrant Card and keys,' Furness continued.

Wordlessly, she handed them over. It felt very strange, doing so, knowing that she would never again be able to enter this or any other police station through the staff entrance.

'There's something we have to do, now, Steph,' said Furness.

She heard sadness in his voice and turned to look at him.

'What's that?'

'We're going to go to your desk and locker, and I am going to use your keys to let you remove your personal effects. It will look to your colleagues as if you have been the subject of a disciplinary complaint and dismissed for gross misconduct.' He shook his head. 'I shall neither confirm nor deny that speculation. I'm afraid it will damage your reputation here among them, and every other person who will never know the truth – and that's everyone apart from us, here in this room.'

She felt crushed. She'd had no idea that the cut-off from her friends would be so quick and so total. She nodded, una-

ble to find words, and they went out, along the corridor to
begin the process.

* * *

Five days passed, a week since her conversation with Stephanie Tabor, and Penny had received no word. She had decided
not to try contacting her former colleague as she didn't want
to appear to be hassling her, but after a week, she thought
she should give Steph a gentle nudge, aware that she might
have been very busy, and a favour for a friend must come
well down her list of priorities. She called in at the police
station as she was passing, glad of an opportunity to rest her
shopping bag on the floor while she waited her turn with the
Front Desk Officer.

He smiled at her shyly. She remembered him as a new-
comer to the service, shortly before she retired.

'DI Sanderson, isn't it?' he said, when the last customer
had left.

She smiled. 'Just plain old Mrs Sanderson these days,' she
said. 'Any chance I can see Steph Tabor?'

The smile went from his face.

'I'm afraid not,' he said.

Penny felt a terrible foreboding. 'Why? What's the matter
with her? Is she out on a job?'

The young man took a step or two away from the counter and started filing papers in pigeon-holes, not looking at
her.

'She's… uh, she's left,' he said.

'Left? What? Gone? Resigned? When did this happen?'

'Last week. She went in to see the Old Man, and came out
escorted by him and a fellow in civvies, and they stood there
while she cleared out her desk and her locker. Then she was
escorted off the premises and the other bloke took her off in
his car.'

Penny stared at him, scarcely able to believe what she was
hearing. 'You make it sound as if she's done something very
wrong.'

'That's the rumour,' he said, stopping his filing and returning to face Penny across the counter. 'Gross misconduct cases get treated like that, don't they?'

Penny drew a jagged breath. 'I can't believe Steph did anything that could be construed as gross misconduct. There must be another explanation. Could she have gone into hiding? Witness protection?'

'I dunno, ma'am. But the Sarge was in the Old Man's office later that day and swears he saw Steph's Warrant Card on his desk.'

Penny was finding herself unwillingly being led towards acceptance of the unpleasant possibility that Steph Tabor – her best friend – might have done something quite out of character. She thought for a moment.

'Any chance I could have a word with DS Furness?'

'I'll ask, ma'am.'

The FDO phoned the DS's Personal Assistant, Penny assumed. She expected to be told there was no chance of talking to Furness, and was surprised when the FDO put down the phone and told her the PA was coming down to escort her to Furness's office.

On the way, they passed through CID and Penny saw the desk which Steph had occupied, its surface bare, as if nobody wanted even to dump a pile of papers on it. The few officers in the room nodded, smiled and waved, but over everything seemed to be a pall of gloom. The PA knocked on Furness's door and left when Penny entered.

Furness stood up, smiling and holding out his hand.

'Penny, how good to see you!'

She shook his hand and sat in the proffered chair.

'How can I help?' he asked.

'What's happened to Stephanie Tabor?' she asked, bluntly.

The smile fell from his features. 'She's, uh, left us.'

'So I've just been told. I hear it's rumoured she's been dismissed for gross misconduct.'

Not a muscle twitched on Furness's face. He drew in a breath. 'I can't comment on that,' he said.

Penny stared at him in disbelief.

'Is that it? Is that all you're going to tell me?' she asked when she'd found her voice.

Furness shrugged. 'Penny, can I trust you not to talk about this to the people outside?' He indicated the CID office.

'If you're going to tell me something that bears on Steph's whereabouts, or what happened to her, then yes, I'll keep what you say to myself.'

'Then let me reiterate, I'm obliged neither to confirm nor deny any rumours about Steph Tabor. The fact is, she is no longer a member of the police service.'

Penny stared at him. She'd expected rather more after the build-up. 'That's it? Nothing else?'

He shrugged apologetically. 'That's as much as I can say,' he said, drawing a hand symbolically across his throat.

'I'll go and see her,' said Penny.

He smiled and rose to his feet. 'Good luck.' He didn't sound optimistic.

The interview was clearly over. Penny thanked him for his time, and went out of the office. Furness's PA saw her at once and came over to show her out of the building before she could even think of chatting to any former members of her team, who'd worked with Stephanie and, until she'd retired, herself.

As she went past the front desk, the FDO held out her shopping bag.

'You left this when you went upstairs,' he said.

'Sorry.'

'You realise that, normally, abandoned bags result in the building being evacuated and the Bomb Squad called?'

She felt her face flush with embarrassment.

'Yes, thank you. I'm aware of that, and grateful that you used your initiative not to implement the procedure on this occasion.'

She took the bag and strode outside into the street. She felt as if her integrity had been somehow impugned, since on the one hand, Furness had made a point of asking for her silence, and on the other, he had then not said anything useful.

Or had he? He'd added the words, "I'm obliged". Somehow, she didn't think he was being obliged solely by consideration of good manners. She felt her spirits rising. Perhaps that was his message: someone else, someone with a lot of clout who could dictate a police superintendent's behaviour, had "obliged" him neither to confirm nor deny any rumour – that also was what he'd said: *any* rumour – concerning Stephanie Tabor.

When, later that day, she drove round to Stephanie's flat and received no answer to her knock, and when she'd then gone round the back and peered through the windows and seen the place empty, she was almost relieved. The inference, she was sure, was that Steph had been spirited away and might be on some very dangerous assignment somewhere, and that the performance seen by other police officers, culminating in her removal from the building, was just that: a performance, designed to start the rumour mill.

No, Penny was as certain as she could be that Steph was not under any sort of cloud in fact, simply doing something terribly secret.

She released a breath she hadn't noticed she was holding and returned to her car, smiling. It was a pity Steph had gone before she could pass on anything she'd learned about Geoff Pearson.

Sudden realisation hit her and chilled her blood. What if Steph had been taken away *because* of the enquiries she'd made about Geoff? Penny knew only one person who might be able to tell her whether she was correct, and that person was Geoff Pearson himself.

The memories prompted by Delphine's diaries had prepared David for the changes to Bletchley to some degree, but he still experienced a slight sense of shock as he got off the train and made his way out into the street. He found himself staring at a female police officer, but felt no sudden recognition. He'd never risked taking photographs of Ann or Penny during his previous visits, and his recollections of what his daughter looked like were unclear. He felt more confident that he would recognise Ann.

He began his visit by stopping off at a coffee bar. The plain filter coffee, containing a high proportion of robusta beans, was harsh on his taste-buds, but he could feel the caffeine waking him up after the long journey.

Using one of the oldest pick-up techniques in the book. Mary, in her role as "Kate Newsome", appeared to slip on the terrazzo floor of the coffee bar, and lost her footing, grabbing for support at David's table, knocking over a bar stool and spilling his coffee.

He caught her before she hit the ground.

'S-sorry!' she muttered.

'Are you all right?' he asked, raising her to her feet. He reached down and picked up the stool. 'Here, sit down.'

'Thank you. I'm so sorry. Let me get you another coffee,' she said, patting her hair, which was a golden blonde instead of her natural brunette. She suddenly stopped and bit her lower lip, lifting an ankle across a knee and rubbing it, baring several inches of her upper thighs.

'Ooh! I wonder if I've sprained it?'

'Let me look.' he said.

She smiled and moved her hand away, stretching out her leg until it rested across his lap. He felt around her ankle with gentle fingers, which she found not at all unpleasant. He glanced up when a waitress arrived with a cloth to wipe up the spilled coffee, drawing his hands away from Mary's leg when he realised how it might look to the girl.

'I'm sorry,' Mary said to her. 'Could we have two more coffees.'

The girl nodded and returned behind the counter. Mary put her leg down, adjusted her position on the stool and tugged the hem of her charcoal grey skirt until it almost reached her knees.

She'd taken time over her appearance, starting with the change of hair colour and a slash of wine red lipstick. The rest of her makeup was just enough to give her skin a healthy glow. Her aim had been to catch his attention without looking sluttish.

'You needn't have worried,' said David. He leaned towards her. 'The coffee's not the greatest.'

'Oh, dear! Should I have ordered hot chocolate or tea?'

David held his hand up against her protest. 'No, no. I am just beginning to get used to it.'

The waitress appeared at his elbow bearing a tray balanced on one hand, while, with the other, she placed mugs of coffee in front of each of them, and the bill in front of David. Mary whisked it to her side of the table and fished around in her handbag for change.

'How much is it?' David glanced at the price-list on the wall. 'Five bob?' He felt in his pocket and pulled out a half-crown.

Mary produced two florins and a shilling. 'Got it! Thanks, but put your money away, I'm getting these.'

David shrugged and dropped the big coin back in his pocket. 'I'll get the next round,' he said.

She patted his knee. 'No need, I'm sure you have other things to do.'

'Not really,' he said. 'I'm on holiday.'

She smiled, curious. 'You're on holiday in *Bletchley*?'

He understood her amusement. 'It's not such a bad place. I used to live here – during the war. So much has changed.'

She glanced at the street through the plate glass window. 'Yes.'

He glanced at her sharply. 'You knew the place in the forties?'

She bit her lip then nodded. That had been a slight slip, when she'd been temporarily distracted by the way his tie was not quite snug-fitting and the urge to straighten it for him.

'Were you a soldier?' she asked.

'Uh, no. Not really. Used to sit behind a desk. Very quiet sort of life.'

'You sound like one of the Station X people.'

'Station X?' he asked, as if hearing it for the first time.

'Bletchley Park. You know.'

'Sorry. I live in France – have done for years.'

'Whereabouts?'

'My home is a farmhouse in Lower Normandy – *Normandie Basse.*'

She leaned her chin on her hand. 'How interesting! You're a farmer.'

'Not I. I teach maths at a high school.'

'Really! Do you have a family?'

He looked down. 'My, uh, wife's dead. We have a grown-up son.'

'Sorry to hear about your wife. When did she die?'

'Last year. Look, I don't want to bore you with all this—'

She rested a hand on one of his. 'Look, I have to be somewhere soon, but I'm sure you've guessed, I like you. Could we meet up later, perhaps have dinner together, or at least a drink?'

He told her where he was staying, an old coaching inn called the Bunbury Arms, not far outside the town. She arranged to meet him there at half-past seven.

* * *

Where ostlers once attended to the equipages of weary travellers, with their landaus, Berlins, gigs and phaetons, the current owners of the Bunbury Arms had roofed over, and set out tables and chairs. David watched from the window of his room on the second storey, overlooking the former courtyard as guests and non-residents began to take their places for their evening meals.

He realised he'd slipped into an easy friendship with Kate, and wondered how far it would develop. He felt she was a woman in whom it would be easy to confide, but it could endanger the relationship if he tried to burden her with his strange history. Maybe one day, when he knew her better.

He smiled and shook his head at the realisation that he was assuming their relationship would last longer than twenty-four hours. For some reason, the image of Édith Solon drifted into his mind for a moment.

He picked up his room key and went down to the yard.

* * *

So there was a live file, Mary thought as she entered the vestibule of the Bunbury Arms. Something dating back to the old days when she'd worked at Station X herself – dating back, she recollected, with genuine abhorrence, to the days she'd allowed herself to be blackmailed into spying for the Germans in order to save her husband's life, as she thought.

And now here she was, spying still, but for the British this time. She didn't mind the subterfuges, the lies that made up her personas, because these were, in her view, all in a good cause, and Mary had been brought up in a very 'Establishment' family which passionately believed the British were innately 'good' and a beacon of light to those less fortunate, born in other countries. She had not liked spying for the Gestapo, but with concerns for her loyalty behind her, the spying game itself, or at least the way she played it, had turned out to be very enjoyable. She was hardly ever bored.

And there, sitting comfortably at a corner table, was the latest man Callum had asked her to spy on, only this time, it was, apparently, a personal matter. Before he saw her, she went into the Ladies' room and checked her appearance, touching up her makeup, and smoothing the tight skirt of her turquoise tailored suit down her thighs, to be certain that the tops of her hold-ups wouldn't show when she was walking.

Satisfied with what the mirror told her, she picked up her handbag and went back into the vestibule. She saw David glance up and see her, and put a little extra sashay in her hip movements as she wound her way sinuously around the furniture. She glanced around at other people in the vestibule, or standing at the Reception desk, at the far end of the room, and was satisfied she recognised none of them. She sat facing David, and crossed her legs.

'So tell me about yourself,' she invited, when they'd been served with coffee and she figured he was relaxed enough to talk.

'I've been teaching mathematics at a high school, until a few weeks ago.'

'You've changed jobs?' she asked, the heel of her shoe dangling from her toes and drawing his gaze to her legs. She tugged at the hem of her skirt, aware that an inch of stocking-top was still visible, and he'd noticed.

'No. I, uh, am on sick leave. Had to have a spot of surgery.'

The dangling shoe stopped moving for a moment. 'Nothing too serious, I hope?'

He smiled uncertainly. 'I hope not,' he said. 'I was apparently attacked. Someone fractured my skull. It was reset, and I was waiting for the all-clear from the doctors.'

'And when is that likely to be?' Mary asked, thinking Callum might find this interesting.

'I was pronounced fit just before I came here. And now the schools are on *grandes vacances*, so I have a few more weeks before I have to go back.'

'Have the police found whoever did it?'

'No, I don't think so.'

'Typical!' she said. 'They worry about drivers having the odd glass or two to drink, but they can't find the thugs who go round assaulting people.'

He grinned. 'There are more drink-drivers than violent criminals.'

'I'm always careful about anything I put in my mouth.'

He digested that for a moment, disguising the fact by glancing at his watch. 'I booked a table for seven-thirty. Shall we go through to the restaurant?'

By the time the meal ended, he had told her a heavily edited version of his life in France, and his loss of memory as a result of his bad landing there.

'Your earliest memory in France was when?' she asked, apparently intrigued.

'Late in 1943. I learned I'd been in a coma for several months, looked after by a wonderful young woman, Delphine…' His voice faded.

'What became of her?'

He swallowed and looked up at her. 'I married her.'

Mary looked a question at him.

'As I told you, she died,' he told her. 'The same day I was attacked. It was an accident, they tell me.'

'How did she die?' asked Mary gently.

'She drowned.' He stared past her, unseeingly, lost for a moment in his memories.

'That's terrible! And a terrible coincidence.'

He nodded. 'I know. At first, I felt sure someone must have killed her, but the police seemed happy that she had simply slipped in our duck pond and been unable to get out.'

'Couldn't she swim?'

He stared at her. 'You know, I have no idea. I never saw her do so. Maybe she had forgotten how, or maybe she couldn't.'

'You never forget how to swim,' Mary said.

'Then I assume she couldn't. Or maybe she hit her head on something, or… But no, the doctor who examined her said there were no marks on her body.'

'So she was given a post mortem?'

'Yes. Only by the local doctor, but he's been around long enough to recognise signs of violence on a body.'

'Does he do a lot of PMs, then?'

'I don't believe so. But Delphine – and I – have been his patients since the war, and I think he did the examination out of some regard for her. It wasn't some stranger who was seeing her body, you know. He'd been her doctor all her life.'

'You have a son.'

'Yes.'

'Any grandchildren?'

'Oliver is not married. He has become somewhat estranged from us – me – in the last year.'

She watched his expression turn blacker.

He told her about his son's childhood, how they'd hoped everything for the best for him, as parents do.

'Don't see much of him these days,' he concluded.

They fell silent for a while as the waiter cleared the table of everything but the small vase of flowers at one side, and the glasses of *vin doux* they'd had with dessert.

'What I'm curious about,' Mary said, 'is what you were doing in France in 1943. I mean, the only Brits there then were SOE agents.'

'I've wondered about that, too. Maybe I was one. Maybe I was a shot-down airman or an escaped POW. I don't know, and I don't know how I could find out.'

Mary studied him thoughtfully a moment. 'I know someone who might be able to help with finding answers.'

He raised a sceptical eyebrow. 'At this length of time since the war?'

'Maybe. I'll contact him in the morning.' She leaned forward and allowed the pointed toe of one patent leather shoe to slide up his calf, and an inch or two beyond his knee. 'But there's something I want first.'

'What's that, Kate?' he asked, slipping a hand below the table-cloth, finding her ankle and allowing his fingers to slide up her leg on the thin film of nylon encasing it.

'Perhaps we can go to your room where I can explain in detail.'

* * *

She woke early the following morning. It had been a useful trick of hers, to be able to set an alarm clock in her head, just by thinking what time she wanted to wake. It had never let her down. The sun was just on the point of rising when she opened the curtains a crack, admitting just enough light to dress by.

She brushed her hair and reapplied lipstick in the little en-suite bathroom. There had been a couple of moments when their romping had transferred most of her lipstick to David and the bedclothes, and seriously dishevelled her hair, but in the end, she'd managed to wriggle free and take control of their love-making. When she returned to the bedroom, David had not stirred, and lay stretched across the bed, the coverings rumpled and creased, snoring gently. She smiled to herself. It had obviously been a while for both of them since their last sexual encounter. Nevertheless, he was much more considerate than 'Orrible Oleg, as she thought of her erstwhile Russian lover.

She let herself out of the room and took the fire stairs down to the vestibule. She'd seen telephones tucked away near the stairway, which were out of sight of most people who might be using the vestibule at that early hour. She barely noticed a short, rotund man, at the Reception desk. He caught sight of her as she picked up a telephone. When she finished her call, he followed her into the stairwell and climbed to the first floor on thick rubber soles which made no sound.

She turned as he followed her through the door into the corridor, a few seconds behind her.

'Oleg!' she exclaimed.

'What a surprise to see you here, Maria,' he said in heavily-accented English. 'I thought you were going to be on holiday in Scotland.'

'Not quite yet, Oleg,' Mary replied.

'Really? And why are you now blonde?'

She touched her hair reflexively. 'A woman can change her hair colour if she wants.'

'Did you know I was arrested briefly and accused of spying?'

'No,' she replied. A more important question occurred to her. 'What are you doing here?'

'Looking for you. I think you've been avoiding me.'

'How did you know I was here?'

He smiled crookedly. 'I asked a couple of friends. They found you for me. They are very good at finding people – and following them. What are you doing here? Who is the man you're with?'

'You had me followed?'

His smile broadened, cold. 'I know all about your meeting on Blackfriars Bridge. The man you met there works for MI6. Do you work for MI6, Maria – or whatever your name is? Are you, in fact, a spy?'

'It seems the police were right to suspect *you*.'

'So answer my questions: who is the man you're with, and what are you doing here?'

'It's a personal matter – and that's all I'm telling you.'

He gripped her upper arm, painfully, and pulled her towards him, until their noses almost touched. 'No! You'll tell me everything I want to know,' he hissed.

'I'll scream!'

He slackened his grip slightly and snorted. 'You think I haven't thought of that already?'

His other hand snaked into his pocket and brought out a linen pad. She scarcely had time to recognise the odour it was emitting. A moment later, before she could react, he twisted her round until her shoulder blades pressed against his chest, and clamped the chloroform-soaked gag over her face. She began to struggle and attempted to call out, but the pad was effective, and only a muffled cry came out. She felt her consciousness slipping away and her struggles weakened.

Suddenly, the pad was pulled away and she was released from Oleg's grip. She fell to the floor and took a moment to clear the fumes from her lungs with deep breaths. Turning her head, she saw David grappling with Oleg, Oleg getting the upper hand, pressing David back against the wall, and pointing a short-barrelled pistol at him. She staggered to her feet and moved slowly towards the two men, approaching Oleg from behind his left shoulder.

The Russian turned towards her reflexively, his gun moving with him. In a blur of speed, David cracked the hard edge of his left hand down on Oleg's wrist, paralysing the nerves for a moment, long enough for the pistol to fall to the floor. As he bent to pick it up, David brought his knee up sharply, smashing the Russian's nose, blood spurting over trousers, the wall and carpet. As he staggered back, David quickly stooped and pocketed the pistol.

He grabbed Mary's arm.

'Back to my room!' he commanded, dragging her with him.

Mary felt the grogginess brought on by the drug receding. She followed David and, as the door slammed behind her, she drew a deep and ragged breath.

'Thank you.'

David was rubbing his left hand where it had made contact with Oleg's. He nodded towards a hip flask on a small table.

'Help yourself to a drink.'

She poured each of them a shot of brandy.

'Now, will you tell me who the hell *he* was, and what he was doing with you?' asked David.

Mary thought quickly. 'He's just someone I knew in London.'

'He said he thought you might be a spy, working for MI6.'

She drank two large mouthfuls of the wine. The effects of the chloroform were fading, though it had left her with a thumping headache which made thought difficult.

'I'm not working for MI6.' Technically, she was doing a favour for a friend, to say nothing of one for herself: last night had been both passionate and tender, and very, very satisfying.

David was silent. She wondered whether he believed her.

'What else did you hear?' she asked.

He glanced at her. 'He called you Maria. Is that your real name?'

She took his arm and sat him beside her on the bed, smiling and shaking her head.

'No. It was just one of those harmless, silly, little things women do: you're at a party, some man comes on to you; for a while it's flattering, but when he wants to know your name, you give him a false one. Stops him finding you later, with any luck. False telephone number, too.'

'He found you. How'd he do that?'

She shrugged. 'I don't know. If he wasn't so horrible, I might have been flattered he made the effort.'

David nodded, apparently satisfied with her explanation, which had not been so very far from the truth.

She studied him shrewdly. 'You told me at dinner that you went to France in 1943.'

'That's right.'

'I'll bet you didn't use your real name.'

He grinned wryly. 'Well, no.'

'So who were you then?'

'A farm worker called Marcel Dubois.'

* * *

'That makes it certain, then,' said Callum, when Mary reported back to him. They were again on Blackfriars Bridge – he liked it, he'd told her, because you could be fairly sure you weren't being eavesdropped.

'So now what?' Mary asked.

'Now I can shunt you off to Norfolk until the Foreign Secretary declares Oleg *persona non grata*. The hotel reported him to the police when their Reception staff noticed him leaving, covered in his own blood.'

'What will happen to David?' she asked, staring down at the river.

'Nothing, for now.'

She chewed her lip for a moment. 'I wouldn't mind seeing him again.'

Callum turned and looked at her. A faint blush stole across her cheeks.

'Mary, I don't believe it: you really like him.'

She turned her head to glance quickly at him. 'I know. I'm just being stupid, I suppose, but I can't help the way I feel.' She straightened up and turned to face him properly. 'I've been your official tart for nearly twenty years. I've slept with men I can't stand the sight of, because you wanted to know what they'd tell me across the pillow. It's true I've sometimes enjoyed these stolen intimacies, but I knew, all the time, that they were simply the currency of our business.

'David was different. He wasn't work – yes, I was with him because you asked me as a personal favour, but he wasn't MI6 business, and I didn't have to drag information out of him he was unwilling to tell me. When we slept together it was because we both liked each other. I haven't had a man make love to me since my wedding night, and even then, Frank was so bloody useless – so *innocent* – that... well, let's just say the Earth didn't move. And it hasn't since – much! – till the other night with David. I want more of that.'

'Do you want to stop working for MI6?'

'I have to give it up if I want to continue seeing him. Besides, I'm not getting any younger. I'm sure you can call on much younger and prettier women to carry on the good work.'

'You could have a desk job.'

She uttered a short, sharp laugh. 'You have to be joking! Can you see me working in an office? Not since Station X days, Callum – and I'm not going to do it again.'

'So, retirement, then?'

'I'm fifty-four, Callum. I've had enough of the spying business.'

'Okay, okay,' he said slowly. 'We're none of us getting any younger. I'll agree to pension you off. You know you'll have to move out of the Square? I'll see if their nibs at the Treasury will agree to give you a thirty-year pension on account of the demanding nature of the services you've performed for Her Majesty. But afterwards, you'll be on your own, you know.'

'I know. Never look back.' She smiled at him. 'Thank you, Callum.' She kissed his cheek.

He swallowed. 'I'll miss you, Mary. Never thought I'd say it, but I will.' He turned back to look upstream towards the setting sun. 'Might be time to think about taking an early bath myself, as Eddie Waring might say.'

'Eddie who?'

'That fellow who comments on rugby league matches on the BBC.'

She rolled her eyes, not having any interest in the sport herself. 'Right!'

CHAPTER 26 – 1999

Stephanie Tabor moved quietly, keeping the distant figure in sight. Her target stopped beside a headstone which had settled slightly to one side, like others marking older graves, and began arranging flowers in a vase at its foot.

The last few weeks had been hard for her. Mark Tanner had taken her from Bletchley police station directly to a flat in London, which she had been told would be her home for the foreseeable future. She'd been ordered to make no contact with anyone from her past, and given a new identity, Laurie Allen, which she didn't particularly like.

And then the training had begun in earnest. Mostly, Tanner went through procedures which she'd learnt as a police officer, but she'd had to learn the careful use of certain *ultra vires* procedures which could be implemented in strictly-controlled circumstances.

It had bothered her that her sudden departure from the life she had always known had meant leaving Penny Sanderson without any explanation, and without having resolved her question about Geoff Pearson. Now she was on the inside, she'd found that information about him was relatively straightforward to obtain. It had taken a couple of weeks of tussle with her conscience , whether to disregard Tanner's direct order not to contact Penny again, or put her friendship with her above duty. In one way, it wasn't as if Penny was an ordinary member of the public: she'd been a middle-ranking police officer until last year, and surely could be trusted to be discreet.

In the end, she'd decided to risk it, and now she had followed Penny on a visit to the graveyard where her mother's and step-father's ashes were interred. While Penny was intent on arranging the flowers, Stephanie slipped through the trees marking the boundary of the cemetery until she reached Penny's car. After glancing round to make sure she was unobserved, she slipped a manila envelope under the windscreen wipers. When Penny read its contents, she would know Stephanie was still alive and thinking of her, even if there were no direct clues as to the source of the information.

Her self-imposed mission completed, Stephanie glanced once more at her friend, and slipped away, unseen.

* * *

Penny lit the paper and threw it after the envelope into the empty fire grate in her lounge. She watched thoughtfully as the flames blackened and charred the pieces, and when the flames had died away, she used the poker to break them up into tiny fragments, light as air.

She was experiencing conflicting emotions: of course, it was good to hear from Stephanie who was apparently all right and more than likely working for MI6 herself: nobody else would have supplied, or been able to supply, the information she'd just burnt.

A programme she'd watched on television a week ago came strongly to mind. It had been a repeat showing of one made in the late nineteen seventies, not long after the government had lifted the veil of secrecy which had covered the workings of much of SOE and Bletchley Park during the '39-'45 war.

It seemed that, thanks to intelligence learned from the work at Station X – SOE's code for Bletchley Park – Churchill was forewarned of the Nazi intention to bomb Coventry. In what must have been one of the most difficult decisions of his life, he took no steps to prevent it happening, because had he done so, the Germans would have known their 'Enigma' codes had been cracked, and changed them, and the Allies would have lost the source they'd relied on almost since the outbreak of the war.

Penny knew she couldn't raise the matters she'd learned about Geoff directly with him because he would have known they'd been 'leaked' to her by someone in MI6, and there was one obvious suspect. Somehow, she had to convince him to disclose his hidden agenda to her voluntarily. She invited him to dinner.

After plying him with a tender roast of beef topside, roasted potatoes and vegetables, topped off with her own recipe for a tasty gravy, Penny sat beside Geoff on the settee, and refilled his glass with a decent claret.

He was looking at her with a slight hint of bafflement in his gaze.

'Is there something on your mind?' he asked.

'Why? Should there be?'

'You must want something.'

'Geoff!' she exclaimed, a touch accusingly, partly to disguise the fact that his intuition was accurate.

'You've made a fabulous meal, provided a good, palatable wine… and you've not done this for me before.' He sipped. 'So I conclude there's something special about tonight.' He took a copious mouthful of the wine, rinsed it around his mouth and swallowed it delicately. 'So, spit it out: is there something I can help you with?'

'I didn't think I was so transparent,' she said, sipping from her own glass before turning towards him. 'Do you remember the day we met?'

'Yes. Very well.' He smiled.

'Tell me again how you found out I was intending to trace my father and had applied for his military records.'

'I thought I'd explained all that,' he said, staring into his glass apart from one quick sideways glance at her.

'You did – but when I think about it, you didn't tell me much. So tell me, Geoff, how did you come to turn up on my telephone, if not quite on my doorstep?'

He continued to direct his attention to the wine remaining in his glass. 'As I think I said at the time, my father mentioned it. And since I was looking at researching my family's history – well, *his*, actually – it seemed sensible for us to pool our efforts.'

'Our fathers having so much in common?'

'Exactly.'

'Your father is still alive, Geoff. You could ask him directly.'

Geoff shrugged. 'He wouldn't tell me.'

'You could ask him to write it down and seal it in an envelope that you could open later – after he's gone.'

He turned to look at her. 'That sounds a mite callous, Penny.'

'But not impossible. I'll ask him, if you like.'

'No!'

'Geoff, it doesn't hold water, you know. Someone in M-I Three-and-three-quarters became interested when I applied for my father's war service records and you turned up.'

'But – '

'When we first met, you asked me to trust you. "Give me the benefit of the doubt", you said. And I did. But you don't expect my questions to go unanswered forever, do you?'

He pursed his lips. 'And tonight's the night my parole runs out?'

She rested a hand on the back of his. 'Geoff! I like you! Really! I would like us to continue seeing each other, but we're not going to if you don't trust me.' She stood up and paced along the rug in front of them, finally turning back to look at him. 'Tell me why you came to me. How did you know what I looked like before we'd met? And whilst we've spent a lot of time researching *my* father's past, we've spent none at all looking into the things you said you wanted to learn about your own father.'

She stood still and waited, watching expressions flit across his face while he gazed at the wine in his glass. She fetched the bottle and topped it up, then resumed waiting.

At last he seemed to come to a decision.

'I need to make a phone call. Private,' he said.

She pointed him towards the back door into her secluded, suburban garden. 'Keep your voice down and the neighbours won't hear. Or go into the greenhouse,' she said.

She went back in the house and closed the door, watching him through the living room window while he spoke a little into his mobile phone, and listened a lot. Three minutes later, he came back into the house and rejoined Penny on the settee.

* * *

In Bayeux, Inspector Dumonde of the *Police Judiciaire* put the phone down after a long conversation with a prosecutor. He called to his sergeant.

'Daniel, *avec moi!*'

The sergeant closed the file he was working on and placed it on a pile at the edge of his desk.

'Yes, Inspector? We have work to do?'

'We're going to arrest Oliver Dubois – or Delacourt.'

The sergeant smiled. 'The prosecutors have agreed to give it a try, then?'

Dumonde sighed. 'Indeed they have. Now it's all down to the woman who made the accusation, Lisette Cornu.'

With another car containing two uniformed gendarmes following them, Dumonde and Sergeant Rappeneau drove to the Delacourt Farm. As they arrived, an ancient, battered 2CV emerged from the yard onto the farm track and turned away from them, towards the next farm. In the yard, there was no sign of Oliver's car and the place looked deserted. The sergeant got out and knocked on the door with his fist. There was no response.

He shrugged and got back in the car behind the wheel. 'Nobody home, sir. What shall we do now?'

Dumonde thought for a moment, then jerked his thumb towards the track they'd come along. 'Follow that 2CV. Somebody knows this place, and might know where Oliver is.'

The two police vehicles turned in the yard and returned to the track, turning to their left at the gate. The track led to the next farm, where the 2CV was parked outside the kitchen door. Sergeant Rappeneau climbed out quickly and was knocking on the door by the time he was joined by Dumonde.

The door opened. A thin woman, grey-haired and wearing a pinafore, on which she was wiping her gnarled and weather-beaten hands, stood there.

'Yes?'

Rappeneau showed her his ID.

Dumonde smiled disarmingly. 'Sorry to trouble you, Madame. I am Inspector Dumonde of the *Police Judiciaire*. We're looking for Oliver Dubois – or Delacourt. We saw you leaving his place earlier and wondered if you could tell us where he might be?'

At the mention of Oliver's name, the old hands stopped their wiping motion and clasped each other.

'He spends a lot of his time at Caen. Got a car business there. What else he gets up to, I couldn't say.'

Dumonde glanced at his sergeant, his curiosity piqued by the woman's manner and tone of voice.

'I wonder if you'd mind telling me your name, Madame?'

'Valéria Le Greq.'

'You know Monsieur Delacourt fairly well?'

'Yes.'

'What can you tell me about him?'

The woman's mouth turned down at the corners. 'I don't think he's a very nice person.'

Dumonde tilted his head attentively. 'Why do you think that, Madame?'

Madame Le Greq backed inside. 'You'd better come in.' She pointed at chairs around the large kitchen table. Dumonde and Rappeneau sat. 'Would you like coffee?'

'Very much,' replied Dumonde, 'but there are more men waiting outside for us. Perhaps you could just tell me… ?'

She drew a deep breath. 'He is cruel, M'sieur. '

'What makes you say that?'

'He was horrible to his mother, especially in the days before her death.'

'How do you know?'

'She and I used to talk. We've always kept an eye on each other's properties if one of us has been away. Back when her father was still working the farm, he and my father would work together on our fields at harvest, and during the lambing season, if we needed the help.'

'I don't know anything about Madame Dubois' father… ?'

She turned away and stared out of the window. 'He was killed by a gang of murderous Boche. Christmas, 1943, of all times. Poor girl. She was very upset – as you can imagine. They turned up, wanting food, and when the Delacourts didn't have anything to give them, they shot her dear Papa. Marcel helped her through the period.' She turned back towards the two men, smiling reminiscently. 'She'd nursed him for months, you know. Don't know where he came from the night she found him, out in the fields. Somehow, Delphine and her father kept Marcel alive while he was in a coma. I suppose Lafarge helped.'

'Lafarge?'

'He was our doctor.'

'Is he still around?'

'He still lives in Sainte Marguerite.'

'And he's known the family – he'll have known Oliver since his birth?'

'Yes.' At the mention of the son's name, the smile fell from her face and the scowl reappeared.

'How lovely people like Delphine and Marcel could have produced a son like him, I don't know!'

'What makes you say he was cruel?'

'For a boy who grew up on a farm, he was cruel to animals. Delphine told me once he'd tried to wring the neck of a chicken but bungled it, and only hurt the bird. She was worried he'd keep trying until he succeeded. Wouldn't let his mother or father show him how to do the job properly – not that Marcel was much good on the farm. Had to be told everything.' She glanced at Dumonde's face. 'Lost his memory, you see. When he woke up, he couldn't remember a thing about his early life.'

Dumonde was beginning to realise how little he knew about Oliver and his family.

'Marcel – where's he?'

Madame Le Greq pursed her lips.

'I don't know, to be honest. Ever since the attack on him, in 1969, the same day Delphine died – which in my view was no accident! – he was never quite the same again. I haven't seen him for a long time. He spent more and more time in England. Retired from his job as a school teacher twenty years ago.'

Dumonde frowned. 'Marcel Dubois was attacked on the same day that his wife died?'

Madame Le Greq raised her hands despairingly. 'A double tragedy, M'sieur. And one which seemed to leave Oliver entirely unmoved. Unaffected. I said he was cruel; he was *unfeeling*.'

Dumonde digested what he'd learned for a few moments, then rose to his feet. Thanking Madame Le Greq, he led the way back to the car.

'Do we know which car dealership Oliver has in Caen?' he asked Rappeneau.

The sergeant leaned over the seat and retrieved a file from the back seat.

'Here,' he said, pointing at a document.

'Let's go. Tell the gendarmes.'

Rappeneau contacted the other car, then led the way back along the track to the road, and the city of Caen.

* * *

With the exception of one thing he was expressly forbidden to tell Penny, or even hint at, Geoff had been given permission to answer at least some of her questions.

'My firm became involved because someone, probably your step-father when he worked for it, set a tripwire for the name David Greatorix. That meant that any enquiry about him made through normal channels would be relayed to MI6. Your request for his military record crossed my boss's desk, and we decided it might be worth letting you run with the matter. I was supposed to look after you.'

Penny watched him through narrowed eyes, feeling annoyed that anyone thought she needed a protector.

Geoff looked as if he expected a response. When he didn't get one, he continued.

'That's about it, really.'

She looked at him in disbelief. 'Oh, no it isn't!'

'Oh, yes it is!'

For a moment, they stared at each other before he grinned. She looked away, amused but not wanting to show it.

'There's the little matter of why you had this "tripwire" in the first place. When I first met your father, he said he "supposed" it possible SOE were worried about a traitor in the French resistance, and that my father had been sent to discover who it was.'

Geoff lifted an eyebrow. 'I didn't realise you had such a good memory.'

'I was a cop, remember. So that's the case is it? I expect your father was much better informed than he wanted me to know, and I guess the traitor story was firmer than supposition.'

Geoff held up both hands in a sign of surrender. 'Okay, okay. That's the truth. And we still have an open file. The French know this, and keep pressing us to investigate again. They want to know who betrayed so many patriotic and true sons and daughters of France to the Gestapo.'

'And that's it?'

'That's it. Any chance of a drink?'

She turned towards the liquor cupboard, but stopped and turned back.

'Geoff, why didn't you just tell me this before? It doesn't, quite honestly, sound like a state secret.'

He shrugged. 'I guess keeping back information is deeply engrained in the MI6 mind-set. I was told not to tell you.' He looked at her wryly. 'But my new boss is of a different opinion, and he authorised disclosure to you tonight, on the understanding that it remains between us. Politically, it's still a bit sensitive, and we don't want the French getting wind of the situation until we're ready.'

'New boss?'

'The last one retired. Got one of those high-flyer types.' He sounded, she thought, somewhat put out.

'Something bothering you about that?' she asked, pouring them both a scotch.

'Not really,' he said, sounding despondent. 'I suppose when you get to my age, you have to expect younger people to become flavour of the month, while we old geezers are being put out to grass.' He took the glass from her with a nod of thanks.

Penny was amused enough by his hang-dog expression that she laughed aloud.

'You poor old thing. And when will you be put out to grass?'

'I already have been. I'm kind of a supply agent these days. You're the only reason they're paying me at the moment.'

'I'll expect my fifteen per cent in small bills.'

He grinned. 'I know you'll think this is just a line, but, frankly, you could have all of it. I've enjoyed working – no! I've enjoyed *being* with you.'

'Not enough to trust me, though,' she pointed out.

She still hadn't decided how, or whether, to punish him. She believed him, and realised it was because she wanted to, and deep down, she felt certain he would never have allowed harm to come to her. It was a nice feeling, one she hadn't felt for years, before John had gone down with leukaemia and started the various systemic failures which had eventually, and fairly quickly, led to his death.

'I was under orders, Penny. If it means anything, I've been sure I could trust you since I first met you, but I was not permitted to tell you what was really going on.'

'Have you told me everything now?' she asked.

There was the briefest hesitation before he nodded. 'Yes.'

CHAPTER 27 – 1971

Mary Hamilton felt fifty-five going on eighteen. She had enjoyed herself with David Greatorix, before he'd returned to France, and had begun corresponding with him. His letters were polite and friendly, and gradually, she realised she'd fallen deeply in love with him.

Oh, it was stupid, silly, and quite unlikely, but she couldn't deny the way she felt, how her heart hammered at her ribs every time she thought of him, and her throat constricted with unsaid passions. She felt like a teenage virgin again. She wanted to skip around, dance, and shout her joy, life was suddenly so wonderful. She was sure this was God's reward for being a Government tart, as she thought of herself, since she'd come out of prison.

And now, in the late Autumn, he'd agreed to let her stay at his farm in Normandy. Surely, she thought, he was edging towards the point at which he'd ask her to move in – even marry her. Oh, if only! she thought, her private prayer. She would be good to him, and good for him, especially if he were to mar... but she must stop thinking like that, she rebuked herself.

The ferry docked at Ouistreham and a few minutes later, she made her way with her luggage and the other foot passengers through the Customs and Immigration controls, still using her false identity. Outside, and formally on French soil, she saw David waiting for her, and walked quickly to him.

He smiled and kissed her – not on the lips but on the cheeks. She didn't mind – he was only behaving like they did in France, and he'd lived there long enough, she knew, to have become used to their ways.

He led the way to his car, carrying her suitcase, and she tucked her arm round his, tripping along beside him happily. The scent of him was familiar, and she inhaled it deeply.

'I didn't realise the ferry took so long to get here,' she said.

'It makes a long day for you,' he agreed, 'especially as you lose an hour on the way.'

'Oops! I forgot to wind my watch on. So it's an hour later than I thought?'

'Nearly supper time,' he said. 'There's a casserole that should be ready by the time we get to the farm.'

'Sounds delicious,' she said.

He grinned at her, and they drove on in silence until he turned off the road onto a farm lane.

'Here we are,' he said. 'These fields were farmed by my wife's family for generations, but after the war, we let them out to the farm next door. I'm no farmer, and really, neither was Delphine.'

'You probably did the right thing,' she said, not wanting to talk about his late wife. She glanced sideways at him as he concentrated on his driving. 'Will you marry again?'

He smiled and shook his head. 'I don't think anyone will have me. The best years of my life are all behind me – rather like my glittering career as a maths teacher.'

She'd dropped her gaze demurely. 'Oh, I don't think that's true,' she said.

'Well, I suppose … One thing I've learnt is that nothing is certain.'

She'd felt her heart swell and begin to thump, so loudly he must surely have heard it. She swallowed hard as the same emotions surfaced in her again now.

They drove between the duck pond and the wall, and turned into the farmyard.

Édith Solon's Mercedes was parked outside the house.

* * *

David had returned from England at the beginning of August. He felt unsure about his future: the woman he knew as

284

Kate had been almost rapacious since their first night in his hotel room. Sex was something he'd lived without for so long he had worried he might have forgotten how to do it, but she'd been both confident and gentle, and they had enjoyed each other many times.

After the incident with Oleg, he'd been left feeling there was something Kate wasn't telling him. She'd stilled his curiosity by taking him back to bed and not leaving until he was thoroughly exhausted – too exhausted to recommence questioning her. Then she'd left him, with a show of reluctance he'd felt was genuine, to return to London.

Their enforced separation had given him time to think. He didn't want it to be true, but all the signs were that Kate was a spy, working for MI6 – whatever she said – and therefore, despite the fact that she had seemed genuinely to like him, it was more than a little possible that her contact with him was deliberate and her affection little more than a performance. But he could be mistaken.

He'd been mulling the matter over two days after his return home. For a change, he went shopping in Vire. His previous visits to the town had been either as an in- or outpatient at its hospital, and he'd been promising himself the treat of exploring the parts of it that were of interest to tourists. He decided the shopping could wait until he'd visited the old castle, and spent a couple of happy hours exploring the site.

Later, he found a major shopping thoroughfare and strolled along it, stopping outside a shop selling men's suits. A new suit, he thought, would not come amiss for the new term, and he could do with some more casual clothes. While he tried to make up his mind which garments to choose, a familiar voice spoke in his ear.

'The one on the left. That would look best on you.'

He turned to find Édith by his side, smiling.

'You seemed to be having difficulty deciding,' she said. 'The suit on the left would be perfect for you. '

'Édith!' he exclaimed, pleased to see her, smiling. 'How nice to see you.'

'How is your head? And the memories?'

'I feel pretty-good,' he said in English. 'And you? How are you?'

'Ça va très bien,' she replied.

He wanted to talk. 'Do you have time for coffee?' he asked, reverting to French.

She glanced at her wristwatch, a mannish Rolex Milgauss, he noticed, with a circular dial which looked big on her slender wrist.

'Maybe a quick one,' she said.

She led them down a narrow side-street. 'This place is one of the best in town,' she told him, drawing him into a small bistro, where they sat at a table close to the window.

David realised he hadn't stopped smiling since they'd met, and neither had she. Was this, he wondered, what they called a 'happy accident'?

The Proprietor, a grand figure in a large white apron, approached. He was also smiling as Édith ordered for them both.

After he shuffled off to bully an ancient, hissing, Gaggia coffee-maker into making exquisite coffee, David and Édith found themselves staring at each other. She was in a suit, looking very professional, but nevertheless it revealed her curves. When he returned his gaze to her face, he saw she was blushing.

'Have you been operating today?' he asked, in an endeavour to direct their conversation onto safe ground.

'Since seven o'clock this morning,' she told him. 'I have another patient to see in an hour's time.'

She clasped her hands under her chin. 'What about you? Are you teaching still?'

'Yes,' he said. 'I think I've sorted out my two pasts, and I accept that, while I have a daughter still, in England, I will never meet her as her father.'

The coffees arrived, the *Patron* still beaming warmly and nodding his head as he turned to serve a couple at one of the other tables.

Édith touched his hand lightly with one of hers. 'Perhaps you shouldn't rule out the possibility altogether. She is still your daughter, you are still her father.'

'Biological father only.'

'I know, but I bet if she knew you were still alive, she would want to meet you.'

He bowed his head. 'I took a decision a long time ago never to try to get back into their lives –and I'm sure it was the right one.' He looked up at her. 'I don't even know my daughter's name.'

She gave his hand a sympathetic squeeze. 'That is very sad.'

'Do you have any children?' he asked.

'No. I've never been married.'

'Really?'

'I once had to choose between a man and a career. I was newly qualified, and the whole field of neuroscience was beginning to open up. Times were exciting and full of opportunities for people of science in the nineteen-fifties and sixties. We had a struggle to keep up with developments – you felt if you took a fortnight's holiday, you would never catch up: it was probably an exaggeration, but that's how it seemed.

'To marry would have meant moving away, and probably never being in the forefront of what I enjoyed so much, ever again. My boyfriend lived in *le Midi,* and I'd probably have finished up as a provincial family doctor. I considered his offer, and eventually, thinking there would be another man who wouldn't want me to give up my work, I turned him down.

'There has never been another man.' She smiled slightly. 'That's not to say I've not had boyfriends, but none of them were men I'd have wanted to marry. One or two were married anyway.' She looked down, the colour still visible in her

287

cheeks. 'Compared to your life – secret agent, married twice, two children – mine has been quite boring.'

'It doesn't sound boring to me,' David said. 'In fact, I'm quite envious of what you've achieved' – he patted his head – 'especially when it came to putting Humpty Dumpty together again.'

She looked up in puzzlement. 'Humpty Dumpty?'

'English nursery rhyme. Humpty is usually represented as a large egg. Falls off a wall and shatters. "All the King's horses and all the King's men, couldn't put Humpty together again". I have this image of my broken skull being like Humpty's shell.'

She thought for a moment, and smiled. 'I suppose there might be similarities. I shall never be able to mend a fractured skull from now on without thinking about Humpty Dumpty.'

He laughed and she joined in. For a moment the atmosphere between them seemed like the true conviviality of old friends. He took her hand and squeezed it affectionately, without thinking, his attention being drawn to it only when he felt an answering squeeze from her fingers. He released his grip at once.

'I'm sorry,' he said, 'I wasn't thinking.'

She took his hand in hers. 'It doesn't matter. Please don't apologise. Unless, of course, you wish you hadn't?' She let go and gazed at him.

'I would only regret touching you if it meant I could never see you again.'

She smiled, shyly. It looked odd but very attractive in a woman closing in on middle-age. 'It doesn't mean that, David.'

She stopped, looked him straight in the eyes.

'Good,' he said, 'because... I should very much like – if you don't mind – to see you again.' He swallowed, only realising as he spoke that he meant it.

She flipped open her handbag and produced a business card and a pen from it. She wrote on the back of the card.

'Here,' she said, handing it to him, 'that's my home number. The hospital's is on the other side. When you want to meet, just telephone.'

'Thank you,' he said, stowing the card in his inside pocket.

'Don't leave it too long.'

'I won't.'

They finished their coffee and she glanced at her watch again.

'Must be getting back,' she said. 'I have things to prepare before this afternoon's operation.'

He rose to his feet with her, leaving payment on the table, and followed her into the street. She turned into his arms, took his face between her hands, and kissed him lightly on the lips.

'Remember, phone me soon!' she said, twisting away from him and setting off towards the hospital. He watched her go, amazed at his feelings, and the realisation that they appeared to be reciprocated.

He became aware that the *Patron* was leaning against the doorway, watching Édith's departing back, and still smiling. David looked at him, and the *Patron* returned his glance.

'A fine woman, that,' he said. 'Your wife?'

'No, no. Not—'

'Mistress, then? I warn you, M'sieur, if she is neither your wife nor your mistress, I could be interested in her myself.' His grin robbed his words of any offence.

'Your wife wouldn't mind?' asked David, glancing over the man's shoulder.

The *Patron* turned sharply, and saw his wife was not there. He looked back at David, who was grinning.

'M'sieur! I am too old for jokes like that.' He patted his chest. 'My heart – I have to be very careful.'

'Perhaps you fall in love too often?'

The *Patron* held his hands out beseechingly. 'That is the trouble, M'sieur. I have a naturally amorous nature. I fall in love twenty times a day, and some of those affairs end disastrously. I cannot keep it up.'

'That is the trouble as you get older,' said David, glancing over the man's shoulder again.

The *Patron* grinned. 'You don't catch me a second time, M'sieur. My wife is waiting for my attentions in the kitchen.' He made the crude gesture of a raised fist, the other hand clamped across his bicep.

'Really? So she has a forgiving nature, yes?'

'What she doesn't know doesn't hurt her, M'sieur. Anyway, I really came out here to find out if you wanted your change.'

'No thank you, M'sieur. Keep it as your gratuity. I must be going. May see you again, if you're still here the next time I visit Vire,' said David. 'Au revoir, M'sieur, Madame,' he added politely, hesitating just long enough to watch the proprietor glance over his shoulder and find that, this time, his wife *was* standing there. David didn't wait to find out what happened next.

* * *

David led the way indoors. Édith loosened her apron and hung it up, then came forward, smiling.

'Édith, this is Kate Newsome,' he said. 'Kate, this is my friend, Dr Édith Solon.'

Édith briefly touched Mary's hand. 'I am just going. I'm due back at the hospital,' she said, glancing at David. 'I hope you enjoy the meal.'

They both spoke in English.

'Thank you for making it,' he said. 'I'm sure we'll do it justice.'

He kissed her on the cheek, and held her coat so she could slip into it. At the door, she smiled at Mary.

'*Bon appétit*,' she said, and went outside.

David went with her to her car, while Mary, who was struggling to understand what was going on, watched through the window. She felt angry that David had not mentioned that he had a 'friend' who was cooking a meal for them. He'd not mentioned having a 'friend' at all, especially a woman, apparently around the same age, but whose appearance made Mary feel frumpy.

When David came back into the room, she was ready for battle.

'You didn't tell me– !' she began, stopping herself and biting her lip.

'Édith was my doctor, after I was attacked. It's only a few weeks ago – just before I went to England – that she signed me off her books, so I was no longer one of her patients.'

Mary felt a spiteful retort spring to her lips but forced herself to keep silent.

'We met by chance a month ago and found… well, we enjoy each other's company.'

It didn't sound like the passion of the century, thought Mary. She made herself smile pleasantly as David took her coat and suitcase upstairs.

While he was out of sight, she examined the food Édith had prepared, tasting the gravy or sauce meant to be poured on the meat. It was packed with flavour, and a tantalising aroma of tomatoes and garlic rose from it. It made her mouth water. She considered pouring salt in it, but David had probably experienced Édith's cooking before and would know she didn't make mistakes like that.

She heard him coming back downstairs. Nothing for it but to grin and bear it, and see what transpired.

The meal held to its promise. Mary was not a good cook. While she'd been working for MI6 and living a life of some degree of luxury, necessary to her work, her domestic arrangements had been looked after by the housekeeper, who had prepared her meals on the occasions she dined at home. Édith was obviously a *cordon bleu* chef. It galled Mary, even while she enjoyed the food.

As she set aside a cleared dessert bowl and dabbed cream from her lips with her serviette, she watched David as he finished his meal and put down his spoon and fork.

'So, where do I stand, David?'

He refilled their glasses with a reasonably good red Bordeaux.

'You're a welcome guest.'

'Is that all I am to you?'

'You're interesting. I don't think I've met a spy before.'

She scowled. 'I'm not a spy! What gave you that idea?'

'Your friend Oleg. If what I overheard is right, he put a lot of effort into finding you, having you followed. I'd guess he hadn't mistaken you for someone else, despite knowing you by a name different from the one you gave me, and therefore, I believe him.'

Mary glowered. 'All right! I was a spy, once. I used to work for MI6. But I've retired. I'm not working for MI6 now.'

David held up his hands. 'Okay!'

She waited a moment. 'Okay? Is that all? Okay? Exactly *what* is okay?'

'That you were a spy but aren't now.'

That didn't tell her anything.

'Yes, but… where do I stand, David? Are we… an item?'

'An item, Kate? Because we slept together?' He pursed his lips regretfully. 'I'm sorry if it meant more to you than a very enjoyable few hours.'

She stared at him, full of resentment but trying not to let it show. 'I'm sorry, too, David. I'd obviously read more into our love-making than there was.' She smiled brightly. 'I know I was due to stay until the weekend, but if you don't mind, I think I'll go back home tomorrow. I – I don't feel comfortable here anymore.'

He nodded. 'As you wish. There's a late ferry: it'll get you back to the UK after dark, but it will give us time for a spot of sight-seeing in Bayeux earlier in the day. I thought you might appreciate seeing the Tapestry.'

She looked at him oddly. 'Is that what you'd intended us to do? A bit of sight-seeing, visiting the tourist spots?'

'You told me you hadn't been to France before, so I thought that would be what you wanted to do.'

'David,' she said, wrinkling her brow, 'we – Oh, God!'

She sat back, appalled at how stupid she had been, to begin to think she might have met a man who would want her for herself, would be a companion for life, when all the time it had just been sex for him. She felt a chill roll through her. Sex, just what she'd offered countless men over the last twenty years, with no more meaning than that. Why on earth, she asked herself, had she thought this was any different?

She stared down at the table-top. 'I think, if you don't mind, I'd rather try to get on the earlier ferry.'

She suddenly couldn't wait to get away.

Chapter 28 – 1999

'Mark, can I have a word?'

Stephanie Tabor waited while her nominal boss propelled himself in his swivel chair across the carpet between their desks.

He regarded the old files spread out before her.

'Been raiding the archives, Steph? Still chasing that little matter of your friend's father?'

'I reckon I can, since it's still an open file.'

'Not on him: he was declared dead in the nineteen forties.'

'Yes, but the file on the reason for his trip to France is still open – as you well know.'

'All right,' he said, waving his arms helplessly. 'I know you can be like a dog with a bone, so what's new?' He swung his long legs up and rested the heels of his boots on the edge of her desk.

'Our friends in the DST have kindly sent me their files on the Resistance leaders who went missing, apparently betrayed to the Gestapo. I've been putting the information they contain into the analysis program.'

The analysis program was some clever software which allowed transactions and relationships to be plotted. It was very useful to the police and intelligence services because sometimes it threw up connections which were not immediately obvious from the raw data.

'And what have you found?'

'They all had contact at some time shortly before their arrest with just one man.'

She tapped a name on her computer's screen. 'Him.'

Tanner studied the diagram the software had created from the information Stephanie had keyed in. His eyebrows arched.

'Who'd have thought it!'

'Clearly, no-one,' she said. 'But then, nobody would have had access to this sort of software fifty years ago.'

She waited for him to speak.

'Should we just hand this information over to the DST?'

'What do you think would be right?' he asked.

'As we know David's still alive, I think it would be a good thing to tell him, and let him take a part in the arrest.'

'I thought you'd say that,' Tanner said. 'Anything for a short break in France, eh?'

'You see right through me, boss.'

'Fibber!'

She grinned.

* * *

The telephone line had that hollowness which tended to indicate an international call.

'Is that *Madame* Sanderson?' asked a hesitant female voice.

'Yes, who's that?'

'Lisette Cornu. You remember, you spent time talking to me in Bayeux and said I could talk to you any time?'

'I remember. What's happened?' asked Penny.

'Oliver has been arrested. The police have decided to charge him with Anne-Marie's murder.'

'That's excellent news, Lisette. Have they found more evidence?'

The girl sounded depressed. 'No. Inspector Dumonde told me they were going to try for a conviction using only my evidence – but I can't remember it!' Her voice rose in her distress.

Penny felt sorry for the girl. Any prosecution witness in a case like the one she was facing was going to be severely cross-examined, a process which anybody, including people of very strong will and self-esteem, would find stressing. In Penny's view, Lisette possessed neither of these qualities.

'Lisette, would it help if Geoff and I came back to Ba-yeux, and were there for you if you need us.'

The girl's gratitude was expressed in voluble French, be-yond Penny's abilities to translate verbatim, but she under-stood the gist.

'Okay, we'll come over as soon as we can.' She obtained Lisette's phone number and promised to let her know when they would arrive at Ouistreham.

* * *

David put down the telephone. Édith put her head round the door.

'Who was that, darling?'

'Inspector Dumonde of the Bayeux *police judiciaire*,' he re-plied. 'Oliver has been charged with murder, and now, it seems, he wants my help. He's asked me to go and see him. He's in police cells at present.'

'Shall I come with you?' She moved to his side.

'I expect you have patients lined up for tomorrow.'

'I could ask someone else to take them on.'

He waved away her suggestion. 'No, no. I'll be all right. I won't have far to walk from the car.'

'I'll load a couple of syringes for you, so you'll be able to keep your insulin up.'

'Thank you, dear,' he said, catching her hand in his and kissing it. He smiled ruefully. 'I seem to have spent half my life being looked after by French wives.'

She patted his hand. 'Delphine and I wouldn't have done it if we hadn't wanted to.' She returned to the doorway. 'Will you be back tomorrow evening?'

He grinned. 'You don't think I've forgotten what the fol-lowing day is, do you?'

'I suppose not. Must be quite a habit for you. Most peo-ple are lucky to celebrate one Silver Wedding Anniversary, and here you are on your second.'

'I've booked a table at *Le Moulin au pré* for eight o'clock, and, if you can get the weekend off, we're going to Paris for a night of decadence at the Hotel George Cinq.'

She smiled at him. 'We haven't been decadent for ages. What a lovely idea.'

'You bring the saddle and stirrups and I'll bring the bridle and whip.'

She shook her head in mock solemnity. 'Now don't you go getting your hopes up, David, we're both a bit old for that sort of thing. Your arthritis gets in the way.'

He groaned theatrically. 'Don't remind me.'

'Would you like some coffee?'

'Yes please, nurse – unless, at this time of night, you think it should be a cup of cocoa and a Viagra tablet.'

'You don't need the Viagra: I'll make sure you don't roll out of bed.'

He groaned again. 'That's the trouble with being married for twenty-five years, your wife has heard all your jokes and nobody ever tells you new ones.'

She laughed and left him to watch the television alone and play with a new mini-disc recorder he'd bought. There was a brief item repeating a report from a few days ago about Oliver's arrest, updated with news of his being charged with murder earlier today. He was described as a leading busi- nessman, and a journalist explained what effect he thought the legal proceedings would have on the chain of motor dealerships Oliver owned throughout France.

* * *

In the morning, David drove to Bayeux and went to see Oliver at the police station.

They met in a small interview room with screwed-down furniture, after David had been obliged to hand over his insulin syringes, tie, and trouser belt.

'What do you think I can do to help?' David asked.

Oliver had been brought from the cells and was sitting opposite his father, his demeanour indignant. He seemed to relax and smiled.

'Do you suppose it's my English genes or the French ones on trial?'

'I don't think murder is anything to do with genes, and in any case, genes don't have nationality. Answer me one question, Oliver.'

'What?'

'Did you do it – what you're accused of. Did you rape and murder these girls?'

Oliver shook his head sadly. 'I'm sorry you even had to ask that question. I thought you knew me better – after all, I'm your son.'

'You do me an injustice if you think the mere accident of your birth somehow renders you incapable of committing serious crimes. You didn't answer the question.'

'Do you think I tell lies?'

'Not as a rule. A simple yes or no will suffice,' David said.

'So you think I tell lies occasionally?'

'We all tell lies occasionally, but not in respect of the really big, important things. Truth is best then, and I'm asking you for the truth now.'

Oliver shrugged.

'If you can convince me of your innocence,' David went on, 'I will do everything in my power to help you.'

'What if I can't convince you, but I'm still innocent?'

'Then as I see it, your only hope is to sow enough doubt in the Court's mind that they can't convict.'

Oliver glanced round. Considering they were alone in the room, the only effect it had on David was to make him think his son appeared unnecessarily furtive.

'The prosecution only have one witness: Lisette Cornu. If she refused to give evidence, the case would collapse at once.'

'What do you want me to do about it?'

'Talk to her. See if she will agree not to give evidence.'

'She's saying she was raped! Why on earth should she refuse?'

Oliver pursed his lips. 'For a hundred thousand francs. Two hundred thousand.'

David sat back and stared at him. 'You want me to bribe her?'

'Yes. Look, father, if she gives evidence, and I were to be convicted for something I didn't do, how would you feel? Surely you don't believe I really did these awful things I'm accused of?'

But to a large extent, David did. Still, this was his son, his last remaining link with Delphine.

His detached self said Oliver must be allowed to face his accusers in a court, but the father in him said, this is my son whom I must protect at all costs.

He knew what he must do.

'Very well, I'll talk to *Mademoiselle* Cornu.'

Oliver smiled. David noticed it barely reached his eyes. 'Thanks… dad.' He looked down. 'After I'm out, perhaps we could go out for a meal or something. Make a fresh start. What do you think?' He looked up.

David saw the hope and nodded. 'That would be good, Oliver.'

'There's just one thing, dad.'

'What's that?'

'I'm in front of the *juge d'instruction* in a couple of days, so do you think you could talk to her very soon.'

'How will I know where to find her?'

'Ask Ramon at the garage in Caen. He'll have her address.'

David nodded, and shortly afterwards found himself outside the police station. An appearance before an Investigating Judge was the French equivalent of the English 'preliminary hearing' or the American Grand Jury. Only occurring in serious cases, such as Oliver's, they had the purpose of determining if there was a case to put before a trial court, and the power to seek evidence.

He obtained Lisette's address and drove to it. She was not home, but her mother, after some persuasion, reluctantly told him she was in a nearby park.

He found her, sitting on a bench beneath the sheltering branches of a beech tree.

There was no-one else nearby. He stopped a few metres away from the bench and waited until she looked up at him through large, heart-shaped sunglasses.

'Lisette? I'm Oliver's father.'

She stiffened. 'What do you want?'

'May I speak with you?'

'Why?'

'Oliver's asked me to tell you how sorry he is.' That was his first lie, but it should have been true. 'He wishes you hadn't been put in the position of having to give evidence against him. I understand there aren't any more prosecution witnesses, and that places a heavy burden on you.'

She looked away. 'Is that all?'

'May I sit down?' he asked.

'I expect so.'

He moved slowly, the arthritic pain in his hips and knees needing no exaggeration, and sat at the far end of the bench, anxious not to seem threatening.

He didn't look at her as he spoke.

'Oliver lost his mother when he was quite young, you know?'

She didn't reply.

'It was a terrible tragedy,' he continued, almost as if talking to himself. 'And one I missed, because someone attacked me on the same day she died, and I was in hospital a long time. By the time I came out, Delphine had been buried and the fuss surrounding her death – she drowned in our duck pond – had died down.'

Lisette had turned and was listening to him now.

'What happened to you?' she asked.

'I was kept home after the hospital. You see, I'd lost my memories of my years in France. Twenty-six years, all gone. I had to relearn things – even how to use my kitchen appliances, how to drive a car. All these had changed since – well, my last memories.'

'So you couldn't remember your *wife?*' Lisette sounded aghast.

David shook his head and smiled grimly. 'Not a thing.'

'That must have been terrible,' she said.

'After a while, I got my memories back, so it wasn't a total disaster, by any means. Whoever attacked me did me a favour. These days I have pretty-well a full set of memories.'

'You never found out who?'

He shook his head. His recollections of that day were hazy in the extreme. He had a vague memory of someone behind him. He felt instinctively it was a man, but that was all.

He turned back to Lisette. 'I hate the idea of anyone being raped. It is a horrible, despicable thing for any person to do to another. Almost as bad as the act itself is the thought of a rapist getting away with it. Murder is even worse.'

He stopped and waited for her to respond. She pushed her sunglasses up over her hair and looked at him.

'You want me to refuse to give evidence, don't you?'

He looked down. 'Oliver is the only child I have. He's told me that he did not rape either you or the other unfortunate girl, and didn't kill her either. I believe him. He wants me to ask you, yes, to refuse to give evidence, but if I was your father instead of his, I would probably urge that if you believe he raped you, you should do your best, whatever the personal cost. There is always a cost to victims of rape, you know what people are like: how much did she lead him on? Is she a slut? "There's no smoke without fire" – to bring the offender to justice.' He touched her shoulder lightly.

'But I'm not *your* father, and I do think, from what the police have told me, that a successful prosecution is very unlikely, and guess who will come off worse if you are *the* prosecution witness and the case is thrown out?' He looked down. 'I suppose I want you to take a balanced view, and see whether you come to the same conclusion. If you do, then a refusal to give evidence will save you from that kind of criticism, and reduce the stress under which Oliver is now living.' He looked up at her again.

'If it's true what I've heard, that you can't remember the incident, then I can't see how you can possibly provide evidence which would clinch a conviction. Can you?'

She stood up and walked a few paces away before returning to stand in front of him. Her jaw trembled.

'I cannot remember having sex with your son. I only know that I did. He doesn't deny that. But if I can't remember, I can't be sure that I consented. I can't be sure I didn't. You're right, of course: I'm useless as a witness.' She drew in a shuddering breath. 'All right, I will refuse. You've helped me see there's no point, and it would probably do more damage than good, especially to me. You can tell Oliver – and the police, if you see them before the hearing – that I won't be testifying.'

David stood up slowly. 'Thank you. If it helps, Oliver is prepared to pay you significant financial compensation, because, although he maintains that what happened that night was consensual, it is obvious to him that you have been severely distressed, and he tells me he never wished for that.' Another lie.

'How "significant"?' she asked, standing close in front of him and staring deeply into his eyes.

'Two hundred thousand francs – I believe that's thirty-thousand or so euros – was a figure he mentioned, but I guess he's flexible about it.'

'If I'd not decided to refuse to testify, were you going to offer money to buy me?'

David smiled wryly, and shook his head. 'No. To be honest, Oliver wanted me to, but you deserve better than that. I figured you had to make up your mind for the proper reasons, not because of money. But let me tell him you'll accept forty thousand – I think that's more than a quarter of a million in francs – and do something with it that you really want but couldn't normally afford. A world cruise, or buy a house, something like that. I'll tell him, if you like. It'll come with no strings attached, I guarantee it.'

'Then I'd be a fool to refuse.'

'I'll bring it to you after the case has been withdrawn.'

'Just to make sure I don't change my mind again?'

'I don't believe you will, but the hearing is set for a couple of days' time, so you would have to move quickly, and it will take a day or two for Oliver to get the money together, after he's released.'

She thought for a moment. 'What will happen to him?'

David looked at her sadly. 'If ever I find out he lied to me, and did the things he's accused of, I will make sure he is punished. In the meantime, I expect he'll go back to his job.'

For what seemed like a long time, she stared at him without speaking. Finally, she nodded once.

'I believe you,' she said.

* * *

Penny was annoyed when she and Geoff arrived the next morning to find that Lisette had given notice of her intention not to give evidence against Oliver.

They had travelled on the overnight ferry and arrived early, ahead of the rush-hour traffic around the port of Ouistreham. They drove to Bayeux and checked in at the DeVries. In a brief telephone conversation with the girl, she learned of the agreement she'd made with Oliver's father.

Then it hit her: Oliver's father – *her* father.

'How do I get in touch with him?' she asked.

'He lives in Vire, somewhere,' replied Lisette, 'but you don't have to get involved with him. I've done what I promised, and I expect he will do the same.'

'Promised? What did you promise?'

Lisette hesitated. 'Well, it wasn't so much a promise by me, more a recognition of the reality – that my evidence wouldn't be enough to convict Oliver, and all I'd be doing is opening the way for the Press to raise questions about me…'

Penny nodded. 'Of course,' she said, her anger dissipated. 'I understand. And you're right.' She frowned. 'Did you say he promised you something?'

'Yes. I felt a bit funny about accepting it at the time, but it seems reasonable.'

'What does?'

'He said he would see that Oliver paid me some compensation. Enough to change my life.'

'Oh,' said Penny.

'It'll do me more good than the thought of Oliver in prison somewhere, getting his food and lodging at the expense of the State. And,' she added, 'his father promised me that if he ever found out Oliver *did* rape me and murder Anne-Marie, he would see that Oliver was punished.'

'And you believed him?'

'Why? Shouldn't I? He hasn't handed over the money yet. He's supposed to do that tomorrow, after Oliver has been released.'

Penny stared past the telephone at Geoff. 'Do you... Do you think I could be with you when he hands it over. Please.'

'Why?' asked Lisette, sounding nervous. 'It's all right, isn't it?'

'I'm not interested in the arrangement you have with Oliver's father, Lisette, I just want to meet him. I think he may be someone I've been looking for for a long, long time.'

'Oh? Who?'

'I'll tell you if it *is* him. Now, when are you meeting him?'

'He's going to take Oliver to get the money, and bring it to me later. I expect he'll phone me.'

'Will you phone me when he does, Lisette? I'm at the Hotel DeVries in Bayeux.'

'Okay,' said the girl, sounding curious.

'Please! It's very important to me.'

'Okay,' Lisette repeated, more definitely.

Penny hung up and turned to Geoff, who was obviously waiting to find out what Lisette had been saying. She waited until they were in her room at the DeVries before she told him.

'It seems there's a chance that tomorrow, I may get to meet my father.' She went over to the wardrobe and slid the door open. 'What the hell does one wear on these occasions?'

For some reason, she found she was weeping.

CHAPTER 29 – 1999

David could tell the moment he saw him, that Dumonde was not a happy Inspector of Police. The man's scowl dragged the corners of his mouth down, and he could barely bring himself to be civil as he led Oliver out of the cells and brought him over to where David was rising painfully from his chair.

'You are free to go, M'sieur,' he said as Oliver strode past him to embrace his father. David nodded his appreciation, but Oliver ignored him as they stepped into the sunlight.

'I gather you talked the bitch out of it,' said Oliver, when they were a hundred metres from the police station.

David turned to stare at him. 'If you're talking about Lisette, then yes, she agreed to withdraw from the case.'

'How much did you promise her?'

'Nothing – until after she'd agreed.'

Oliver smiled. 'Excellent! You mean, she didn't want paying?'

'She does now. I told her you would pay her a sum of money in compensation – because, Oliver, I'll tell you frankly, I'm not at all sure I believe you're innocent, so you shouldn't get off scot free.'

Oliver halted and turned. 'What? How much?'

'Forty thousand euros. A bit more than a quarter of a million francs.'

'*What*!' Oliver's dark complexion turned even darker. 'You promised that slut a quarter of a million francs of *my* money?'

David nodded. 'She's not a slut, Oliver. She is young, and may be a little too trusting, but she is not a slut, nor a bitch.'

'Oh!' Oliver scoffed. 'You don't believe all those innocent airs, do you? Remember she and her friend went with me voluntarily.'

'Do you think nobody knows about GHB, Oliver? Do you think there was no trace of the drug in their bloodstreams, or the glasses which contained their drinks?'

David had no idea whether the glasses had been preserved for forensic examination, but he was pretty sure that Oliver did not know, either. It would do the man good, thought David, to fear there might yet be some evidence that could see him put away.

'They still went with me voluntarily,' Oliver insisted, his voice quieter.

'Under the influence of GHB, "voluntarily" doesn't mean a lot. Nor does the idea that the girls consented to sex.'

'What do you know about it?' demanded Oliver.

'Just because I'm eighty and arthritic doesn't mean I can't use the Internet. Besides, have you forgotten – I'm married to a doctor.'

Oliver frowned and began to walk away. David caught up.

'The bank, Oliver. That's where you're going.'

'No way!'

'Oh yes! Otherwise, that nice policeman might just be feeling your collar again, this time for attempting to pervert the course of justice, and there'll be two willing witnesses, me and Lisette. You can be put away for a long, long time on that charge. You're not short of money: give the girl the forty thousand. Either a banker's draft made payable to Bearer, or cash.'

'It would never stick.'

David laughed. 'Oh, I think they'd believe a story that you asked me to offer her the money if she'd withdraw from the case – after all, that's exactly what you did, back there in the police station.'

'Yes, but you didn't; you just told me. You offered her money *after* she'd agreed to pull out.'

'I don't think that's the version the Inspector would hear.'
Oliver stopped again and stared afresh.

'You'd lie?'

'In an instant, if it means getting justice for Lisette.'

'But – I'm your *son!* You can't set me up to go to prison.'

David pursed his lips and let the silence speak for him.

'You bastard!' Oliver spat.

'I'm a bastard, and you're over a barrel, son. The bank!' David nodded in the direction of the establishment in question.

Oliver glared at him, but slowly turned and led the way into the building.

* * *

Lisette glanced at her watch. 'It's about time,' she said. 'I'll go first. Give me five minutes. I'll keep him there until you arrive – don't worry!' she added.

Penny nodded. Her stomach was feeling queasy. Geoff rested his hand on her wrist and beckoned one of the waitresses. They were in the café named for Duke William and his wife, Matilda, near the square in front of the Bayeux law courts. Beyond the bridge over the River Aure was the quiet square in the centre of which stood the fine bronze statue of the nun, Catherine of St Augustin.

Geoff ordered another glass of the house Merlot. The girl brought it over and placed it in front of Penny, who felt her hand shake as she lifted it gratefully to her lips.

She turned to look at Geoff. 'I can't believe it, you know – that I'm going to meet my true father for the first time. I'm shaking. It's ridiculous: I'm a grown woman, I've had to cope with many of life's unpleasanter people and incidents, and yet I'm nervous as hell.' She gulped more wine.

Geoff grinned.

'Look on the bright side,' he said. 'Most girls don't remember the moment they first set eyes on their father, being just a little too tiny and not good at focussing at the time. You're going to remember this moment forever.'

'What if he doesn't like me?'

'You might not like him. My guess is that you'll like each other well enough. But liking isn't what it's about, is it? Like him or not, that man *is* your biological father, and whatever you think of each other won't change that.'

'But all the same…'

He glanced at his watch. 'Come on, it's time. Drink up.'

Penny checked her hair. 'Oh, God! Do I look all right?'

'I'm sure He thinks you do. And so will your father.'

She sighed deeply and rose to her feet. 'Let's go.'

While Geoff settled their bill, she walked outside and turned towards the bridge. The river, fast-flowing beneath her feet, gurgled and bubbled as she came to the point where the trees lining the road parted to reveal the vista of the square to her.

Round the edges, cars were parked, people strolled. Leaves shimmered in the breeze, but Penny had eyes only for the couple stood in the centre, by the statue.

The man's back was quarter-turned towards her. He was stooped, slightly, and with a shock, Penny realised she'd seen him before – in the street at Bletchley when she'd been having coffee with Stephanie, and on the *Pride of La Manche*. As she approached, Lisette, who could see her over the man's shoulder, obviously said something Penny couldn't hear and the man turned round.

She stood still for a moment, and they stared at each other. She slowly moved towards him, and felt her emotions rising as she did. He took a half-step towards her, and held out his arms. She walked towards him with a lump in her throat, her resolve to stay calm totally undone when suddenly tears began to roll down the old man's cheeks. She took the last two steps into his arms and for a long, long time, it seemed, they just held each other.

He gently pushed her away and simply looked at her face. 'Lisette says your name is Penny.'

She brushed tears from her eyes and nodded. 'Penny Sanderson, these days, but I was born Penny Greatorix.'

'Then I must really be your father.'

She nodded, finding speech difficult, and hugged him again.

'You didn't hug me last time we were almost this close,' he said in her ear.

She pulled away this time. 'When were we ever this close?'

He smiled at her. 'I don't suppose you remember a lost motorist, thirty-one years ago, in 1968, in the middle of Bletchley? You were looking very smart in your police uniform, and you gave me directions to some street I named at random off the street map. Unfortunately, it was the red light district, in those days.'

'Why would you ask for that?'

'Because you were trying to help me, and I really didn't need helping: I knew where every place I wanted was, but you seemed fairly insistent and you'd have been suspicious if I'd not acted lost.'

'Did you recognise me? If so, why didn't you tell me who you were?'

'Not at the time. I saw a young woman about the age I expected you to be, with eyes the same colour as mine and your mother's.' He coughed, embarrassed. 'I have to confess that I used to stroll past your home – Ann's home – from time to time, and eventually, I was there as you were leaving – I presume for a late shift. In uniform. That was when I knew it was you who gave me directions to the Red Light district.'

They were interrupted by Geoff. 'Are you two able to cope with visitors? Only Lisette and I are feeling a bit ignored.'

Penny turned. Lisette was beside him, and they were both smiling broadly.

'Is it true that this is your father, Penny?' asked Lisette.

Penny was grinning, too and was unable to stop. 'Yes. And he was just going to tell me why, when he met me thirty years ago, he didn't identify himself.' She turned back to David.

'The answer is, I didn't recognise you then. Having met you now, I know it was you then. But I'd decided I wouldn't identify myself, anyway: you and your mother had made a new life for yourselves, and so had I. I didn't want to risk upsetting what you had. Everyone would have believed that I was dead. What do you think would have been the effect if I'd turned up on the doorstep? Ann had remarried, you had a stepfather – and I didn't know whether you'd been told who your real father was.'

'Callum was a really good dad. I knew my father was David Greatorix, and I used your name until I got married.'

David indicated Geoff. 'And is this your fortunate husband?'

'No, he died last year. This is Geoff Pearson. Apparently you knew his father when you both worked at SOE.'

'Derek Pearson,' supplied Geoff.

David thought for a moment before shaking his head. 'No, can't say the name rings a bell. But then, my memory of those days has never been good.' He looked from one to the other. 'We obviously have much to talk about. Lisette,' he added, turning to the girl, 'thank you for bringing us together.'

She smiled again and waved a banker's draft. 'Thank you for this. *Au revoir*, everyone, ' she said in English before turning and leaving them to their reunion.

'You must come to my home,' David said.

'Dad,' said Penny, 'you know about mum, don't you?'

He took her arm in a gentle grip. 'I know your mother died some years ago – '

'1990.'

'Right. And your dad died in eighty-five. I found out from the electoral rolls and the death indexes. I'm your biological father, Penny, but Callum was your real, true dad.' He glanced briefly at Geoff then back to her. 'So if Geoff's not your husband, where is he?'

'John died last year, of leukaemia.'

'I'm sorry. Any children?'

'One son, Alexander. He did anthropology at university and spends a lot of his time these days in the Middle East, working for an oil company. Can't see the connection myself.'

David snorted. 'No. Nor me. I have a son, Oliver.'

'I know,' she said, 'we've met him. Used the name Delacourt, but then we found out his legal name was Dubois. Later still, we – I – learned through Geoff's father that your cover name in 1943 was Marcel Dubois.'

Geoff coughed. 'Excuse me, but how far is it to your place?'

'Ah!' exclaimed David, 'I am very forgetful.' He kissed Penny lightly on the cheek. 'We will continue this conversation at home – better still, if Geoff will drive your car, you can travel with me and we can catch up on family business.'

'That sounds like a good idea,' she said, and turned to Geoff. 'Will you mind?'

'No, not at all.'

They set off in convoy for Vire.

* * *

If Édith Greatorix was surprised when her husband brought guests home on their Wedding Anniversary, she didn't show it.

David introduced Geoff and then turned to Penny.

'And this, my dear, is the step-daughter you didn't know you had, the daughter whose name I never knew,' he said. 'Édith, meet Penny Sanderson, née Greatorix.'

'My dear!' exclaimed Édith, stepping forward to embrace Penny who found herself blushing. 'How lovely to meet you.'

When Édith released her, Penny smiled at her father.

'I never thought it was true that when old men remarried, they chose women young enough to be their daughters – until now.'

Édith laughed and the men smiled. 'I thank you for the compliment, but I have a good ten years on you!'

She insisted that the visitors stay overnight.

'I had booked a table for dinner. I'll phone the restaurant and see if they can fit two more in. If not, I'll cook a meal here.'

Penny raised her hands in a negative gesture. 'No, no. Dad was telling me – I'll call you "dad" if it suits me,' she admonished David who had opened his mouth to protest her use of the epithet – 'it's your Silver Wedding, so you must go out, just the two of you as you intended. Geoff and I will forage in the town centre and find something for ourselves, won't we, Geoff?' She turned to him.

'Of course,' he agreed.

'Absolutely not!' said Édith, firmly. 'Tonight is a double celebration. We shall all dine together – and that's final.'

Penny graciously allowed her objection to be overridden, and later that evening, both couples dined out together.

At the end of the meal, Geoff sat back and dabbed his lips with his serviette.

'I suppose this is the end of your quest, if that's the word?' he said to Penny.

She glanced at David and smiled. 'I set out to find my father, and I've found him – still alive and living with his third wife,' she said.

'Glad I was able to help,' said Geoff, a little pointedly.

'I was going to say,' Penny went on, smoothly, as if he hadn't spoken, 'that of course your help has been invaluable – yours and your father's.'

He smiled. 'But my, uh, quest, is not altogether finished,' he said.

'And…?'

'I had a phone call from my boss on the drive down here.'

'What does he want?'

'I have a few questions for David, then – '

'Questions for my dad?'

'Yes. You'll remember, the reason he was sent to France in the first place? Find a traitor? File's still open.'

She nodded. 'Oh, yes. But it's a long time ago, surely?'

'It is, indeed, but the French would like the matter re-solved. My boss has an idea about it, but wants me to talk to you, David, if you don't mind.'

'Of course, but perhaps in the morning? I am rather tired this evening.'

'Tomorrow will be fine,' said Geoff.

Édith Greatorix enjoyed cooking when she wasn't being "Doctor Solon" at the hospital. Breakfast the next morning was a choice between a light and more typical French one, or a cooked one in recognition of English preferences.

Geoff took the opportunity, as they all enjoyed coffee afterwards, to bring up David's mission in 1943.

'I was not really trained as an Agent,' David said. 'I'd been working on decryption – they thought my grasp of mathematics would be helpful in that respect. I suppose it was, but once they had their computers up and running, much of the slog was taken out of the job.

'Anyway, they had this other problem, in France. It seemed that there was a pattern of not just our Agents, but local Resistance leaders in the area, around Bayeux and Sainte Marguerite-en-Bessin, who had been taken by the Gestapo and killed. The assumption in London was that someone was betraying them.

'They decided to send me to try to identify the traitor. I was not to make contact with any of the groups directly, and indirectly only in my character as Marcel Dubois. One real Agent was sent ahead, and was supposed to meet me when I landed. I think he was supposed to keep me out of trouble, and I don't know what happened to him.'

'The Gestapo followed him when he went to meet you. It seems he had been betrayed, too. He was killed at the landing ground,' said Geoff. 'The wonder is that they didn't find you.'

Penny looked at him oddly. Clearly the man knew more than he'd told her before. Maybe he'd only recently been briefed.

'Well, of course, I didn't know that,' David continued. 'In fact, thanks to a very bad landing, I didn't know anything.'

'We know about the memory loss and how long it lasted,' said Geoff. 'But now you appear to have remembered everything, can you recall whether you ever found the traitor, or even suspected someone?'

David shook his head. 'No. When I came out of my coma, I was simply the man named on my fake French ID, Marcel Dubois. And so I remained.'

'And, not knowing you had a wife and child in England, you married Delphine Delacourt, the woman who'd found you the night you landed, and looked after you while you were unconscious,' Geoff added.

Édith poured everyone more coffee and sat down to listen. 'This is fascinating. Do go on,' she said.

'There's not much more to tell,' replied David. 'Several years later, I began to recover snatches of memory. I remembered the name, Ann, and the place, Bletchley. I remember my first visit – Delphine didn't come with me, but wanted me to go to England to see if it prompted any more memories. It was the year of the Queen's Coronation.'

He turned to Penny. 'It was the first time I saw you. I could scarcely believe I had such a beautiful daughter, and I didn't even know her name.'

His eyes moistened. He took Penny's hand in his and lightly kissed it. When he released his hold, she took his hand in both of hers and smiled as tears slipped unheeded down her cheeks.

'I wish you'd said something,' she said.

'As I said, I figured it would be too upsetting all round. After all, I was married, with a seven-year-old son, and your mother had obviously found a new partner in Callum. I decided that, although I would have liked to, it was better for all of us if I didn't. Of course, I returned nearly every year during the summer holidays, and would make sure you and your mother were okay. I did that until you left school and, I guess, went to university?'

'Oh, we were okay. Callum was a good father. Did you know he and mum both worked for MI6 after the war?'

315

She noticed that Geoff looked away, out of the window.

'Did you know, Geoff?' she asked.

He looked back at her and nodded. 'It was Callum who set things up so Six were always told when David – Marcel – came to Britain. The trouble was, so much time had elapsed that we didn't know which Marcel Dubois – and there were lots: very common name, apparently – was David.

'After Callum retired, the matter was filed, until the French government reminded us that the question of who the traitor was had never been resolved, and they wanted him. Or her.

'You turned up, in a manner of speaking, at just the right time, wanting to find your biological father, which fitted in rather well with our needs. So, I was sent to work alongside you.'

'You could have told me,' Penny said.

Geoff shrugged. 'Orders, OSA, whatever.'

'I hardly think something that happened in 1943 would count under the Official Secrets Act.'

Geoff shrugged again. 'I can only tell you what I was told. Technically, I think I'm in breach of it now.'

'They amended it in 1989 to restrict the range of kinds of disclosure covered by it.'

'Yes, ma'am. Sorry, ma'am,' said Geoff, contritely.

Penny grinned. 'I remember it well because Steph and I were both seconded to Special Branch shortly after the new Act came into force, and there were people moaning that it would lead to a flood of information leaking out. They'd be appalled that the government is thinking of enacting a Freedom of Information Act.'

David sighed. 'So, to cut a long story short, I never did find out who the traitor might be.'

Penny sipped coffee thoughtfully. 'It must have been someone in your community in forty-three and forty-four.'

'No obvious suspects come to mind,' he said.

Geoff put down his empty cup. 'The only people Penny and I know who were around at the time, apart from yourself and Delphine, were the Le Greq family at the next farm, Doctor Lafarge and Albert Lebrun.'

'The Le Greqs were active in the resistance, so it's not likely to have been any of them,' said David.

'Let's not rule them out yet. Whoever it was might well have been a member of a group, to know who the various leaders were. I suppose that includes Albert, but quite honestly, having met him, I don't think he'd be the one.'

'That only leaves Lafarge, and he was a medical man, and not unreasonably, opposed to all the killing and brutality. He wasn't a member of any group, either, but he helped us all. I mean, I owe him my life, for God's sake!'

Geoff's cell phone rang. He answered it while the others waited in silence.

'Okay,' was all he said before closing the connection.

He turned to the others. 'My boss wants to meet us. Apparently he's in France with his Number Two. He suggests one o'clock at a bar in Sainte Marguerite-en-Bessin which Penny and I know well. I think I mentioned it once when I was talking to him, and I suppose he's trying to get a flavour of rural France while he's here.' He turned to David. 'He particularly included you – and Édith – in the invitation.'

* * *

Henri Lafarge was definitely beginning to look his age. He'd stared into the bathroom mirror that morning and for the first time wondered if he could be bothered to shave. He told himself he was a proud Frenchman, even at eighty-three years of age, and he was not going to appear in the bar looking like a peasant. The fact that Albert had always appeared with plentiful stubble was one of the things Lafarge didn't like about him.

He combed his thinning, silver locks, the hair still retaining its natural curl, which had attracted the interest of more than one of his female patients in the past, before the natural pigment had stopped colouring it black. He hadn't minded having silver hair, but his vanity prompted him from time to time to apply a judicious quantity of black boot polish to his moustache, which, without such treatment, appeared more dark grey than silver.

He picked up his cane, black ebony with a silver ferrule and grip, fitted his trade-mark broad-brimmed hat on his head, and set off for the bar near the main junction around which Sainte Marguerite had grown.

The marble shrine opposite the bar took the form of an elaborate diorama.

Lafarge traditionally touched the brim of his hat in a salute as he passed it, a compromise gesture between making the Sign of the Cross and not acknowledging it at all. He wasn't particularly religious, but on the other hand, he liked to hedge his bets.

A two-metres-high back wall curved round behind the representation of Calgary like a theatrical cyclorama. In front of that were three crucifixes, with Christ on the largest of them, in the centre, flanked by the two robbers. In front of all three, within touching distance of the street and separated only by a marble trough, filled to overflowing with scarlet geraniums, were the entwined grieving forms of Mary Magdalene and the Blessed Virgin. But today, the shrine was a mess. It looked as if someone had driven a heavy vehicle into it, smashing the fragile marble and scattering pieces everywhere. He bent to pick up some of them, and found himself looking at the sad face of Mary Magdalene, the tears clearly visible on her white cheeks.

Lafarge found himself grieving for her, for the destruction around him, and for the fact that she grieved for her Saviour. He tried to smooth the tears from her cold cheeks, becoming suddenly aware that Albert, white stick in hand, was by the door to the bar. He put Mary's head down gently and crossed the road, hoping the destruction of the shrine would not bring down divine retribution on the village.

He felt depressed by the damage which had been done, and was subdued as he followed Albert into the bar. Albert led the way across the wooden floor to their usual table, the

middle one on the left. Serge came over, smiling, a glass of
Merlot in one hand and a Pastis in the other.

'Good day, gentlemen,' he said. 'How are you, Albert?
Doctor?'

Lafarge had spotted a pair of unfamiliar faces sitting at
the table to his left and wondered if Serge's somewhat unusual bonhomie was an attempt to impress them with his
friendliness.

'We're fine, Serge – aren't we, Albert?'

Albert appeared to look past him. 'Yes.'

Lafarge raised his glass and sipped, realising as he did that
the man sitting at his left was trying to catch his attention.
He studied his appearance for a moment, his mouth twitch-
ing at the sight of snakeskin cowboy boots visible below his
jeans.

The man saw him looking. 'Not real snakeskin, unfortunately,' he said in good but accented French.

'We, uh, don't see many boots like that in Sainte Marguerite-en-Bessin,' Lafarge commented.

'No? Well, they're just a foible of mine.'

Lafarge smiled politely and turned away.

'Er, I was wondering if you could help me.' The foreigner
was speaking again.

'Yes?'

'Yes. I've been researching the way the Agents of the
British Special Operations Executive worked with the
French resistance in World War Two. Any chance you and
your friend could help me with that?'

Lafarge was about to refuse when Albert leaned across. 'I
was in the Resistance, M'sieur. What do you want to know?'

Beyond him, the door of the bar opened to admit six
more customers. Lafarge recognised David Greatorix and a
woman who might be his present wife, then the two who'd
come to talk to him, Pearson and Sanderson, if he recalled
correctly, and finally two men whose body language was such
as to make Lafarge suspect they were police.

Serge had been in his customary place on the public side of his bar counter. Now, with a look of pleased surprise on his face, he hurried through the flap to stand behind it and beam at the manna coming his way.

'Messieurs, 'dames...' he began.

Lafarge wasn't the only one staring. There were more people in the bar than he could recall seeing any time since the Liberation party in 1944.

'Perhaps we could sit at your table?' asked the man in the cowboy boots, moving as he spoke and before Lafarge could object. On the other hand, the woman was quite beautiful, he thought, and when she sat opposite him, he had no wish to drive her away.

'I'm Mark,' said the man, 'and this is Stephanie, Steph.'

At that moment, Geoff leaned across the table. 'Doctor Lafarge, isn't it. Geoff Pearson. And do you remember my friend, Penny Sanderson?'

At the mention of the name, Steph turned to find her friend staring at her with such surprise that it made her giggle.

'Hi, Pen. You see, I'm not dead, and I did survive my departure from the police – and Bletchley.'

Penny sat at the table to Albert and Lafarge's right, Geoff sliding along the bench next to her.

She shook her head. 'I wish you'd told me, Steph. I can keep a secret, you know.'

Mark turned to her. 'My fault, Mrs Sanderson. And I'd be glad if you forgot about meeting her here, when you get back home.'

'There's been altogether too much forgetting things,' said David, ushering Édith into the seats on Lafarge's left vacated by Mark and Steph.

Finally, the two whom Lafarge thought were police sat at the table on his right, opposite Geoff and Penny, and between him and the door. Drinks had appeared in everyone's hand, and the bell on Serge's till was tinging merrily. The bar owner had a grin fixed to his face, and he kept wringing his hands as if frightened it was all a dream and he'd wake up to find his bar empty.

Lafarge turned his attention back to Mark.

'As you will have gathered, I am Doctor Henri Lafarge. My colleague here is Albert Lebrun.'

Albert held his hand out and Mark and Steph shook it in turn.

'Pleased to meet you, M'sieur Lebrun,' said Mark.

'Albert.'

'Very well, Albert. You were in the Resistance. Was that round here?'

'Yes. Quite a lot of us old men – and old women – were in the Resistance.'

'Quite a few didn't live to see Liberation, did they?'

'No,' said Albert.

Mark turned to Lafarge. 'And you, doctor, were you in the Resistance?'

'No. I'm a doctor. I was opposed to all the shooting and killing.'

'But you treated the wounded, didn't you?'

'Of course. It was my calling–'

'The wounded of both sides?'

'Yes, of course. I am – was – a humanitarian,' replied Lafarge, unaccustomed to being questioned and then having his answers interrupted.

'So would it be true to say,' Mark continued, 'that whilst you weren't actually a member of the Resistance, you probably knew everyone who was?'

'Of course. I was the only doctor for miles around. Naturally, anytime a member of the Resistance got hurt, I was summoned to assist.'

'You worked in the hospital at Bayeux as well, didn't you?'

'Yes. I did a lot of work there.'

'Treating injured members of the German army.'

'When necessary. This is no different from your Nurse Edith Cavell, who treated soldiers of both sides, German and Belgian without discrimination, in 1915.'

'You must have met officers of the Gestapo.'

Lafarge blinked. People were looking at him. 'Yes. They were brought to the hospital.'

'They would have befriended you, wouldn't they? After all, you were helping their side.'

On Lafarge's left, David had been listening to the interchange with growing interest.

'They let you remove equipment from the hospital, and supplies, didn't they, doctor?' he said.

'Not very much, M'sieur Dubois.'

'You're being modest, doctor. You told Delphine and me that you could usually source what was needed for the local population.'

'Yes, indeed,' added Albert, 'you supplied me and other groups with the Syrettes of morphine.'

'Morphine, eh?' echoed Mark. 'I'll bet that wasn't something most people could get their hands on.'

'Look! What is this?' demanded Lafarge. 'Is this what the Americans call the *Third Degree?*'

Mark held up his hand. 'No, no, certainly not, doctor. Let me see if I've got this right: during the war, you were a humanitarian. Were you also a patriot?'

'Of course.'

'What did that mean to you?' Steph asked.

'I wanted my country to be at peace. I wanted the war to be over and things back as they were.'

'And that would be achieved as soon as one side beat the other.'

'Of course!'

'Which side did you think was going to win, doctor?'

'I never had any doubts about the outcome.'

Mark leaned forward. 'With respect, doctor, that doesn't answer the question.'

'What would you know? You're too young. You weren't there.'

'As I seem to recall,' said David, joining the debate for the first time, 'most of the locals did not want the Germans taking up permanent residence. While some, inevitably, had to appear to be complying with the Rules of the Occupation, nearly everyone I knew wanted the Germans out of France. But you never seemed to want that.'

Lafarge stared at him indignantly. 'Is that some kind of accusation?'

'Only if you take it as such. The point is, you wanted the fighting to stop; most people wanted to drive the Germans out, and in effect, have the Allies win the war. But you, I believe, were simply appalled by the casualties, the lost lives. Especially, you wanted the Resistance to stop, because every time they killed German troops, the Germans would respond by raiding villages, massacring many, if not all, of those who lived there, and torching the places. That, I believe, you hated. Am I right?'

'Yes. Yes, you are right!' Lafarge was visibly upset.

It felt to him very much as if he was at the centre of a witch hunt, and all the time his conscience was prodding him from the inside as hard and as painfully as the questions of those around were prodding him from the outside.

'We can prove that you knew every one of the local Resistance group leaders, Doctor Lafarge,' said Mark, 'every man and woman who were arrested and murdered by the Gestapo around here.'

'So what? I wasn't the only one.'

'Actually, you *were* the only one. Do you know what the mathematical probability of *that*, and that you *didn't* tip off your Gestapo friends, is?' Mark glanced at David. 'I expect our mathematician friend, here, could work it out.'

'What do you mean, "Gestapo friends"?'

'I remember you telling us that you were allowed little perks by the Gestapo in return for patching up their troops and the prisoners they'd been over-zealous with,' David told him. 'That, I'd say, means you were in their pocket. After all, in our community, you continued to live well, never short of food or petrol for your car. They looked after you, didn't they, doctor. And in return, you tried to shorten the war by giving them bits of information which would reduce the chances of the Resistance killing Germans, and thus prompting one of their acts of retribution – didn't you?'

'It would have been natural to respond to their apparent kindness with the odd act of kindness, from yourself,' said Steph. She smiled at him.

It was a gentle smile, he thought. He had been provided with beautiful girls during the war by the Gestapo. They had smiled sweetly, too, and he'd talked to them about when the war would be over, and then... then they would talk about the things which made the fighting worse, the sabotage which inconvenienced the Occupying Forces so much. And they would agree with him, that some of his fellow-countrymen were stupid, provoking German anger, which in the end only rebounded on the innocent.

'It was simple arithmetic,' he said quietly, 'a straightforward matter of balancing one life against many; better to sacrifice the one, who directed the action against the Germans, and save the many who would otherwise be killed in retribution.'

'From the best of motives, saving more lives than it cost,' she said quietly.

He found tears welling up and brushed them out of his eyes.

He nodded. 'Of course, not everyone would see the clear sense of what I did. No doubt some would have regarded it as betrayal, but it was just to save French lives.'

He was aware that the nearest policeman had stood up and was showing him his warrant card. 'Henri Lafarge, I'm Inspector Alain Dumonde of the *Police judiciaire,* and I am arresting you in connection with war crimes.'

Lafarge stared at him. 'I'm eighty-three, man! What is the point? Why go through it all, bringing back bad memories, for God's sake?'

Suddenly Albert turned towards him, bright blue eyes seeming to be fixed on his.

'Did you betray me, Henri?'

Lafarge stared at him. 'No, Albert. I would never have done that.'

'How else would they have known when and where I was? They'd known for months, the animal who blinded me said.'

Lafarge chewed his lip. At the time, Albert had simply been one of the local leaders. He couldn't remember for certain – on more than a few occasions, he had taken wine before going to bed. Maybe Albert's name had slipped out during one of his conversations with the girls.

He shrugged. 'I don't know.'

'But you betrayed others, like Serge's grandfather?'

Lafarge swallowed. Serge was staring at him from behind the bar. Every conversation in the room had stopped and they were all looking at him.

'Yes,' he whispered.

'You bastard!' – Serge.

Lafarge stared at him, chewing his lip again. 'You don't understand: I wanted the war to end quickly. It was a case of sacrificing the lives a few people for the sake of the many.'

'People you knew, people who thought you were their friend.'

'You can't think I would have done it if I could have found any other way, do you? You cannot imagine how diffi-cult it was to name people who were my friends, even though that's all I did. What the Gestapo did with the infor-mation I didn't realise for some time – after all, resistance fighters were often killed or captured anyway. I didn't know it was what I said that was causing it.'

He sagged abjectly against the table.

'That's good enough for me,' said Albert. He pulled one of his lapels forward. Stuck in the back were two three-inch long hatpins. Tugging them out by their bejewelled heads, one in each hand, he drove them deep into Lafarge's ears before anyone could move to stop him.

Lafarge screamed and collapsed. The room erupted with exclamations of shock. Dumonde bundled Albert out of the way, into the arms of Sergeant Rappeneau, then leaned forward to see the damage to Lafarge's ears. He felt a hand on his arm.

'May I see, Inspector? I'm Doctor Édith Solon from Vire Hospital.'

He moved aside so she could pass him and get close to Lafarge. The man's eyes were closed and his breathing was ragged. Blood leaked out from both ears.

Édith shook her head and called for some kitchen towels, which Serge reluctantly supplied. 'I daren't remove them,' she said, 'I might damage his brain.'

Dumonde was already on the phone, and nodded.

'He needs to be scanned, so we can see exactly where they lie.' She stood up and moved back to her chair, opposite where Albert had been sitting. Lafarge showed no signs of returning to consciousness.

'Is he going to die, Doctor?' asked Dumonde.

'We're all going to die, Inspector,' she replied, 'with him, I don't know whether it will be sooner rather than later. At eighty-three, with a regular diet of red wine, there's a chance it'll be sooner, and the hatpins will only hasten that moment, even if they haven't actually damaged any part of his brain necessary to life.'

Lafarge opened his eyes as Dumonde was slipping handcuffs round his wrists. Pain was etched across his face.

'I knew you wouldn't understand,' he said, 'that's why I never said anything.' He twisted his head until he could see David. 'And you, M'sieur Dubois–'

'Actually, my name is David Greatorix. I came to France to find you.'

Lafarge shut his eyes in anguish for a moment. 'Bloody English! I should have known. No wonder your son hates you.'

'How do you know that?'

'We've been friends for a long time. I was a member of the FAF, like him. I could understand his anger when he discovered he was half English, and how that made him hate both you and, especially, his mother.'

'His mother was the kindest, most generous and loving woman–'

'But she married you, a foreigner. She must have known you were a British spy. She married you and had your children.'

'Child.'

'But wasn't she was pregnant when she went up the aisle, with a child she miscarried five months later?'

'And your point is?'

Lafarge's expression was sickly. 'It was God's judgement on her. She deserved what she got.'

'Why do I think you're talking about the manner of her death rather than the stillborn child?'

'Take it whichever way you want. I knew, when Oliver came to me and told me to sign off her death as an accident, that he'd killed her. I think he meant to do you in as well. As I think the English say, he *lost his bottle.*'

David stared at him. He'd read the expression, "his blood ran cold", but it was the first time he'd ever experienced it for himself. It was all he could do to keep his composure. He turned to look at Édith. She covered his hands with hers.

'Poor David,' she muttered. 'How terrible.'

He stared at her, a desperate look in his eyes. 'I won't believe it unless he tells me himself.'

'We can go to the farm on the way back to Vire.'

He shook his head. 'Not you, Édith. Just me. I'd prefer to have this conversation with him in private. Please.'

'Are you sure you'll be all right?'

He smiled at her, took her hand and kissed the backs of her fingers lightly. 'I've done all right so far. I'll be home for tea. You can go back home with Penny and Geoff.'

She sighed. 'I have a feeling that I should be with you,' she said. 'I think this is not going to go well. You're no spring chicken yourself, David, so don't get yourself into a situation you can't get out of. Especially, don't get into a fight with Oliver! He's a lot stronger than you.'

He grinned grimly. 'I don't plan on engaging in fisticuffs with him, for sure, but I do think he deserves the chance to explain what the doctor meant.'

Paramedics arrived and led Lafarge outside, accompanied by Dumonde.

'You get in the ambulance with him, Sergeant.'

'What about… ' Rappeneau jerked his head towards Albert.

Dumonde looked round to make sure they were not being overheard. 'Maybe we'll have to come back for him another time.'

Rappeneau nodded. 'I understood your grandmother was one of those taken and shot by the Gestapo.'

Dumonde waved a finger at him. 'Don't repeat that to anyone, please.' He watched as David came out of the bar and got into his car alone. Édith got into Geoff and Penny's car. Dumonde scratched his head and watched them all depart.

CHAPTER 31 – 1999

It was late afternoon when David arrived at the farm where he and Delphine had lived, and which was now home to Oliver, when he wasn't staying in a hotel somewhere. The place looked forlorn, and it was obvious to the casual observer that it wasn't much lived in.

David parked in the yard and called Oliver's cell phone.

'Yes?'

'Oliver, will you come to the farm, please. I need to talk to you. It's urgent.'

'I'm busy.'

'Please, Oliver. This is the last time I shall ask you this.'

'Why? What's happening?'

'Tell you when you get here.'

'You're *in* the farm, now?'

'I'm your landlord. Of course I have a key.'

'Don't go rummaging around,' said Oliver, sounding sulky. 'I'll be home in half an hour.'

David let himself in. Despite it being late summer, the place was chilled and he gathered together kindling and paper to light the kitchen fire. As the flames grew, making the wood crackle, blacken and smoke, David opened the small cupboard beside the fireplace, lifting the board out of the bottom and peering inside the hidden cavity, where Delphine and her father had kept his fake ID papers while he was unconscious in 1943. He sighed as he stared at the thing which filled the space now. After a few moments, he lifted it out and put it in his coat pocket.

A car pulled into the yard. It was too soon to be Oliver's. When he looked out of the window, he saw it was Penny, Geoff and Édith. He went outside.

'I know what you said, darling,' said Édith, 'but we thought we'd better be on hand. Just in case, you know.'

David grinned ruefully. 'I promise not to lay a finger on him.'

She tapped his nose with the tip of a finger. 'It wasn't Oliver I was concerned about.'

'You can all wait somewhere else,' he said.

'Where?'

He glanced round. The *gîte* he and Delphine had made out of the former cow byre was dark and empty.

'In there,' he said, pointing. He pulled a key off his key ring. 'And please stay there until Oliver or I leave.'

It was a compromise they could all accept. David watched to make sure Édith, Geoff and Penny went inside and closed the door, before re-entering the kitchen of the farm house.

Half an hour later, Oliver's new black Mercedes pulled into the yard, stopping sharply alongside David's smaller Citroen. David watched his son climb out from behind the wheel, and walk swiftly towards the door, like a man anxious to be somewhere else.

David poured coffee and was adding milk as Oliver entered.

'I see you're making yourself at home, father.'

'It was my home before it was yours, Oliver.'

'Someone in the *gîte*?' Oliver jerked his head towards the yard. 'Car out there.'

'Short-stay guests,' David replied.

He pushed a coffee cup across the white wooden table towards his son.

'Thanks. Now what's so urgent?'

'How well do you remember the events of 1969?'

Oliver pulled a chair from under the table and sat down. 'It's a hell of a time ago. Obviously, mum was killed and you were, nearly.'

David sipped coffee and studied Oliver over the rim of the cup.

'Interesting choice of words, that, Oliver. "Mum was killed" – not "Mum died". How did you know she was killed?' He felt proud of the fact that his voice retained a measured calm, making the question sound very casual, a simple matter of interest.

'I meant that she died. Everyone knows it was an accident.'

'Because Doctor Lafarge said so?'

'Yes. You can't argue with a medical finding thirty years ago.'

David sipped again. '*I* can't, but *he* can. As I understand it, he is even now, as we speak, recanting.'

Oliver stared at him. 'He can't. There's no evidence.'

'Apparently he can. He says he didn't do a very thorough post mortem… because you more or less told him to write off your mother's death as an accident.'

'I…? He says *I* told him?' Oliver stood up and strode round the kitchen, returning to stand by his chair. 'Why would he do anything I told him?'

'My guess is that you outranked him in the FAF. You were both members.'

Oliver's face darkened then paled. 'Who says?'

'He does. I have to admit he was under severe duress at the time. He'd just admitted betraying all the Resistance group leaders in the area to the Gestapo, thus leading directly to their deaths, and one who survived after the Gestapo officer interrogating him shoved a pair of hatpins in his eyes as a parting gesture, shoved those same hatpins into Lafarge's ears. Shame and pain, Oliver. Shame and pain. They incline people to spill all sorts of beans.

'And I remember what you thought of your mother for marrying an Englishman. Even less than you thought of me for being one. I suppose there was enough anger in you to kill her, if an opportunity offered. And it did offer, didn't it, Oliver, that day by the duck pond?'

Oliver stared at him, his lips clamped together in a thin line.

David continued. 'Don't bother admitting it, if you find that too hard to do. I'm sure Lafarge's testimony will be adequate. It's likely the police are already on their way.'

'Lafarge is obviously a weak-willed coward.'

'I agree. I don't think he's ever killed anybody in his life – unlike you.'

'You haven't killed anybody, either.'

David sipped the last of his coffee and marvelled at how he could still appear calm.

'Actually, son, that's not quite true. The night your mother delivered the dead foetus that would have been your older brother or sister, we were out with Albert Lebrun – the man who had his eyes put out with hatpins a few hours later. As she was helpless for the moment, a German soldier lifted his rifle and was about to shoot her. I shot him first.'

'I didn't know.'

'No. It's not something I'm proud of, except that my job as Delphine's husband was to protect her from all harm, and I did that.'

Tears suddenly pricked his eyes. 'I only wish I'd been able to protect her when the ultimate threat to her life arose from a direction we'd neither of us expected. But I'd been laid out with a – a hammer or something.'

'Even if you'd been there,' said Oliver, 'I don't believe you'd have done anything. You Englishmen haven't got the guts.'

'Oliver, I owed your mother my life, just as you owed her for yours. Bearing in mind that you had shown yourself to be heartless, and totally unworthy of her love and mine, really – what would you have done in my shoes? Protect her by killing you, or let you kill her and say nothing about it? Where do you think my loyalty should have been – if I'd been there and not unconscious with a hole the size of a, what? A hammer? A spanner? in my head.'

'A wheel brace.'

'Are you sure about that?'

'Yes.' He was sullen now.

'Did you actually mean to leave me alive?'

Oliver stared at him and slowly shook his head.

'So that's one murder and one attempted murder. Makes me wonder about the girl in your hotel room.'

'I'm not saying any more about her. The charges have been dropped.'

'So they have, but it only takes one.'

Oliver took a step towards him. 'Pity there aren't any witnesses to our conversation.'

'That's true, there's nobody here but you and me.'

Oliver took another step closer. 'By the time anyone gets here, they might find your body, overcome with smoke, after you let the kitchen fire get out of control and it burnt the place down. I'll be in Caen, of course.'

'You would do that, Oliver? You'd kill me, despite knowing that Lafarge has confessed and you'll have to stand trial anyway?'

Oliver laughed. 'I can be out of the country by tonight. They'll never find me.' He took another step. 'Now do you want to take this sitting down, or standing up, like a man?'

David stood up. Oliver raised his hands towards his father's neck, but was distracted when David pulled his minidisc recorder from his left jacket pocket and put it on the table.

'Evidence,' he said. 'Your confessions.'

Oliver laughed again. 'I shall just take it away with me and destroy it.'

His attention was caught again when David drew his other hand from his right pocket. In it, he held the pistol he'd picked up when Oleg had dropped it all those years ago in the Bunbury Arms, and which had been hidden in the cavity beside the fireplace.

He raised his arm and looked his son squarely in the eye.

'No, Oliver. I think you've run out of options.'

His finger was squeezing the trigger when the door burst open and Edith stood there, Penny beside her.

'David!'

'Dad!'

But reaction times after more than eighty years are slow. Oliver, however, was turning away when the pistol fired. The bullet entered his abdomen on the left side and exited on the right, burying itself in the wall.

In the seconds after the gunshot, Oliver turned an incredulous face to his father before crumpling to the floor. A pool of blood began to spread from both wounds. Édith crouched beside him, and demanded towels. David put the pistol on the table and walked outside, passing Geoff on his way to investigate the shot, in the doorway.

After a few minutes, Penny came outside and joined him.

'He's dead.'

David looked at the daughter he'd loved from afar for more than forty years and nodded.

* * *

Stephanie Tabor was writing the final note in the MI6 file on David Greatorix. Across the office she shared with Mark Tanner, she watched him swing his long legs off his desk and stand by the window, staring out in the street. He still wore cowboy boots. She wondered about the wisdom of breaking her rule about having a personal relationship with a work colleague. There were times like this, when he didn't know she was staring at him, that she allowed her imagination to indulge in such flights of fancy.

She turned back to the file and picked up her pen. She had written most of the story: it was unfortunate that everything in it would remain an official secret for another fifty years. Which meant no one could give evidence about the events leading to Oliver's death. The pistol, which had borne David's fingerprints, and mobile phones used by David and Oliver, had been picked up by Geoff Pearson, so there was no direct evidence the French police could use to prosecute.

David and Édith had moved to England, and now lived quietly, not far from Penny's home. David had received a substantial sum from the British Government to compensate for his injury while on active service, and Édith had taken her pension a few years early, though Philippe at the DST had seen to it that no actuarial reduction was made in view of what he called her "services to France".

Geoff Pearson had proposed to Penny, been accepted, and never again wore his trousers to get in bed with his wife.

THE END